UNDER
TIBERIUS

UNDER TIBERIUS

TIBERIUS

A NOVEL

Nick Tosches

LITTLE, BROWN AND COMPANY

New York Boston London

Copyright © 2015 by Nick Tosches

Little, Brown and Company
Hachette Book Group
1290 Avenue of the Americas, New York NY 10104
littlebrown.com

First Edition: August 2015

Little, Brown and Company is a division of Hachette Book Group, Inc. The Little, Brown name and logo are trademarks of Hachette Book Group, Inc.

The publisher is not responsible for websites (or their content) that are not owned by the publisher.

The Hachette Speakers Bureau provides a wide range of authors for speaking events. To find out more, go to hachettespeakersbureau.com or call (866) 376-6591.

Frontispiece: Allegorical illustration showing the transformation of Mercury in the form of a snake nailed to a cross, from a treatise reputedly written and illuminated by Nicolas Flamel (c. 1330–1418) (vellum) / Bibliothèque Nationale de France, Paris, France / Bridgeman Images

ISBN 978-0-316-40566-9

LCCN 2015935824

10 9 8 7 6 5 4 3 2 1

RRD-C

Printed in the United States of America

UNDER TIBERIUS

S OME YEARS AGO, IN THE SPRING OF 2000, I WAS SPENDING MY days in the Vatican, studying several unique manuscripts in the course of my research for a novel.

Access to these manuscripts required high academic credentials. I had none. But in the end, after several meetings and interviews that seemed at times to be interrogations, the Vatican Library had given me identification cards authorizing the access I needed to both the Archivio Segreto and the Biblioteca Apostolica Vaticana. These cards, which bore the seal of the Vatican, attested that the Vatican had bestowed an honorary doctorate on me.

I was under constant supervision, or surveillance, during the days of my research. But I was very fortunate that the guardian who had been appointed me was a kindly old prelate who was more devoted to librarianship and learning than to the Head Librarian in the Sky and the recondite hierarchical ambitions of the Vatican, all of which he seemed to have waved away long ago.

One afternoon, as we walked toward a destination in the vast underground maze of one great chamber that on this day was eerily deserted and silent, we passed a long, high wall of partitioned shelf upon partitioned shelf of strapped-shut leather tubes that cast a soft penumbral patinated glow in the dim lighting from the vaulted ceiling above them.

The old prelate and I upon first meeting had begun our brief, tentative conversational exchanges in Italian. Slowly, by interjecting phrases of English into our talk, he let it be known that his English was more fluent than my Italian. And so, after a few days, we spoke almost exclusively in English.

"What are these?" I asked, gesturing to the leathern tubes that seemed to be countless in their dark wooden places of rest in the wall that seemed to be endless. I was sure that they were papyrus scrolls.

Very, very ancient scrolls, as the leather cases that held them were ancient themselves, and the wood of the shelves appeared to have been there for centuries.

He nodded with a slight smile, as though sensing what I had surmised, and affirming it.

"No one knows all that is here. Some of them are three or four thousand years old, maybe older." He paused, then slowed his pace as we proceeded. "The even older writings, the clay tablets, are in a vault in a room that diverges from the start of this passage. Back there. We passed it a while ago. Some of these scrolls may be as old as some of those tablets. No one knows. That's the trouble with this place. There has never been a complete and serious inventory of what is here."

The passage of leather-cased scrolls led to a wider passage. He called this the place of books before paper. Piles and piles of the earliest codices: sheets rather than scrolls of papyrus or parchment, bound together between wooden covers. Most of these were from about two thousand years ago, among the oldest codices to have survived.

"Look at this," he said. "The first books. Heaped and strewn like trash in the basement." He mumbled something about *ratti*—rats, something about *uno caseggiato bassifondo*—a slum tenement; then he shook his head. "They say that Pius VIII sent his servants down here to fetch kindling to keep his fireplaces roaring in winter."

Looking at this mess, he turned still as stone, as if he had been looking at it all his life.

I picked up a codex. There was very little wood left of its original covers. The dust of the ages seemed to be the only solvent holding it together. The old man did not mind that I had raised it in my hands. I very carefully opened it, turned its friable, torn leaves. My fingers were filthy with its dirt. I slowly, gently turned a few pages, looking at what remained of the faded ink on those pages. It was written in Latin, in an elegant hand. I tried to make out the words, tried to make sense of them.

The elderly priest joined me in looking at the page. "Good parchment. Good atrament: looks like cuttle-fish, the best the Romans had. And the hand-writing: adept. A bit shaky, but adept. No cheap job, this one."

He placed his own fingers to the pages, and, while I continued to hold the codex, removed my free fingers from the pages and let his take their place. He was reading the Latin far more ably and with far more alacrity than I had managed, and he pronounced the words in a whisper as he read.

"*Tristissimus hominum,*" he whispered. He repeated the phrase, no longer in a distracted whisper: "*Tristissimus hominem.* 'The gloomiest of men,'" he translated. He seemed stunned. "This is a book about Tiberius," he said. "By someone who knew him. *Knew him.*"

His fingers moved backwards through the pages with a professional care that did not hide his intent and rising but expressionless excitement.

Suddenly he stopped, his eyes fixed on a single word. The word was *Iesvs,* the Latin form of *Jesus.*

"*Iesus.* And here, again, in the accusative: *Iesum.*"

He muttered something to himself in Italian, something that I could not clearly hear. Then he looked to me. It was as if he had discovered something that made every other discovery in the last two thousand years seem as nothing.

"This piece of overlooked kindling is the memoir of a man who knew both Tiberius and Jesus. It may be the only real proof that Jesus ever existed."

He put the codex in his black briefcase. "You must say nothing of this," he told me.

I nodded. We made our way to the file cabinet that held one of the medieval manuscripts I wanted to see for my research. We were both so fouled by the soot and dirt of the codex that we went first to a large wash-sink nearby. He was with me; he located the manuscripts for me. But he was a thousand miles away.

When I called him the next morning, he told me that we would not be able to meet again for another two days. And that we should meet at a certain café in a certain secluded little piazza a considerable distance from the Vatican.

At the café he explained that he had torn two pieces from two sheets of the codex and had them tested at the library's laboratory. He had told the chief technician nothing about these scraps, only that the analysis was a matter of urgent importance. Every analytical test had been performed. The frail scraps had been exactingly examined by transmission electron microscope, by scanning electron microscope, by ion and electron microprobes, by energy-dispersive X-ray spectrometer. Microscopic particles of the ink had been subjected to chemical analyses. The scraped-goatskin parchment and the black ink on it were of the same age, and dispersive penetration tests showed that the ink had been laid to the parchment since their making. Furthermore, the visual evidence of the nature of the pen that had been used—a calamus of the internal shell of the cuttle-fish — and the form of uncial script of the fragments corroborated the technical conclusions.

"It's real," he said.

Seeing that he had somewhat lost me along the way, but not knowing quite where, he paused, then said: "This calamus, the ancient Romans called it a *calamarius,* a sort of horny flexible pen made from the bone in the cuttle-fish, the ink-fish. The word *calamari* comes from this, but *calamari* is squid; cuttle-fish are *seppie.* Latin, Italian: the cuttle-fish is *seppia.* Somebody got confused. Probably an American."

He smiled, then was silent and drank his coffee. A double espresso with a lot of sugar. Then, pointing to his heart, he took some pills, drank some water. He asked the waiter for another double espresso.

"And while they were doing this, I was doing this."

He unclasped his briefcase and removed a fat dark-brown button-and-tie kraft envelope. Placing it on the table, he then placed his pale, spidery veined hand upon it. He unwound the string from the closure, then carefully withdrew the topmost of the sheets of paper within it.

It was thick fine white paper, and the image on it — the first page of the codex — was far more clear, darker and sharper, than the original. To be sure, the torn areas and the black smears here and there were also more striking; but the text had magically been restored, from faded to vibrant characters.

"They set it up for me, the scanner in the laboratory, tuned it to do this with one of the scraps I gave them. While they worked on the scraps, I worked on this. And while I did, I translated it."

Again he placed his hand on the envelope. He raised the second little cup of espresso to his lips and drank as I tried to translate the Latin. I found the uncial script to be daunting; and

7

years away from this most powerful of languages had taken from me much of my familiarity with its declensions and cases.

The first words that appeared, the first words that emerged after those words forever lost to the attrition of the ages, on a worn-away area of parchment that appeared as a gray stain on the scan, were *sub Tiberio:* "under Tiberius."

"It's real," he repeated. "The laboratory dates it to the first century, to about two thousand years ago. It's the memoir of an old man written for his grandson. An old Roman aristocrat of equestrian rank. What he writes dates it to about the middle of the first century. He wanted to leave this behind for his grandson, who was a child at the time. He wanted his grandson to read it when he grew to be a man, so that he could come to know his grandfather after he was gone. Nowhere does he address his words to anyone else. It is all for the grandson. And it seems to me to be at times as much a sort of—*obliquo, perverso,* how do you say?"

"Oblique, perverse."

"Yes, yes. It seems to me to be at times as much a sort of oblique last-rites confession as it is a memoir."

He looked to the sky, breathed as deeply as he could, smiled as his eyes followed the movement of a swallow over a small, medieval church across the piazza.

"All my life," he said—to me, to the sky—"I have doubted Jesus: the reality of Jesus, the historical existence of the Jesus of this Church. There was simply no real evidence. He appears nowhere in any record or document of the day. The odd, cursory references to him in Josephus and Tacitus have long been regarded as insertions by monastic scribes in the Middle Ages. Even the greatest of modern theologians, biblical scholars, and Christologists, from Crossan to Sanders and the rest, now agree that most of what is in the gospels could never have happened, and never did happen."

He moved his hand across the dark-brown envelope. "This proves that I was wrong. This, and only this, proves that I was wrong."

His smile deepened, grew more serene, as he became more immersed in the blue sky and the slow movement of the wispy clouds of this lovely spring morning.

"In fact, it is the earliest portrait of him, older even than the gospel of Mark. And the only portrait of him drawn from life."

"I see a raise in your future," I said with a grin. "I see one of those white cassocks and red beanies."

"And I see danger." He was no longer smiling, no longer facing the sky. He looked directly into my eyes. "If I were so much as to be suspected of having any knowledge of this thing, I'd be out of here on my ass. And worse," he added cryptically.

"Then why are you trusting me?"

"Because you once wrote a book about Michele Sindona. It is not that he trusted you enough to talk to you. It is because it was a book involving many secrets and many people. And you are still here. And that is because you betrayed no one." After a pause he added: "And because there is something about you that I like." He shrugged. *"Homo sum."*

"Where is the original?"

"I threw it back where we found it. Where you found it."

"And what do you want me to do with this?" I gestured to the envelope, handed him back the sheet he had given me.

"Give it to the world."

"I don't think my command of Latin is up to the job."

He placed the page I had returned to him in the envelope as gently as he had taken it from the envelope. From the bottom of the envelope, he pulled out sheets of cheaper paper that were folded into a bundle.

"Notes I made while reading it as I scanned it," he said.

"These will help you with some of the difficult words and sentences and passages. As for the rest, that is up to you."

"If it is all that you say it is, if it proves that there was a Jesus, if it is the earliest and only first-hand account of that Jesus" — and I still did not really believe that any of this was true — "then why is it so dangerous?"

"Read it and you will see."

He closed the envelope and gave it to me.

About a year later, at home in New York, I finished the novel I was working on. The old prelate and I kept in touch, but the codex or the contents of the envelope he had given me were never mentioned again. Only in 2004, after receiving word of the death of the old man, did I turn in earnest to what lay in that envelope. Almost every Saturday morning for three years I studied for at least an hour with a Latin tutor. I took again to reading the red-covered Loeb editions of my favorite Latin authors, trying to shift my eyes as little as possible from the Latin text to the facing English text of these volumes.

One day I rediscovered my favorite opening line of Catullus, in his nameless Poem XVI, written as a response to critics: *"Pedicabo ego vos et irrumabo"* — "I will fuck your ass and fuck your mouth." This sort of thing, as much as re-reading Virgil and Ovid, renewed my love of Latin and fueled my enthusiasm.

Then, finally, I read what had been given me; and then, as had been foretold, I knew.

I was fortunate that what I read had been written at a time when the Romans were not commonly writing in *scriptura continua,* a style of writing without word dividers, without spaces or other marks between words or sentences. What I read and worked with was written with *interpuncta,* crude dots used to divide words and sentences, a style that fell into disuse during the second century, when most writers in Latin reverted to continuous script.

I translated, then I translated again. I studied the translation until I was confident. Then I studied it until I was sure. I decided to use only one long section of the codex, for much else in it, the earlier parts of it, seemed somewhat prosaic and of slight interest except to historians of early first-century Rome. I decided to use the first two legible words of the original ancient work as its title. I also decided to put my name to it, rather than the name of the man, Gaius Fulvius Falconius, who nearly two thousand years ago wrote it in Latin for the eyes of his grandson, and for his grandson's eyes alone.

—*Nick Tosches*

1

I SPEAK TO YOU ALONE WHO BEAR MY BLOOD. I SPEAK TO YOU from beyond the kingdom of light, from beyond the kingdom of darkness. I speak to you, my grandson, from the grave.

Your father, who was my only son, was reduced to ashes in your infancy, and your mother followed him to the perfumed flames before two years more had passed. Even if this had not been so, you would have come to know me only through their tales, and therefore the truth of my life would have remained unknown to you.

This would mean nothing were it not that the devious path and wrongful turns of my life led me somehow to an understanding of things. The older I have grown, the rarer I have observed this gift to be.

You have been given this book, corded with my leaden seal and with my patrimony, on the morning on which you will have put aside the crimson-edged toga of a boy and taken on the white toga of a man.

As pronounced in my testament, this will have been when the light of the first dawn of your seventeenth year has come upon you.

By now you know well that a philosopher is a lover of wisdom, from the words for "love" and "wisdom." I have read the works of many philosophers. I have spoken with others. They are as actors on the stage. No man who espouses wisdom possesses it. I myself never loved or courted it. Our word for that thing, *sophia,* that philosophers profess to love is not so distant from our word, *sophisma,* for turning knowledge toward deceit. This was my love.

But the skies and winds of the days and nights of this world bring mysteries. The seeds of wisdom sprouted in the dirt of my sins. Like a woman scorned, she, Sophia, came to me.

It is she whom I wish to give you. She is the better part of my patrimony, with which you cannot buy her. I can do so, or attempt to do so, only through the story of my life. There is no other way.

Thus this book. My desire to reach the end of the journey of which it tells and my desire to postpone my own end are one. I am old. The vomiting of blood grows more frequent. If I try to walk, I fall. But these words run fresh and clear and strong, like a stream in a strange but well-remembered woods.

2

H E WAS NOTHING UNTIL I FOUND HIM. ANOTHER DIRTY little half-shekel thief, no different from the thousands like him who infested the provinces.

Jews. Israelites. Children of Sem, who they believed to have been born without foreskin and to have lived for four hundred years, father of them and the Arabs and all the rest of the hook-nosed mongrel Semitic tribes of the wastes beyond the Great Sea.

They called themselves these things — *iudaeii, israeliti, filii Sem* — and all manner of other things, and the sons of this one, that one, and of others upon others. As many yowling whelps and moaning scurvied old dogs of as many of these promiscuously inbred and intermixed clans of these multitudes as there were, just as many were the names by which they called themselves, in Greek, in Latin, in the babblements of their own bestial tongues, all of which they called Iebraeus. And likewise as various and inbred was the confusion of their primitive gods and beliefs. No matter how astute their skills at the swindlings of money-lending and currency-trading, they were fools for the taking, if not for the touching.

He could barely write his name, or that of the vicious god whose mark the particular branch of his foul race bore. In truth, he knew less of that false god than I did. As he was without learning, so he was without trade. He knew only to loiter, to connive, and to pilfer.

His eyes alone distinguished him from the other young wastrels who scurried through the streets like unweaned rats. The lie of sweet innocence in those soft, pale-brown eyes struck me the moment I chanced to look into them. They were eyes destined for greater games, greater gains.

It was I who envisioned and devised the means of those gains.

3

I HAVE TOLD YOU OF HOW THE WELL-CULTIVATED SEEDS OF MY
dedication to the art of oratory came to distinguish me among
the peerage for my success in representing accusers and the
accused, the innocent and the guilty alike in legal cases brought
before the Senate. I have told you of how this success was brought
to the attention of the emperor by his consuls, of how I entered
the emperor's court in a curule position, of restoring the fallen
dignity of our family's equestrian rank, and of being raised
above it.

My writing of speeches for the emperor differed from my
work as an advocate in two significant ways. I was now writing
orations to be delivered by another, as if he himself had composed them; and I was now no longer representing the innocent
and the guilty alike, but only the guilty, the same single guilty
man every day.

The lies that I placed in the mouth of the emperor grew from
eloquence to grandiloquence. But for occasional moments of
benevolent grandeur, which satisfied his vanity well, every measure he enacted and every devious path he pursued was for his
own gain at the expense of the populace and often of the
aristocracy as well. It pleased him that the words I wrote for
him were claimed to be his own. This pleased me also. To be
the concealer of his perfidies was a perfidy from which I wished
to be concealed.

To be sure, the speeches I wrote were more than duplicity, more than malfeasance. They were the recasting of horrible truth into beauteous falsehoods. His betrayals were turned into acts of beneficence, his thefts into acts of charity, his evil into good.

All words are mercenary. The same words that served Virgil serve the most wicked among us. The poet and the bringer of ruin are one. Oratory is the craft of convincing through words of forceful elegance. Morality is not elemental to it.

To veil the source of the words to which an emperor gives voice, a speech-writer is referred to as an advisor to the emperor. When we are moved by words at the theatre, it is against all reason that it is to the actor who has uttered them that we immediately respond, rather than to the unseen author of the words. So much more so if the Senate is the stage and the emperor, in all the imposing gravitas of his presence, is the actor. No one has ever asked his neighbor if he heard tell of what the emperor's speech-writer said on this occasion or that. He asks if he heard tell of what the emperor said. It is the puppet that gains the attention of the crowd, not the hidden puppeteer.

It is curious that in discussions with the princeps as to the illusions or effects he wished to bring about through his speeches I came in time to be closer to him than his actual appointed advisors. Slowly he drew me into the shadows of the secret truths that my words must hide with compelling splendor. This complicity was necessary to better achieve what he sought. He lavished gold on me at times. He promised me a praetorship at times. I knew that the lavishments, to insure my fidelity, were grudging and loath, and the promises, toward the same end, were hollow.

We were of a kind in a way, Tiberius and I—he reaching and grasping from on high, I from far below.

I had come to his court in the fourth year of his reign. It was in the ninth year of his reign that I saw madness overtake him. His carnal appetites, which had been always depraved, became ever more grotesque. He all but forsook appearing in public, and thus my oration-writing all but ceased and my role became that of a confidant who sometimes was called on to compose and impose what sense I could on lunatic proclamations or proposals of deranged laws. A confidant in the confidence of a madman.

He developed a custom of being carried on many mornings to the Tullianum, where those awaiting execution were brought out to kneel before him in a row. Strolling down the row of them, he looked at their faces and, knowing nothing of the crimes for which they had been condemned to die that day, often ordered that one or two of them be set free.

I asked him how he chose among them, and he said he encountered the faces of the innocent in his dreams. I asked him how he knew that he was not encountering the faces of the guilty in his dreams. He told me that he no longer merely enjoyed the honors due a god, and that he was no longer merely god-like. He told me that he had in fact become a god, and that nothing that was not good could enter the dreams of a god.

It seemed to me that he was very sincere in telling me this. It also seemed that the visible pleasure he derived from looking into the faces of those about to die was equally sincere. He told me that he could sense the rapidity with which their mortal hearts beat.

He could not see that all of Rome, from the streets to the Senate, had turned against him. He had abandoned them, they felt. He cared nothing for their welfare, they felt, or for that of Rome itself.

They were right. He had once been hailed as a great warrior and conqueror. Now he was looked on as a threat, a liability, a creature to be more despised than pitied.

He had his long periods of lucidity, but they grew fewer and briefer. All the while, there was within me a rising blight of agitation and confusion. I knew what I was not meant to know, and I did not know what to do with what I knew.

The princeps had but one surviving son and successor, Drusus, from his first marriage, to Vipsania Agrippina, whom her father, Agrippa, had betrothed to Tiberius when she was an infant in swaddling.

Lest your tutors have painted pretty pictures in a palimpsest of the truth, you know the politics of the late Republic, the first imperium, and the Julian and Claudian clans. They speak for all politics. One need not lay waste to time by learning the political history of our world. It is all the same, ever repeating. Different names, different faces. But all and always the same save for the extraneous detail of the embroidery. One need learn but a span, and learn it well, to understand eternity. For eternal is the nature of man's treachery, greed, and bestial hunger for power, which, well-groomed, is the essence and sum of politics.

Trust no man. Above all, trust no man of wealth who speaks of his concern for the welfare of the people or the common good.

Just as our first princeps, Augustus, had compelled the divorce between Livia, the mother of Tiberius, and her cousin Tiberius Claudius Nero, the father of Tiberius and a conspirator with the sicarians of Julius Caesar against Octavian before he had been raised to the title of Augustus, so it was Augustus who, on the death of his general Agrippa, compelled Tiberius to divorce Vipsania and marry her mother, Agrippa's widow, Julia, the daughter and only natural child of Augustus.

This was before Augustus, seeing those with claim to the succession perish—his grandsons by Julia and Agrippa, and his nephew by his sister, Octavia—and foreseeing Tiberius as his successor, adopted him, rendering him then the stepbrother as well as the third husband of his daughter, Julia.

As happy as was the fifty-year marriage of Augustus and Livia, the mother of Tiberius, just as unhappy was the marriage of Livia's son Tiberius and the daughter of Augustus, a termagant in whom the ways of a whore and the overbearing airs of an arrogant aristocratic bitch resided in full, equal, and abominable measure. After a while of wretched discord, Tiberius and Julia lived apart.

Augustus himself showed little liking for the man Tiberius had become. As a boy-soldier, Tiberius had accompanied Augustus, riding at his left side, on his triumphal entry into Rome after forcing the suicide of Marc Antony in Egypt. That noble boy-soldier, now in command of Rome's armies, had grown into a character so dissolute and wanton in his ways that his idlest degeneracies extended far beyond all conjecture and rumor. As much as Augustus had come to loathe Tiberius, he made a show of praising and supporting him, all for the sake of keeping power in the family hold.

A man orders another man to divorce his wife and marry her mother. He then adopts the man, whom he increasingly dislikes. The adopted son knows nothing but misery in his marriage to his former wife's mother. The enmity between the two men increases. But the one has ensured that his power will be passed to a man who has been configured into a shared lineage, even as he considers that man to be unworthy and undeserving. And he who has allowed himself to be configured and brought to misery has done so to ensure that power will be bequeathed to him.

What sane man cares so for the course the world's power will take after he is dead to it? A decomposing corpse, or a handful of tossed ashes, can feel nothing, know nothing. What satisfaction could Augustus have hoped to derive after he was but ashes in his pompous mausoleum on the Campus Martius? Were all his arrangements only to inflict a final revenge on the world? Were they a final raging against mortality? The man to whom power was passed descends slowly from misery to madness. Are such incomprehensibilities, manifest in the ways of these men, inherent in the malady of power?

When he succeeded Augustus as princeps, Tiberius made a great show of his own, affecting both humility and reluctance.

This show of humility was not long-lived. When addressed by senators as "master," he took offense, declaring this title to be an insult to his stature and power. He was, he said, master only to his slaves. To his armies, he was imperator. He was princeps to all, and of all. The title he dictated to be used on his coinage was Tiberius Caesar Augustus, Son of the Deified Augustus. While affectedly demurring in Rome to be regarded as a divinity, he allowed elsewhere, in Italy and farther lands, priests to be ordained in cults that worshipped him, temples and statues to be dedicated to him, and sacrifices to be made in his name.

His first act upon his accession had been to put to death Postumus Agrippa, son of his wife Julia by a previous marriage, grandson of Augustus, and a former potential heir to the throne. He had proclaimed this execution to be the fulfilling of a deathbed desire with which Augustus had entrusted him. That Augustus had years ago disowned his grandson lent a note of credibility to this claim. Few dared ask why, if he wished his grandson's execution, he had not seen to it himself rather than merely exiled him.

This world is a world of lies. If we seek truth, we must look to where no man speaks.

Tiberius looked often for guidance and counsel to an Egyptian of Greek blood named Thracyllus. This man was an astrologer, a soothsayer, a magician. It was he who had assured Tiberius that it was written in the occult signs of the stars that he would become emperor, thus insuring his lucrative employment until the day of his death, which came mere months, unforetold, before Tiberius's own. The emperor consulted Thracyllus almost daily. He bestowed Roman citizenship on him under the name Tiberius Claudius Thracyllus. Whatever of deception I did not learn through oratory and politics, I learned from Thracyllus the seer.

You have heard the story, be it true or not, of how Julius Caesar, while a quaestor in Farther Spain, dreamt one night of raping his mother, and, ordering that his soothsayer be brought to him, was told that it was a great and wondrous dream, for it augured that Caesar would one day ravish and conquer the world. It was among the oldest and slyest of ploys, to see the finest of fates in the future of a master of rank. If by chance the prophet were to be right, his gain would be considerable. If he were to be wrong, nothing would be lost.

At the same time, with Thracyllus installed in the luxury of the palace on the Palatine Hill, Tiberius banished all astrologers from Rome save those who begged his forgiveness and swore to abandon their black art.

He established the Delatores, a virulent and feared group of men whose duty it was to arrest and bring to his judgment all who were suspected of speaking, even privately in their own homes, against him or his rule.

He had studied rhetoric under Theodorus of Gadara. He could write and speak well. But not well enough to weave spells of lovely lies around his public doings. At the same time, he was much concerned that the rhetorical flourishings I wrote for him be taken as his own. Thus I was assigned also to compose several brief circumlocutions that he could memorize for seemingly extempore occasions. I was even to compose a series of Greek epigrams and a long lyric lament on the death of Lucius Caesar, all of which were recited and peddled as his own. The lament was especially sardonic, as Lucius Caesar was the second son of his wife Julia through her marriage to Agrippa, and detested by Tiberius on principle. The entire matter of writing verse to which he might put his name was in fact sardonic, as he took little pleasure from poetry. His only true pleasure lay in watching others suffer. That was his poetry. He devoted his leisure not to meter or rhyme but to devising implements and methods of torture. It is my consolation that I was never much of a poet, and thus the poetry with which he is credited is quite lackluster.

He spoke often of the love and happiness he had known with his first wife, Vipsania. It was difficult to accept him as capable of love or happiness. Perverse pleasures from perverse lusts, yes. What we call love, happiness: no. It may be that these are things that none of us knows. It may be that they are chimeras dreamt by us that we sometimes deceive ourselves into glimpsing during our waking moments. We long most for what we have never had and will never have. But it seemed that Tiberius never even dreamt these things, much less pursued them. If he did, if only for one errant, forgotten breath with Vipsania, it remained, like light caught in amber, in the eyes of their living son, Drusus. There were times when the emperor would halt Drusus, hold him by the jaw or the back of the neck, and look into those eyes. It was said by all that they were the eyes of his mother. And what does our name for amber mean? "Tears of the daughters of the god of the sun." The amber of the eye holds many things.

I had come to know much of the amatory appetites of the emperor. I knew he much preferred to irrumate than to be fellated, and he preferred to irrumate than to fuck. He favored young girls, those whose breasts were just budding. Young boys held almost no interest for him. But he enjoyed the Siphnian

fingerings of children, boys and girls together, who were trained
to minister in this manner, their little fingers lubricous with oil of
rosemary.

He was a loquacious expounder and critic of the imperfections
of the cunt, as well as of the imperfections of woman in general;
and for him cunnilingus and anilingus were the only unnatural
acts, the latter being acceptable if performed on, not by, him.

He was at times a paedicator of young men, many of his soldiers among them, but never paedicatus to them.

He bragged, with some exaggeration I am sure, that he never
had sex with a woman who was unbound, either by rope or thong
or shackle. This, he said, not only held them subject to his will but
also rendered all the more lascivious the especial undulations of
their haunches that we call *crisandum*.

The older he became, the younger the girls with whom he
consorted. Their breasts far from budding, they were often little
more than babes. They were brought to him by willing, even
eager, parents. It is remarkable what a mother or a father of little
means will do for a single coin of brass.

There were rumors that some of these children were not seen
again. I believed these rumors to be untrue. I know, however, of a
lute-player whose name was Aquilina. The emperor retained several girls to provide him with music when and as his whims and
moods desired. Aquilina was by far the most beautiful of these
girls. She did not live beyond her fifteenth year, and when death
stilled her, the emperor ordered her body cleansed, anointed with
perfumed unguents, and brought to him that he might bestow on
her remains his blessings.

There was an image of which I could not rid myself. I saw
Vipsania—a vague, shifting face and form that I never knew—
bound and captive at the moment that Drusus was conceived.

I was close to Drusus and believed him to be a good man and a good son, who knew his father to be a monster yet felt the blood that tied them. He was prone to drunkenness and to sudden outbursts. I prefer such visible flaws in men to those that lie hidden. These outbursts sometimes seemed to well up from a need to break free and be unbound from an unknown inner bondage of his own.

But this is phantom-talk such as fool physicians make. Let us just say that Drusus was a violent-tempered drunkard, and I liked him. We were about the same in years. We watched the downfall of his father together, though through quite different eyes, quite different amber.

Would Drusus retain me in his own imperial court? Should I tell him what I knew, or did he already know what I knew? Should I tell the princeps himself in one of his lucid moments, without knowing what his reaction might be, in lucidity or derangement? Drusus, as I had witnessed often and as I have said, was a man of unpredictable violent tempers. His father more so by the day. Should I keep my silence, leave the court with my gold and finery, go my way, and let the dice roll and come to rest as they might? Or might such a flight later be seen as a sign of involvement on my part, with retribution due?

I grappled with these questions. Perhaps because what I knew seemed to be madness, and he was mad, I decided at last to reveal my knowledge to the emperor. I really do not recall what the line of my thoughts at that time was. It very well may have been that, as it was Tiberius and not his son and heir, Drusus, who held the riches, I should likely be rewarded handsomely for my life-saving loyalty.

I grow impatient and short with myself at how I say what I say to you. It is as if I am living through those days again. This is no time to live my past again. There is no time to live the past again. I want only to tell it, and that is all.

There are occasions, too, when I pause to craft flourishes of oratory in this narrative. As it is said, the habits of youth accompany us in age. But I have not here set out to compose a literary work of ornate inflections, subtle sonorities, and poetic filigree for the eyes of posterity. I have set out to write a plain and simple narrative of my life for you alone, and I must stay that plain and simple course. The time to deliberate upon eloquence is gone. Cicero long ago said that no man is so old as to think he cannot live another year. In the infirmities of my age, I am that man who disproves his wit.

We sat together in the garden, Tiberius and I. We drank good wine of smoked Alban grapes and watched the flight of birds in the vernal blue sky. I remember it was the ides of Maia, the day of the full moon of the goddess of spring, daughter of the god of the sun, in the ninth year of his principate.

"Would you say that the man closest to you is the prefect of your Praetorian Guard?" I asked.

"Yes," he said. "I would say that I trust young Sejanus more than I trust any other."

"And are you fond of Livilla?"

"I care only that she be a good wife to Drusus."

"And you know that Sejanus and Livilla have been quite involved behind your son's back?"

His eyes did not turn from the sky.

"I've had her as well," he said. "I'm surprised you haven't."

I had, but I said nothing of it.

"Her cunt is a sewer," he said. "Her mouth is a sewer. Her asshole is a sewer."

"And you know that as they copulate they conspire to kill both you and your son so that Sejanus might rule?"

His wrath was upon me like a sudden storm. I was jealous of Sejanus, he inveighed. I was an invidious ingrate. I was seeking gain through vicious betrayal.

Looking back, I think that what truly enraged and offended him was that I had the temerity to know what he, as a god, did not know. I had impugned his sagacity, or his all-knowing divinity.

Then he fell silent. His eyes were on me as on a dog who had misbehaved. Then his eyes were not on me, and nothing more of the matter was said.

The summer was a beautiful one, and the warm night winds through the gardens brought an air of fable to the moonlit frolickings and cavortings of the mad Tiberius, who danced, declaimed, and deified from tree to tree, bush to bush.

As the night winds grew cooler and summer neared its end, young Drusus was murdered by his stepmother and Sejanus in concert. The response of Tiberius to the death of his son was to embrace Sejanus all the more tenderly, proclaiming him "the partner of my labors" and commanding statues of him to be raised throughout the precincts of Rome.

I took a few dictations from Tiberius for a treatise he fancied himself to be compiling on the occult communications of butterflies, but during the three years afterward I wrote no more speeches for him, because he made no more speeches. For that matter, he became all but unseen by the public. Sejanus employed his own speech-writer, and I was pleased with that. I did my best to avoid the prefect. I idled and drew my pay, which was handsome.

One quiet afternoon, I woke in open sunlight in the gardens and undertook removing myself to the shade nearby where cornel trees blossomed. My thoughts wove through the softening golden light and lengthening shadows in the bright of the sun that could no longer be seen. I did not hear the approach of Tiberius as he came stalking to me.

He stood before me. He beheld me as if I were a stranger, an intruder. He dismissed me with imprecations.

"Go now," he commanded.

It struck me full as I beheld him that there was little trace of the Tiberius I had known twelve years ago and more. He had been an august and imposing figure then. The sixty-seven-year-old man who stood before me now, trembling with madness, was stooped and emaciated, toothless, with sores and scabs on his withered bald head, and a face of red blotches that could not be hidden by the cosmetic plasters on them.

I went to my chamber to fetch my robes, my writing tools, and my gold. The gold was gone. Not one aureus remained in the leather pouch that had grown full through the years.

Thus was I banished to the Judean provinces, to a clerical post in the capital city of Caesarea Maritima, on the farther shore of the Great Sea.

"I am too merciful."

These were, or so I thought, the last words I would ever hear from him. Unlike his Thracyllus, I made no pretense of reading the future in the stars.

4

M Y WIFE, YOUR GRANDMOTHER AELINA, AND I HAD GROWN apart through the years. No man who serves an emperor can be a good husband. I saw to it that she and our young son, your father, were well provided for in every way. Duties, and idleness, at the palace had kept me from home for long periods, but she and your father were very dear to me. On the quay at Ostia, when I bade them good-bye before boarding for Judea, I shared with them my sincere belief and hope that I would be with them again soon. My duties in Caesarea Maritima would not be so consuming as they had been here, and I would be able to return to visit them in a matter of months. It was truly my desire to renew my family life, and I declared this to Aelina while holding her close in my arms. From the ship I saw that she wept, and your father consoled her. I was never to see her again.

It was not long after I left that Tiberius withdrew to Capri to rule in absentia, leaving Rome to Sejanus in his stead.

Was it fear that drove the princeps Tiberius from Rome, or was it, following the death of his son, a complete loss of concern for the world? Or was it both?

The conspirator and the emperor now shared the consulship, the one as a dictator in Rome, the other as a man who now pursued little but the gratification of his senses, and who dwelled on an island that was many miles and far away.

The diviners said that Tiberius would never be seen again in

Rome. He had a great palace built for him on remote Capri. He called this palace but a villa, and he dedicated it in name to Jupiter, the foremost of the gods, the god of sky and storm and thunder.

In the same year that Tiberius left Rome for Capri, an equestrian of the Pontii family, Pontius Pilate by name, succeeded Valerius Gratus as prefect of Roman Judea. He lived in a palace built by Herod, the murderous client king of Judea. As king of the Jews, Herod had hated his kind as they had hated him. He had a succession of ten wives, and sons by most of them. He killed two of these sons with the same nonchalance with which he killed many rabbis. After his death, other sons of his reigned as client kings throughout Judea.

Valerius had been Tiberius's man, and had served more than ten years under him. Pontius Pilate, appointed in the eleventh year of the reign of Tiberius, also formally served the emperor, who was now in self-imposed exile. But he was Sejanus's man.

It was he, Pilate, born like me to the equites order, whom I was condemned to serve in a god-forsaken land. But before ever I came before him, I felt myself drawn to him. It was not my will, nor my desire. It was merely something that I felt, a vagueness, a feeling beyond which I could not see.

My voyage, by light, fast-sailing liburna rather than by heavier galley, was good. The moon and fine summer winds were with us, filling our sail for long spells. The oarsmen were strong, and preferred the pain of hard rowing to the pain of the lash. There were days, a good many of them, when we must have made a hundred and twenty sea-miles or more.

To a Jew banker not far from the harbor I sold a brooch of emerald set in gold, my golden serpent bracelet with eyes of black onyx, and one of two rings, each of gold and with a ruby flanked by a pair of six-pointed Indian diamonds. The rings were identical.

They had been given to me by Tiberius, in the ninth year of his principate, at about the time I first sensed madness overtaking him. They were, these rings, an astoundingly generous and sumptuous presentation that indicated both my rank in the equestrian order and my place of high distinction in his court. The inner bands of both rings were inscribed with my name, his, and the year.

The ring that remained is mine still, and is destined to be yours.

Also in my possession, sewn into my cloak, were three magnificent pearls, the most precious and valuable of all jewels, and these, from the Indian ocean, were the most precious and valuable of all pearls. These, as always, I kept in secret, never mentioning them, and never losing sight of my cloak.

After all his tedious wheedling, weaseling, lying, and arch imposturing, it was only by forming a sort of consortium with two of his neighboring hagglers-in-avarice that the Jew banker could summon sufficient money to satisfy my desire and demand to be only modestly swindled.

I wandered slowly in the general direction of the palace, which I could see atop a promontory that jutted out into the sea. The well-guarded residential palace of the proconsul and those under him was called the Palace of Herod, after he who had built it.

In a dark by-way, I came upon my loiterer. The marble of the palace, which glowed pale blue in the distance, was immediately overtaken by something that glowed pale brown, like amber, in his eyes.

If there was thought in my mind, it left me in that moment. He saw my gaze and smiled. It was a smile of faint, aloof malevolence, a curse of a smile.

As I had wandered vaguely toward the palace, so thought, vague and wandering, returned to me.

The shabbier streets of this place and time were filled with ranting or mumbling messiahs, with howling or gesticulating claimants to prophecy, some of them alone and ignored, some of them drawing a sparse group of passing listeners, some of them gathering crowds. I thought of gods and men.

This sort of thing was not unknown in Rome, though it was much less noticeable. Among my earliest orations for Tiberius was one on the occasion of his decree abolishing the cults of the Egyptians and the Jews. The oration justified this on the grounds that the increasing proselytizing of these cults posed a dangerous threat to the established, time-honored nature of Roman worship and thus to the integrity of the traditional fabric of Roman society itself. Public displays aside, he himself believed in no god or gods, except perhaps, later, himself. His true concern was that the growing number of Roman converts to the Egyptian and Jewish cults was a peril to the foundations of his own power, which rested on the authority of the autochthonic gods.

The Jews claimed that they sought no converts. But their forced conversion and forced circumcision of the multitudes of Idumaea, conquered by them under Hyrcanus II, the high priest and king of Judea, spoke otherwise. Herod was of the Phoenician-Syrian stock of Idumaea, where he was born. His grandfather was among the conquered.

All who embraced the Egyptian and Jewish cults were ordered to burn their cultic vestments and destroy the idols and other accessories of their worship. Priests of Isis were crucified, the statue of Isis in the great Iseum, in the ninth administrative region of the city, was demolished, and the Iseum itself was shut. As for the Jews, who were a more numerous and significant presence in Rome, the actions taken against them were less severe. Some Jews of military age were drafted and removed to the most unhealthy marshes, there to die more than to serve. Some Jews of elderly years who did not worship the gods of Rome were simply expelled from the city under the threat of being reduced to slavery if they remained or revisited.

But Isis returned to Rome, as did the principal god of the Jews, who in their Book and rites had a confusion of many names, some of them denoting plurality and some singularity, one of which, rarely uttered, was an incomprehensible guttural muddlement, like the attempt to speak of a man whose tongue has been torn from him.

And new converts they did make, for unfulfilled by one thing, man will seek fulfillment in another. An old toga will be put away for a new one, though there be little or no difference between the two. As from one wife to another, so from one god to another.

But of late in Rome, and all the more intensely here, one could sense among the Jews a growing search for a portent, a promise, a coming of the new. A new day, a new life, a new age? Were they waxing weary of their weary old god himself, or gods themselves? Old gods do die, and new gods do appear.

Anxious anticipation was rife in the air. For a thousand years, their Book had promised them a final, consummating savior. His time, many felt, had now come. Unbeknownst to them, endless expectation may have been their truest and most enduring captivity. Enough of this ancient promise, this eternity of waiting, complaint, and moaning. They wanted fulfillment of a thousand years' prophecy. They wanted it now.

There was among them a history of redeemers and deliverers. The demigods of their Book were such. All histories are lies. We have our she-wolf, our Romulus and Remus. The Jews favored a history of oppressions and slavery. Their Book tells of captivities in Egypt, in Babylon. Captivities that never were. Deliverances from them that never were. Yes, histories are lies, but the nature of the lies that are embraced tells us something of the nature of those who embrace them.

Perhaps they had come to see themselves as captives under Roman dominion. Only rarely were they slaves. The slaves of Rome were then as now brought in their greatest numbers from Asia and Africa, with lesser numbers from Spain and from among the Gallic, Germanic, and later the Britannic tribesmen. And there have been many natives to our own soil to be enslaved for theft or debt. Jews were free in their own land to work and worship as they would. Julius Caesar himself had bestowed legitimacy on their cult. Far more Jews owned slaves than were slaves themselves.

Whatever it was they sought, the long-overdue fulfillment of prophecy—their final, consummating savior—was central to it. This was evinced by the mangy messiahs thick as flies in the offal and shit of the streets.

In the breadth of an instant, an ocean of thought seemed to be mine. Or was it but the single crashing down of one immense wild wave of envisioning?

I saw the high priests of the cults of Rome—the riches of Mithras, the riches of Cybele, the riches of the pontiffs of the temples of the Capitoline Triad of Jupiter, Juno, and Minerva. I saw the riches of the high priests and the rulers of the synagogues of the cults of the Jews in Judea, compounded by riches gotten through those with whom they were in league, the usurers and money-merchants in the yards of their temples.

I saw wealth beyond imagining. I saw the principate of the other world, and the vast treasures of the real world that derive therefrom.

I saw that every prayer was a profession of the ignorance and benighted folly of he who knelt, that he who prayed avowed

himself a fool for the taking. I saw lambs to the slaughter. I saw
fortunes falling from the hands of believers into the coffer of the
believed.

I saw many things in that lightning bolt of an instant, that
fulmination of a breath between a lowering and rising of the
lashes of my loiterer's eyes.

I had given Tiberius dignity, had given him counsel and fine
words of commanding and enchanting powers. I had created the
lie of him and the illusion of him. What I had done, I could do in
the dream-world. Different words, different calculations, but the
same game.

What I had done, I could do again. I had cultivated a god in
whom no one but himself believed. I could mold and fashion of
other clay a new prophet, to whom those seeking a new prophet,
and then the masses beyond them, would flock. With no master
to serve, no master to restrict or command me, my craft would be
free to flourish to the fullest.

It was strange, but there was no uncertainty in me as to this
unsavory loiterer with his eyes that seemed, like obsidian, to hold
in them the magic of the most powerful of the elements — earth,
air, water, fire — commingled. He was my man, this loiterer. There
was something eerie in my sureness. There was something eerie in
it all: this place, this moment, the sinister otherworldliness in the
late afternoon air, the weave of light and gloom. A sense of presentiment moved through me, then was gone.

I returned his look with one in kind, and I strode casually to
him. As I approached, he regarded me with a slightly different
but no less malevolent smile, one that implied I was soon to be a
victim, perhaps not of him directly, but of something of which I
knew nothing.

We were face to face. He no longer smiled in any way, nor did
I. Without words I told him that he was nothing, no one, a lowly

Jew peasant in thrall to almighty conquering Rome, and that he stood before a Roman citizen of rank.

He absorbed this wordless meaning written in my stern face and stance, and suspicion came over his demeanor.

And so we faced each the other. I introduced myself to him.

"I am Gaius Fulvius Falconius, son of Marcus, grandson of Lucius."

He did not speak. I looked into those lambent eyes, the likes of which I had never before seen.

He was toying aimlessly with a plane-twig, holding it in both hands, or moving it occasionally from one hand to another. Now in the unpaved street, he used it to write six Greek characters.

"I am he."

I read aloud the name in the dirt: Iesous. It was the common name that we would render as Iesus in Latin. He corrected me, saying it rather as something like Iesua. I took this to be Hebrew, but I was right only in ignorance. I was later to learn that a dialect called Aramaic had much displaced Hebrew as the written tongue of the Jews, and that much of their Book was written in this related language.

Hebrew, however, was the spoken tongue among them, along with Greek and often Latin. I also was to learn that the common name of Iesous, or Iesus, or Iesua, was but a form of the commoner Ieosua, or, as we have it, Iosua.

I can only trust that you have heard, or will hear, these names, Iesua and Ieosua, pronounced by a Jew in the Hebrew tongue, as their true sounds are not represented by any combination of characters in Greek and Latin, and our spelling Iesus gives rise to nothing that sounds of his name, unless perhaps in the case of a grave speech impediment. It involves a rising of the tongue toward the palate that I have encountered elsewhere only among a few unlettered Germanic and lately Britannic tribals.

Yes, it would be good for you to have his rightful name, as he and I here begin to travel forward in this account.

That you could hear the sound of my own voice is a dream that can never be.

My loiterer raised his head from the name he had written in the street, but did not look directly to me.

"Born of dirt, son of nothing," he added.

Surmising that, like most of his countrymen, his Latin was wanting at best, I had spoken to him with words of Greek preceding my name when introducing myself; and it was in Greek—a slovenly and a heavily accented Greek, but Greek nonetheless—that he now said what he did.

It was perhaps his intention to make mockery of the manner in which I had introduced myself, but I felt no insult. I was indeed pleased to have evidence of his own innate gift for words, wry as they were.

"Why are you here?" he asked.

"I come seeking you."

Pretense left him. He appeared to be puzzled, in a wary way.

"Tell me," I said, looking round, then back to him. "Which of these saviors will save you?"

He beheld them, the messianic rabble, with the same mean smile with which he had met my initial gaze. That smile seemed to extend not only to the confusion of expectation and disappointment, impatience and resignation, ranting and yowling, that filled those streets, but to the dusty foul air itself of those streets. Three small, slender shadow-figures, fast and furtive, fled past us.

In answer to my question, he gestured to the dirt in which he had written his name, much of which already had vanished in the wind and the dust.

"Such was my hope," I said.

He sighed wearily, echoed my words guardedly: "Such was your hope."

"It can do us no harm to eat, drink, and talk."

"I no longer play the catamite for money," he said. "These buttocks lack meat, but they are not for sale."

"It is not your buttocks I want. It is your soul. And it is not money I speak of, but riches. The sort of riches that would make their sort seem as paupers by comparison."

I threw a slight nod of my head to the northwest, in the direction of the synagogue courtyard where I had sold my jewels — the direction of the Jew money-lenders and currency-traders.

"A new and vaster kind of temple-wealth," I said.

Again from him, that weary sigh.

We chose an inn. It had not been his fortune to eat there, he said, but he assured me that I should like it, as it was owned, tended, and frequented by men of Rome. We took a table and benches apart from the others who ate and drank. A few, mostly Roman soldiers, regarded us askance, but with little malice or pronounced disapproval. I could not tell if it was because he was a Jew, or because he was unwashed and disheveled, or both. We were told what was on offer. I took a portion of roasted baby pork, he a plate of deep-sea oysters and garum. Two fresh breads were brought to us, oyster-bread for him, bread of emmer for me, and wine.

"I am forbidden by the Book to eat such things," he said, gesturing to the oysters.

I looked at him.

"All that have not fins and scales in the seas, they shall be an abomination unto you," he said in a tone of mock gravity. Then in the tone that was his own: "So commands the Book."

He savored the oysters and garum, tore off a piece of bread, ate it, washed it down with wine.

"And the swine," he said, returning to his tone of mock gravity, "though he be cloven-footed, he cheweth not the cud, and thus he is unclean to you."

I cut off a piece of the charred suckling pig, placed it with my knife on his plate. His eyes closed with pleasure as he ate it.

"It seems to me that your Book denies you much," I said.

"It denies me nothing. It denies to my people any delight in this world which their God is supposed to have created."

He told me of a legendary hero of the Book, a man named Job, on whom the one true God, as a sort of game, inflicted all manner of torments, woes, and pains, taking from him everything: his family, his property, his health. But not once did Job raise his voice in protest or anger at this God. For this he is an exemplar, much to be admired and much to be praised.

"That," said he, "is the one true delight of the Jews under their one true God—to suffer."

We laughed together, he more meanly than I. He offered me an oyster, which I took, without garum. It was fresh, delicious, pulsing yet with life from the sea.

Eating the rich, warm bread, he told me of a bread of his people, unleavened and bland, called *massa,* not to be confused with our good barley-bread of similar name. This tasteless bread is to be eaten during their holy spring feast, when no other bread is permitted.

"In the Book, it is called 'the bread of affliction.' It is true. The Jew's delight is to suffer."

I told him of our Altar of Bad Luck, Mala Fortuna, on the Esquiline, not far from the old necropolis.

Do you know the place? Have you been there yet, to that old disreputable stretch between the old altar and the old necropolis? We caroused there many a night, we boys of the age you are now, roaming amid the cheap wine-shops and the young whores who haunted the dark overgrown grounds of the necropolis in their diaphanous unsashed gowns of salacious mourning, caressed by the summer moon, and by us. One warm night my father caught me about my idle mischief there. After a good stern calling-out and a clap to the side of my head, he laughed and mused aloud how he had gone about the same boyish carousings there more than thirty years past. I tell you, those were good days. There was continuity between generations then, shared passages between father and sons.

"Yes," I said, more to myself in reminiscence, than to him in conversation, "the Altar of Bad Luck."

"Here there is no other kind," he said.

He shook his head as if it were beyond his understanding, all of it.

"Bread of affliction," he muttered.

"Why do you cultivate a beard?" I asked.

"Because it is the custom of my people. It is believed to be a sign among them that one has renounced vanity."

"So it is, therefore, an affectation, a vanity of its own?"

"Yes."

"You speak of 'my people' but of 'them' and not 'us.' Are you not one of 'them'?"

"In blood, yes. In belief and ways, no."

"You do not believe, then, in the many-named god, or gods, of your people?"

"I left behind me those fables when I was little more than a child."

"So why, again, the beard?"

"To appear to be one of the many. To be indistinguishable."

A very good reason for a petty thief and cutpurse, which I surmised him to be, and which he was.

After chewing intently, he corrected me, saying: "It is not a

41

matter of god or gods. My people believe in only one God, almighty. The plural names of the oldest days, the days of other gods, have been artfully if unconvincingly explained away. He has for very long been held to be one, and one alone, and the one true God."

"And you do not believe in him?"

"If I believe in anything, it is as the Persians believe: that there is a force for good and a force for evil at play in this world. I do not believe in the Persian gods, but at times, yes, I believe in the forces that they embody."

"You are an educated man," I said. "To know of Persia, to know of what Persians believe."

"I have kept my eyes open, my ears open, in this world. I have learned much beyond what the rabbis teach." He paused. "We have taken much from what they, the Persians, believe. Much of Persian source is to be found in some of the scriptures of our Book."

"You know the Book very well, it seems."

So much was obvious, and I said this only to maneuver the conversation.

"The fables of the Book are like nursery songs that are put early into us. But they are nursery songs that haunt us from the cradle to the tomb."

"In the Book, there is truly the prophecy and promise of a coming savior?"

"It is written in the Book, in the scripture that is called the book of Isaiah. He speaks much of the wrath of our God, this Isaiah. And he prophesies the coming of a great savior, and he tells of the signs, the deeds and attributes, by which this savior will be made known."

We had, then, in this Isaiah, map and manual for the journey before us. He would be the Vitruvius of our kingdom come. As had been prophesied, so we would fulfill; and the words I would give to the voice of the Messiah would further attest, beyond all refuting, the truth and the grandeur of him.

I laid open my scheme to him. All my thoughts, all that passed through me in the fulminous infinite moment I had experienced, I laid open to him.

As I spoke, words came forth from him as well. Words of ridicule, words of querulous dismissiveness. His declarations grew calmer and less frequent, and were overtaken by questions. These questions were at first cynical and disputatious; then full of doubt and hesitance; then, in the end, complicitous.

He sopped the last of the bread in what was left of the olive oil, and drank the last of the wine. There was but one more question from him:

"So tell me, Gaius et cetera et cetera, son of this one, grandson of that one. How are these hypothetical riches to be divided between us?"

I slowly raised the blade of my knife and just as slowly lowered it vertically to cleave in twain the air between us.

"Straight down the middle."

Those eyes of his glowed, as if there were no wine in him, and he smiled.

He had no home. In bad weather, he explained, he lodged in brothels. In good weather, the vaulted recesses of the streets offered many a fine enough bedchamber. When he said this, he ran his fingers over the handle of the dagger in the sash of his rough and soiled linen tunic. As he did so, I became conscious of my own dagger, iron and double-edged, that hung in its sheath from my leather belt. Its grip was inlaid with gold and ivory, the golden claw of its pommel clutched a great single sapphire of deepest blue that I had brought back from Ethiopia in the youthful days of my military service. Like my one remaining ring of gold, ruby, and diamonds, and my secret pearls, my dagger would not be sold to any Jew. It would not be sold to any man, and no man would take it from me.

The hour was late. An owl under old eaves across the way seemed to lay claim to this lost little corner of deserted darkness, where there were very few lighted lamps.

We took rooms at the inn where we had eaten. The rooms were small and shabby, but after my long voyage at sea, and compared to his usual sleeping arrangements, they presented themselves as luxurious.

I found in my satchel the perfunctory letter of assignment that I now knew I would never place in the hand of Pilate or his adjutant.

I slept with my wealth beneath the reed-filled mattress-sack on which the weight of my body lay. My tired thoughts, wending their way to dark dreams, were good.

I had nothing to lose. Or so it then seemed.

5

You may think me a scoundrel, my dear boy. But look into yourself and see, even at your own young age, your thoughts, your shames, your feelings of guilt. Know that all men are scoundrels, but that the honest among them are few. Never trust a man who claims to be pure in his thoughts or pure in his motives. To yourself at least, be honest and not a liar, and never a believer of your own lies any more than the lies of others.

The gods are imagined things, and all of them are false. Cupidity is real. I should rather be accused of fraud than of faith.

I want you to understand these things. I want you to feel the understanding of them in the marrow of your being.

Keep with you always the apothegms of the Seven Sages. Above all, the words of Bias: "Most men are bad." And the words, too, of Thales: "Know thyself." And of Pittacus: "Know thine opportunity." Few have gone wrong under the guidance of the Seven Sages.

To seek wisdom is to pursue the greatest thing that a man can possess. To attain it is to achieve his greatest glory. To ignore it is to commit the greatest sin against himself and the fast-extinguished life he has been given.

Wisdom is like a snake that moves unseen in the grasses where we stand. Many men go their lives without even glimpsing it, and others, glimpsing it, flee from it. I speak not of the common little tamed snakes that are kept as pets in homes to catch vermin, nor of the common little tamed snakes that crawl openly in the places of the sick and in the temples of oracles. These and the snake of wisdom are not one. Tiberius kept a snake, of which he was quite fond. I was told, after I left the court, that he one day found it dead and much consumed by rats and ants. Yet Tiberius possessed no wisdom. His mind was in the same state as that of his dear snake, dead and much consumed by creatures that feed on the dead.

The snake that is wisdom, rarely seen, and from which many men flee, is no common tamed thing. It is more a horned viper. The snake that winds round the rough-hewn staff of Asclepius, the two snakes that wind round the winged herald's staff of Hermes, our Mercury. The serpent round the spear-headed staff of Minerva, our embodiment of wisdom, our Sophia, or the serpent at her feet. These are representations of the viper of wisdom. In the case of the entwined snakes of the caduceus of Mercury, one indiscernible from the other to our eyes, the one snake is the serpent of ignorance, the other is the viper of wisdom. So alike they appear, so different they are.

Men saw Hermes as the god of thieves and trickery. Men see Mercury as the protector of thieves.

Regard well the caduceus. Listen well to what moves in the grasses near you. Fear not the viper, for what is deadly venom to the fool is nectar to him who would know wisdom.

And I? Be I wise man or fool? I do not know. But I do know that these are the words of a man too old to lie. Death is no longer the supreme terror. The supreme terror is being taken by death with a lie on one's lips.

6

THE SKIES WERE KIND TO JESUS AND ME AS WE JOURNEYED. Storms were few. What little rain there was, refreshed. The late summer winds were pleasant. We moved easily, slept well. The early mornings brought us balm-dew.

I remember the breezes and the butterflies and the birds, the stars and the fire-flies and the glow-worms. I tend not to recall as vividly the mosquitoes and the ticks and the scorpions and darting adders. Such is memory. Such are its ways.

As we traveled, he told me of things that were in the Book. At night, in silence, by our fire kindled with tinder scrub, flint, and pyrite, I composed the plain-sounding but carefully crafted words that would be his sermons, his teachings, his wisdom and his forewisdoms, his seeings and his foreseeings.

From the Way of the Philistines, the ancient trade route between Cairo and Damascus, we crossed the Sharon plain on the highway that led from Caesarea, past Narbata, to Gitta. There we took the southeastern road, which in time brought us to Sebaste.

When we reached the fork of the road at Sebaste, we veered to the left, which took us south on the Beth El-Shechem highway through the fertile valley east of Mount Gerizim. The way was lush with trees.

Just beyond the city of Shechem, we found springs of cool delicious water that issued from the rock of Gerizim.

Above one of the springs, there was a tree that grew out sideways from a crevice in the crag. The tree curved upward from years of seeking the sun. Beneath it, in a recess of smooth stone, there was a deep pool. We lingered there, and as we did so, it occurred to me to seize the opportunity to introduce him to cleanliness.

He demurred at first, but I would have none of it.

"It is good for a holy man to have about him the look of the ascetic, the humble, the scorner of worldly comfort. Yes, that is good. But no one wants a savior who stinks of his own shit."

Removing my clothes, I told him to do the same. Lowering myself into the water, my garments in hand, I told him to do the same. Rubbing my wet garments against the stone, then swirling them about in the water, I told him to do the same. Laying them out on dry risings of stone at the pool's edge, I had him do the same. Scrubbing all over my body, face, and hair with my hands, I had him do the same. There was a spreading film of scum in the water round him, and a millipede as well, though I was not sure that this slithering louse had not emerged from the elements rather than from him. I bent my knees and immersed my head beneath the water, then rose, splashed about a bit, and climbed out into the sunlight. He did the same.

After that baptizing plunge, we rarely came to a stream without his stopping to free the sash from his tunic and bathe. He became something of a dandy in this way.

He had not the usual coarse wiry hair common to the Jews of the region. His skin, too, was more fair. Indeed, looking at him, you might think that his true father were other than the man he believed to be his father. I bought him a wooden comb, and he took to combing locks and beard alike as he came forth from his ablutions. He cursed sharply to comb from his hair some scorpions of small size. He began to follow my example of breaking off sapling twigs, chewing their ends to pulp, and brushing my gums, teeth, and tongue with them. Going further, he gathered the leaves from mint and hyssop plants whenever he found them, and chewed them long and ate them, until there was an ethereal air in his breath and speech.

I told him of the finest and most lavish baths of Rome, built on natural hot springs. I told him of their tranquil cultivated gardens of exotic foliages, their dining-rooms of savory delicacies. I told him of their steaming heated rooms to bring forth purifying sweat, whereafter awaited cold pools to close the pores and invigorate the blood humor. I told him of the scrubbing-stones of tufa, of pumice, and of the sea-sponges. I told him of the scented balms, rare ointments, volcanic muds. I told him of the massagings of the bath physicians, the painstaking ministrations of the depilators with their razors and tweezers. I told him of the various specialized skills of the depilators.

"Ones to remove the unsightly hair that grew from nostrils and ears. Even ones to tend to the hair of the anus."

He looked at me, unsure as to whether I had made this last statement in jest.

"Yes," I assured him. "*Depilatio podicis.* The depilatory grooming of the asshole."

"I should like very much to visit such a place," he said.

"You will," I told him. "Our way is long, but it leads to Rome. The wealthiest of Romans have all the facilities and attendants of the most luxurious baths under the roofs of their estates. So will you. You will witness the building of your own temple in Rome, and the building too of your own private villa. Then you can bathe away your life in luxury and leisure. Your riches will be such. As will mine."

Thus I foresaw it. I beheld him as he allowed himself to imagine it.

But I amused myself at the same time by thinking of a man coming to Rome with no Latin other than the two words constituting the careful tidying of the anus.

All along the way south from Shechem, we came upon towns and villages. We procured food, drink, and supplies as we needed them from every town, village, and settlement through which we passed.

We had much dried fruit, such as raisins, figs, dates, apricots, pomegranates. We had smoked and salted meats, smoked and salted fish, dried pulse. We cooked good meals with water boiled in our clay pot, which hung with the rest of our possessions from the stalwart dun jack donkey that was our beast of burden. There were butterfat and whey in goatskins. There were cheeses, leavened and unleavened breads, olive oil and vinegar in which to immerse them. Our wineskin was never empty, and we never wanted for spring-water.

He reprimanded me for paying for what he said he could as easily steal. His most exasperated rebuke came when I tossed a coin to a blind man who was offering almonds for alms.

I told him that we were about to assume a posture of purity and innocence, and that this was a posture that could be brought down by the least transgression.

"You shall steal no more," I commanded him, "except from God."

With our bare hands, we sometimes caught and gutted fresh fish for the fire. There were wild boars, and we hungered for them; but neither of us knew to hunt except by trap, or dogs and pig-stick, and as we stopped only to camp when the sun fell, there was no time to trap, and we had no dog, bay dog or catch dog or otherwise. But my good Jesus did once drive his dagger into a rabbit, and, with garlic, hunks of old bread, and choppings of a yellow-flowering fennel plant that we dug from the sandy soil, it made for delicious stew.

We lived well for the most part, and were often as gay as two boys on an adventure. My legs, which in recent years had grown weak, were renewed in strength.

We made our way to the south, to the city of Bethlehem, in the hill country, west of the lake that is called the Dead Sea. Bethlehem was known in the Book as the city of the patriarch David, the house of the patriarch David, who was born there in time out of mind. Isaiah of the Book prophesied that there would be born a child, a son, on whose shoulders all holy authority and governance would rest, and he would become known as the mighty God, the Father everlasting, and the Prince of Peace. This holy authority and governance was likened by Isaiah to a key, the key to the kingdom, the key of the house of the patriarch David. Other prophets in the Book also looked to Bethlehem, to the house of David, for the birth of the new god, the bearer of the key, the Prince of Peace.

Whenever we came upon natural beauty, we rested. If the cool of evening was in the air, we settled down for the night amid that beauty. Walking slowly, we advanced less than ten miles, or five of his parasangs, in a day, and even less when the way was steep or treacherous. This afforded us much time to converse at leisure, to more deeply come to know one another, to learn from one another, to discuss and lay the finer points of our scheme.

We progressed slowly also because we both were lazy by nature. This shared inclination to a languid pace rendered all the more comfortable our traveling together.

Somewhere in the countryside, south of a settlement where fig trees, olive trees, and almond trees were in abundance, we spent the night in a grassy place that was rich with the rare, wondrous scent of balsam, though there was not one balsam tree to be seen.

"We come upon almond trees bare of almonds," Jesus said. "Fig trees and olive trees whose fruit is not yet ripe enough to harvest. And here we are, in the dream-like midst of balsam trees that cannot be seen."

"Well, they are quite small trees," I said. I was sitting, and I raised the flat of my hand to a bit over the top of my head.

"Yes, small. But not so small as to be invisible." We slept that night without dreams.

After some days, my companion let it be known to me that he himself had in fact been born in Bethlehem, or so he had been told. It was, he said, an accident, for his family was of Nazareth, very far to the north, in Galilee. But his father came from Bethlehem. When, early in the third decade of his reign, Augustus decreed a census for the taxation of the joined provinces of Syria and Judea, those who did not abide where they were born were obliged to register where they were indeed born. It was on this return to Bethlehem that his mother, who was heavy with him, gave birth. In youth he had known only Nazareth, but this was the tale of his birth that had been told him. Every time it was told, his mother added that his was a breech birth, and so had caused her more pain than the births of her other children.

I had no memory of any such census decree, nor had I ever heard of any such decree, or any such census. I told him this. It also struck me as very unlikely, indeed nonsensical, absurd, for a census to oblige men to return to their places of birth to be registered. I told him this as well.

"It has always seemed the same to me," he said. "That is why I have made no mention of it until now. As I say, it is a tale that

I was told. It is as if I had been told this tale to veil something from me."

He shrugged, exhaled, and spat.

As he reckoned that he was born in the year of a census that we both felt was more fable than truth, he confessed that he did not know when or where he was born.

His earliest memories, he said, did indeed date to the third decade of the reign of Augustus, to a time when Marcus Ambivulus was the Roman prefect of Judea. I knew that Ambivulus had overseen Judea and Samaria from the thirty-sixth to the fortieth year of the reign of the emperor Augustus.

For him to have been aware, in his days of earliest memory, of the name of the prefect, he would have been of about the age when children of Roman families of rank began their schooling, in their seventh year.

I was now in my fortieth year. By the looks of him, he was about ten years younger than I. This would place his birth somewhere near the twenty-fifth year of the reign of Augustus, before Roman soldiers were first garrisoned in Judea, and before Coponius, the first prefect of Judea, briefly preceded Ambivulus. Of those days, he remembered nothing, though he had heard much of them: the time before the Roman troops, and the time of trouble upon their arrival.

I figured him, then, in the summer that we met, to be about in his thirtieth year.

To not know when or where one was born. To not know one's age. Were these a blessing or a curse? In some way, did they free a man from time and place?

I asked him if his family, his parents and siblings, were still alive.

"Not to me," he said, then said no more. I let his silence be, then spoke lightly:

"Odd, considering the tale of your birth, that you never before considered you were the bearer of the key, the Prince of Peace."

This brought back the now familiar smile to his face, and the soft wry laugh that was barely there.

The fire was but an embering. The stars in the vast black of the calm luxuriance of blissful night bade us leave our thoughts to ember as well.

One night, not far from Shiloh, in the Ephraimite hill country, we made study and repeated recital of what was to be his first pronouncement, made on our departure from Bethlehem. I gave it to him in Greek, he gave it back to me in Greek. I advised him, assessed his performances, encouraged him. He put to memory the words and the practiced delivery of them. He set them into Hebrew and put to memory those as well. I could not understand the latter, but I could feel power in them. As for his Hebrew-accented Greek, I felt it to be near perfect for our purposes: the universality of our message represented by the inherent cosmopolitan nature of the Greek language, but imbued with the deep and unmistakable intonation of a sense of Hebraic past, present, and future.

"I have come from the town of my birth, to which I had journeyed in search of guidance..."

At Bethany, which was but a few miles southeast of Jerusalem and a few miles northeast of Bethlehem, we did the same. I could feel, hear, and see the hesitation and self-consciousness lifting from him and being borne away into the night. I closed my eyes. The sound and presence of him overtook the dark with a low seductive majesty.

"I have come from the town of my birth, to which I had journeyed in search of guidance..."

We drank much wine that night, for we were to assume the pretense of austere and abstemious men before the next night fell.

He stood, turned away, walked a few paces, and pissed, letting his head fall back easily as he did.

"Ah," he sighed. "If only this were the mouth of a young virgin whore instead of a roadside ditch."

We shared laughter and more wine. Then we slept, and rose the next morning in the dark and the dew.

The road became but a path. This path grew obscure and rugged in turn, then steepened as we ascended the foothills of the southern part of the mountains. The final few miles of our journey to Bethlehem were thus the most difficult of the miles we traveled to get there.

The northern outskirts of the vast desert Wilderness of Judea, in parts still unknown and unexplored, lay between Bethlehem and the Dead Sea. An unprovisioned man could perish if he lost his bearings in that desert before reaching Qumran on the western shore of the Dead Sea, or the oasis of Ein Gedi, the spring of the kid. On the table-land of Qumran, I was told, there was a great settlement of the sect known as the Essenes. Fewer in number than either the sect of the Pharisees, pretenders to highest sanctity, or the sect of the Sadducees, pretenders to the sole righteousness of sacred written law, the Essenes were a mystical, ascetic coenobitical lot that seemed forbiddingly self-miseryed even to others of their blood. They forbade the presence of women among them. Yet there was such a growing number of devout but despairing souls in Judea driven to join the Essenes, perhaps as an alternative to suicide, that the sect was the only group on earth whose population increased without procreation.

The Pharisees believed in the resurrection of the dead and in judgment-day. The wealthy Sadducees, comprising the aristocracy and priestly classes, did not believe in the resurrection of the dead. For them, there was no immortality of what we call the psyche, no afterlife, and, comfortingly, no reward or punishment beyond the grave. The Essenes were enigmatic in their view of the resurrection of the dead, which involved the separation of body and psyche, a separation that they strove to effect in life. Where the Pharisees saw judgment-day, the Essenes saw wholesale apocalypse.

The Sadducees had much influence on Hyrcanus II, the Hasmonean high priest and king of Judea who conquered Idumaea, and forced its people to convert, and its men to be circumcised.

It was good to have knowledge of these things, the natures of the players among whom the dice were to be cast.

Soon and at last we could see it above us. Bethlehem.

He told me of the meanings of the names of the Beth-places we had passed, and the Beth-place we were about to enter. By this time I was aware that *beth* was the second letter of both the Hebrew and Aramaic alphabets, but I knew nothing of its meaning as a word, which is also the same in both the Hebrew and Aramaic tongues, so very similar are they.

"Beth-El, the house of God. Bethany, the house of misery."

"House of misery?"

"Yes."

How this strange land intrigued me, exhilarated me. This beautiful land with its pall-cloud of suffering. More and more it seemed to be a vast theatre open to the sky, filled and eagerly expectant, the stage set and all riggings ready, awaiting only our entrance, and the breaching of the pall, and the bringing forth through that breach the light of imminent deliverance. A people that could be led by neck-iron to misery could be led to radiance, hope, and joy. And, after them, the miserable victims of other gods and unanswered deprecations.

"And Bethlehem?" I said.

"The house of bread."

"The bread of affliction?" I laughed.

"No. A different bread, *lechem,* a bread that is more than bread. A bread that signifies food, life, sustenance of all kinds."

The three of us slowly approached the entrance to the town: Jesus, the donkey, and myself.

"Remember, my Lord," I said in a low voice. "We seek together, but it is you whom I reverently follow in our seeking."

"And what is the Greek again?"

"Christos."

"Yes." And then he intoned from memory. "He called me *christos,* and I knew not this word; and I learned that it was the Greek for our Hebrew *mashiach,* our Aramaic *meshichah,* which mean 'anointed' and nothing more. The Book describes priests as anointed. I am no priest. We are told in the Book that Cyrus the Great was anointed by God. I am not great, and I do not worship Persian or Babylonian gods, as Cyrus did. Why, then, should I be called anointed? Why, then, should I be called by him *christos,* or, in the tongue of his native land, *christus?*

"I did ask of him an answer. And he, who knows not the Book, said unto me —"

"Enough. That is for our journey to Nazareth."

He began anew, modulating his tone to a humbler and less assured effect: "I have come from the town of my birth, to which I had journeyed in search of guidance —"

"And that is for tomorrow morning. Rest your voice, work your pantomime, and let us remain in this day."

"Yes, my son."

We laughed quietly, and it did us good, helping to allay the undercurrent of anxiety within us. We looked at the donkey trudging just slightly ahead of us. We stopped, gazing down into the valley whence we had come. We drew deep breath and entered Bethlehem.

7

BETHLEHEM WAS A PLACE OF HILLS UPON A HILL. IT WAS A wonder that a city had grown on terrain that seemed so unwelcoming and so uncompromising. In conforming to the rocky hills, it was a labyrinth of narrow, constricting pathways of sharp sudden turns, sharp sudden inclines, and sharp sudden declines. It was a city built of limestone on a highland limestone ridge. It was a city of sun and moon, where the pale buildings took on the hues of dawn, day, dusk, and dark.

Many people were about, but it was oddly quiet. An old man sang an old-sounding song as he went about gathering the dung of dogs, which was much used by tanners to bate their hides. His voice and his old-sounding song were for long moments all that could be heard. It was a plaintive song of no beginning and no end. It was as if the rest of Bethlehem were listening to it, or stilled by it.

We found the synagogue. It was one of the few buildings made not of limestone, but of darker, more somber rock and mortar. Its small courtyard sheltered only two money-lenders. Nearby, another two men sat at a shared table carving small figures from olive-wood. It was explained to me by Jesus that they were figures of demons. He spoke a question to the carvers. One of them answered. He nodded and then he added to me that the little olive-wood demons were to ward off the evil eye. He said some words from the Book to me, something to the effect that he who hasteth to be rich hath an evil eye.

He scrouged one brow, arched the other, and he looked at me. I could not immediately discern if there was more jest than pondering in him. This place, Bethlehem, was working some sort of subtle sorcery on my equilibrium.

He entered the synagogue, as I had instructed him to do. If the priest was there, he was to seek counsel. If the priest was not there, he was to make a show of prayer. We both assumed and hoped that the priest would not be there. While I waited, I walked some paces to where I found myself looking out on the desert southeast of where I stood, and seeing in the distance the grand domed roof of Herodium, the fortress palace of Herod, the king of the Jews. Once staffed by so many attendants, servants, and slaves that it was a town unto itself, the palace complex of Herodium was now as deserted as the sands that surrounded it. Herod, who had built the port of Caesarea, who had built the great temple of Jerusalem, had built Herodium for himself and his untold stolen, blood-stained riches. Now it was his tomb.

As I gazed on it, there came to me the whole of what Jesus had recited to me from his memory of the Book:

"He that hasteth to be rich hath an evil eye, and considereth not that poverty shall come upon him."

When did poverty come upon Herod the Jew? Only when death robbed him of breath in the ripeness of his years.

Jesus emerged from the synagogue, and I walked to him.

"The priest is not to be found," he said. His tone was natural, but he spoke so that the men in the courtyard, and likely some passers-by, overhead him. One of the demon-carvers, the one who had answered him, looked toward him, then down again to his work.

We found an inn near to the synagogue. There was a manger, and we had our good donkey tended before we took our room.

It was our plan to have our evening meal and then remain awake until well after midnight.

The sun was setting. Wisps of the ghosts of red, orange, yellow passed over the limestone, and the first brightling star appeared in the sky.

The pallets in our room were much inviting to us after our nights of hard ground. But we must stay awake. Looking directly to the cramped plank beneath the window, I saw, near to the oil lamp, a simple clepsydra such as those that measure the passage of an hour in brothels and courts. We fetched water and filled the timepiece to the hour-mark. Assured that the clock was in fine working order, we decided we could sleep in turns, one sleeping an hour while the other sat guard an hour. I worried that one of us might fall asleep on guard, considering especially the slow, soft droplets being so conducive to sleep. Jesus assured me that we would not allow this to happen. We would each take two alternating turns of sleep, two turns at guarding the clock.

I was awakened from my second turn at guard by the hand of Jesus gently shaking my shoulder.

We ventured into the middle of the night. I have described Bethlehem as quiet by day. Imagine it at this hour. Yet lamps did burn in some windows.

In the synagogue, we stood in silence and allowed our eyes to adjust to the darkness.

Synagogues offered shelter to wayfarers. We wanted to be sure there were no sleeping wayfarers.

A rat scurried from pilaster to pilaster. There was nothing else.

I watched him remove his sash, fold it to the ground, and kneel on it. I watched him bow his head, and I heard him speak aloud his humble, reverent, and heartfelt petition for much-needed guidance.

"I implore thee. Bestow on the senses with which thou hast blessed me, or breathe into me, a sign."

He was good. He was very good. And so was I. Never before had I written for the theatre. Do not take me wrong. I was no Aeschylus. But I was good. I was very damned good.

8

THE NEXT MORNING, BEYOND THE CITY GATES, HE STOOD UPON a rock. I sat in the grass beside him. I had not yet deduced the proper distance that should be maintained between us, the span of hands that evinced both deference and closeness.

Across the way, there was what appeared to be the fallen remains of a pyramid of eleven stones. Was it emblematic of something? Had it been an olden shrine of sorts? Was it nothing at all, a mere random configuration of fallen rocks? We were never to know, but I can see it to this day.

Many passed our way, some coming from, some entering, Bethlehem. Again and again, for as long as they paused to hear the words he spoke, he would speak them.

"I returned here," he would begin, again and again, "to the city of my birth, in the hope of finding here, where I drew my first breath, a sign of guidance, which I could not find elsewhere, though the journey of my seeking has brought me to many a place.

"For perplexity is mine. Within me, mingled winds await direction.

"In the good synagogue of Bethlehem, I prayed. In the good synagogue of Bethlehem, I supplicated. In the good synagogue of Bethlehem, I implored.

"The mingling of the winds neither diminished nor found direction, nor were lifted from me.

"There was a voice that then did speak unto me. Could some

unseen man be making mockery from the shadows? No. This voice was not from the shadows. This voice enfolded me. This voice was low and strong. It issued from within the synagogue itself and did fill the air of the synagogue, though there was no speaker.

"He whose voice this was did call me by my name, though I had not revealed my name. And he whose voice this was did call me *christos,* though I knew not this word; but later learned that it is the Greek for our Hebrew *mashiach,* our Aramaic *meshichah,* which mean 'anointed' and nothing more.

"The Book describes priests as anointed. I am no priest. We are told in the Book that Cyrus the Great was anointed by God. I am not great, and I do not worship Persian or Babylonian gods, as Cyrus did. Why, then, should I be called anointed? Why, then, should I be called by him *christos?* Why should he speak to me in the ancestral tongue, but for this one word?

"I did ask of him an answer. But there was no answer. And he spoke then of a key. But there was no key.

"And then there was no voice. As it had come, so it had gone. And perplexity is now all the more mine.

"Please, any among you: do you know of this voice in the synagogue? Do you know of this talk of keys?

"Please, my brothers, my sisters, I seek not alms. I seek only knowledge. This voice unnerves me, and I do not understand this talk of keys."

As I said, many passed our way. Some of them merely glanced at him. Some paused, then moved on. A child pointed to him and made laughter, at which his parents smiled to him. One man listened long, then slowly shook his head, as if gravely concerned, and continued on his way. A large group of travelers gathered before us awhile, talked among themselves in hushed tones, then were gone.

And so it went the better part of the morning.

"I am tired," he said at last, when there was none to hear but me.

"Do not weary," I told him. "Do not allow the strength of your words to lessen."

"You are sitting," he said. "I am standing. And my throat and mouth grow parched."

I raised the goatskin of water to him.

The noonday sun was upon us now. I recalled the street-corner prophets of Caesarea. The madder they were, the more idlers they attracted. But while the ravings of the insane could attract crowds, they could not attract followers. As dispirited as I grew this long morning, I remained convinced that my way was the only way, that my way was the true way.

Three men passed in silence. One of them turned slowly round and retraced his steps.

"It was David whose voice you heard," he said to Jesus. He spoke simply, calmly, in earnest.

He spoke then by memory from the Book: "And the key of the house of David will I lay upon his shoulder."

The man looked into the eyes of Jesus, as into what was ineffable, as if those eyes held something of the colors of the final setting of the sun.

He was a young man, but intense in his bearing. There were early wrinkle-lines below and at the corners of his eyes, the creases of too much study by too little light.

"Bethlehem is the city of the house of David," he said. "You, who were born here, are of the house of David. It is upon your shoulder that the key has been laid, or is to be laid, as was very long ago ordained by the Lord. The key of David is the key of the power and the authority of the Davidic dynasty, the kingdom of our people, Israel."

"And why the lone word in Greek?" asked Jesus, as if he was of considerable suspicion and doubt.

"Because the koine tongue of Greek is the koine tongue of all the world. The key to the kingdom is to no one place alone, not only to Israel, but to the world."

This man captured us as much as we had captured him. It had not occurred to me, this perspective of Greek being the language of the world as a reason for its utterance by the voice. I had been thinking more along the line of conveying a sense of the humbleness of Jesus, a man to be shown as one who knew Greek but was not so fully literate as to have all its less common words in his vocabulary.

The young man's companions looked on from a distance. He summoned them to him by a gesture of his hand and arm.

They spoke together in whispers. Occasionally, one of them looked to Jesus, or to me. I heard the word *mashiach*.

"And who is this Roman?" the eldest of them asked, in Greek, evidently so that I could understand his words, though they were addressed to no one in particular. There was in his voice no implication or disparagement, no undertone or overtone. It was simply a question.

We were well-prepared for this inevitable eventuality. Jesus said to them:

"He is my devoted friend, who has accompanied me in my journey for some time. He believes that he will find guidance in me, as I seek guidance from whom or what I do not know."

"A Roman who serves a Jew," another of them commented.

"He knows not the Book, but he seeks the way," said Jesus, with words I had not provided him.

It was I who then spoke, saying in Greek: "I heard the voice also, though it spoke in Hebrew and I could not understand it."

Jesus and the others ignored my words.

"You have explained much," Jesus said to the young and studious man who had first approached. "But still I do not understand. If what you say is true, I ask you this: Why me?"

"Why you? Why the foundling Moses? Why King David himself, for that matter?"

"The questions that are most profound are always without answer," commented the second of them.

The third of them then addressed me: "And what is it that you seek, to which you believe he will lead you?"

I delivered my words with poetic grace and force, a single line in the dactylic hexameter of Homer, ending with an ancipital foot of the two grand syllables of the Greek genitive, *theou* to our monosyllabic *dei*.

"I believe that in following him I will find the kingdom of God."

Nothing more, nothing less. It was indeed the rhythm and not the meaning of these simple words that struck with might.

Heed this, my good grandson; for he who controls rhythm, controls.

"You seem to have more faith in him than he himself has in him."

There were smiles in a friendly way all round, save for the look of Jesus, which remained somewhat confused and apprehensive.

"It is as you have said. The chosen are at first blind to what the unchosen can see, and in turn can see what the unchosen cannot."

When I said this, I was thinking of blind Homer, and surely not of my loiterer.

The three men introduced themselves respectfully. The first of them asked Jesus if he would tell them his name.

He told them his common name in a common enough way. There was no openly sly dawdling in the dirt with a stick.

They repeated his name and nodded among themselves. "Where will you go now?" one asked of him.

"To Nazareth, to the town of my home, to bid farewell."

"It is a long way."

"I have much pondering to do. I seek to hear further voice."

"Surely the voice of David is here and nowhere else."

"I sense now that the voice I seek is everywhere, within me and without me. I await it."

The one who had first approached him asked with some hesitance if he might join us on our journey.

"As I say, I have much pondering to do."

The young man seemed disappointed. It was unclear if his companions sought to join us as well.

"Meet me in Galilee," said Jesus. "Meet me in Simonias. I will do what must be done in Nazareth, then will go to the holy town of Simonias. Await me there as the day begins, at sunset, on the second day, *yom sheni,* after the first *shabbat kodesh* of the new moon, the Sabbath following that which now approaches. It is a matter of ten days, nothing more."

By this, the young man seemed heartened. He nodded to his companions, who seemed heartened as well.

"I have never heard Simonias called holy."

"I sense it to be so," said Jesus. "I know not why."

All the while, he assumed the air of one who endured a great burden dutifully and without complaint. Furthermore, one got from him the impression, which issued from the mind of the beholder independent of that air, that this burden was the burden of divine radiance, the unique unweighable weight of the key upon his shoulder.

"There is no synagogue in Simonias. But the town is small. You will find me there, at that hour when the fallen sun brings forth that day."

Jesus wandered some steps away, and I conversed with the men. We spoke awhile of the Greek philosophers, the philosophers of the elements, long before Socrates, and of the flaws in what Cicero called, in Greek, the logic of Socrates. Thence we spoke of the putative meanings of the word *logos* itself; and thence of other things.

I learned that one of these three men, he who had first spoken to Jesus, was a Sadducee priest, a member of the *kohanim* who controlled the Holy Temple in Jerusalem. Another was a Sadducee rabbi, or teacher of Jewish law, in Jerusalem. The third and eldest of them was a subaltern to the vice-justice whose office was under the high priest of the Jerusalem temple and above the sixty-nine general members of the legal council known as the Great Sanhedrin, the supreme high court of Jewish religious matters. This high court of the Sanhedrin convened in the Hall of Hewn Stones in the north wall of the Temple, with doors leading both to the inner sanctuary of the Holy Temple and to an outer city thoroughfare.

I learned that it was under King David that the sacerdotal leaders of the Jews were divided into twenty-four orders of priests, all of whom were descendants of Aaron. I made good note of this.

Jesus wandered back to us. The men walked with us until the road became twain, and, for now, we departed from them.

9

FOR SOME TIME ON OUR JOURNEY FROM BETHLEHEM, JESUS and I discussed the prudence of aligning ourselves with men of aristocratic and conservative nature such as these Sadducees must be.

"If they were Pharisees," said Jesus, "we would worry over the prudence of aligning ourselves with Pharisees. If they were Essenes, we would worry over the prudence of aligning ourselves with Essenes. In truth we have aligned ourselves with nothing. Those men just happen to be Sadducees. There will be Pharisees. There will be Essenes as well. It is good to be embraced by all. Especially by the ruling class. You want money? Well, it is the Sadducees who have it."

This struck me as sound thinking. Our experience with the Sadducees had strengthened him, given him confidence, and rendered him sanguine.

"There will come a day," he said, "when men of all sects and sorts will follow us. Those of different gods, those of no god. They will be ours. If the words you have given me can make fools of earnest men of much study and solemnity, they can make fools of all."

We stopped the night in unfortified Gabaon, where we decided, perhaps prematurely, to celebrate the auspicious beginning of our venture.

On the road from Caesarea to Bethlehem, Jesus had been

given to masturbating almost as frequently, and as openly, as he pissed.

"It is my calmative," he said.

Out of some misplaced sense of decorum, I had abstained. I indeed had grown sick of seeing his disfigured cock, which in youth had been mutilated to emulate the cock of his tribe's great Sem, believed to have been born without foreskin. I had grown sick of his brutal gruntings, sick of his countenance of palsied pain, sick of the sound, like that of a man taking the thrust of a dagger, that came from his mouth when he ejaculated. I had told him to take his imaginary lovers to the bushes.

Now, at the brothel-house in Gabaon, I was filled with good Lebanese cooking, Roman wine, and lust. I drank with a whore on my lap, Jesus with a whore on his. There was no telling who was more drunk, he or I.

The whore he grabbed said that she would not take the *membrum virile* of a Jew into her mouth. I was dismayed.

"But you are a Jew yourself," I said to her.

"It is unclean."

"His mentula, or the taking of it into your mouth?"

"Both," she said. "It would command a higher price."

It was then that I saw her game.

"Save your money," said Jesus. "I'll fuck this pig where it shits."

I loudly rhapsodied on the loveliness of our expression *culibonia,* used only to describe a whore who offers anal intercourse.

"But who is it who gets thus fucked?" he yelled in loud response. "She or the Roman who comes to her?"

All the while, he was drunkenly laughing. He shoved the whore from his lap, laughed all the more as she fell to the floor.

"Who will take the mentula of a Jew in her mouth?" he called out.

Several whores rushed eagerly to him. One was a Roman, another an Arab, the rest of them Jews.

"Who will pay *me* to take my mentula in her mouth?" he demanded more than asked. "For I tell you, it is the mentula of your savior."

They laughed all around. I kicked at him, called him a fool, and told him to shut his jaws.

The prospect of casting my seed into my chosen whore and waking from sound sleep in her arms presented itself to me as blissful.

To my drunken, squinting eyes, she was the most voluptuous girl I had ever seen. I was no adulterer, for, in my stupor, the mother of your father did not exist except in an ill-remembered dream.

I spent my pent seed almost immediately, and woke sickly with what appeared to be a bloated sun-rotten corpse beside me. Worse: a bloated sun-rotten corpse that snored.

Steadying myself, I searched the other chambers for Jesus.

I found him with two half-naked whores at his feet, listening silently as he spoke.

"No woman is unholy. No man is holy who believes her to be, for woman is the vessel, deemed by God, that brought that man, and every man, unto his life."

As if on direction of a prompter, the cry of a babe was heard from a whore's chamber above us.

"Yes," continued Jesus, "cursed was Eve, but blessed was she, too. No woman's body belongs to any man, but to her and the Lord alone."

These were indeed my words. They were not written, however, for an occasion such as this, nor a setting such as this.

The women who reclined at his feet looked to him with eyes of adoration. They were younger than he. One of them stroked his ankle, softly, almost maternally.

I went downstairs for bread and wine.

Later, as we made our way along the northern road, he asked me what my whore had cost me.

"A silver shekel."

"You were robbed."

"And what did you pay for the brace of them?"

"They would take nothing. In fact, one of them gave me this."

He reached inside his tunic and lifted forth a slender golden necklace with a single perfect pearl.

I snatched it from him, put it in my purse. We had agreed from the outset that I was to be the banker of our enterprise.

"Our first offering," I said. "We shall remember and cherish it always."

I patted the donkey's rump, then, more smartly, I patted the rump of Jesus.

I shook my head and recited to him in surly reprimand his mis-spoken words of the night before: "the mentula of your savior."

He looked away, hastened some steps ahead of me, and moved on.

10

THE CUSTOMARY ROUTE, FOR JEWS, FROM THE SOUTHERN
province of Judea to the northern province of Galilee took
them by steep descent to the Jericho Valley Road, whence, north
of the Dead Sea, they traversed the Jordan to Perea on the eastern
bank, then, farther north, in the Decapolis region, they crossed
back across the river as it neared the Sea of Galilee, where one
road continued north along the Sea of Galilee, past Tiberias,
through Magdala, and on to Capernaum, and another road veered
northwest to Nazareth.

It was a tortuous route, and was taken solely to circumvent
the province of Samaria, which lay between the provinces of
Judea and Galilee, and through which one must pass on the more
direct route, west of the Jordan.

The Jews hated the Samaritans, and the Samaritans hated the
Jews. It was a deep and fierce hatred rooted in the mists of time,
in the earliest days of the Book. The Samaritans held their ways to
be the truest and ancient-most ways of the faith of the Israelites,
and the Jews of other tribes held them in contempt and denounced
them as worshippers of false gods, such as Nergal, the war-god of
Babylon. And so there were hate and howling and bloodshed
without end between this tribe of Semites and the other tribes of
Semites. As they all looked the same, it is difficult to understand
how these God-crazy Jews knew which, one or the other, of their
kind to hate, spit upon, or slay. When I asked about this, I was

told that it was a simple matter, as the Samaritan dialects of Hebrew and Aramaic were identifiable to the discerning ear.

Jesus was not opposed to traveling directly through the land of the Samaritans. He had neither care nor fear about the matter. It was at times such as this that he showed himself to be so unlike others of his countrymen. We encountered no trouble in Samaria. They seemed, the Samaritans, as good a people as any other, as bad a people as any other.

We searched for an easy path through the foothills west of Mount Ebal, but there was none. Had we known what lay before us, we would not have entered those foothills.

At last we reached the town of Bemesilis. We looked back on the formidable terrain that we had endured. We looked ahead to the easy passage of the Jezreel Valley between Mount Carmel and Mount Gilboa that lay west of the Sea of Galilee.

The foothills of Mount Ebal had taken much from body and spirit. But the ordeal was behind us. After food, drink, and rest, we felt a sense of strength, confidence, even elation. We were told in Bemesilis that men, Roman troops among them, had been known to die trying to make their way through those terrible precipitous foothills. But we had more than survived. We had prevailed. We felt like victors. Conquerors of rock-slides, earth-slides, crags, hunger, and thirst, but conquerors nonetheless.

As for our good dun donkey, we were proud, even envious of him and the way he had negotiated the foothills.

"Are we still in Samaria?" I asked.

"I don't know," said Jesus, shrugging his shoulders. "Why do you ask? Do you feel enmity in the air?"

"I feel only amity."

"Then we cannot be in any of the lands that you Romans call collectively Judea."

As I said, we felt strong, confident, elated. Having emerged from the foothills of Mount Ebal, we could do anything. As we approached the luxuriant welcoming meadows of the Jezreel Valley, with the majesties of Gilboa and Carmel rising into the slow-rolling white clouds of the endless blue, our talk was imbued with all that was in us and around us. Each and every breath was full of the miracle of breathing.

We decided that it was as good a time as any to hazard a healing.

In the fields ahead, there appeared a small village. A stream of spring-water rushed nearby us. Though he had bathed at Bemesilis, he wanted to bathe here again, and launder his tunic. As he did this, I lay on my back and watched the movement of the clouds. I turned to see him run through the locks of his head of hair and the locks of his beard the teeth of the wooden comb I had given him.

11

THERE ARE THOSE WHO FEIGN INFIRMITY. THERE ARE THOSE who seek sympathy, pity, or attention while affecting a condoned manner of subsisting on charity rather than toil.

In this settlement without name, we came upon a man who by means of clutched stakes dragged himself and his seemingly lifeless lower limbs about on the ground, moving from the shade of one tree to another, following the movement of the sun. He appeared disinterested in the fate he seemingly had been dealt, and bored and impatient with it. Occasionally someone threw a small copper coin to him.

"What would you give to walk again?" I asked.

"I have nothing to give," he said bitterly. "And dead legs cannot walk."

I gestured to my Jesus. "He can restore life to those legs. And in so doing, he can endow you with the power to heal others, to do what physicians cannot. There is more coin in that than in crawling about like this."

"I am curst. For many years have I moved about thus, low, with the crawling things, upon the earth."

"But curst not by God, I sense. He who here stands before you can raise this curse from you. He can make you to rise. But he too, while he is among us and of mortal body, must live; and, as it is written, man cannot live by bread alone."

The man knew these words of the prophet, taught me by my Jesus, and he spoke them in full:

"He might make you know that man shall not live by bread alone; but man lives by every word that proceeds from the mouth of the Lord."

"The words of the Lord are his, and spoken through him." I gestured again to my Jesus, who stood silent, pure, and gentle. "He wants not for them. It is the price of the bread that concerns him, as it concerns me, as it concerns thee. It is but this humble price that we seek in return for restoring you, raising you, and giving to you the gift of restoring and raising others in turn."

"You speak more as a demon than as a holy man."

"Demons have no need for bread."

I beckoned him to follow us. He dragged himself behind us from the shade of a tree to the more isolated shade of a quiet blind alley between two small buildings.

He lay at the feet of Jesus. I receded and looked on. I saw Jesus lower himself. On bent haunches, knees, and ankles, he placed one hand to the man's head, the other across the man's prone legs. I saw him let his own head fall back with closed eyes.

I heard him invoke the names Iao Sabaoth and Adonai. I heard a low chanting in a language that was not a language. "Rise."

The man appeared to struggle to lift himself upward by the force of his arms. He grimaced. His arms collapsed beneath him, and his head was sideways on the ground. He lay with labored breath.

Jesus was standing again. He reached down to the man. The man grasped his wrist.

"Rise."

The man's legs were doubtless weak unto atrophia. I went to them, lowered my own right hand. The man grasped the wrists now of both Jesus and me. He half-rose, fell, rose again, staggered, fell, almost taking us down with him. I could hear the man's labored breath. I could hear Jesus cursing under his own breath.

At last the man stood upright, roused by the promise of scheme and fortune.

I exacted coin from him. Looking down at what he put in my hand from the purse round his neck, I looked at him with chagrin.

"The price of bread is but a few prutot," he protested in a most unconvincing and disingenuous way.

"Yes, we seek bread. We seek also the building of a new and greater Holy Temple, exempt from corruption, greed, and aristo-cratic despotism. Have you neither gratitude nor concern for what is good and right?"

He hesitated a moment. My final words to him were stern with impatience: "It is nothing compared to what shall be yours. For he who has been graced with a miraculous healing, it is then within his powers to so grace others."

Confused by this Janus-talk of humble bread and great tem-ples, and eager to present himself to the others of this place as one who had been transformed and blest by the touch of miracle— as a new man, exalted and attracting awe instead of mere pitiful attention and sympathy, offerings of substance instead of small bits of copper cast to the dirt—and still toil not, he surrendered the full, paltry contents of his purse.

He followed us upright, if unsteadily, into the sun, and men did make much wonderment.

"His heart was pure, and he is healed," I told them. "Now others who are afflicted, if their hearts be pure and there be no darkness upon their houses, he can help them."

The conditional clause "if their hearts be pure" was all-important, as it transferred the blame for any failed healing from the healer to the supplicant.

As for the condition that there be no darkness upon the supplicant's house: truth be told, there was a darkness, real or imagined, on everyone's house. Were there not, his neighbors would be quick to see one, as well as the transgression, committed yesterday or generations ago, that had brought it on that house.

In excitement and wonderment, the settlement elders asked who this healer was. He answered them simply and humbly.

"My name is Jesus," he said gently. "Jesus of Nazareth."

"He comes on his way from Bethlehem," I said. "There the voice of David spake to him, and priests and teachers of the Holy Temple in Jerusalem have told him that the key to the kingdom hath been laid upon his shoulder."

12

As I have made clear, more than any other people to be encountered, the Jews were much given to woe and lamentation. Their afflictions very often existed only in their minds.

These, who had brought on themselves an infirmity that was not feigned, were easy enough to cure. It demanded subtlety and nuance to instill in the self-afflicted a sense of shame and guilt for conditions that had been born of shame and guilt.

They must be made to see and feel that the Lord now deemed that they had suffered enough for him, and he wanted them to suffer no more, but wanted them now to look to his light and serve him in joy. This reward from God for their suffering must not be turned away, as that would be an affront unto him.

This subtlety and nuance of words and manner was a quite delicate process, but in the end it could be worked with ease. I discovered that the words *light* and *reward* were very instrumental, very effective. I would come to use them more in my pronouncements for Jesus. For are we not, all of us, self-afflicted?

There were, of course, those whose afflictions were very real. These we strove to avoid, but many were the times when the ranks of the latter infiltrated the ranks of the former in their desire to be healed.

In Nain, after rousing one of the self-afflicted, a woman in her youth, from the bed in which she had lain wailing for many seasons, we were approached in the street by a man who seemed to be of dignity and means.

"My daughter is in need of you," he said to Jesus.

"And what has befallen her?" I asked him.

"She has no sight."

We were not prepared for this, but my Jesus did not fail me. I was about to tell the man that we had not with us the medicative that, with the laying on of hands, restores sight; that this balm was gathered from rare plants far away; that the season of these plants had passed; and that we would return in due time.

But before I could speak these lying words, Jesus did speak, and he asked the man if he might see the girl.

The man led us to a house that was indeed distinguished among the other dwellings of Nain. He brought forth the girl, who was but a child.

With the assent of her parents, Jesus took her little hand in his, and together they walked to a tree where flowers grew, and they sat together between two roots that protruded reachingly from the earth. We saw him pluck and give to her a flower, and we saw them speaking, but we could hear nothing of what was said.

He stroked her head. After some time, he took again her small hand in his, and they returned to us. The child was smiling.

"She is not afflicted, nor curst. She is blest. She sees what we cannot. The Lord has given her this gift. Hers is a world of light and visions that far surpasses the world of your own seeing. She sees colors unknown to your rainbows. Her sun beams more golden than yours, and the riches of black night are many-fold to her, for all the more in number are the constellations that are hers to see and read in wonder.

"Others who cannot see the vileness that surrounds us can be said to live in darkness. But your daughter, who can see holiness and glory where others see none, lives not in darkness but in illumination. In time, through the gift that has been given her, she will bring great gifts to you and to others."

He closed with words that every man and woman yearns to hear:

"Your child is special among other children, and deserving of adoration."

He bowed his head gently toward the little girl, then to her parents, who looked on her with new soft gladness.

We made as to move on, but the man bade us wait but for a moment, as I had suspected and hoped he would so bid.

Bringing his wife and child into their home, he came out to us and laid three heavy gold aurei in the hand of Jesus.

Jesus put the fistful of gold to his breast, thanked him in a manner of deep sincerity, told him of the building of the new and greater Holy Temple to which his generosity would contribute. He passed to me the gold, as if in regard for the purity of his sanctified hands.

"And I thank you," said the man, "for delivering me from the blindness that was mine."

We passed two men whom I had not seen before. They looked on Jesus, and I heard one of them say in a hushed voice to the other:

"He comes on his way from Bethlehem, where the voice of David spake to him. Priests and teachers of the Holy Temple in Jerusalem have anointed him and proclaimed that the key to the kingdom hath been laid upon his shoulder."

I had told as much to an inquiring stranger while Jesus was in conference with the unfortunate child. I had used the same words with which I had answered the elders of the settlement south of here. But now, in the echo of these words, there were anointing and proclamation, where in my words there had been neither, but only the exaggeration of making plural the one priest we had encountered among the three men outside the gates of Bethlehem.

There would be no whores, no drunkenness from here on. People knew us. There was too much at stake. Jesus knew this without my telling him.

"And I shall witness the building of my own temple in Rome, and the building too of my own private villa. I shall bathe away my life in luxury and in leisure. My riches shall be such."

"Yes." I smiled.

"And I shall become drunken in my private feastings, and my concubines will be beautiful and many."

"Yes."

"And I shall have the most finely groomed asshole in all of Rome."

We smiled together for a long time, then the smiles faded from us. Rome was far.

We spoke not again of the little girl.

13

Mount Tabor rose before us as we descended to the plain of Esdraelon, making our way to Japha, on the high ground that once, in the dew of time, had been the land of the tribe of Zebulun.

Of the twelve tribes of the Book, eleven were either lost to unknown fates or absorbed into the tribe of Judah. The tribe of Zebulun was one of those lost to an unknown fate.

The tribe of Judah had become the kingdom of Judah, and our David of the key, our David who was descended directly from Tamar, daughter-in-law of Judah and mother of twins by Judah, became the king of Judah.

Our King David committed adultery with a woman called Bathsheba, the wife of a Hittite soldier in his army. David ordered the murder of her husband most ingeniously, commanding his other troops to withdraw from him during battle, leaving him, alone against many, to be killed. David then took Bathsheba as one of his wives, and she bore him his successor, Solomon. It was said in the Book that Solomon, a man of revered wisdom, had seven hundred wives and three hundred concubines.

"But we do not know if his asshole was clean," said Jesus in concluding his little story from the Book.

And as we passed the town of Endor, he told me of the witch of Endor, who, according to the Book, did summon through her necromancy the spirit of the prophet Samuel. A king seeking guidance from the ghost had asked her to do this. This king of something or other was by name called Saul. The spirit of the prophet was so incensed at being roused from his peaceful sleep in the house of the dead that he berated the king and predicted his end, as well as that of his entire army.

The next day, Saul's army was defeated in battle, and Saul took his own life.

We looked to one another and laughed.

"And so it is written," he said in a voice deep with mock gravity.

"The more I know of it, the more queerly intriguing the Book becomes. I do wish someone would translate it."

"Perhaps someday in our old age we can work on it together."

"Someone should. Such lurid comedy and lurid tragedy commingled. It is like Sophocles buggering Aristophanes, to the rhythms of a chorus of moon-mad gods, so ever-changing, irascible, many-faced, and various is its almighty one true God."

He did not know the names of these makers of plays. I should not have expected him to know them. But he said nothing. When he did speak again, it was to ask the value of an aureus.

"It is different at different times. It represents about a month's pay to a legionary soldier."

"And how many of them would make a man rich?"

"A great many of them. A great many for you. A great many for me."

"How many of them do you think are in the Holy Temple?"

"A very great many of them. A very, very great many of them."

A hawk flew high above us. We watched it swoop down in the distance on its unseen prey.

We wondered to each other at what birds might think as they looked down in flight on all the pitiable earth-bound creatures, men and beasts, below. Did they in turn wonder at us? At why we could not, or did not, take to the sky? At the lowly wretchedness of us, who would never know freedom, as they did?

Our wondering became wordless, and it was in silence that we walked the rest of the way to Japha.

Only two men who were traveling north, as we were, had passed us on the road from Nain. Yet when we arrived at Japha, we saw that our coming was awaited. Several men came forward to receive and welcome us with much interest and perfunctory bowing. They whispered among themselves. One of them used the word *mashiach*.

Yes, talk travels fast, and it is magnified and embellished along the way.

We could see the village of Nazareth. We passed through two small settlements as we neared it. The gatherings awaiting us grew from one settlement to the next. The closer we got to Nazareth, the more sullen he became.

In Nazareth, we heard again the word *mashiach*. My priests and teachers of the Holy Temple who had told Jesus that the key to the kingdom was on his shoulder, who had become the priests and teachers of the Holy Temple who, as others told it, had anointed him and proclaimed the key to the kingdom to be upon his shoulder, were now the high priest and elders of the Holy Temple, and the key was now golden, and all was as had been long-ago prophesied, long-ago promised, and long expected.

He was Jesus of Nazareth, and Nazareth was proud of him. This pride was evident in the fabrication of fond remembrances of his youth that were heard here and there. The few who had true memories of him, the few who remembered him as he really was, seemed not to be heard.

We walked through the streets, which were not many.

"This is a very small place, with a very small synagogue, and little else," said Jesus. "For me, there are only ghosts here. Ghosts and scavenging dogs and bad memories."

He drew heavy breath. "I wish to leave this place," he said.

"You did."

"Again. Now."

"There is your pronouncement to be made."

"I will perform no healing. I do not like these people. I will do no healing among them."

I laughed quietly. "It's not as if you're actually helping anyone," I said.

He shot me a look as if it were a stone aimed from a sling. His look was true. He had helped the blind child in Nain, and he had helped her father and mother. He had brought the self-afflicted back to more salutary lives. He had helped those two whores in Gabaon. He had even helped that groveling scoundrel in that nameless settlement to become a higher class of scoundrel.

Then there was no more sling, no more shot. Not for me, anyway. He grew calmer as he looked about. It was not a pleasant calm. It was as if he had simply wearied of anger and disgust.

"My father was a carpenter here. I worked with him. Most of our work came from the city of Sepphoris. I measured. I cut. I planed. I joined. I was better at wood-crafting than he."

"Why did you quit? It is a good trade."

"My father was a vile man. He had his way by force with my sister when she was a child. My mother did nothing. My brothers could do nothing. They were too young, closer in age to my sister than to me, and they did not comprehend. I struck him in the head with the hammer-end of an iron adze. The blow almost killed him. My regret then is my regret now: that I did not strike a second blow, or a third. But I let him live, and, like you, I was banished."

I let time pass before I spoke. "You could have taken your skills to Sepphoris. You could have taken them anywhere. To the capital, Caesarea, itself."

"When I see planks and nails, I see him."

The synagogue was nothing but a dwelling in ill repair. It was the Sabbath, and when others entered into this dwelling, we entered with them. When it was time to read, the attendant hesitated. He well knew which few of the congregants could understand and say aloud what was written, and on any other Sabbath he would have passed the scroll to one of them. But custom demanded that, should there be a visitor among them who could read, the scroll should be given to him. The attendant's hesitation derived from his not knowing whether or not Jesus could read. He reached out with the scroll slightly and tentatively in the direction of Jesus, and Jesus put forth his hand.

As I had been told by Jesus, the scroll would be one or the other of the first two parts of the Book. He had prepared a brief passage from each. The scroll turned out to be the part known as Prophets.

Jesus opened the rods of the scroll so that the parchment unfurled to a random place. He looked down and pretended to read the words on the small section of parchment before him, though the words before him were much different from the words he pretended to read:

"The Spirit of the Lord is upon me, because he hath anointed me to preach good news to the poor. He hath sent me to heal the broken-hearted, to preach deliverance to the captives, and to recover sight to the blind, to set at liberty them that are oppressed, to make known the year of the Lord's favor."

He closed the scroll and returned it to the minister, who was as surprised as the others. The few eyes in the room that had not been on Jesus were on him now.

When the congregants left the synagogue, he stood before it, and addressed those who gathered.

"When I am asked who I am, my answer is always that I am Jesus of Nazareth. For it was here, in Nazareth, that I was a child; and it was here, in Nazareth, that I reached my manhood. It was here, among the good people of this good town, that I earned my daily bread through daily work, with callused hands and the sweat of my brow. I was not alone in doing so, for this is an honorable place, of honorable people, with a long and honorable history.

"Our ancestors gave to this place the name of Nazareth because it is indeed the *neser*-shoot of a flower, a most glorious flower that drinks purest spring-water that flows to the south of here, where she overlooks the plain of Esdraelon, which is like unto a field of Eden that the Lord spared for us, and our flower, to gaze upon.

"I have returned to Nazareth on this day because this town and its people are dear to me. It is here, at this moment, as I stand before you that I now give voice to words I have not before uttered.

"For I say that I have been told by those from Jerusalem to whom I bowed that I am the fulfillment of the very words of the prophet Isaiah to which the scroll did open to me.

"And I have been told by those from Jerusalem to whom I bowed that the key to the house of David has been laid on my shoulder: the key of which the Lord did tell the prophet Isaiah.

"And the prophet Isaiah spoke of a shoot, and said that fruit would in time be borne by the branch of its growth, and that the Spirit of the Lord will rest in him who was that borne fruit—the Spirit of wisdom and of understanding, the Spirit of counsel and of might, the Spirit of the knowledge and fear of the Lord.

"The shoot is Nazareth, from which I have come and to which on this day I have returned to tell you, my fellow Nazarenes, of the Spirit that is upon me, and of the key, and of the shoot—our shoot, the sprout of us all, Nazareth—from which I came.

"With you alone did I want to share these words. For it is here, now, that I commit myself to the ministry that has been appointed me."

He told them of the new temple he had been ordained to build. He told them that the sprout of Nazareth would be the corner-stone of that temple. The sounds of the gathering swelled. A Sabbath-song and joy were among them. They turned to the minister. Yes, he told them, the Book forbade the handling of money for any transaction on the Sabbath; but this was no transaction. It was *tzedakah,* charity, and furthermore a very special and unique occasion for it. If the Lord had wanted them not to contribute to the corner-stone, he would not have brought Jesus to us today. Jesus knew the Book. If he did not know that this Sabbath giving was sanctified, he could easily have waited the day.

In truth, Jesus was as unaware of this interdiction as was I, and we were silently very grateful for the minister's intercession.

The offerings were many. This was not a prosperous place, but those who did not give what their means allowed, gave beyond their means. The minister himself gave from his own purse and from the funds accrued to the synagogue for good works. Only a few used the strict letter of the proscription as an excuse not to give.

There were those who felt their donations entitled them to a blessing. My quick-witted Jesus blessed them all at once, bowing his head to them and raising his palms with arms bent at right angles.

He knelt, kissed—or seemed to kiss—the threshold-stone of the synagogue, where many had trodden. This was his inspired doing, and the gathered beheld it in solemn delight.

There were offers of food and lodging, and the synagogue was open to us. "Come sunset," observed the minister with a smile, "the niggardly ones will have no pretext for their closed fists."

But Jesus was set on escaping Nazareth, and did not look back even as voices called warmly to him.

The little village with the little synagogue was behind us. A young boy began to run after us, but his mother called him back to her.

"Sepphoris is only a few hours away. From there, it is even less time to Simonias." He looked at the sky for a while. "We will meet the priest there, maybe the others as well."

We counted the money. It was a substantial amount. The pouch in which I kept our money was becoming heavy with the weight of copper, silver, and gold. We soon must store it safely in Caesarea. Safely? With whom in Caesarea would it be safe?

He was silent for some time. He seemed not to want to say what he did when at last he spoke.

"I saw my brother James, and my mother there. They stood not far from those who gathered near me, but they did not come forward. They were not in the synagogue. I saw them later, when I delivered my nonsense. Your nonsense."

"It worked well enough."

"The shoot of the beautiful flower that is Nazareth."

He said these words in a way that brought grudging laughter to me. He began to laugh as well, ungrudgingly.

Then he quieted again; then he spoke again.

"I did not see my sister or my other brothers. I did not see my father. Maybe he is dead. That would be good. They could have told me, my brother and my mother. But they did not approach. I wonder what they felt on seeing me again. I wonder what became of my sister. Their faces were inscrutable to me."

He inhaled deeply, and slowly exhaled. The slow expulsion of his breath seemed to lighten him.

"They were not among those who gave," he said, almost off-handedly.

"Maybe they gave through another, not wishing to impose themselves on your moment," I said, knowing there was no truth in these words.

He laughed darkly and unopenly, as if unto himself alone, as if at all the world.

Man is a haunted thing.

14

THE CALENDAR OF THE JEWS IS ALIGNED MUCH MORE STRICTLY with the moon than is our Roman calendar. In the Hebrew calendar, every one of their twelve months begins with the appearance of the first slender crescent of the new moon's emergence from darkness, with the sunset that is the beginning of each of their days.

Whereas our year begins on the first day of Januarius, the month of Janus, theirs begins with the appearance of the new moon of the month they call Nissan, whose name derives either from the word for a budding or from the word for signs and miracles. They are not in agreement as to from which of these ancient words the name Nissan derived. This first month of their year, Nissan, is the month of their great feast of Pesach, another word over whose origin and meaning they argue. Their Nissan comes in the midst of our third and fourth months, Martius and Aprilis.

The dark moon that overtook us after the Sabbath ended on the evening we spent in Sepphoris would show the first, falcated trace of its rebirth on the evening after next. Then, as it rose from the sunset, the new month of Tishrei would begin. This is a name whose meaning is little argued, as the possibilities are too numerous, so tangled and countless are its contending roots. Some say these roots extend to Babylon, to Assyria, to places unremembered.

Tishrei was a month of many holy days, which the Jews called by names such as the Feast of Trumpets, which began on the very sunset of our arrival in Sepphoris, and the Day of Expiation, which came with the ninth sunset following the Feast of Trumpets, and the Feast of Tabernacles, and others whose names I do not remember.

This month of Tishrei, the seventh of their months, comes in the midst of our ninth and tenth months, September and October.

It was indeed this Feast of Trumpets that Jesus wanted me to witness in Sepphoris, the great cosmopolitan city that was the capital of Galilee and, for a time, the capital of all Judea.

The stern and severe God of the Book had ordained the Feast of Trumpets to be, as Jesus said it was there written, "a day of joyful blasting."

He told me that of late some rabbis, who felt this to be quite unlike their angry God, were trying to convince their fellow Jews that this feast was the anniversary of God's creation of the first man and woman—Adamus and Eva, as we would call them—who disobeyed him by seeking wisdom, a transgression for which all men and women, descended from them, must continue to suffer. This was, said these rabbis, the birthday of those first sinners, the commencement of a new year of suffering. Little attention was paid to them, as it was generally held that God had spoken what he had meant to speak regarding the Feast of the Trumpets.

He told me, too, that in places less cosmopolitan than this, the atmosphere would have been far more subdued. For the gloom-loving Jews, this day was looked upon in its holiness as another day of abstinent requital, another Sabbath-day, different from others only by the call of the trumpets. But in a city such as this, the presence of many gentiles changed the tone of the feast, and many of the less gloomy Jews happily partook of that changed tone, that mood of celebration, freedom, and abandon.

And what a joyful and glorious blasting it was! I had never seen this side of the Jews.

Lamps and blazing torch-staves filled the moonless night with light. There was merriment, and there was dancing such as to pulverize underfoot the bread of affliction. And the sound of the horns! The very stars above seemed to frolic in their glitterings.

The trumpets sounded not at all like the various instruments of brass we know. The dominant of them is an actual ram's horn of large size, which is blown with such force as to cause a deep chthonic rumbling drone to build within its big curling curves and issue sonorously from its natural hollow. The others, which accompany it, are long, straight, elegant clarions of silver. Here, in Sepphoris, when the traditional priestly music ended, other musicians appeared with other horns, and the music made by them became more freely, more rousingly sublime.

Oh, what a noise, and oh, what a night!

Romans and Africans sang together. Arabs shook timbrels and sistra and banged on goatskin-headed drums and pans. Many were the colors of the sounds that wove through the joyful Hebrew blasting. Even our donkey took to happily braying.

For sweet uncounted hours, there was no world but this. No Rome. No Tiberius. No new temple. No nothing. Only the here and now of life, and life alone.

"This is my Judea," said Jesus. "These are my people." I smiled to behold him.

By this time, I no longer looked upon my loiterer as merely a means to an end. He was no longer but an instrument for me to play, no longer the ram's horn of my own artful blowing. The wall separating us, the Jew and the Roman, was crumbling. Except for physical differences, and differences of language and circumstance, we were two men of like mind and temperament. The distinguishing marks of tongue, snout, and cock were trifles now. What had begun as conspiracy, each wary of the other, had slowly become camaraderie. We conspired now in the truest sense of the word: we breathed together.

The boughs, leafy branches, hanging vines, and flowers of lush scented gardens swayed in the warm breezes of the night.

There came over me an endearment for these people who were his people.

There came over me a guilt for what we were doing to them.

"The food of Lebanon is here," said Jesus. "The wondrous food of Persia is here. Wines from Syria, wines from Rome. Women from every nation of the world.

"No one in these crowds knows us. Let us break our vow just once, on this night. Let us have wine and women. Let us drink and fuck under the stars."

The man approached us slowly.

"I am Simon, son of John, of Bethsaida," he said. "I fish the Sea of Galilee. As yesterday was the Sabbath, of course I did not cast my net."

Hearing these words, I felt the guilt lift from me.

At hearing the formal manner in which the man introduced himself, I remembered how Jesus had once thrown back at me the words with which I had introduced myself to him, addressing me on the night of our meeting as Gaius et cetera et cetera, son of this one, grandson of that one. I smiled to remember that evening, which seemed now to have been so very long ago.

"I was on the eastern shore, far south of my home, south even of Tiberias, when I took my fish to market at Gath-hepher on the eve of the Sabbath. There is no synagogue there. So it was that I came to be at the synagogue in nearby Nazareth when you read from the prophet. And I was much stricken by your words in the street. I have come here seeking you."

Jesus was no more in the mood for this bore of a boor than was I. This was a night for abandon and joyful blasting, not for business.

"What sort of fish do you catch?" asked Jesus.

I could hear the sarcasm and ambiguity in his tone, as if he were belittling the intruder.

"Mostly tilapia."

"That is what all who fish the Sea of Galilee seem to catch. Tilapia. Nothing but tilapia. Always tilapia. Day after day, year after year, generation after generation: tilapia."

"This is so."

"And why have you come seeking me?"

"I wish to follow you."

The undercurrent of annoyance and aloofness that I sensed in Jesus was mistaken by the fisherman to be an air of casual ease, so he ventured a sprig of jocosity:

"I am sick of tilapia."

"He seems a good man," I interjected, in the way of calling back Jesus to the matter of our business, as much as we both wished this night to be a respite from it.

Jesus looked the fisherman up and down. He was a sturdy man of about the same age as Jesus himself, perhaps a few years older. In his beard were streaks of gray, which lent the lie of sage experience to his demeanor.

"So you wish to be a fisher of men?"

"Your words yesterday moved me much, and I feel much in your presence. I believe that you very well may be the *mashiach*."

Assuming the full character of his dramatis persona, but still not wholly without a hint of lingering resentment, Jesus responded to him with words that were both cryptic and curt:

"You are Simon, son of John, of Bethsaida. You will be called Cephas."

This name of Cephas in Hebrew is also their word for "rock," as our Roman name Petrus is also our word for the same. I was later to ask Jesus why he re-named the man in this way.

"Because the man seemed as slow and witless as a rock" were his words. "But a rock is also stalwart, and the symbol of strength immovable. As such, I felt that he and others would perceive this as a name of good and trustworthy honor."

When the faithful tilapia-man joined us, it occurred to me that it would be for the better if we disposed of the word *follower* in favor of *messenger,* as the one suggested a lowly going behind, like a laggard retinue or servile lickspittle, while the other suggested an exalted and active going forth, like the chosen bearer of an important message from on high. Thus the fisherman would be the first of what we would call our *apostoloi,* as the Greeks denote what we know as *nuntii,* the messenger-delegates of a mission.

Jesus demurred.

"If I am to be seen as a rabbi, a teacher, it is pupils that I need, not messengers. Would you entrust this man with a message? The wit of the sender would be brought into question. A sack of tilapia, yes. The Word of the Way, or the Way of the Word, or whatever it is? No, definitely not."

What he said was true. So it was that the fisherman who rose one day as Simon and went to sleep as Peter, who woke another day as a follower and went to sleep as a messenger, in the end rose and slept as a pupil, a learner of the Word of the Way. Or the Way of the Word. Or whatever it was.

Thus the fisherman became the first of what in Latin would be called our *discipuli,* our devout and dedicated learners of the Word and the Way. Or it might be said that he was the second, as I myself had long and well posed as the first, even as I was the author of the teachings, the disciplines of the Word and the Way, to be learned and taken to heart. Jesus and I used the Greek word for "pupils," *mathetai.*

We were not in the mood for our first *mathetes*—Simon or Peter, or whatever you will; follower, messenger, student, or whatever you will—on the night he came to us. But in time both Jesus and I came to like him. He was indeed a good man. And no finer an inlicitator could we have hoped to find than we did find in our Simon Peter, for the best of shills are those who do not believe they are shilling but believe they are advancing truth, and the most desirable of all accomplices are those who are unaware of the conspiracy of which they are part.

His discipulate was of benefit to us. It seemed to benefit him, too.

When he came to us amid the joyful blasting, Jesus tried to get rid of him for the night. The stars still spoke to us of wine and women, and the fisherman and his expectations could wait until daybreak.

Jesus granted him the night to fetch his belongings, and told him to meet us in the morning.

"Fear not to travel by night, for the spirit is now with you," he told Simon Peter, who looked to him but did not move.

"I say, what of your possessions?" Jesus pressed him.

"All that I need is with me."

"What of your boat and nets?"

"Don't worry for my boat. All boats on the Sea of Galilee are safe. The Jordan is unnavigable. Even if a man were to survive the rapids and had a team of other men to tow him over the sandbars of its southerly current, he could go only to the Dead Sea, where there is not one fish to be caught, and from which there is no way out by boat. No. My little boat is safe, as it always has been. If a storm destroys it, the same storm would destroy it if I were there."

"He tells us what Strabo neglected to tell us of Galilee," I said, seeking to halt his excursus. Neither of them knew the name of the geographer, or what I was talking about. I looked to the stars and thought of the nearby inviting grass beneath it. I could taste the first, long draught of wine. I could feel the warm soft flesh of recumbent thigh horripilate to my caress. But the fisherman talked on.

"As for my little cast-net, I took it with me to Nazareth, and when I set out to find you, I gave it to the minister to store. My great-net is in Bethsaida, with a friend who often fishes with me."

There was to be no getting rid of him for the night. Jesus and I retired to a good inn. Simon Peter went to make his bed on a knoll in the public gardens. He was the only one of us that night to lie under and rise to the morning star of heavenly Venus.

I wonder, do you still call this brightest and most beautiful of stars after her, as Virgil had Aeneas do? I have always much preferred it to Lucifer, as this bringer of light was known of old.

Recalling the words of Jesus to Simon Peter—"You will be called Cephas"—I recall too that, in our myths, the father of Lucifer was called Cephalus, a name cognate to our word meaning "pertaining to the head," and thus in many instances also relating to rock.

15

WE ATE A GOOD MORNING MEAL OF STEWED BARLEY AND calf marrow, sardines, eggs, bread, and ewe-milk. The cook, a big-bellied Syrian, pressed food on us even after we had eaten more than our share.

The new member of our cohort, Simon Peter the fisherman, had much to say on the subject of sardines.

Jesus and I glanced to one another as he expounded on size and species.

Then we discovered that all of his expounding on sardines was based on hearsay. He had fished only inland waters all his life.

"Tell me, Simon, son of John, of Bethsaida, who is called Cephas," Jesus interrupted him in his recounting of hearsay. "Do you see God? Describe him to me. Tell me how you see him. Describe him as you would a sardine."

At this, Peter Simon fell still. His hesitant silence was long in passing. Then he began to put words together slowly.

"I see God not as I see a man. I see God as a sort of running brook, a brook that is more of soft light than of water. A brook that gives forth light that runs through everything, that seems to stream between this world and another."

"But you do not see him—you do not see this brook—when you look outward, is that not so? You see him, do you not, only when you look inward?"

"This is true."

"Then why do you feel that he, the God that you see, the brook that you see, does not reside within you, and only within you?"

"Within me only?"

"Others see no brook."

"But it is..."

He had no words to follow these, and Jesus let silence be with silence.

We had much time before meeting the priest in Simonias at sundown. There was splendor in the sky of the day, which was warm with cool light breezes from the west. We wandered.

Not far from Nain, we came upon a funeral procession. The body of the only son of a widow of that place was being carried to a burial ground north of there. Some in the procession recognized Jesus from his visit to Nain, where he had ministered saving grace to the blind girl. Her gift of inner seeing was now apparently regarded as beatific, and the hue of her father's exaltations was heard and known throughout the village.

It was one of those who recognized him that besought him to raise the dead son to life.

In my consternation, all became suddenly abstracted. The splendor of the sky was no longer there, and I knew not what to do. But an accidental glimpse of the widowed mother struck me like a mote of sand in my errant eye. The look on her face suggested to me that she did not want to see her son alive again. The look on her face suggested to me that she was terrified of her son being returned from the dead.

She immediately countered my glimpse with a contortion of her face into a great weeping and wailing. I looked to Jesus, and he to me. We both had suspicious minds. Having read this far, you may be inclined even to call them criminal minds. And, as is said, a suspicious mind sees everything on the dark side. But there seemed to us to be a false note in her wailing, a forced trace in her weeping. Simon Peter stood by, as if he himself were without breath, watching.

I drew close to the body of the boy on its wooden bier. I could smell the myrrh and aloes from within the linen winding-cloth that enwrapped his body. Enlacing the scent of these funerary resins was an altogether more bitterly unpleasant scent, which issued from the separate cloth of his head-wrapping. I recognized this noxious odor. It was not the smell of death. It was the foul smell of imperial Roman stealthy political maneuverings, the smell of the murder of Drusus by Sejanus and Livilla, and of many another calculated mourning.

It was the stench of henbane. I parted the head-wrapping with respectful care. The acrid scent filled my nostrils.

There are those who, to induce trance and visions, ingest small doses of henbane, the rank extraction of the purple-streaked yellow-flowering plant. Priests and devotees of various gods do it and call it holy ritual. Others do it in the name of no god and simply, and more honestly, call it pleasure. Occasionally one of them ingests too much — an imperial portion, so to speak — and dies. Occasionally one of them takes only a bit too much and is lost to a stupor between life and death, the "deep sleep" that the Greeks call *coma*.

In closing the head covering, I surreptitiously put one of my fingers to one of the boy's nostrils. I felt the warmth of faint latent breath.

Had he taken a drop too many in his quest for thrillsome delights, and was his mother overly eager to be rid of him? Or had she put a drop too few in the wine she had served him? As with brews of thorn-apple, which can bring stupor and coma but rarely death, henbane leaves its survivors with no memory of the event.

"There is nothing that can be done," I announced to Jesus. "The boy is dead."

I went to him as if in sadness, and I whispered to him, all the while making gestures of sadness, contradictory to the nature of my whispers, for the lookers-on to see.

Jesus went to the wicked widow, and said in a consoling way, "Do not cry, good woman. Your dear son is not dead. He sleeps."

She wept now in relief, believing this to be the end of the matter.

Jesus went to the body, drew aside the head-wrapping, covered the boy's nostrils with his hand so that air could neither enter nor exit them, drew open the boy's mouth, brought his own open mouth down full upon it and into the henbane stench of it howled of Iao Sabaoth and Adonai and howled on in a language that was not a language, and as the body of the boy jerked with a horrid gasp, Jesus fell to the ground as if to show that he had drawn from the boy into himself, and the mother of the boy fainted where she stood, and many in the procession fell to their knees to pray, and Simon Peter with them.

Amid much panic and rapt terror, Jesus, on his feet again, made as to calm them with words that brought further frenzy and dismay: "He only slept, my brothers and sisters. He was not dead but only slept."

I went humbly mannered among the many processioners, collecting offerings for the new temple. This was somewhat difficult, not because they were hesitant to give—they were quite eager to give, and well they gave—but because they were almost as dazed and disoriented as the risen son, who remembered nothing of poisoning himself or being poisoned, and was quite alarmed to hear that he had been dead. Of course, the mother, for the sake of appearances, gave more than her neighbors.

We had done it. Many besides our disciple Peter had seen it. As surely as God had breathed life into the mouth of Adamus, so Jesus had sucked death from and breathed new life into the mouth of one of the faithful. We had done it, and there was no one to say we had not done it. On that aimless afternoon, under that sky of splendor, we had wagered out of the game every other would-be savior, redeemer, prophet, messiah, sage, mage, and madman gathered round the dice. We had done it. We had raised the fucking dead.

As we moved on, Simon Peter appeared visibly shaken. Jesus said to him: "He only slept. He was not dead but only slept."

The disciple looked on him with awe.

Traveling with Peter, who was but the first of many to join us, we now were forced to be doubly wary. There could be no open talk between Jesus and me when he was near. This presence of innocence, no matter how good-hearted, was difficult for us, but it was also good for us, as it behoved us to play the game all the more, to live it and to breathe it, rendering it all the more convincing, all the more real, until we and our roles all but merged.

When we needed to discuss words that I had written for him, or plans to be laid, or moves to be made, Jesus would send Peter to pray, and we would have to listen carefully for his return.

Jesus took to saying nonsense that was taken by Peter, and others whom we encountered, as profound enigmas to be delved.

"Man has two arms but only one heart," he would say, and there would be the slow contemplative stroking of beards and slow nods of deep pondering.

"I am the son of man," he would say, and there would be the slow contemplative stroking of beards, slow nods of deep pondering, and, when we returned months later to the town where he first said this, we found men still engaged in interpreting it.

"What do you mean when you say that you are the son of man?" asked Peter of him one day, feeling that his closeness to Jesus was such that he could ask; but asked it of him reticently, circumspectly, also feeling that one should tread carefully in the presence of a man who could raise the dead.

"Is not a sardine the son of a sardine?" Jesus smiled. "When you ask things of the brook within you, do you receive answers? Do you know yet the true nature of the brook that you call God?"

"No. Tell me."

"I have never seen the brook within you that you see. I believe you, but you must discover its source. I feel that I have failed you in not leading you to it."

"You have not failed me."

"Then you have failed yourself."

"Others call you the son of God. Why do you never call yourself the son of God, but always the son of man?"

"Because I am the son of man. I am the spawn of your brook. I am the son not of man's seed, but of his imagining. This frail body that you see was born of the flesh of man and woman, yes, but it is my fleeting form and nothing else. All else of me, the unseen part of me, was born of the imagination of man."

"But you command the imaginations of men. It is not the imaginations of men that command you."

Our good man Peter had a way of confusing himself, of entangling himself in his own words and thinking. Sometimes he could extricate himself, sometimes he could not.

"You are right," said Jesus. "It is I who command, but only because I was imagined into being to do so. The imagination of man, of whom I am the son, is fearful; and thus was I born to be fearsome, that man might protect himself and allay his fears through me. Truly, I am the son of man."

"And so—"

Regardless of what, if anything, Peter was about to say, Jesus answered what may or may not have been his question:

"Yes. I am the son of man. And it is man who is the son of God."

He had entered dangerous ground. I, careful not to outstep

the bounds of my disciple's role, tried to warn and halt him, not with the words I said, but the tone of voice in which I said them:

"I feel, my Lord, that we are beginning to understand." But on that late afternoon following the evening of the joyful blasting, that late afternoon following the raising of the dead, that late afternoon when we approached Simonias with the dirt of distant hills turning the color of copper all around us, Peter was without words for almost all the way, stricken dumb by what he had witnessed on the road not far from Nain.

Entering Simonias, we were hailed by a crowd that rushed toward Jesus, then stopped respectfully not far from him.

"You have spoken great words that portend great things. David's key is on your shoulder. The panther has lain before you in peace and eaten from your hand. You have made the lame to walk. You have graced the blind. To the faithful you have delivered gifts from the Lord. Lightning has struck you and issued from you as a rainbow. You have this very day raised from the dead the only son of a worthy widow."

Several moved closer to him, to kneel and kiss the hem of his tunic.

A chant rose among them: *"Mashiach, mashiach, mashiach…"*

In my mind, there rose a contrapuntal chanting: *"Merda, merda, merda…"*

As grand a city as Sepphoris was, so negligible a speck in the dust to the southeast of it was the hamlet of Simonias. The people who came forward to us were, then, a significant number of its populace.

"You honor us," said one of them. He was the oldest of those who gathered. His beard was long and full and white, brindled with silver and tarnished with yellow.

"It is I who am honored," said Jesus.

"What brings you to our town, where the plain ends and few visit?"

"I feel it to be a hallowed place."

These words were met with self-satisfied approbation all round among those who stood before us.

"Will you speak to us?" asked one who stood close to the old man.

"I have come here to meet a priest."

"We have no priest," the old man said. "We have not even scrolls, or men to read them."

"But a priest will be here with the setting of the sun. I have asked him to meet me here. Why Simonias, he asked. I told him the same as I have told you: because I sense it to be a hallowed place. He comes from the Holy Temple in Jerusalem."

They took in breath as one. Some repeated their entreaty, seeking exhortation from him.

"Perhaps," said Jesus, "you would stand to gain more from the words of the learned priest."

"We wish to have words from you," someone said, and the others voiced their agreement.

Jesus moved to the shade of a date-palm tree, so that the shadows of its weaving fronds might pass over him in a hypnotic way as he spoke. They went to the date-palm, and he smiled gently to them. He glanced above for a moment. Others joined those who gathered.

"This tree bears good fruit in its season, as do you, through your work, and through your children. This life is a life of fruitfulness. It has by God been so designed."

I immediately recognized this as one of my omnipurpose homilies, one that was simple and dulcet, but subtly edged with the lace of revolution. He wove Greek and Hebrew, that everyone in this rustic backward hamlet might understand him.

"The seasons of a tree are many. The seasons of a man are few. We are told in the Book that some prophets of old lived to be many hundreds of years old. But these are not the reckonings of the years these prophets walked the earth. They are the reckonings of their years as was measured by the depth of their wisdom. Thus a prophet may not live to see his eightieth year, but may be said to have possessed eighty upon a hundred and more years of wisdom. I am sure that some among us here today, if their ages were to be calculated in wisdom-years, would be said to be very old indeed.

"Yes, we dwell on earth for only a span. But I am here to tell you that, though we perish, yet we live on. The loving arms of God await our spirits as the grave awaits our bodies. This, too, is as designed. For your good works will not be without reward. And beyond the grave, there will be neither toil nor years, for there will be only the fruit of your good works, and they will be yours for all eternity, which is vast and not to be measured by the years of man or the years of his wisdom."

He paused long and let his eyes wander among theirs. They were in the thrall of what he said and his manner of saying it.

"But something approaches. Something glorious with light, dark with terror. A light as you have never before known. A darkness as you have never before feared. Yes. Something comes.

"You say that I am the possessor of a key. You say that I have made the lame to walk. You say that I have graced the blind. You say that I am of deliverance. You say that I have raised the dead."

Oh, how pleased I was to hear him add these two lines to what I had written. He was brilliant.

"These things that you attribute to me, I tell you that they are as nothing to what approaches."

He raised his right hand before him, and before all who gazed on him, and he slowly turned it.

"If this frail hand can do as you say, imagine the powers that lie in the hand of my Father: the powers of the light and dark of what approaches.

"And I tell you that these are the last of days." His gentle smile in time returned.

"A great and holy new temple is to be built. That, and the spreading of the Word, is our mission.

"I know that you are poor. As I have said, I came here only because I felt a summoning to do so. I do not expect or ask any offering of you for the building of the temple, for you can ill afford it."

Many of them turned to look at one man who stood with them.

"I want you to know, however, that the name of Simonias will be carved into the corner-stone of the temple, and that it will be yours to share in spirit and in flesh, and will welcome you, as all others who do prepare for what approaches."

The man to whom others had turned retreated. He returned and put a coin into the hand of Jesus. From where I stood, I could see the soft gleam of gold.

A young man approached Peter. They studied one another, then smiled with recognition. The young man was also a fisher of the Sea of Galilee. They spoke for some time, and then the young man came to Jesus.

"I want to follow you," he said.

"No one follows me," said Jesus, more so that the others who gathered could hear him than to respond to the young man. "Men walk with me."

"Then I want to walk with you," said the young man. "Will you have me?"

"I will have any who believes in the Way."

Oh, no, I thought. Two disciples, two fishermen. Was this to be a tilapia expedition or a mission that merely smelled like one?

And we would have to start defining this "Way" of ours. Vagaries could get one only so far.

"Look to my disciple Gaius here," I heard Jesus saying. "He is a gentile by birth, and a Roman too, and even he is accepted among us, for he has accepted the Way."

Maybe I had that one coming.

The young fisherman introduced himself. His name was Andreas, or such was the name that Jesus put on him.

We must try to bring the Sadducee priest into the fold. He would attest that a figure of the established religious authorities had seen the divine supremacy of our Way, whatever that might be. And, if I had rightly understood, the Sadducees were of the mon-eyed aristocracy. If we could open his family's purse-string, other aristocratic purse-strings very well would be opened to us as well.

As if my thoughts had invoked him, our priest stood before us.

On our meeting at Bethlehem, the priest was accompanied by two men, one a Sadducee rabbi and one a subaltern to the vice-justice of the Sanhedrin. With him again now was the rabbi. As at Bethlehem, the priest wore garments of pure linen, but not the embroidered sash or other trappings of the attire that distin-guished him in Jerusalem.

The priest stepped forward to kiss the cheeks of Jesus in greeting, and then my own.

Jesus introduced the priest to our new companion, the disci-ple Peter. Together Jesus and the priest ambled off. Making way for their aimless path, the gathering dispersed into smaller groups, each of which fell into discussion that was in turn pensive and excited. Peter and I and the rabbi walked in tandem behind Jesus and the priest at a respectful distance, but we could hear much of what they said. Our young Andreas tagged along at a farther length, happily telling those he encountered that he now traveled with Jesus.

"I have heard much of you on my journey here," the priest told him.

"No lightning struck me, and there was no rainbow," said Jesus. "It was merely a storm such as we all survive."

"I heard nothing of thunderbolts and rainbows. I heard of the restoring of the lame and the blind. I heard this very day, crossing the plain of Esdraelon, that you have raised the dead."

"He was not dead, but only slept."

Peter was about to speak out, but I restrained him with a staying hand and a look that advised silence.

"How does a man who has done what you have done—how does such a man speak with such modesty?"

The two men's steps upon the ground were of equal pace, but the mind of my wily Jesus was one step ahead of the priest's.

"Modesty? I fear that I have none. I fear that arrogance consumes me. These deeds of which you speak, these deeds that have been attributed to me: they are not of my doing. They are nothing."

He beheld the palms of his hands, and the priest beheld them, too. The sun was now setting, and the palms of his hands took on a rosy glow.

"These deeds are not of these hands. If these hands had power, I would have them bring well-being and understanding to all.

"I am asked, and so I do; and always I expect nothing to happen, but something happens. Yet I have tried to effect things through these hands by my own wilfulness—simple things; the healing of my own aching feet—and I cannot. It makes me feel very insignificant. It makes me feel that this mortal shell I occupy is a plaything of capricious behests that are not my own.

"Why should one inconsequential man among the multitude of worthier men who went to the grave this day be raised from the dead?

"It makes no sense. It cannot be justified. It seems to me nothing more than monstrous spectacle, putid trumpery for the entertainment, not the edification, of the low-minded.

"It is the words that I am given that I would have them acclaim and noise abroad. Therein lies my arrogance."

"So you still hear the voice of David?"

"No."

"Then what is the source of these words that you are given?"

"The voice of another. A different voice. One that is not audible to others, unlike the voice of David, which my good companion Gaius heard as clearly as I. This voice speaks in elemental tones that are not words and yet are words."

"If it pleases your arrogance, know that much is said, too, of the words that you speak."

Jesus appeared gratified to hear this, but the true gratification was mine.

"Do you never feel that what you call monstrous spectacle is a way to summon the attention of people, to prepare them to more fully hear and heed your words?"

Jesus hesitated, as if thinking, then answered.

"No," he said. "I feel that the Word is of more awe than the hideous sight of a corpse staggering forth from his bier only to one day die again. How can the author of so wondrous a Word be also the author of so cheap and abominable a display as befits a cheap and abominable magician?"

"Perhaps it is a metaphor."

"Metaphor," grumbled Jesus. "Metaphor for what?"

"For the new life and resurrection of which I have heard tell you proclaim. Perhaps it is an emblem of these things."

"If this is true, it is an ugly metaphor, a shoddy emblem. And what of a single lame man who is made to walk while all the rest of the lame of the world are left lame? Is there a metaphor, an emblem, in that as well?"

"There is again a raising, a rising, in it."

"This is why you are a great rabbi. You can speak in endless circles round anything, until the circles tighten to form a noose to throttle the truth."

The priest laughed, but when he spoke again, it was in earnest.

"It is you who are the great rabbi," he said. "It is you whom we have come to follow; you who were addressed by the voice of David in Bethlehem as *mashiach,* and are now addressed as *mashiach* by many people in many places. Yes, we have come to follow you on your way, if only for a while, to hear your Word as it unfolds."

"I am honored to hear this."

The snare I worried over had been fashioned and entered into by the prey.

"You know," said the priest, "that we of the Sadducees have been taught that there is no resurrection, no life hereafter. You do espouse and proclaim these things, do you not? We wish to hear more of this 'new life' of which you are said to tell. We know that your meaning when you talk of these things is much different from that of the Pharisees."

"I know little of the teachings of these schools. To me, these are all more to do with temple politics than with the Word and the Way. For me, there is only the Word, there is only the Way."

"We believe in the word of the law as written in the Book. Is it not a new Word that you reveal?"

"It is the Word that lies before and beyond what is written. It is not new, but only unpronounced."

"And we of the Sadducees have been taught that oral law is as nothing, that the written law is all."

"The elemental tones are not oral. Nor do I speak of laws. How is it that you can accept and defend the raising of the dead, but not the Word of him who uses my voice as he uses my hands to perform such things?"

"I accepted you on the day that I met you. I have for far longer accepted the one who seems to dwell at times within you. This has nothing to do with acceptance, or even with the doctrine and nature of my officiating as a priest.

"It has to do with feeling. And I do feel, in Jerusalem and throughout the land, a shaking in the air. I feel that something is coming, or something has come."

Jesus did not say that he had told the people of Simonias of the great approaching. It would be better that he heard tell of this from the townsfolk.

"It will be good to have you with us," Jesus said.

"You call those who follow your teachings your disciples."

"As are called those who follow any teachings."

"And you are aware that this word, *talmidim,* which is the same in Hebrew as in Aramaic, is found but only once in the Book."

"And you are aware that I am not so learned as you."

"It occurs only once, spoken by God to the prophet Isaiah, meant by God to describe those who were taught of him."

This Isaiah was becoming a haunting to us. The priest spoke the words from the Book:

"Bind up the testimony, seal the law among my disciples." Jesus looked to him.

"The testimony," said the priest, "is the written law. It is the doctrine of the coming of the *mashiach,* the coming of the Messiah."

Jesus was silent awhile, then spoke: "This is most curious."

The priest was silent awhile, then spoke: "It is a part of the shaking in the air."

And so it was that Aaron the priest and the rabbi Ephraim joined our merry glorious-doomsday band.

Now there were more eyes close upon us.

Aaron seemed unlike a temple priest. He seemed lacking in avarice and ambition. Ephraim seemed unlike a rabbi. He had a carefree and jovial side to him. Peter took Andreas under his wing like a younger brother, so that at times it was hard to tell whose disciple the young man was.

It was good to have as our disciples learned men of the Book as well as unlettered fishermen, men of the city as well as men of the countryside. It gave our mission an air of universality, widened our appeal.

I must say that it was strange to be the only gentile in our traveling troupe of players. And stranger still to be in a troupe in which most of the players were unaware of the heavy iron masks they wore. A fool was a fool, no matter his erudition or lack of it. I sometimes amused myself comparing the ways of the cosmopolitan aristocrat to the ways of the agrestian bumpkin, who were united in their unknowing folly.

But we are all fools, are we not?

Winter came, but in this beautiful land, the climate did not much change. So, as fools, we wandered on.

One afternoon, we came upon a spring and rested. The sun was low in the deepening blue and lavender-flowering sky, immense, like a vast planchet of gold, an enormous aureus not yet struck. We gazed at it, as if spellbound, watching it grow as it descended, turning from soft gold to apricot, from apricot to orange, from orange to cinnabar, from cinnabar to blood-red scarlet.

The perfect sphere sighed the last of its light on us, and in the deepening blue and lavender-flowering sky, we saw a great bird that was bigger than a man, a bird whose head was of white, whose body was pale brown, whose wings and tail-feathers were so dark to our eyes that they appeared to be black. If it was as long as a man, the span of its broad wings surpassed the length of two men.

None of us had ever seen such a thing in the sky before. It passed slowly, effortlessly, alone.

At last, when the creature could no longer be seen by us, the priest spoke.

"I believe it was a griffon vulture," he said.

Not only had we never seen such a creature before, I and the fishermen had never heard of it before, either.

It was the rabbi who then spoke, saying: "The first bird to appear in the Book is the raven. There are many others. But the griffon vulture is the bird of God's power. It is the bird of all power."

"So this sign in the sky is good?" asked Peter.

"Its strength and longevity are noted," said the priest. "In times past, many did make of the griffon vulture a false god."

"Is its song known?" I asked.

"It has been described as a harrowing," said the priest. "A dreaded, not to be forgotten sound."

Jesus continued to stare into the sky, even though all was very near to darkness.

The rabbi let the priest become silent, then spoke words from the Book:

"Where the slain are, there is she." Quiet fell again.

"And who is it in the Book who speaks those words?" asked the younger of our fishermen.

"God," the rabbi answered him. "It is God who speaks those words."

16

O NE NIGHT, AS WE PREPARED FOR SLEEP IN A CLEARING
amid trees, the Messiah went off wandering through the
tall pines, ostensibly to commune with his elemental tones but
more likely to lay his healing hand to his cock and make his bestial
sounds. I laid me down and after a while closed my tired eyes to
the stars and the risen first-quarter crescent of the waxing moon.
I could hear the subdued and quiet talk of Peter the fisherman
and Ephraim the rabbi. Peter said:

"You are a very learned man. Our Jesus is not so learned as
you. Yet you follow him, as I have come to follow him."

"There are many degrees and kinds of learning, an infinity of
them, between knowledge and wisdom. I believe that wisdom is
holy and lies beyond the reaches of learning. I believe that he
possesses it, in its truest and profoundest form. I believe the gift
of being in his presence, the gift of witnessing his deeds and hearing his words, will lead me to the light that is in him, and to a
greater light that lies before him on this road to the unknown that
he travels, and we with him."

Then I heard the voice of Jesus, returned from his solitary
love-making. He asked the rabbi why the third and eldest man,
who was with them at Bethlehem, was not with them now.

"He is a subaltern to the vice-justice of the Sanhedrin. The
position of the vice-justice is high, between that of the chief justice and the high priest of the Holy Temple in Jerusalem. His

superiors — indeed all of the sixty-nine members of the Great Sanhedrin, the supreme high court of Jewish religious matters — would not look kindly on his taking leave, especially and certainly not on his taking leave to convene with a man such as you."

"A man such as I?"

"Yes. A man such as you, who speaks and seeks the Word and the Way. The Sanhedrin care only for their own authority, their own share of the Temple's riches, and they are not tolerant of any conceived threat to their status, that is to say, any conceived threat to the established observance of sacred judicial law."

"So, these Sanhedrin would be against me on the ground of fixed motive? That is not justice."

"It is to them."

"But does not the Book they defend, from the first prophets to the last, speak much of the Messiah to come?"

"Yes. But they wish to delay his coming, for it is not in their best interests."

"So, these Sanhedrin, they go against the words of God and his prophets while defending the law of the Book?"

"You could say that, yes. It was the Lord himself that told the serpent in Eden that there would be born of the generations of Eve a savior who would strike a great blow to the serpent. The Sanhedrin are devout as regards the Book's foretellings and prophecies of the Messiah's coming. But they do not want him to come now.

"The very last of the Book's prophets, Malachi, to whom God spoke only thirteen generations ago, was told by him: 'I will send my messenger, and he shall prepare the way before me; and the Lord, whom you seek, shall suddenly come to his temple.'

"Can you imagine the Messiah coming suddenly to the Temple? Can you imagine the terror with which the Sanhedrin might look upon the prospect of this prophecy's fulfillment?

"No one knows who is meant by the messenger, but most agree

that the messenger and Lord of our seeking are one, embodied in the Messiah anointed by the God of judgment and justice himself.

"These words come very close to the end of the parchment that is the end of the Book.

"God goes on to demand: 'Will a mere mortal rob God? Yet you rob me.' He is speaking of tithes and offerings to a corrupt temple.

"He then warns: 'Surely the day is coming.' It is like unto that coming of which you speak, that shaking that Aaron feels in the air.

"And God's very last words, with which the Book ends, threaten that the true law, as he gave it unto Moses, must be obeyed 'or else I will come and strike the land with total destruction.'

"Worshippers heed these words. The Sanhedrin, to whom they seem to be addressed, shrink from them."

When Jesus spoke, there was a hushed excitement in his voice:

"But whose temple? It says only that he shall suddenly come to *his* temple."

"The Holy Temple in Jerusalem, I assume. This is the temple that rightfully belongs to both God and the Messiah."

"But I am to build a great new temple. This is our only reason for accepting donations and collecting funds."

The seriousness in his voice was so convincing that even he seemed convinced of what he said.

"Yes, I have heard you tell of it wherever you speak. I and the others gather what we can for this."

"Which temple, now, do you believe was meant?"

Then came the voice of young Andreas, who was, like me, believed to be asleep but was not:

"It is clear to me," he said.

Neither Jesus nor the rabbi seemed to pay his words any mind. There was no sound from either of them. I could not see if they even turned to look his way. Then there was no sound at all but for the crickets in the grass.

17

THERE WAS TALK OF A MAN WHO WAS CALLED BY MANY NAMES.
Some of these names were Aramaic, some Hebrew, some
Arabic, some Greek. Some said he was an Essene, some said he
was an itinerant beggar, or a self-appointed priest. As many were
those who told of him, so many were his names and natures and
physical features.

It was said that he spoke of a Messiah and was a great baptizer
of people, much given to rivers and streams and immersions of
the faithful in their waters. It was said that Jesus had been among
the faithful who had come to him, and that on beholding
Jesus, the Baptist had humbled himself before him, saying that
he was not fit to bless him who was blessed beyond himself and
all men.

And as many the people who told this tale, so many were the
places where it had occurred.

The source of this legend was unknown to us, but it was good
for our purposes, so we let it be said and we profited from it, as we
let be said and profited from all the tales of little miracles that
Jesus had performed as a child in Nazareth, all the tales of greater
miracles that he had performed in the more recent times of his
ministry. Many of these miraculous doings were beyond our
imaginations, and we often wondered at the seeds of the imaginations from which they had sprouted. But when asked about them,
Jesus responded with an almost imperceptible smile, an even

more subtle lowering of his head in vague affirmation, and a silence of profound humility.

His nuanced affirmation seemed not to affirm anything to do with the miracles of which he was asked, but rather to dismiss them as trifles while affirming something unspoken that lay beyond them. As for his silence of deep humility, it had been developed to perfection by him from the near-silence of his taking no credit for raising the dead: "He only slept."

When we heard that we had fed five thousand with two fish and a few loaves of bread in the Decapolis desert, those who told of this received the almost imperceptible smile, the even more subtle lowering of his head in vague affirmation, and the silence of profound humility.

There was even an explanation as to how five thousand people had come to be gathered in the desert. They had gathered, of course, to hear the Messiah speak. And how could the voice of Jesus be heard by the farthest of such a multitude? This, too, was a miracle, of course.

When we heard that this cripple or that had been cured by him: the almost imperceptible smile, the even more subtle lowering of the head in vague affirmation, the silence of profound humility.

Our dear disciples, the fishermen and the learned men alike, often wondered at these tales, which were told as if they had happened in days just passed. Why, they wondered, had they seen or known nothing of these things?

They were hesitant to speak of this to Jesus, but not to me.

It troubled me that I had no answer. One morning, the rabbi provided me and the others with the answer we sought, I in my way, they in theirs.

"I believe our Lord is several in his oneness, as the aspects of God."

The priest spoke of Pythagoras, saying:

"His was the most scientific of minds the world has known. He traveled as far as mathematics, reason, and logic could lead him. Then he came to the spheres where they did not enter; where they, and he with them, ceded to the mystical."

To these words I made as to agree with the rabbi and the fishermen, and things were well.

So it was that the people of Judea, wherever we journeyed, and wherever we did not, worked our miracles for us. Our concern—my concern—was to keep them from saying our words for us. The miracles, the cheap tricks, they craved were of little matter. The pith and substance were in the words. Let them become lost in interpreting all they wanted, so long as they did not embellish them too much with their own tales of what was said.

I saw that the Word and the Way, the Way and the Word should indeed remain without precise meaning. Let them mean all things to all men, and let them discuss these things.

New disciples joined us. Some remained. Some returned to their families. I remember some of their faces, some of their names.

There was the errant tax-collector, Levi, who always seemed to be scratching at himself, and who said little but obeyed. There was a second Simon, who was also given another name by Jesus. There was a Thaddeus, a drifter of Canaan, I believe, and a most somber man. There were other fishermen. There was a gentile, a Roman by birth, like me. There was an Eleazar, a merchant of crude wares, whose two young sisters were eager to have congress with the Lord, were hard to resist, and were hard to have return to their home. There was for a time an elderly man whose good cheer I will not forget, but whose name has long escaped memory. He could not go far with us. There were others, many others.

At this time, in the cities of Judea, politically minded young Jews were aligning themselves with one or another of several idealistic groups advocating change in society.

The Herodians were led by Pharisees and Sadducees of the priestly caste, along with soldiers and courtiers of Herod Antipas. Young Jews recruited to the Herodians foolishly espoused a renewed dedication to rule by the dynasty of Herod, king of the Jews and hater of them. They believed in their ignorance and folly that such a return to despotism might bring about a more perfect theocracy. The young Jews did not see through to the ulterior motives of the aristocratic priests who lured them with talk of this more perfect theocracy.

The Zealots were more radical in their cause. The Herodic rulers, after all, were mere client kings and puppets of Rome. The Zealots, though they too sought a more perfect theocracy, advocated a revolution against and freedom from Rome itself.

Other groups were taken less seriously. Some of these fell apart as quickly as they appeared, only to be revived later. One of them was the Sicarii, who took a boyish delight in calling themselves by this menacing name for dagger-wielding assassins. They were as laughably tough-talking flower boys to the Zealots.

Rome saw these groups as being as potentially dangerous as they were naive. This was particularly true of the Zealots. Rome had been distressed by its share of rebellions, and the one invariable fact she knew was that every rebellion began with the rumor of rebellion.

Thus a certain God-fearing young man of unweathered innocence who professed himself a Zealot had to be coaxed from among our disciples. His name was Barnabas, or something like that. Serious in the way that only innocents can be, he was altogether a nice enough boy. He spoke of the injustice of taxes, as if others did not see and feel this as he did; and his talks about this with our disciple Levi, the quondam tax-collector, were most entertaining. But we had to rid ourselves of him.

We could not be seen as out to ruffle the feathers of Rome. To conquer Judea under the Romans, we must not be construed to be at enmity with Rome. In this way, someday, we would command the faith of Rome as well.

It was at this time that I wrote one of my most masterly pronouncements for my Loiterer and Lord, words that would be received well and with strong approval by any Roman authority whose ears they reached.

Jesus would begin this pronouncement, which was to be repeated many times in many towns, by asking that someone in the crowd bring forth to him a coin of tribute. Never was it merely a coin that he asked be brought to him, but always a coin of tribute. This was to ensure that it be a Roman denarius, as older Jewish coins were not accepted as tribute, but only the Roman denarius, which represented the capitation tax levied on every Jew.

He would hold the face of the silver coin to the crowd, who knew that it presented the profile and name of Tiberius. He would move his arm in a long slow sweep before them. Sometimes, if the coin was of a new minting, it reflected intense sunlight into the eyes of those who stood before him.

"Whose image is this, and whose superscription is this?" he would ask with some force.

The force in his voice never failed to rouse most of them to call out in response: "Caesar's!"

To which he would declare with increased force: "Render therefore unto Caesar the things that are Caesar's."

Never would he cease the long slow sweep of his arm, or lower the coin during these words, but only when he lessened the force in his voice to say what he said next:

"And unto God the things that are God's."

In placing Rome before God, and in placing the obligations due Rome before those due God, our Lord could be seen as a propagator for the authority of Rome as much as a propagator for the God whose Messiah he was. The powers of state and God were set in equation, and men could go so far as to here sense a syllogism: powers were deserving of tribute; Rome and the God of the Jews deserved great tribute; therefore Rome and the God of the Jews were powers in like kind and measure.

Thus, for now, our safe passage was insured among both Jews and Romans.

After every performance of this display, the man who had brought forth the denarius would step forth to retrieve it, whereupon I or one of the more devout disciples would hold the coin to him and ask, in the presence of onlookers: "Tribute for Caesar or tribute for the building of the new temple?" Invariably, though often begrudgingly, he would give it up for the latter. When he did this, others in the crowd tendered their coins of godly tribute as well. Thus this pronouncement served more than one end.

As we traveled, we were sometimes mistaken for Essenes, as women were not seen among us. But in fact many women were taken by our Lord. At times, this presented problems, for our Jesus must appear to be chaste in every way.

There were walks in the woods with women who came to our camp seeking the presence and guidance of our Lord. I would follow after them for a distance, then post myself to be sure that his beast noises could not be heard by me, and thus not by the encamped disciples.

But there were too many women, too many woods, too many walks. I had to lay down the law.

"Would you sacrifice a kingdom for a whiff of spoiling tilapia?"

He looked at me. He smiled. His chest moved with silent laughter. He understood.

Sometimes the women who followed him brought problems of a more absurd nature.

There was much talk of a woman who traveled after us from town to town, city to city, settlement to settlement, desert wilder-

ness to desert wilderness. She was called Maria—not to be confused with the fair sister of our Eleazar, who bore the same name:
a name to which Jesus always reacted with occluded eyes, as it
was, too, the name of his own mother—and Maria the Magdalene, after Magdala, the town whence she claimed to have come,
on the shore of the Sea of Galilee, near Tiberias. And she was
called simply the Magdalene. Between ourselves, Jesus and I
called her the Magdalen Hag.

Many were the tales of her beauty, but not one of these was
ever taken up by any who chanced to see her. She was a toothless
crone of eighty-six who walked with a staff, cackled unpredict-
ably, and was given to muttering nonsense. The tale-tellers who
had never seen her spoke of the romantic desires she harbored for
our Lord. I believe these desires to have been real, as she was
much given to drooling and offering to rub his tired limbs with
balm. It was also said that she was a prostitute who had changed
her ways upon experiencing the light of Jesus. She may in truth
once have been a prostitute, but if so, it was age and not the light
of Jesus that changed her ways.

We never knew the source of her means, which allowed her to
follow after us again and again; and she came always bearing gifts.

The Lord did allow her to rub his feet with aromatic oil on an
occasion when she presented him with several olden coins of
heavy gold; but he stayed her rough and gnarled hands as they
moved above his ankles. She worked her wiry gray hair like a
cloth upon his oiled feet.

There was another woman, also said to be of most stunning
beauty by those who had never seen her. The name by which we
knew her said much: the Hemorrhaging Woman.

This unfortunate woman was in years beyond the moons of
her natural bleeding, and even then her bleeding was in no way
natural. She bled horrendously, and more days than not. She had

come to our Lord to be healed of this affliction, the like of which we had never witnessed. Jesus could of course do nothing for her, but said to her:

"No woman can bleed so profusely and live. This truly is a sign from God that you are most special. He has chosen you to suffer for many. Not only do you bleed without losing life, but your reward will be great indeed."

This uplifted her, and she followed us for many weeks, cooking for us when we spent our nights in the countryside. She was a very good cook. But what a blood-sodden mess, attracting mosquitoes and flies, and leaving puddles of gore to be stepped round wherever she went. We liked her, but were relieved to see her go.

For a very long time, we remained in or close to Galilee. Known as both the Nazarene and the Galilean, the Messiah had a strong hold there that grew stronger by the day. We discussed the need to journey farther, but we were slow to do so. Then one night something befell us that precipitated our farther journeying and taught us that it is dangerous to have known whereabouts for too long. It was a miracle of sorts, in that we escaped with our lives.

Whether the Baptist lived or was a phantom of rumor, we knew that others who proclaimed themselves to be the Messiah were very real, and that none of them was pleased with the new fame of Jesus and the shadows of increasing anonymity to which it consigned them. The most angered of these, we knew, was the man who called himself, and was called by others, the Egyptian. This particular Egyptian was one of a few who went by that name. All of them claimed to have spent years in Egypt, but none of them could speak a word of either older Ptolemaic or even Roman Demotic.

The Egyptian who harbored anger for Jesus was a Jew who went in a Jewish-made approximation of the old-fashioned striped head-cloth worn by men in Egypt. His preachings had been cobbled together from second-hand mis-readings of the Sibylline

Oracles of the Jews and the alleged teachings of the Egyptian cult of the ibis-god, Thoth, which had passed piecemeal into Greek as the nonsensical "secret wisdom" of Thrice-Great Hermes.

The fading impression of the man who called himself the Egyptian, or the men who called themselves by this name, was such that Jesus himself was sometimes rumored to have journeyed early in his life to the treasuries of learning in Alexandria. To these rumors, I had Jesus answer:

"I have sought God nowhere but here, in this land that is my home."

We were far to the north, near the raised road to Tyre. The disciples had been sent to Sidon, to procure provisions and to minister to the poor with bread and kindness. We were to meet them there and enter twin-harbored Tyre together in the morning, crossing over the bridge that Alexander the Great was said to have built in fulfillment of a prophecy in the Book.

We had seen two spring-traps set for birds, but not the pit-trap set for venison or big cat or whatever might fall to it. We heard the sudden cry of its catch, which was the cry of a man. Then three men were upon us with daggers.

Jesus struck one of them in the face with wood aflame from our fire. I drew my dagger, and another of them took it to the hilt in his gut as he flung himself at me with his own dagger raised to strike me. As Jesus, our prince of peace, no longer carried his dagger in his sash, I took the knife from the gutted man's hand and hurled it to him on the ground. Seeing that the two remaining men were poised above him and ready to strike, I grasped my weapon with both hands and drove forward its long blade into the back of one, while Jesus in one continuous movement took from the dirt the dagger I had tossed him and deeply slashed the other man above his ankle. The man wailed his pain as Jesus rose and with a fast sweep of his arm, cut open the man's throat and was bathed in a rush of blood.

Only then did we see that the man still vomiting blood from his neck had worn a striped cloth on his head. This head-cloth now lay in the dirt beside his fallen body.

I heard words come from my mouth, hearing them as if I had heard them somewhere before:

"No matter whose hand holds the knife, it is always truly the hand of God that wields it."

He looked at me with disgust as I said them. I was half-mad with trembling. There was frenzy in my breath.

"Even now do you compose pretty words for me?" he said. I could hear the trembling frenzy in him as well.

"Have you never killed before?"

"No," he said. "I have not. And you?"

"Once, as a soldier."

This was a lie. Even at such moments, when all falls from us, men and their lies are not easily parted.

We knew without saying it that we now must kill the man who cowered in silence in the pit. He could not be left there to die, for he would not die. Whoever had laid the trap would be round, and the man in it would live to tell.

We had no spades with which to bury him alive. Jesus peered into the darkness of the pit, where a shadow breathed in pain, and he said to that shadow:

"Raise your hand to me, that I might help you."

"You will not help me. You will kill me as you have killed those whom I guided to the place."

He was no guide. He was a fourth killer, now trying to exculpate himself through subtle lying.

"If we wished you harm, we had only to leave you here to die in this hole we dug for fallow deer. We had only to take our spades and bury you alive in minutes with the soft earth that was dug to makes this hole."

The lies of these men, and my own, could almost be tasted in the cool of the darkness.

We watched his hand rise toward moonlight. Jesus grasped its wrist with both hands. I grasped Jesus round the waist, and together we pulled the man from the pit. Pain was thick in the gasps that came through his clenched teeth. The white of jagged bone shone through the flesh of his leg. He could not move. He could only lie crying in the dirt.

"Go ahead," I said. "Heal him."

The daggers were gathered up, and we robbed the corpses of what money was on them. I removed the striped cloth from the blood and dirt in which it lay.

Blood-drenched linen clung to us uncomfortably. When we came to a stream, we cleaned ourselves, our tunics, and the daggers. The moonlight showed the blood like a pool of blackness spreading around us in the slate-colored water. I raised a stone and put the striped cloth under us. With the blades of daggers, we scraped beneath the nails of our fingers. We stepped forth shivering.

We moved slowly under the moon to Sidon. The sun began to rise. I could see that his damp old tunic was still pink here and there with lingering stains. A tunic of beggarly-gray fustian was gotten at a stall in the little market of Sidon. I told him that at Tyre he would have a new tunic and robe of the finest flaxen linen and immaculate white.

Before he could discard the stained tunic and draw over him the tunic of gray fustian, the young disciple Andreas approached us. As a fisherman familiar with the rosy tints of blood that were not to be washed away, he beheld his Lord as if to question him.

"An injured beast shed blood on him," I said.

"And did him no harm?"

"The injured beast came to him meaning no harm."

"And what became of the injured beast?"

"It was healed and now roams free again."

When Andreas told this story to the other disciples, the injured beast had already become a leopard.

Jesus laid his hands to the forehead of a self-afflicted boy who had been brought to him on a makeshift litter.

As he did so, I stared at his fingernails, looking for traces of darkened blood that the blade had failed to scrape out.

The self-afflicted child opened his eyes and smiled before the face of Jesus, and his parents wept and knelt before him.

"See that he gets his fill of vinegar with his bread," he said to them. "And keep him from the presence of the dead."

A farmer came to him and said that a curse had been put on his fields, which for seven years had yielded paltry grain while the fields all round his had been harvested full and lush.

"Your seven lean years will now be followed by seven years of plenty. This curse is lifted and will not be on your fields again."

He paused to tell a woman who stood with her small daughter:

"This child is special. She is a lamb not to be sacrificed. Someday she will bring you grace, and someday she will bring you more prosperity than you have ever known."

The disciples had apparently done much good here. Many of the townsmen called fondly to them as we made to leave. Some rushed forward to kiss the hem of the tunic Jesus wore, and to utter to him some of his own teachings that they variously especially liked, teachings that the disciples had spread among them, or that already had made their way to them otherwise.

"This tunic is of your town," he told them as they brought their lips to its humble edge. "It will keep you close to my breast, as you already are."

The nails of his toes showed blood, which could easily be taken for dirt.

Thence to Tyre.

18

Exorcism is easy. All one needs is the right drunkard and a knowledge of drunkenness.

I speak not of a man who is drunk, but of a man whom the need for drink has come to define, so that he is no longer really a man but rather what is left of a man — the dregs of a man, whose every atom doth scream for the dregs of wine. His sanity lies in pieces behind him, like so many crumbs of bread. Dragged down by wine to the doorway of death, he would enter therein for more wine, or, for want of it, would relinquish himself with his own shaking hand. Drink was his obsession; and a man obsessed is a man possessed — by a demon, as it were. And demons were indeed often seen, along with all manner of other terrible phantoms, by a man such as he. Yet somewhere in him an ember of hope seeks rekindling by an unknown breath. Such is the right drunkard.

The drunkard is more suggestible, and more fearful, than a child. If you tell him that there are sores or boils or a skin rash upon him, he will excitedly examine himself and see with alarm what you told him was to be seen. If you tell him that he will not live to see the sunset of the new day, he will believe you and become distraught with panic.

It was a new entertainment among the Jews, this casting out of demons. We tried to give the people what they wanted. But we found it quite strange that men and women who had given little thought to demons now felt their presence all about. In the thousands of years of the tales of the Book, only once does there occur the expulsion of a demon.

A woman known as Sarah, in the Persian lands, was prey to Asmodeus, the demon of lust. He did not enter her or take possession of her; he merely lingered close by. He so desired her that he slayed on the nights of their marriages to her, before consummation, the seven successive husbands she took. As she prayed for death and its deliverance, the angel Raphael, sent by God, came to free her of the demon.

Asmodeus is called by the Book "the worst of demons," but the Book says nothing else of him. Except for the Satan, to whom allusion is made here and there in the Book, there is little concern in the Book for demons. And I wonder, if Asmodeus is said to be the worst of them, and he could neither seduce nor rape the woman Sarah, what menial piddlers these imagined demons must be.

Only the heart, liver, and gall of a fish, and the smoke from the burning mixture of them, are mentioned by the Book in connection with this sole exorcism. Our fishermen were put to use in procuring and preparing a paste of these stinking things.

I remembered the two men in Bethlehem carving their little olive-wood demons to be sold as amulet trinkets. It seemed so long ago.

Yes, we found it quite strange that men and women who had given little thought to demons now felt their presence all about and sought riddance of them. But slowly we sensed this strangeness to be only part of a greater strangeness in the air. For such was the air of those days, whose every breeze seemed to whisper foreboding, whose every stillness seemed to bear presentiment, whose every aspect seemed to possess a darkening shadow. The demons thrived in the strangeness, the eeriness of those days.

After crossing the raised sea-road to Tyre, we came upon the right drunkard on a hillock very near to the walls of that town. He was sprawled close to his wineskin in the sandy soil and weeds.

Jesus stood over the drunkard, and the drunkard stirred and drank. Jesus said to him words from the Book.

"Woe unto them that rise up early in the morning, that they may follow strong drink; that continue until night."

The words of God as revealed to Isaiah, whose ghost now seemed to be always near. These words were said by Jesus only that he might ascertain the nature of the drunkard, only that he might see if he was the right drunk.

The drunkard shrank from him, hurkling with dread and muttering sorrow. His watering red eyes, set deep in yellowed skin, were the eyes of one who saw horrible things. He was the right drunk.

"This man is possessed of a demon," said Jesus.

"This man is drunk," said the priest.

"Yes, that too," said Jesus. "But his drunkenness claims only him. I sense that the demon seeks to claim many men."

He called to Peter to bring the paste of fish heart, liver, and gall. Peter brought the phial to him.

"Do you wish to be free of the demon that is in you?"

The drunkard tried to rise, staggered, and fell again to the ground.

"Yes," he said. His body shook violently. "Yes!" he cried, then wept and affirmed, wept and affirmed.

Jesus knelt beside him, took him by the hair, and with the paste signed his forehead with the *beth* that is both the second character of the Hebrew alphabet and the word whose meaning is "house." The man writhed and gasped.

"In the name of God, I declare the vessel of this man's body to be my home. No longer will you dwell here, demon, and you will eat of him no more."

The drunkard again shook violently, and Jesus moved as if withstanding a strong sudden gust.

"Away from us, demon! Away!"

Seeming weakened, he lowered his head and let fall his shoulders. With the aid of my hand, he rose.

"You are cleansed," he said to the drunkard. "Do you feel your freedom?"

The wretch nodded rapidly and repeatedly. He seemed to be much confused and abstracted.

"You can now take food again," Jesus told him. "You need not drink. Your thirst for wine was of the demon, who now is fled."

The drunkard continued to nod, rapidly and repeatedly, seeming now even more confused and abstracted. Jesus turned from him, toward the walls of ancient Tyre. People were watching us from the gate. The closer we got, the more excited became their welcome.

"It was Azazel who possessed him," Jesus said to us as the acclaiming grew among those who awaited. "She let her name be known to me as she rushed from him to the desert wind."

"But Azazel is a demon, not a demoness," said the rabbi. His tone was one of deferential perplexity. "The Azazel of Leviticus, the Azazel to whom a scapegoat is sacrificed on the Day of Atonement. Azazel is a he-demon."

"Azazel is of both male and female aspects. At times they roam together and are one. At times they roam apart and are two."

The rabbi, like the others, received this elucidation with a look that expressed an effort to understand.

"Were other things addressed to you in the rushing forth of the she-Azazel?"

"Yes. Unspeakable things."

One of the men milling at the gate of Tyre asked why we had tarried with the drunkard on the hillock. As was usual in a situation that might result in seeming lack of modesty on his part, Jesus allowed one of the disciples to say what he would.

"The man was possessed of a demon," a disciple said. "He is possessed no more. Please be accepting of his return to a sober life among you."

Another of the men at the gate said that he had for a long time suspected that a demon had taken up residence in the poor wretch. The speaker had known him for many years. Before his descent, he had been a fine young man.

But what a story this was to become! We were to be celebrated for it far and wide, for the drunkard did in fact convalesce and become sober again and did eagerly lay the blame for his wretchedness on the demon of our invention and expulsion, which he believed to have been real.

Some months later, Jesus performed an exorcism that was most exceptionally delightful in that the drunkard was so hoarse, parched, and scorched of throat that in forcing out words, it truly sounded as if a demon of otherworldly voice spoke from deep within him. This gave good fright to all.

For every miracle affected, the talk of men greatened it and multiplied it by three. Such was their hungering for these tawdry ticks.

"It is as I told you," Jesus said to the priest. "I worry lest the Word be lost to these ostentations."

"God knows his way," the priest would say. "As we follow the path you make for us, so you must follow the path he makes for you." There were times when the exaggerations and fabulations of the people grew so preposterous as to tax their own credulity and prove an embarrassment to us.

On the western shore of the Jordan, for example, there was much praise for an exorcism we were said to have performed across the river near the town of Gerasa. As the tale had it, a possessed man there had run from his cave at the sight of Jesus and thrown himself at the feet of our Lord.

"Come out of this man, you evil spirit!" Jesus was said to have reprimanded the demon within the man, and the possessed man, or the demon within him, was said to have cried:

"What do you want with me, Jesus, son of the most high God? In the name of God, please do not torture me so!"

At which, Jesus was said to have asked the unseen demon its name, eliciting the reply:

"My name is Legion, for we are many."

It was said that there was a hillside nearby on which grazed a herd of some two thousand pigs.

It was said that the demons begged Jesus to be allowed to enter the pigs if they must vacate the man. It was said that Jesus granted permission, and the legion of demons left the man and entered the pigs, whereupon the pigs rushed down the steep hillside into the Sea of Galilee, which now also happened to be nearby, and there the two thousand pigs drowned themselves.

The possessed man was said to have been restored and at his ease, and the swineherds were said to have run off and reported this throughout the countryside and in Gerasa, whose people were said to have pleaded politely with Jesus to leave the region. And so it was said that we had come to be here, on the other side of the river, among these other, more appreciative and sophisticated people, as they said themselves to be.

It was in the town of Scythopolis that we heard this tale. I believe it was then and there that we decided to evict no further demons and to let all right drunkards be. If we could not prevent such gross and overly outrageous tales from circulating, we could at least not encourage them.

Jesus spoke twice at Tyre, once before sunset, again at daybreak. He spoke of the Word and he spoke of the Way. He spoke of the will of God the Father, and he spoke of what was and was to be.

We collected much money from the good people of Tyre, including a number of Romans. Phoenician gold and silver shekels were in abundance. Many who lived in this place of busy commerce seemed to have prospered well. The merchant at whose home Jesus had spent the night gifted him most prodigiously.

Our donkey was becoming heavily burdened with the wealth of the new temple that was never to be. Surely we were tempting, and soon could not but attract, the bands of thieves and highwaymen who shared with us the roads and ill-gotten gains of Judea. We had overcome the Egyptian and his men by good fortune, not by prowess. Fortune might not be with us were we caught, alone and unawares, by highwaymen or footpads. We were at risk also when spending our nights in the towns we visited. Our treasure-sacks were becoming too ponderous to lift, and the donkey that bore them needed good guard. I worried again over what to do to safeguard our growing riches.

What ways were open to me? Again I thought of Caesarea, the provincial capital. Surely in that seat of Rome's power, there must be at least one respectable and well-established Roman argenter who was of such wealth and probity as to be entrusted with the extensive and complex finances of the Roman prefecture here. I could easily deposit our fortune with him, either as *vacua pecunia,* bearing neither interest nor risk, or as *creditum,* to be lent out by the argentarius at the conservative fixed legal rate of twelve per centum per annum. Many Roman citizens deposited all their capital with an argentarius. I was a Roman citizen of equestrian rank, with much money to deposit.

But such an agent, who worked for the prefecture but was not a member of it, would nevertheless be subject to answering to the prefect, Pontius Pilate. While Pilate ostensibly served under

Tiberius, he was the chattel of Sejanus, who had arranged his appointment. This was the praetorian prefect, perceived by Tiberius to be his bosom friend, who had murdered Drusus, the son and heir of Tiberius, and pressed Tiberius to flee Rome, where he, Sejanus, now played at princeps.

You will remember the circumstances under which I was banished from the court at Rome.

It was Pilate whom I had been banished to serve. But I had not entered the palace walls at Caesarea, and the curt letter of assignment that bore the seal of Tiberius was still with me, still unpresented and still unopened.

When I thought of the argenter, who was faceless, I thought of Pilate, who was faceless; and then I thought of Sejanus, Tiberius, and Drusus, whose faces were quite clear. And then I thought of the order of assignment I had disregarded. And then I stopped thinking of the argenter in Caesarea, though my mind would return again and again.

I thought of Jerusalem, where the wealthiest of the Jews deposited their money at the treasury of the Holy Temple.

Though the Book forbade Jews from lending money at interest to their own kind, this prohibition was ignored rather than feared. Here alone did the devout dare to defy their God so openly. While Roman law limited money-lending to a certain rate of simple annual interest, the consortium of Temple-affiliated usurers not only imposed much higher rates, but also often the treachery of compound interest.

Thus the riches of the rich and the riches of the Holy Temple.

But I was no Jew, and Jesus was more wary of this notion than I. What might become of our wealth so securely on deposit, if the Temple heard tell that this wealth was for the building of a new temple dedicated to a new Way?

Were this Rome, it would have been so easy, with my own

good strong house, and the argentarii of the aristocracy at their places of business all about the forum. But this was not Rome.

We acquired a second donkey, divided the burden of wealth in ox-hide sacks between the two beasts, and made our way.

There were days when we did not recognize half of those who came and went in our fluctuating band of peripatetic disciples. It would be easy for a man with designs on our wealth to infiltrate us and steal away with the donkeys. He could put miles between us and our riches while we slept.

Jesus suggested that we fix iron bells and clappers round the necks of the asses. But what can be fixed can be unfixed; and it took but a piece of rag wadded into a bell to silence a clapper.

I remembered exacting those first petty coins from that false cripple in that valley settlement without name. It was so long ago, when we did not know what lay before us. Much was now behind us.

There were quiet nights when I lay awake feeling that we should put an end to it. We could vanish silently, sail to Rome with the sea wind, and live our lives of ease. We could do it now. Right now. This very moment. Or before dawn broke. It was just a matter of wandering soundlessly off to Caesarea with our donkeys, then to the harbor. I told Jesus of these thoughts. He told me that, on quiet nights of his own, he was given to these feelings, too.

"I once dreamed of happiness," he said. "Now that I have the gold to buy it, I dream only of more gold. It seems that there are many sorrows among the uncounted riches in those sacks."

We looked to the stars for a long time. Clouds moved across them. A very light rain began to fall.

"It seems that the night itself is pierced with sorrows," he said.

"Did you truly dream of happiness?" I asked him after a while.

"I should say that I once yearned for happiness. Yes. I yearned for happiness, and now that I have the gold to buy it, I yearn only for more gold."

There was more silence, another wordless stagnancy, between us.

"I ask," I said, "because I have never dreamt happily. My dreaming has always been unpleasant. On the few occasions when I saw happiness in my dreams, I woke only to the more dire unpleasantness that this rare happiness was an intruder in the house of dreams, come only to bring disappointment in the house of my life."

Again there was nothing but the very light rain and the darkness without stars.

"We all wish each other good night and sweet dreams," he said. "But are sweet dreams to be had by us?"

For lack of an answer, or words of any kind, I forced the ghost of a stillborn dismal laugh.

"That is what the Book is," said he. "The Book and all its curses and doomings and prophecies. It is the Book of Bad Dreams."

"Or simply the Book of Dreams."

"Which is to say that it is the Book of Life."

"One and the same."

"Would you pay for a sweet dream?" he asked.

"Yes," I said.

"And for the idle promise of one?"

"No," I said.

"Yet that is what we sell," he said, "and grow rich in the doing."

The light rain felt neither good nor bad. The constellations were there, somewhere, but they were not ours to see. And nothing more was said by us that night, for it was not ours to say. Our eyes were heavy. We seemed alone in all the world. We could extinguish it at any time, by entering the house of dreams. The house that awaited us. The house that we dreaded.

The morning was a spent, still mist that stank of dung and human excrement. Slow steps made sucking sounds in the shallow mud and silt. Low groans and thick congested coughing could be heard from disciples who were not yet awake. The sky had no color.

I told Jesus of my dream, in which I stood unsteadily on a jagged rock very high above a raging sea, having no knowledge of how I had ascended to this pinnacle, and, much more disturbingly, of how I was to manage a descent from it that would not be fatal.

"And you?" I asked.

"I dreamt I fucked that ignoble cunt of a mother of mine," he said without hesitation.

I took this as an indication that he was familiar with the tale of the dream of Caesar, and to bring the jest to rest, I said:

"A great and wondrous dream, for it augurs that you shall ravish and conquer the world."

But I was mistaken. He had never heard the story of the dream of Caesar. Scratching and fingering the humidity-stuck folds of his scrotum and looking at me curiously, he shook his head and walked off a few paces to piss in peace.

Even-song and morn-song. Dream and dirt. One and the same.

Our riches seemed now to grow with the strangeness in the air of these days. It did not occur to me, nor to my Lord, that we furthered this strangeness with every forward movement of our mission, spreading it through the land as we spread the Word and we spread the Way.

19

W E FOUND HIM HIS TUNIC OF FINE FLAXEN LINEN AND
immaculate white. For a robe, we settled on one of simple
deep cerulean blue. Dyed with indigo, it was of the color worn by
the humbler classes in Rome, though it was of better making. The
eye of Jesus was at first taken by a robe of red. But I advised
against this, explaining to him that red was a color worn by the
Roman aristocracy. Like violet, I told him, it distinguished men of
wealth and privilege from the common people.

The tunic was of pure linen, the cloak of pure wool, for the
law of the Book commanded that no Jew wear clothes of wool
and linen woven together.

He gave the coarse gray tunic to a beggar in rags, and cut
quite a figure as we departed Tyre.

Old men with staffs, in turbans and knitted skull-caps, men of
business, men of labor, women with scarves and veils on their
heads followed us to the shore, and children ran with them.

The trees were beginning to bud again. We spent the week of
the Pesach in Capernaum, by the sea.

I had been in this land now for almost a year. With the help of
Jesus and synagogue men and their scrolls, I had learned something
of the rudiments of the language of the Book. I had learned enough
to know that no one truly understood the language of the Book.

The parataxis of its language disallows clear understanding.
Ancient vestigial intermediary word-forms are ambiguous or

unsolvable. The omission of verbal connective elements results in shade upon shade of possible meaning. The elusive allusions and arcane syntax of its divine and prophetic pronouncements are like ominous rainclouds that do not burst open.

The Hebrew of the Book describes mysteries in mysterious ways. The more learned the scholar, the more acute his awareness of this, and the more acute his vexation.

I did not learn the language of the Book, you might say. I learned the unlearnableness of it. That and some words here and there of Hebrew and Aramaic.

It was in Capernaum during Pesach that I first tasted the unleavened bread of affliction, of which Jesus had told me. It was not so bad that you would spit it out, but it was so bad that you would not raise it to your lips a second time unless you were very hungry and with nothing else to eat.

This bread of affliction was not the stuff of Romans. I was a Roman, and furthermore I was dearly missing Rome. I found a small inn with a table outdoors beneath a willow tree, and was served good Roman bread, olive oil, sausage of wild boar with much garlic, and a cup of wine.

The town was quiet with the undertakings of Pesach. Many had left to make pilgrimage to Jerusalem.

There were spring breezes from the sea. As I ate and drank, I composed words of beauty on a wax tablet. Though they were only now beginning to flow, I felt them to be among the finest I had written for my Lord. I had learned to cultivate the powers of mysterious portent that were of the Book, but to express them in a clear and simple way, which seemed much appealing to the people, and also a most fresh and welcome relief to them. It was not a storm-god I gave them, but his son, a new god, a god of comforting warm breezes instead of fulmination; a god who embraced them, and who was in turn embraced by them.

Two disciples came upon me, the young fisherman Andreas and the priest, Aaron. Soon they were joined by Ephraim, the rabbi.

"We observe the holy Pesach, and our Gaius feasts," said the young fisherman with a smile, emboldened by the company of the priest and the rabbi.

As I had taken a liking to the young fisherman when he had joined us at Simonias, so I now took a disliking to him. The once affable young dolt had become an arrogant young dolt. My disliking was stronger than the liking had been. He had removed himself from under the wing of Peter, and no longer looked to him as an elder brother. The priest and the rabbi had shown kindness toward him, and he saw this kindness as their acceptance of him as an equal, which he was not, and which they certainly did not feel him to be. It is always the most inferior of men who espouse the lie that all men are equal. His manner of speech to me was an impudence that raised my hackles.

I wanted to smack this little wisp-whiskered calfling, this tilapia hatchling, more *viridis* than *virilis*.

Do you think your God even knows of your existence? I wanted to demand of him.

I wanted to tell him that his God was dead. I wanted to demand of him further: Do you think that you are other than the most insignificant and stunted sapling grown from the humus of your dead God's putrid decomposition?

May you choke to death on your bread of affliction, I wanted to tell him.

But I did not. I breathed and let my sudden anger subside and dissipate. I would not have the peacefulness of the previous moments stolen from me. The breezes through the overhanging tree, the pleasures of my food and drink, the calm, flowing composition: I would not allow these to be lost. I wished that Jesus might happen by, sit with me, and savor the good bread and pork sausage, that the calfling and the priest and the rabbi might see him do so. And Jesus did come by, but he did not take the bread or the meat into his mouth, but merely gazed on us.

To the hatchling, I spoke calmly, but with a note of angry rebuke that I could hear, even if he could not.

"God does not care what you eat. God does not care what you wear." There was no response, and I continued, saying what came to me. "Adam and Eve went naked before him, and were forbidden one food alone: the fruit of the tree of the knowledge of good and evil."

The priest and the rabbi seemed indulgent, even supportive, of my right to speak.

"And what was the nature of this tree and its forbidden fruit?" I asked.

"It was a fig tree," said the titmouse.

"The Book," said the priest, "describes it only as —"

I interjected the next word that would have come from his lips, the Hebrew word, plain and simple, for "fruit," a word very much like our word for the fruit of the pear tree. He was startled, not by the impolite manner of my interruption, but by my acquaintance with, and utterance of, this ancient Hebrew word.

"No fruit from the branch of a tree rooted in this earth bears the knowledge of good and evil," I continued.

"And why," I asked, "did Adam and Eve's taste of this fruit cause them immediately to feel shame at their nakedness?"

There were no answers forthcoming. I sensed that the priest and the rabbi had answers at the ready, but that they would rather hold their tongues and hear me implicate myself further. Jesus stood behind them like a divine presence, all-knowing but silent. And so I went on:

"It is because the forbidden fruit, the knowledge of good and evil, is the secret truth unrevealed in the Book's fable of creation. It is the secret that precedes the fable. It is inherent in God, but at the same time unknown to him. It is the secret of the creation not of the world, but of the creation of the creator himself."

I saw Jesus furtively rolling his eyes to me.

"You speak blasphemy," said the priest.

"And at Pesach," squeaked the titmouse. Again I wanted to smack him.

"And what of the serpent?" said the rabbi.

"The serpent?" said I. "She is wisdom. The serpent is wisdom."

"Blasphemy," repeated the priest. There was no anger in his voice. He seemed merely to be making a casual observation.

"Blasphemy," echoed Andreas. The priest glanced at him with impatience. I was not alone in finding the boy irksome.

I felt that I had suffered enough of this. I wanted only to return to my bread and my sausage, my wine and my wax tablet, and my quiet. With a turn of pleasant mischief, I decided to draw from my sleeve the gentile lot, and to lay the matter all on my loiterer.

"I am but a disciple of our Lord's," I said. "I am a gentile, unlearned in Hebrew and the profundities of the Book. I will say no more. Ask the Lord, not me."

They looked to the Lord, whose eyes no longer rolled, and whose face was now a beatific blank.

My bread, my sausage, my wine, my wax tablet, my quiet. They were mine once again.

From where I sat, I could see, through the breaches in the swaying willows, the synagogue that marked the center of Capernaum. It was of two stories, built of limestone, with carved ornamentation of some skill: stylized plants, fruits, Stars of David, figures from the legends, and geometric patterns like those of the swastika of India. The synagogue rose above the other structures of the town, and further distinguished itself by its blushing paleness amid the town's buildings of black basalt.

I could hear the hushed sounds of afternoon prayer. The streets were all but empty. The taverner, a few fellow Romans and other gentiles, a Jew or two who may have been unbelievers. Each of us cast a solitary shadow that made us appear to be alone, apart, and excluded. As in fact we were.

As I have said, I missed Rome dearly in the bloom of that Judean spring. All the more dearly did I miss my good wife and son, your grandmother and father.

From the innkeeper, I bought for a widow's mite a small, brittle round of the bread of affliction. In the deserted street, I crushed it in my fist and let the crumbs fall to the ground.

Little birds gathered to delight in them. I felt a smile come to my face as I watched them, their small feathered throats aquiver with chirrupings and pipings of a carefree happiness that laid waste the dirge-like prayer of those who could not fly.

20

T HAT NIGHT, WHICH WAS THE LAST NIGHT OF PESACH, WE SAT
alone on a bench of stone on the grounds of the synagogue.
The donkeys were tethered nearby. The younger of them grazed
on a tuft of spring grass and weeds that grew amid what remained
of very old paving-tiles. The other, the one who had been with us
from the outset, looked to the stars. We watched him do this,
wondering what figures he saw in the constellations.

"Why did you let him speak to me as he did?" I asked.

"Whom?"

In the light of the waning moon, I could see the faint wry
smile on his face, which told me that he sensed the pique in my
question and knew the answer to his own.

"That goat pellet of yours," I said. "The runt of your motley
litter."

"Thou speakest disparagingly of our devoted disciples."

"It is a new Way of which you preach. A new God, a new Way.
Do you know that I was fully expecting you to sit down and share
bread and wine with me?"

"That day will come." His eyes moved from the donkey to the
stars from which the donkey's eyes now turned. "They are not
ready for your pagan sausage yet." The older donkey joined the
other to graze on the grass and weeds that grew amid the broken
paving-stones. "And they are not my litter. They are ours."

My eyes moved to the stars as well.

"Do you see a great bear there?" I asked him, raising high my arm and pointing to the bright star that marks the upper part of the tail of our Ursa Major.

"I see a great leopard. You see a bear because you were taught to see a bear. I see a leopard because I was taught to see a leopard. If they had taught us to see a salamander, we would see a salamander.

"We see what we were trained to see, and cannot free ourselves from seeing as we do.

"Teaching is often a dangerous thing. To be taught is often to be impaired. Children are punished for their innate imaginations, and trained to see and do alike, as one might domesticate a free and wild dog into a household pet. Teaching should encourage individuals, not liquefy them into a leaden homogeneity to be poured into uniform molds to cast leaden minds that are all of a kind."

"Everything we are taught is a lie."

"And what of our teaching?"

"As I have said."

"And so the great bear and the great leopard become a great salamander."

At this, we shared quiet laughter.

"So, tell me," he said. "What ever were you talking about? 'The serpent is wisdom.' The secret truth that is hidden in the fable. Tell me. Please. Really. What ever were you talking about?"

I drew slow breath and looked at him. I had taken it for granted that he had fully understood what I had been talking about; but now it was clear that he had not.

"How did the God of your Book come to be?" I said. "How did all the gods of all the peoples of all the world, throughout all the eons, come to be?"

"By the invention of man," he answered plainly.

"Yes. And why did man invent the gods? Why did he invent

the God of your Book? Of what use to him was this God? What need did he have of this God?"

He pondered for a moment. He seemed less at a loss for an answer than for a way of expressing it.

"As a manifestation of his sense of inferiority, his sense of being lost in this world. As a justification of the ways of this world. As an eternal anchorage in the killing-sea of tossed and fleeting mortality."

"No," I said emphatically. "I am surprised at you. If not as a god, then surely as a thief, you have the answer in you."

"I believe what I have said to be true. If the answer is not in what I have said, then I have not the answer."

"What is felt as one with shame in the moment that Adam and Eve cease to be divine and become mortal? When they eat of—"

"Fear."

"Yes. To be human is to be fearful. Most men are composed of little else but fear and shame."

"This I know."

"When is this tale of the creation supposed to have been concocted?"

"I do not know. They say that Moses was the first writer of the Book. A thousand years ago and more."

"All tales are first told by firelight. And so it is with the invention of the gods. We will never know when your God was born. It was probably so long ago that the secret in its telling was forgotten and unknown to those who first set it to skin in the Book, if indeed it was known beyond the earliest teller. For it is as they say: if a thing is known to more than one, it is not secret.

"So, a thousand years ago and more, or five thousand years ago and more, a flame danced in a campfire in the night, and this tale was told. What is that word with which the tale begins?"

He pronounced a word of three syllables that was something like *beresit*.

"And this word carries the meaning of 'in the beginning,' does it not?"

"Yes, but not exactly. It is an odd formation. It means 'in the beginning of.'"

"Of what?"

"It does not say."

"And the next word we encounter is the name of God in the plural, is it not?"

"Yes. *Elohim*."

"This Book of yours is high holy wreckage and massacre of meaning from the outset."

He smiled broadly and nodded his amused agreement. Light from the stars moved in his soft, pale-brown eyes.

"It all must have been very different as told into the dancing flame of that long-ago campfire. The rabbis are crafty, the rabbis are wily, but they cannot rabbinize away an 'in the beginning of' that falls abruptly in a sheer drop to nowhere and nothing. They cannot rabbinize away their one true God being introduced as more than one.

"And nor can they explain why the fruit of the tree of the knowledge of good and evil imparts nothing but shame and fear. The fruit was forbidden because it held the knowledge of good and evil. Were fear and shame the sum of this knowledge?"

"Perhaps," my good Lord uttered, "perhaps." It seemed as if he would say more, but he did not.

"The forbidden enlightenment in the forbidden fruit was the knowledge that man created God. For this inelegant tale with which your Book begins is not the tale of the beginning. It is the tale of the tale of the beginning. In telling of God breathing the first breath into Adam, the tale breathes the first breath into God.

"So it is that Eve and Adam are of a sudden in shame and in fear. They are in shame because they know that they go naked not before God, but before those who made him. And they fear those who made him. Their children, their kindred, their fellow-kind. Cain, the first born of all men, and Abel, first slain of all men, and Cain's sister-wife, from whose incest we are all derived, and on.

"So, why did man invent the God of your Book? Of what use to him was this God? What need did he have of this God?

"To protect him from what he feared. That first breath that man breathed into him was the breath of his protectorship. As man feared, so he invented God to thunder forth commandments that might protect him from and forfend what he feared.

"Man fears being killed. Thus he has his God thunder most fearsomely: 'Thou shalt not kill.'

"Man fears his wife being fucked by another. Thus he has his God thunder most fearsomely: 'Thou shalt not commit adultery.'

"Man fears being robbed. Thus he has his God thunder most fearsomely: 'Thou shalt not steal.'

"And, less forcefully but fully and formally: 'Thou shalt not covet thy neighbor's house, thou shalt not covet thy neighbor's wife, nor his manservant, nor his maidservant, nor his ox, nor his ass, nor any thing that is thy neighbor's.'

"The gods of the Greeks and Romans are embodiments of the forces of nature, and reflections of the natures of men. Your God is a dictator against the natures of men. You speak so eloquently of the evils of teaching. Your God is a teacher, a rigged mouthpiece, that teaches in behalf of the self-interests of frightened men who created him that they might hide behind him. His inventors were forgotten, but he was not; and the imagining grew greater than the imaginers."

"And why would men adjure and endure so angry a God?" he said, as if not to me, but to the night.

"Some men take to rough hemp rope and pillory. Some men enjoy the lash."

"I knew a whore in Caesarea who made good coin lashing politicians and priests and such who came to her in garments of disguise."

I smiled at the grace, balance, and justice of this. His mind seemed to drift back to the days before we met. With a long breath, I said the last of what was in me then.

"The serpent, who in the tale is coeval with God, maybe older than him, is the only one in the fable who speaks the truth and leads man to knowledge, of which there is of course no forbidden species. The serpent is wisdom."

He whispered into the night the word *nachash,* which in the fable is the serpent's name.

"Chokmah or Hokmah," I said, "Athena or Sophia, Minerva or Sapientia, she has been known always by a feminine name. Wisdom is a woman. The serpent of wisdom is a woman."

I let myself fall silent. I had talked too much. I looked at the mounds of donkey shit as if they measured the accumulation of my gross long-windedness.

"Who is it who said 'Know thyself'?" he asked.

"The maxim has been attributed to many. I myself believe it to have been Thales."

"You have helped me to know myself," he said.

"Maybe you can help me to know what I have long yearned to know. Did man invent God before or after he invented good and evil?"

He smiled to me, as if to say: you ask of me the simplest things.

I had gone on and on speaking of wisdom. His eyes bespake it more deeply without sound.

"Man first perceived gods in the forces of nature," he said.

There was no tone of conjecture in what he said. He spoke as if stating facts. "Then man conceived good and evil. After inventing this unnatural morality, he recast his storm-gods into gods of morality, for the reasons you have expressed.

"Morality. Gods of morality. They are one and the same infirmity, one and the same disease."

"So," I said, "we are spreaders of disease."

"Yes. Physicians of a kind, you might say."

Earlier we had wondered if the donkeys saw figures in the constellations, and what they might be. Now I wondered aloud if they had their gods as well.

"If they do," said Jesus, "we can be assured that they are saner than ours."

The others were sleeping that night in the synagogue. We decided to sleep in the open night air. Each of us tied one of the donkeys' tethers round a wrist as we laid ourselves down.

"Thou shalt not snore," said he, in a most theatrically pious tone. Then his voice was again his own, natural and relaxed:

"And, speaking of the Shalt-Nots of the Commandments, you are quite right about the new words you have composed. They are beautiful, and I shall be proud to pronounce them. I will give them my best."

"Good," I said. "Otherwise, I would have your darling little Andreas deliver them."

Our laughter rang low through the dark silent night. We were not so very far from the synagogue, and for a moment it occurred to me that one or more of the others might have heard us. But I really did not care. Nor, I felt, did he.

The seven days of Pesach ended. From the synagogue there came voices that wove together lament and joy. I was told that it was an ancient song, a song of deliverance and freedom from slavery.

But all men are slaves, and always will be. Imprisoned in the bodies in which they are born, confined by the circumstances of their lives, they can measure their relative freedom only in small increments; and these grains of salt can be had only through man-umission. Like all salt, the salt of freedom can be bought only with cast coins. And freed slaves often become the slaves of their freedom.

Jesus blessed the people of Capernaum, and I told them of the pronouncement that was to be made on the eve of the new moon, three days and a short distance thence. Coins in plenty were gathered for the building of the temple of the Word and the Way.

We went southward as far as Magdala. As we had expected with some dread, the most vociferous of those who met us at the entrance of that town was the old hag Mary the Magdalene, who had followed and haunted us in former days. Yes, old as she was, she still lived. We learned from the townspeople of Magdala that she had long claimed to have been restored to fertility by Jesus. More than that, she also claimed that she had borne a child by him. This child, whom she called Bar-Jesus, which in the Aramaic way meant "Son of Jesus," was a bundle of old cloth rags that she carried about cradled in her arms for a time. The eventual disappearance of the "child" was easily explained by her. An angel of God had come to take it away, for as Jesus was the Son of God, so little Bar-Jesus was the grandson of God.

Those who told us this made scoff and sport of it. But Jesus did not. And when Mary drooled from her toothless gums and reached out to fumble at his robe, he looked into her eyes, which were now opalescent with the milkiness of lost sight, and said:

"Woman, have you no shame?"

This was said for the hearing of those gathered about, who responded with approbation. It is doubtful that doddering old Maria could hear or understand what was said.

We say: the fewer the fangs, the finer the fellatrix. I do believe that this saying was first said by salivating crones like our Mary the Magdalene.

Preceding us to Magdala was the rumor that, while we were at Capernaum, our fisherman Simon Peter had caught a tilapia in whose mouth he found a silver coin. One of the Magdalenes specified the coin to be a tetradrachm. Another expressed awe at this miracle.

We were nonplussed. What a paltry excuse for a miracle this seemed to be. A trifle of a miracle, if a miracle at all.

"But surely," said Jesus, "it is not all that uncommon for a fish to take into its mouth a coin that finds its way into the sea."

"No," replied the man. "But how did you know to tell Peter to bring forth the first fish he caught in the lake, for there would be in its mouth a four-drachma coin? That is the miracle of it."

Men invent rumors and others corroborate them to be a part of them, to say: yes, I was there. Other men transmit these rumors to seem to be possessors of privileged communication. All these men yearn to be party to something, even if at times they know not what.

As always, Jesus took the praise for this new miracle in silence, with an air that was more humble than dismissive. Simon Peter knew that there had been no such fish with a coin its mouth, and that no such fish had been foretold. But his pleased smile was greater than his surprise. The rumor showed him now to be looked on as especially close to Jesus, and as an important participant in his Lord's miracle-workings, and this appealed a good deal to his vanity. It mattered not to him that the miracle was only hearsay and had never happened. All that mattered to him was his prominence in this hearsay, and he basked in his moment of slight celebrity.

The face of the younger fisherman, the tick Andreas, showed a perturbed and envious look.

I found satisfaction in his look.

The rabbi looked to the priest, and the priest looked to Jesus, who had moved on.

Some new disciples whom I barely recognized, and whose names I did not know, looked to each other, then all around.

What a bunch we were.

Magdala was a city of shipbuilding. Many of the best of boats used for fishing the Sea of Galilee and plying its shores were made here. Crafted of oak and cedar, strong-masted and well-rigged, some of these boats could carry a dozen or more dragnet fishermen or passengers, under sturdy sail, oar, and rudder, in the gentlest or harshest of winds.

The resinous compounds used by those who fashioned big sails and bigger dragnets from bold-woven flax were held in secret by the several masters whose workers used them. Though men of sail differed in their estimations of the sail-makers' wares, none knew for sure the precise recipe of these various mixed resins. Of the liquid bitumen, of deep dark shades of blue and purple, used by the shipbuilders to seal and waterproof the seams of hull-boards, more was known than of the closely guarded compounds used to fortify the sails.

Magdala was also known for the excellence of its cured fish, and the recipes of the various ways of smoking, salting, drying, and pickling fish were more occult than those of the sail-makers' compounds. The various fruitwoods used in smoking were numerous, and no smoker made known to another the wood that he used. This was especially true of those who used a combination of woods, such as one or more fruitwoods set to smoke together with berry-bearing alder-wood. The aromatic sprigs and spices that were added by one curer to salts for drying, and to brines for pickling, were unknown to the next.

So esteemed was the fish cured at Magdala that it was not only sold throughout Judea, but was transported in barrels to Caesarea and Tyre and thence by ship to every distant port of the Great Sea. It was the smoked tilapia of Magdala that gave Rome her taste for this manner of curing, which she later applied to every swimming thing in the Great Sea and the inland waters of Italy. A great many Romans, as you know, came to prefer the smoked to the fresh.

The synagogue at Magdala was old and small, and nowhere near as elaborate as the synagogue at Capernaum. It was as if the business of God here was of less importance than the business of shipbuilding or the business of curing fish. To one side of the synagogue door, there was a crude black mosaic adumbration of a boat under full sail. To the other side of the door, there was a crude black mosaic adumbration of a fish. As with some parts of the plaster that covered the walls, some pieces of these black mosaics had fallen away.

This impression was wrong. The industry of this city, its shipbuilding and its fish-curing, was conducted under the supervision of God, and those who conducted it bowed daily before him.

Jesus spoke briefly at the little synagogue, at the midday hour when workers took some rest from their work.

"I walk among the good people of this good city," he said, as if he felt a deep liking for them. "I see the men wielding mallets and laboring at the joinery that will send forth rugged craft, and I remember my youthful years as a carpenter.

"Our sweat is as one. The bread and wine of our reward, like the burden of our taxes, are one. I am, like you, of the land and waters of Galilee. Two who travel with me on my mission are also of Galilee. They have fished our waters in your craft. They are fishermen who now also are fishers of men."

As I was hearing this, my mind returned to the night Simon Peter came to us, that glorious night of the Feast of the Trumpets, in glorious Sepphoris, as we yearned for wine and women. "So you wish to be a fisher of men?" he had asked Simon, extempore, with irritation. I was surprised that he recalled those words.

"I walk among the good people of this good city," he said, the sound of a deep liking still in his voice. "I delight in the fine smells of your cured fish, and I remember that this frail earthly body of mine has its earthly hungers. In this, surely, we are also one.

"But I say unto you, there are labors and hungers of the spirit that call us to a new Word, a new Way."

He smiled and looked gently among them. They were his to summon and to sway.

"You concern yourselves with a bit of silver in the mouth of a fish."

His smiling words were met with smiles and a soft rippling of subdued, complaisant laughter.

"Come to meet me when your work is done on the eve of the new moon. Come to meet me at that place of quiet beauty that you know as the Hill of Riches. Forget about that bit of silver in the mouth of a fish. It was nothing, it means nothing. I will give you the Word that has been given to me. I will show you the Way that has been shown to me. I will fill your ears and hearts with gold."

There rose a stir of buoyant anticipation among the people of Magdala.

I was astonished. I had given Jesus only a few hasty lines to pronounce. The rest were his, and spontaneous.

We feasted on cured fish, bread dripping with vinegar and rough-pressed oil, warm wine and cool spring-water. The priest, the rabbi, and the others were as buoyant with anticipation as the men and women of the city.

"These words that you will speak," said the priest. "When did they come to you?"

"The elemental tones of these words were in me for a very long time." The Lord washed down salted fish and bread with wine and water. "But their articulation was exceptionally elusive. I feared that their meaning was such as to be beyond my comprehension. Then, in a sudden wave, all was revealed. And there was simplicity where I saw complexity and difficulty."

The newer disciples made as if they understood what he was saying.

I did not press the people of Magdala for offerings, but said only in a light-hearted way to one small group of them:

"If fish give us silver, what give you for the building of the temple?"

The building of boats and the curing of fish had made rich men of many of this city. We were benefacted well and generously. Much to our surprise, even one of the usurers stepped forward to place a coin of modest worth into the hand of Jesus, who tucked it into his cloak and kept it always as a token of sardonic good luck.

We procured a third donkey, whose seller would accept no payment for it, and purchased a third leather packsaddle and set of sacks.

I swore that with the new moon, something must be done. I thought again of the Roman argenters in Caesarea, and my trepidations. But my concern for our growing caravan of treasure now overshadowed all else.

Women of the town adorned our new donkey with colorful ribbons, and smiled to our Lord like blushing brides.

On our way north to Gennesaret, with the others moving for a while more slowly behind us, Jesus looked to our trinity of asses and let forth a laugh.

"Virtuous beasts, our friends here, don't you think?" he said.

"I should say so. Virtuous indeed. We take the money and they carry it for us without complaint."

"High time to give them names," he said. "If I can give names to asinine disciples, I can give names to noble asses."

He brought to mind something I had wondered about.

"And why do you give new names to these men?"

"Only to some of them."

"But, even then, why?"

"To lessen their sense of identity, to take a bit of their selves from them. To lay the touch of subjugation to them."

I asked him the names of the new disciples, and he told me.

I asked which of these were their true names, and which of them had been given them by him, and he told me. I asked him if he recalled the names of the disciples that had come and gone. He said that while he could recall some of those come-and-gone disciples and some of the names of those come-and-gone disciples, he could not recall which of them was known by which name.

"And when you give them new names, how do you choose the new name?"

"I just pluck them from the air. A man tells me his name is Simon, but to me he looks like a Peter, so I tell him that henceforth he will be known as Peter."

Jesus then commented on Aaron, the Sadducee priest, and Ephraim, the Sadducee rabbi, whom we had met long ago, at Bethlehem, and how, when they had joined us in Simonias, it seemed they would be with us for only a time before returning to Jerusalem; and yet they still followed.

I said that it was not good that they were Sadducees, for by their being in our company, people might see Jesus as also affiliated with the Sadducees.

"You must be perceived as associated with no established sect. You are the Messiah, and you must be seen as above and beyond all known sects. We must induce the priest and rabbi to relinquish their sect and embrace in full both you and your teachings."

"That will come," he said, and he seemed to believe it would.

Once again, I expressed my recurrent feeling that we now had enough. We could vanish. We could live out our days in luxury and indulgence in Rome. And once again, he admitted to the same feeling, but said that this feeling in him was always followed by the feeling that we were not yet done, not quite yet.

"And to think that it was I who had to convince you of this adventure on the night that we first met," I said.

There was from him that familiar laugh that remained silent within him, to be seen only in the smile on his face and the movement in his chest and belly.

This subject and this silence were uncomfortable. I returned idly to the matter of the disciples' names.

"And so you changed Simon into Peter, but you let Andreas, the tick, remain Andreas."

"That is not his name," said Jesus.

I watched the hind gait of the new donkey. It was rather soothing and hypnotic, until its asshole opened to allow the release of a ponderous piece of shit.

"His name is Judah, or Judas, or some such thing. And he was not born at Simonias, but somewhere to the south. A place called Kerioth, I believe."

He saw my impassive expression, and took it to be what it was not. The truth is that I was barely listening to what he said. My mind had drifted back to thoughts of Caesarea and Rome, thoughts of your dear grandmother and father, my wife and my son, to whom I wanted to return.

"If it makes you feel any better, I don't like him, either. But we can't order disciples away from us. Their bitterness would be such that they would renounce us and make calumny against us. Their denunciation would be dangerous. One thing that we have learned is that people believe lies as readily as truth."

He muttered something about the coin in the mouth of the fish.

In turn, with a feeling of incongruity, I heard myself mutter something:

"Trust and mistrust alike ruin men."

These were not my words, but when I said them, I could not remember whose words they were, or where I had gotten them.

A light breeze descended. Jesus returned his attention to the asses. He looked with fondness on the dun jack donkey that was our first, with us since we crossed the plain of Sharon.

"Faith," said he.

He looked with fondness on the second of them, the white-bellied jack of black that was the youngest of the three.

"Hope," said he.

He looked with fondness on the third of them, the new mottled gray jenny from Magdala.

"Charity," said he.

21

U NKNOWN EVEN TO JESUS, I HAD AT TYRE PURCHASED A
good deal of opium from an importer who supplied the
renowned Roman pharmacopolist of that city.

I was not interested in henbane, from whose death-like coma
we had raised the young man of Nain as he lay bound for burial
on his funeral bier. Nor was I interested in mandrake, that other
stinking plant poison that in small doses brought phantoms and
visions, and in larger doses eliminated political and personal enemies. These were drugs for murder, narcotics with which those of
low class and ill-breeding played a dodgy game in seeking to lace
the stupefying effects of their palled wine with crude illusions
and apparitions.

It was the stuff of gods, opium, praise-sung and rhapsodied by
Homer, Virgil, and Ovid; the wondrous stuff, opium, that, mixed
with his cup of hemlock, sent Socrates smiling to his death as if
entering a place of bliss; opium, banisher of pain and sorrow, bringer
of enchantments—it was opium, and opium alone, that I wanted.

The opium of royalty, which was of prohibitive cost in large
amounts, was that which bore the seal of Anatolia. The importer
assured me that the opium of Egypt and India surpassed the
Anatolian, and that the higher price and prestige of the latter had
more to do with the glamour of its luxury seal than with its quality. I was also told by him that the best grades of Egyptian and
Indian opium were often of higher purity than the Anatolian,

whose weight was often augmented by adding undetectable shavings from the lanced poppy pods to the thick opium juice that these pods yielded.

He told me this not because he had no Anatolian opium in stock, but because I had presented myself as a potential long-term buyer, and he surmised that honesty would in the end prove more profitable than the wiles of single-purchase selling.

A libra of Egyptian opium, round and wrapped in linen, was set before me. It was expensive, he admitted, but it was also the best to be had. Pure, unadulterated, uncontaminated, from the recent harvest, which was one of the finest in years. He unfolded the linen and lightly pressed his forefinger into the black substance to illustrate how very fresh and soft it was.

The big, thick, heavy libra was far more than I wanted. Its weight was about that of an old Republican cast-bronze coin. He brought down several unciae of the same opium: much smaller rounds in smaller wraps of linen.

I asked him how much opium, taken at once, might kill a man through poisoning. He looked at me suspiciously and asked me why I wanted the opium. I told him that it was for cultic purposes, to be used in rites. I told him that I was the agent of a priest, who knew much more than I. I told him I was merely curious, and that I wanted to be party to no mistakes or mishaps.

"The cult of Ceres?" he asked casually.

"No, another," I answered casually.

"Liquid opium is for killing," he said. He gestured to phials on a shelf. "It is also good for rites," he said, "as it mixes well with wine. One bottle of that size, a mere hemina, half a sextarius, can kill any man. The same bottle can produce a dozen or more cups of most potent ritual wine."

He fetched a parcel, drew back its linen, and revealed to me several lumps of about the size and color of walnuts.

"These cakes contain, each of them, the equivalent of a cup of cultic wine. They are of the best Theban opium, the same as we have here"—he passed a hand over the big libra and the lesser unciae—"mixed with honey, egg, almond paste, and fruit. Uncooked, unbaked, these cakes may be eaten quite delightfully."

As they appeared to be roundish lumps, or misshapen balls, I asked him why he called them cakes. He told me that he called them cakes because that was what they were called. He brought the heel of his hand down hard and fast on one of the lumps, flattening it into a small roundish thing that looked like a fritter waiting to be fried.

"Behold!" he announced. "A cake."

Sensing the merchant's growing impatience, and growing doubt that I might be the potential long-term buyer that I had presented myself to be, I said at last, to ease his impatience, renew his hope, and ensure a good price: "I shall take some of each." And so I purchased six uncials of pure opium, six phials of liquid opium, and two dozen cakes. As he counted the coins I pushed toward him, he gave me the recipe for the cakes, should I wish to make more with the pure opium I had bought. He said in a confiding manner that chestnut honey was the best to use.

The opium was hidden amid the treasure carried by our good dun donkey. I knew that I wanted it for a purpose, but I did not know what the purpose was. Now, on our way to Gennesaret, we came upon a very small settlement of so few people that it seemed more an encampment than a place of residence. The families dwelled in modest tents. They told us that there once had been more families, more tents. Now they were all that remained. They called this place Tabgha, and they were rightly proud of the natural beauty that was to be seen in every direction, all around, from this place that was barely a place.

It was then that I knew.

They had heard tell of the anointed Jesus, and they were most honored to have his presence. They had but one small young lamb with which to feed themselves on this day, but they asked if they might share it with us, even though our number was almost equal to their own.

We could smell and see the roasting kid that was being slowly turned on its spit over smoldering embers. I had Jesus instruct the others to proceed ahead of us to Gennesaret. I had him tell them that he felt a vague sense of having been summoned to this unknown place, for something that was not known to him.

They wished to take one or two of the donkeys with them, but Jesus stayed them.

Their figures grew small in the distance. I called Jesus to me, and told him of my design. He was disinclined to it. He said that it was not right to experiment on these poor and kindly people. I told him that it would be a gift to them that they would cherish always.

At last, he agreed to play his part. He said that he would follow my lead. This would be impossible, I told him. These people spoke no Greek or Latin, and I spoke no Hebrew or Aramaic. It must be he who guided their vision. I would lead them to the threshold of that vision, but mine was not a speaking role.

From what I did, what I saw, and what he later told me, I give you my account of what transpired in that place that was barely a place on that sigh of a spring afternoon that became a sigh of infinity.

Jesus told them to bring forth their goblets, that they might share in good wine with him. The men smiled happily and fetched their homely drinking-bowls, most of which were of wood, and a few of which were of hammered metal. The women among them held no cups, and we feared that they would not drink.

"No man nor woman ever became drunk on this wine," Jesus

said. "It is the wine of the grapes of Eden, to whose wild-growing vines my Father did lead me."

The men gave their assent. All was ready: our wineskin, filled with good wine from a vineyard near Magdala; our waterskin, filled with good water we had drawn that morning from dewy rocks near here; one of the phials of opium; and one cake for each of the tent-dwellers. While preparing their potions, I could hear the voice of one of the men, followed by the voice of Jesus.

"We have heard from some who have passed our way that you are the savior for whose coming men have looked to the East for as long as there have been men. If you are that savior, will you save us?"

"From what do you wish to be saved?"

"From this forsaken existence, in which the beginning of life is the beginning of death. As you have said, it is beautiful to look on the world from here. But the world does not look on us. We are all that remain of a forgotten, dying tribe."

"Your tents tell me that you are nomads. Why do you not resettle near a place of more people?"

"Our tents tell you wrong. It is true, we once were nomads. Our people were, long ago. But here these tents came long ago to rest, to be moved no more. A place of more people would not be a place of our people. This alone is the place of our people. So I ask you: can you save us from our end?"

"But your end will be in glory. Where you see death, I see rebirth."

"You will save us, then?"

"You have been saved, but yet do not see it. Salvation is yours."

I saw that they were all gathered on the grass, and that as the man and Jesus had spoken, the rest had listened. I distributed the cups and the cakes, which I had pressed into rounds. Each man and woman recognized and raised a hand for his or her own cup. For Jesus and me, I reserved simple wine and water.

Jesus looked to the kid on the spit, which faced skyward, unturned and weirdly still, over the smoking embers.

"That lamb once trembled, but trembles no more. He will feed many."

He held his goblet of wine and water in his left hand. In his right hand, he held one of the small discs of cake. He held these things to the center of his breast.

"This is my blood," he said, in a plain-speaking way, raising his goblet of wine. "Drink of it."

We all took our draughts.

"This is my flesh," he said, in a plain-speaking way, looking for a moment to the spitted lamb, then raising the round of cake. "Eat of it."

The mystery of his words overtook them, and me as well. They ate. There was relish in their eating of the cakes and their drinking of the wine.

Though most of them were silent, Jesus conversed calmly with others of them, softening and slowing his voice as he did so, guided by the looks of languorous pleasance that softly and slowly stole across their faces. The emptied drinking-bowls sat or lay beside them.

The blend of potion and cakes seemed to be potent. All seemed to have entered a peace of rarest sweet dreams.

One man opened his eyes. Bearing his weight on his elbow, he did his best to sit upright. He smiled at what he saw, or did not see, or thought he saw. The rest of them lay as if slumbering, but were awake in their reveries.

There was but one child among these people. It could not be seen, but could be heard to cry. I followed the sound of its cry, tilted the dregs from one of the cups to its lips, and soon it slept and did not cry. The quiet was now such that, except for the song of a bird far away, all that could be heard was an occasional faint crackling from the embers under the lamb.

"Look at me," whispered Jesus to the man nearest him, and he placed his hand on the man's bare shin. The man stirred only slightly, and did not open his eyes.

"Do you see them?" asked Jesus, in a voice that could be heard by all.

They remained as if in sleep.

"A thousand and more," said Jesus. "There, in the valley. Your people. They have returned."

There was much smiling among those who lay upon the grass with eyes closed. Here and there, a sigh of happiness could be heard among them.

"An elder comes first. Then a bride and husband. They are young. What a wedding feast this is to be! Beyond the thousand, another thousand, and still more.

"They call your names. They say beautiful things. Their tidings are wondrous. They are so very joyous to see you here.

"I have but two more cakes, and little wine. But on this blessed day, two will become as two thousand, and little will become as an endless flowing. All will eat, and all will drink. This feast will not be forgotten. Tabgha will be celebrated.

"Do you feel the embrace of those who have returned to you?"

As winds pass through leaves, deep and visible undulations of felicity passed through those who lay in the grass. We could hear the sough of dreamers who did not sleep.

Moving stealthily, we strewed among them bright ribbons from our mottled gray jenny-ass, Charity, two half-eaten sweet-smoked fish of Magdala, a crust of barley bread, some coins of brass and some coins of silver—cryptic evidence and mementos of the great wedding feast that never was.

We stole away, toward Gennesaret. The moon was pale in the afternoon sky, like the ghost of a moon from another age.

"There," I said. "That wasn't too difficult, was it? Now tell me the nature of our miracle, before I hear it twisted all round by a complete stranger who was not there."

"You have attended a wedding feast. A most marvelous wedding feast. The living and the dead were there. Thousands of them. Neither vanishing Tabgha nor the world, neither you nor I nor anyone else, has ever before known the likes of such a feast."

"They were good people," I said after a while.

"Now they are better," said our Lord.

It was good to travel alone, just the two of us, if only for this short distance. As we walked toward Gennesaret with the setting sun, we devised a sort of code by which Jesus could address me and gain my attention in the presence of the disciples without attracting their notice.

As Jesus contrived, whenever he henceforth uttered the phrase "the beloved disciple," or "the beloved disciple," it would be a signal that he spoke to me, or of me, or for my ears specifically.

He expressed a desire to indulge in opium, to experience that place of peace, contentment, and rare sweet dreams that was descried in the faces of the tent-dwellers. I told him that there would be time and opium aplenty for this in Rome. We could not now risk the possibility of our Lord making inappropriate revelations.

He asked me the direction to Rome from where we were. I looked to the dimming sun, calculated our position, raised my arm high and straight, and pointed to the northwest.

"My riches," he said. "My well-groomed asshole. My sweet dream-like luxuriations. Our friendship and our laughter."

I smiled to hear these words from him. For a while, all else drifted from my mind. There were only beloved Rome and the life of ease and amity of which he spoke.

We discussed the great pronouncement that lay ahead, the articulation of the new *logos,* the new Law, the efflorescence of the Word and the Way. I spoke awhile of the rhetorical devices by which the tropes of divine command could be interwoven with lyricism.

"Many of my people," he said, "like the gentiles who delve their ways, speak of the Ten Commandments of the Book. But enfolded in that ten are tens upon tens. For the God who was made to deliver them was made to much expound in his deliverance of them.

"If a Jew buys another Jew as his slave, the slave is to serve him for six years and be freed in the seventh, without payment.

"But if a Jew sells his daughter as a slave to a fellow Jew, she is not to go free as male servants do.

"If a Jew seduces a virgin Jewess who is not pledged to be married and sleeps with her, he must pay the bride-price and take her as his wife. If her father refuses to give her to him, he must still pay to the father the bride-price for virgins.

"As the commandment against killing is to protect Jews alone, the Book extols the slaughter of outsiders and even innocents who are born of the enemies of Jews. 'Happy shall he be,' says the Psalmist of the Book, 'that steals away little babies and crushes their skulls upon the rocks.'

"And there is much punishment by death. Anyone who curses his father or mother is to be put to death. Anyone who disobeys his father or mother is to be put to death. Anyone who has sex with a beast of pasture is to be put to death. Any man who has sex with another man, or any woman who has sex with another woman, is to be put to death. Anyone who works on the Sabbath is to be put to death. Any daughter of a priest who prostitutes herself is to be put to death. Anyone who fails to obey the decision of a judge or priest is to be put to death. Any woman who falsely claims to be a virgin at the time of her marriage is to be stoned to death by the men of her town at her father's door, for she has brought disgrace to Israel. Adulterers are to be put to death.

"Seeing as all Jews, by their own account, are descendants of congress between a brother and his sister, it is curious that anyone who commits incest is to be put to death. In accord with this commandment, and all the others, there should be no Jews. They should all be dead."

I laughed, and he waited for my laughter to end before he said:

"All blasphemers are to be put to death. All false prophets are to be put to death. Sorcerers and necromancers are to be put to death."

I understood the implications of these words, but I made light of them, saying:

"It is as you have said. It is surprising that there are any Jews left to be executed, or Jews to execute them."

"There is death everywhere: 'You are to take life for life.' And where there is not death, there is vengeance. 'Eye for eye, tooth for tooth, hand for hand, foot for foot, burn for burn, wound for wound, bruise for bruise.' This vengeance of *quid pro quo* is called the apodictic law.

"Much of what I say, I have learned from the rabbi."

I recognized from our own word, and from Aristotle, the word he used to describe the law of an eye for an eye.

For no reason, it brought to my mind a similar-sounding Greek word, *apodiabolosis,* the consignment to the rank of a devil, the making or treating of someone or something as diabolical. Yes, I thought of it for no reason. And now, as this is written, I can think of no reason why for all these years I have remembered it coming to my mind. It is odd, is it not, that memory persists and sense lapses? Odder still, it now strikes me, that I should address this question to you, dear boy, who are, fortunately, many years from the paradox of which I speak. Yes, odd. Odd, odd, all of it, odd.

"You are the rabbi," I told him.

We entered Gennesaret, a town that occupied a small fertile crescent on a plain near the Sea of Galilee, which in this place was called the Lake of Gennesaret. There was still good light, and we soon came on most of the disciples. They were curious as to the outcome of our Lord's feeling that he had been called for some reason to pause at Tabgha. Peter and the priest asked me about this. The others asked Jesus directly.

"There was a need to feed people," I said.

"Yes," said Jesus. "Gaius is right. The poor of that place. A wedding party that came that way. There was a need to feed people."

"The people here were already aware of the pronouncement you are to make," the priest said. "When we went among them to tell of it, we found that they knew."

"There is excitement here, and much expectation," said Peter.

A crowd began to build around us. Most of them merely gazed on the Lord, but some ventured words.

"And is there a synagogue here?" asked Jesus. "For it is rest, and rest alone, that I need tonight."

Peter answered that the synagogue was humble, attached to the home of the dairyman who served as its priest and attendant.

"We have scrolls, and he can read them," one of the crowd said of the dairyman.

"A man need not have scrolls, or be able to read in them, to be a man of God. Nor is goodness measured by what is written or what is read."

"Is this one of the things of which you will speak?" another of the crowd asked.

"I will speak of many things," said Jesus. "But, good people of Gennesaret—and I have revealed this to no others—heed not only what I say, but also what I do not say. For there will be found as much meaning in what will not be said as in what will be said."

Where in the great cunt of creation did he pluck these sayings of his? I was proud of what I composed for him. But often, ever more often, I was taken aback by words that came to him spontaneously, uncomposed, with the ease of careless breath.

Nor was I the only one taken aback. The crowd looked to him. The disciples looked to him.

The sun was now down, and only its train of soft last light remained.

"And now I myself must heed the call of rest, that I might serve you the better."

The dairyman welcomed us and brought us simple food to eat. He humbly asked Jesus to bless the modest synagogue with whatever brief prayer he might care to kindly utter, in voice or in silence.

"But this place is already much blest," said Jesus at his gentlest. "It is I who felt blest on entering here. It is I who feel blest to be here."

The dairyman appeared to be moved. He lowered his head and said: "It is a blessing that you have deigned to rest here."

Jesus placed his hand on the man's shoulder and asked him for more milk and perhaps just a morsel more of chicken.

In the cool of the next early morning, we walked among the people of Gennesaret. Like many of the towns of Galilee we visited, it was a place of many fishermen. Simon Peter spoke to the men about nets as much as about the Lord, and it was pleasant to witness this, for he had a guileless and charming way of interlacing faith and fishing, and simple men were much drawn to him and his way.

Our young fisherman Andreas, on the other hand, eschewed talk of his trade, seeking increasingly to be regarded as a confidant and an aide of the Lord. He strove to imply and give an impression that he had been singled out and chosen by Jesus on the day when he attached himself to us at Simonias.

Before midday, there arrived from Capernaum a merchant laden with wares to sell and a tale to tell.

He told of a great feast on the afternoon past in the plain not far from here. With only two fish, a few loaves of bread, a little wine, and a handful of small cakes, the Messiah miraculously had fed five thousand men, women, and children. And with a purse containing but three shekels he had gifted all with silver and gold enough to pay Roman capitation tax and Jewish temple tax, and more.

We were reclined in the shade of an oak, hearing this. After the modest answer given yesterday to their question about what had taken place at Tabgha, the disciples were as awe-struck as the townsmen whom the merchant addressed. The disciples beheld Jesus, as did the townsmen; and when the heads of his audience turned, the merchant's eyes followed them, and he beheld Jesus as well. Following suit, I too looked upon him, and I am sure that I was alone in discerning the hint of self-satisfaction that was in his heavenly eyes.

Jesus had plucked a young acorn from a low branch, and his fingers played idly with it as we lay on our sides in the shade. As we rose to walk through the town, he discarded this acorn, tossing it to the rich grassy earth. A young woman rushed forth to fetch it, grasp it close, and hold it to her heart.

22

WE HAD CHOSEN THIS PLACE THE FIRST TIME WE SAW IT. Carved by winds and rains and all the natural forces of time out of mind, this overhang on a hillside amid the cliffs and knolls that rose west of the shore of Galilee seemed to have been set there by those forces solely for us, and to have awaited us since pictures were first seen in the night stars above.

What had first astounded us about this shallow rock-shelter was that it appeared as an arched proscenium. Ascending to it by carefully negotiating outcrops that served us as precarious stepping-stones, what next, and all the more, astounded us was that it was indeed a proscenium of sorts, in that it looked down on a circular terrace, a verdant hollow of a plain, enclosed by what, from the height we had reached, could clearly be discerned as a distinctly curved wall formed by the surrounding hillsides, at the center of whose sweep we found ourselves standing, looking down and all round us.

We had been able to see the shore from there. All the hills sloped toward it. Fishing boats appeared as small dark spots on the placid water. Two of the small dark spots were not far from land and very close to each other. What had astounded us next, astounded us most. We heard a voice call from one of these small dark spots to the other.

"Do you have any idle hook-line we might use for the day?" the caller could be heard to ask in an almost conversational tone.

"Yes, but no idle hooks," came another voice in like tone. These voices were lucid to our ears. This place was a vast amphitheatre; and furthermore, its acoustic properties were better than those of any open theatre of human device. Those of the amphitheatre of Statilius Taurus were as nothing compared to this place. The auditorium *cavea* of that grandly designed Roman amphitheatre was far surpassed by the undesigned verdant hollow of this place near a cove in the middle of nowhere.

We had been very eager to discover if words spoken from the hillcrest could be heard on the shore, as words spoken from the sea had been heard on the hillcrest. I descended the croppings and made my way to become a small dark spot in the eyes of Jesus. I stopped and stood close to where the water splashed over the smooth black stones.

"And I say unto you," he said unto me. And I heard him say it unto me.

"This is it. This is the place," I said.

"I believe it is," he said. "I believe it is." Then I heard his easy laughter.

Neither of us had much raised his voice.

We were silent and still for a while, he high in his vaulted proscenium and I down and afar at the water's edge, overpowered by the magic and far-reaching beauty of our amphitheatre. I envisioned our vast grassy auditorium filled with the audience that would be ours. Unlike any Roman audience, ours would not be segregated to sit according to rank or wealth or sex.

The elements were beyond our control. Too much wind could carry away his voice or diminish its equal distribution. Gray cloud coverings could steal the effect of the changing, softening hues upon his appearance as the setting sun moved over him in its arc. Bad rain could ruin it all.

Yes, the elements were beyond our control. But the rest—I could take care of the rest. I began to compose with increased inspiration.

We walked together through that place, seeing caves and grottoes around us in the soft stone hillsides, seeing birds that flew above us and delicate wildflowers that grew at our feet. But for the remains of an ancient lime kiln we happened upon, it seemed that we were the only ones who had ever walked here. But soon great multitudes would come, and would be filled with the Word and the Way.

As we watched the play of light on the hillside and sea, and especially on our proscenium, the importance of the sun's arc was clear to us. Thus we had chosen to begin in the late afternoon, with the golden sun full upon him, that we might end with the sunset of the new day, with the vesper-colors resplendent through the hills and sky behind him.

"If only there were a God," he said. "If only we could buy the clemency of the weather through prayer, propitiation, or the sacrifice of a son."

I did not like the last phrase of what he said. I knew he was speaking of a figure from the Book, but it made me think of your father, my young son to whom I hoped to soon return.

"Don't you Romans have a god of weather?"

"Jupiter, the king of the gods. He is also the weather-god."

"Perhaps a petition in your native tongue?"

"He receives an infinity of prayers and offerings. But in the end, he seems only to work for himself."

As it was, we could not have hoped for a more beautiful sky or more splendid aurulent beams and light, calm, soothing breezes.

The changing ochers of the earth and the rocks, the glimmer and iridescence of the sea, the deep and deepening of the blue above, the lush white clouds that shared in the increasing dusk-radiances to the west, where he stood in his plush blue robe—it was perfect. All was in accord, beyond the powers of any God or gods.

"I know what the beloved disciple is thinking," said Jesus that morning, as he prepared to ascend. "He is thinking: What if they do not come?"

Our code worked well. Some of the disciples believed "the beloved disciple" to be a figure of speech, a form of synecdoche, used by Jesus to refer to all of them as if he were referring to one of them. Others believed that there was an especially beloved disciple, whom Jesus did not name out of consideration for the feelings of the others. Each of these believed the beloved disciple to be himself, or speculated jealously at which of the others it might be.

And he was right. I was then thinking: What if they do not come?

From the hillside, he looked out and waited. From the grass below, we looked out and waited.

They came. Through every path and passage, they came.

In truth, there were thousands. And they continued to come. Through the morning, into the noontide, they came. From every city, town, village, and settlement where this pronouncement of the Word and the Way had been bruited, they came. From places unknown to us, where this event had been noised abroad from places known to us, they came. Even those of Tabgha, still joyous from their feast of dreams, were there. Thousands upon thousands, they came.

The priest looked awed, as if witnessing something from the Book, or even something not yet written into the Book.

How many other priests were there that day among the humble, and how many rabbis? There is no telling.

And how many cutpurses and thieves were there, as at every congregation? Besides our Lord, I mean. I did my best to keep the disciples near to me, that they might unawares form a protective phalanx between the pressings of the crowds and Faith, Hope, and Charity, which I kept tethered closely to me.

The stone slab on which I alternately sat and stood was not unlike the stone seating in a Roman theatre. But around me, and all others, there were no plastered, painted walls aspiring vainly to majesty. Around me, and all who were here, was only true majesty.

Gazing at these masses, which reached to all the hills around and almost to the sea, I knew that there would be no more talk between us of vanishing. Not now. I knew that we would not relinquish this mysterious road, nor would it relinquish us, until it reached its end, wherever and whatever that might be. I felt a reckless excitement at this prospect. I felt also a fearsome foreboding.

Jesus made the gesture of pressing his right hand to his heart, and he maintained this pose until all were silent and all was still.

And then he opened his mouth, and then I heard him; and the thousands upon thousands heard him.

His voice. My words.

23

A ND THE LORD SPAKE, AND HE TAUGHT THEM, SAYING:
"Blessed are the poor in spirit: for theirs is the kingdom
of heaven.

"Blessed are they that mourn: for they shall be comforted.

"Blessed are the meek: for they shall inherit the earth.

"Blessed are they which do hunger and thirst after righteousness: for they shall be filled.

"Blessed are the merciful: for they shall obtain mercy.

"Blessed are the pure in heart: for they shall see God.

"Blessed are the peacemakers: for they shall be called the
children of God.

"Blessed are they who are persecuted for righteousness' sake:
for theirs is the kingdom of heaven.

"Blessed are you, when men shall revile you, and persecute you,
and shall say all manner of evil against you falsely, for my sake.

"Rejoice, and be exceedingly glad: for great is your reward in
heaven: for so persecuted they the prophets which were before you.

"You are the salt of the earth: but if the salt has lost its savor,
with what shall it be salted? It is thereafter good for nothing, but
to be cast out, and to be trodden under foot of men.

"You are the light of the world. A city that is set on a hill cannot be hid.

"Neither do men light a candle, and put it under a bushel, but
on a candlestick; and it gives light unto all that are in the house.

"Let your light so shine before men, that they may see your good works, and glorify your Father which is in heaven.

"Think not that I am come to destroy the law, or the prophets: I am not come to destroy, but to fulfill.

"For truthfully I say unto you, Till heaven and earth pass, one jot or one small mark shall in no way pass from the law, till all be fulfilled.

"Whosoever therefore shall break one of these least commandments, and shall teach men so, he shall be called the least in the kingdom of heaven: but whosoever shall do and teach them, the same shall be called great in the kingdom of heaven.

"For I say unto you, That unless your righteousness shall exceed the righteousness of the scribes and Pharisees, you shall in no case enter into the kingdom of heaven.

"You have heard that it was said of them of old time, You shall not kill; and whosoever shall kill shall be in danger of the judgment:

"But I say unto you, That whosoever is angry with his brother without a cause shall be in danger of the judgment: and whosoever shall say to his brother as if to spit on him, 'Raca, void and vain,' shall be in danger of the council of the Sanhedrin: but whosoever shall say to him, 'Nabal,' or, 'Moreh, you cursed fool,' shall be in danger of the Gehenna of hell-fire.

"Therefore if you bring your gift to the altar, and there remember that your brother has anything against you, leave there your gift before the altar, and go your way; first be reconciled to your brother, and then come and offer your gift.

"Agree with your adversary quickly, while you are in the way with him; lest at any time the adversary deliver you to the judge, and the judge deliver you to the officer, and you be cast into prison.

"Truthfully I say unto you, You shall by no means come out from there, till you have paid the last copper coin.

"You have heard that it was said by them of old time, You shall not commit adultery:

"But I say unto you, That whosoever looks on a woman to lust after her has committed adultery with her already in his heart.

"And if your right eye offend you, pluck it out, and cast it from you: for it is profitable for you that one of your members should perish, and not that your whole body should be cast into hell.

"And if your right hand offend you, cut it off, and cast it from you: for it is profitable for you that one of your members should perish, and not that your whole body should be cast into hell.

"It has been said, Whosoever shall put away his wife, let him give her a writing of divorcement:

"But I say unto you, That whosoever shall put away his wife, except for the cause of fornication, causes her to commit adultery: and whosoever shall marry her that is divorced commits adultery.

"Again, you have heard that it has been said by them of old time, You shall not swear falsely, but shall perform unto the Lord your oaths:

"But I say unto you, Swear not at all; neither by heaven; for it is God's throne, nor by the earth; for it is his footstool. And nor by the city of Jerusalem; for it is the city of the Great King.

"Neither shall you swear by your head, because you cannot make one hair white or black.

"But let your communication be, Yes, yes; No, no: for whatsoever is more than these comes of evil.

"You have heard that it has been said, An eye for an eye, and a tooth for a tooth:

"But I say unto you, That you resist not evil: but whosoever shall smite you on your right cheek, turn to him the other also.

"And if any man will sue you at the law, and take away your coat, let him have your cloak also.

"And whosoever shall compel you to go a mile, go with him two.

"Give to him that asks you, and from him that would borrow of you, turn you not away.

"You have heard that it has been said, You shall love your neighbor, and hate your enemy.

"But I say unto you, Love your enemies, bless them that curse you, do good to them that hate you, and pray for those who despitefully use you, and persecute you;

"That you may be the children of your Father which is in heaven: for he makes his sun to rise on the evil and on the good, on the Philistine as on the godly, and sends rain on the just and on the unjust.

"For if you love those who love you, what reward have you? Do not even the publicans and heathen tax-gatherers do the same?

"And if you salute your brothers only, what do you more than others? Do not even the publicans so?

"Be you therefore perfect, just as your Father which is in heaven is perfect.

"Take heed that you do not your alms before men, to be seen of them: otherwise you have no reward of your Father which is in heaven.

"Therefore when you are doing your alms, do not sound a trumpet before you, as the hypocrites, the actors, do in the synagogues and in the streets, that they may have glory of men. Truthfully I say unto you, They have their reward.

"But when you are doing alms, let not your left hand know what your right hand does:

"That your alms may be in secret: and your Father which sees in secret himself shall reward you openly.

"And when you pray, you shall not be as the hypocrites are: for they love to pray standing in the synagogues and in the corners of the streets, that they may be seen of men. Truthfully I say unto you, They have their reward.

"But you, when you pray, enter into your closet, and when you have shut your door, pray to your Father which is in secret; and your Father which sees in secret shall reward you openly.

"But when you pray, use not vain repetitions, as the heathen do: for they think that they shall be heard for their much speaking.

"Be not you therefore like unto them: for your Father knows what things you have need of, before you ask him.

"After this manner therefore pray you: Our Father which are in heaven, Hallowed be your name.

"Your kingdom come, Your will be done on earth, as it is in heaven.

"Give us this day our daily bread.

"And forgive us our debts, as we forgive our debtors.

"And lead us not into temptation, but deliver us from evil:

"For yours is the kingdom, and the power, and the glory, for ever. Amen.

"For if you forgive men their trespasses, your heavenly Father will also forgive you:

"But if you forgive not men their trespasses, neither will your Father forgive your trespasses.

"Moreover when you fast, be not, as the hypocrites, of a sad countenance: for they disfigure their faces, that they may appear unto men to fast. Truthfully I say unto you, They have their reward.

"But you, when you fast, anoint your head, and wash your face;

"That you appear not unto men to fast, but unto your Father which is in secret: and your Father, which sees in secret, shall reward you openly.

"Lay not up for yourselves treasures upon earth, where moth and rust corrupt, and where thieves break through and steal:

"But lay up for yourselves treasures in heaven, where neither moth nor rust corrupts, and where thieves do not break through nor steal:

"For where your treasure is, there will your heart be also.

"The light of the body is the eye: if therefore your eye be sound, your whole body shall be full of light.

"But if your eye be evil, your whole body shall be full of darkness. If therefore the light that is in you be darkness, how great is that darkness!

"No man can serve two masters: for either he will hate the one, and love the other; or else he will hold to the one, and despise the other. You cannot serve God and Mammon.

"Therefore I say unto you, Take no thought for your life, what you shall eat, or what you shall drink; nor yet for your body, what you shall put on. Is not the life more than food, and the body than clothing?

"Behold the fowls of the air: for they sow not, neither do they reap, nor gather into barns; yet your heavenly Father feeds them. Are you not much better than they?

"Which of you by taking thought can add one cubit unto his stature?

"And why take you thought for clothing? Consider the lilies of the field, how they grow: they toil not, neither do they spin:

"And yet I say unto you, That even Solomon in all his glory was not arrayed like one of these.

"Therefore, if God so clothes the grass of the field, which today exists, and tomorrow is cast into the oven, shall he not much more clothe you, oh you of little faith?

"Therefore take no thought, saying, What shall we eat? or, What shall we drink? or, How shall we be clothed?

"For after all these things do the gentiles seek; for your heavenly Father knows that you have need of all these things.

"But seek you first the kingdom of God, and his righteousness; and all these things shall be added unto you.

"Take therefore no thought for the next day: for the next day shall take thought for the things of itself. Sufficient unto the day is the evil thereof.

"Judge not, that you be not judged.

"For with what judgment you judge, you shall be judged: and with what measure you mete out, it shall be measured back to you again.

"And why do you behold the speck that is in your brother's eye, but consider not the beam that is in your own eye?

"Or how will you say to your brother, Let me pull out the speck out of your eye; and, behold, a beam is in your own eye?

"You hypocrite, you play-actor, first cast out the beam out of your own eye; and then shall you see clearly to cast out the speck out of your brother's eye.

"Give not that which is holy unto the dogs, neither cast your pearls before swine, lest they trample them under their feet, and turn again and tear you.

"Ask, and it shall be given you; seek, and you shall find; knock, and it shall be opened unto you:

"For every one that asks receives; and he that seeks finds; and to him that knocks it shall be opened.

"Or what man is there of you, whom if his son ask bread, will he give him a stone?

"Or if he ask a fish, will he give him a serpent?

"If you then, being evil, know how to give good gifts unto your children, how much more shall your Father which is in heaven give good things to them that ask him?

"Therefore all things whatsoever you would that men should

do to you, do even so to them: for this is the law and the prophets.

"Enter you in at the narrow gate: for wide is the gate, and broad is the way, that leads to destruction, and many there be which go in there:

"Because narrow is the gate, and constricted is the way, which leads unto life, and few there be that find it.

"Beware of false prophets, which come to you in sheep's clothing, but inwardly they are ravening wolves.

"You shall know them by their fruits. Do men gather grapes of thorns, or figs of thistles?

"Even so every good tree brings forth good fruit; but a corrupt tree brings forth evil fruit.

"A good tree cannot bring forth evil fruit; neither can a corrupt tree bring forth good fruit.

"Every tree that does not bring forth good fruit is hewn down, and cast into the fire.

"Therefore by their fruits you shall know them.

"Not every one that says unto me, Lord, Lord, shall enter into the kingdom of heaven; but he that does the will of my Father which is in heaven.

"Many will say to me in that day, Lord, Lord, have we not prophesied in your name? And in your name have cast out devils? And in your name done many wonderful works?

"And then will I profess unto them, I never knew you: depart from me, you that work iniquity.

"Therefore whosoever hears these sayings of mine, and does them, I will liken him unto a wise man, which built his house upon a rock:

"And the rain descended, and the floods came, and the winds blew, and beat upon that house; and it fell not: for it was founded upon a rock.

"And every one that hears these sayings of mine, and does them not, shall be likened unto a foolish man, which built his house upon the sand:

"And the rain descended, and the floods came, and the winds blew, and beat upon that house; and it fell; and great was the fall thereof."

And it came to pass, when Jesus had ended these sayings, the people were astonished.

For he taught them as one having authority, and not as the priests or the rabbis or the scribes. And his doctrine brought them new life.

And there rose, echoing and resounding through the sweep of the hills, from the thousands upon thousands, the cry of the affirmation of the truth: "Amen!"

Then again Jesus made the gesture of pressing his right hand to his heart, and he maintained this pose until the twilight obscured him.

As reposed and silent and still was the figure of him receding into darkness, just as jubilant and animated were the multitudes on whom evening also fell. Their departure and dispersal were slow, for they talked with much excitement among themselves, stranger to stranger, kinsman to kinsman, elder to young, man to woman, man to man, woman to woman, city merchant to country peasant, synagogue-man to sinner; and almost all of them turned repeatedly to behold him, for one last time, again and again, on this day that would never be forgotten by any of them.

And the day that was yesterday became the day that had been tomorrow.

24

YES, MY WORDS. AND A FEW OF HIS OWN. HE HAD DELIVERED the proclamation in Aramaic, with some Hebrew, and only here and there a retention of the original Greek in which I had composed it, such as when he left as they were the forms of the Hellenic *hypokrites,* in its sense of denoting a stage actor or dissembler. I did, however, recognize his references to the Pharisees and the Sanhedrin, and knew that there were no such references in my original. Nor had I written anything about spitting. Beyond these instances, I cannot say what words of his own he added to mine, and he would not later expound much to me on this.

I sent the disciples to make their ways amid the flowings of the masses toward the passes and paths of the surrounding hills, to gather alms for the building of the new temple. The priest and the rabbi did not move. I looked at them and ordered them to do as the other disciples were doing. They followed my order with reluctance, but they followed it. I derived pleasure from commanding them. Their self-exalted status had meant increasingly little to me. Now it meant nothing.

I sat with the donkeys, awaiting the descent of our Lord from the mount.

Andreas, *raca* and *nabal,* returned with the fullest bag, the most money, intent on proving his avid dedication to our Lord. He held it out to Jesus, who would not touch it, but with a desultory gesture directed the mite to give it to me. Andreas did this with a look that made me want to rip the weaselish face and invidious eyes from his skull. I grabbed the bag from his hesitant clutch.

The priest and the rabbi were reticent beggar-men. Their bags were light. Peter, as usual, cast his net wide and gainfully. From the others, the ones whose names and faces often changed and were not worth remembering, came bags of varied weight.

There was now no doubt that we must get straightaway to Caesarea. The sum of our wealth was dangerously great.

As we moved through the moonless night, Jesus looked to me and said with an exhausted smile: "Such a bounty of shit as could not be produced by Faith, Hope, and Charity together in a week." He muttered to me some of the words I had written for him:

"That whosoever looks on a woman to lust after her has committed adultery with her already in his heart."

"To please the women and bring to the men all the more of the shame they so enjoy, and all the more of protection from trespasses against them as regards their wives."

"I thought," said he, "that in equating the culpability of the thought with that of the deed, you were implying that if one has thought the thought, he may as well do the deed."

"You have an indecent and degenerate mind," I told him; and together we laughed awhile.

It was then that I asked him about the changes he had made to the text.

He looked a bit surprised that I had noticed. "Nothing but a modulation here and there to rouse what lies innate in these people."

For the most part, I let it go at that. But I did ask him one further question:

"And the remarks about the Pharisees and the Sanhedrin?"

"I insinuated that the Pharisees represented ways without

meaning. Nothing more. And I made no insinuations again the Sanhedrin, but referred only to their authority."

"Don't you feel that it is dangerous even to make mention of these powers?"

He reverted in a tired way to the tone he had used on the mount. But now there was humor in his voice, which was hoarse with weariness:

"And I say unto you, May your Father which is in heaven fuck the Pharisees, as the shepherd fucks his flock; and may your Father which is in heaven fuck the Sadducees, as the shepherd fucks his flock, and may your Father which is in heaven fuck the Essenes and the Zealots, as they do fuck each other. Amen."

At this we both laughed. The Sadducee priest, Aaron, who walked ahead of us, turned. Had he heard our Lord's words, or merely our laughter? We cared little.

Jesus fell quiet for a moment, then said in earnest:

"The people are sick of sectarian imperatives and primacies that do them no good. Besides, without risk, there is no gain."

At his mention of risk and gain, I told him that we must make our way to Caesarea, to there arrange with a good argentarius to safe-keep our money, which was now not only the fortune of which we had dreamt, but also a constant and increasing liability. Faith, Hope, and Charity, and our own profound but precarious good luck, could bear no more.

And so we turned south on our western course, toward the Great Sea and Caesarea.

It troubled me to see the fatigue with which Jesus suffered. He uttered no words, and I could hear the scrape and shuffle in the dirt of his feet, which he was barely able to raise from the ground in his labored forward motion. When we came to Narbata in the middle of the night, I insisted that we halt. I secured a room for him, and one for myself. I let the disciples fend for themselves.

I was sick of the disciples. Affable Peter. The good, down-to-earth rabbi. The rodent Andreas. The gentle failed farmer who was new to us. I was sick of them all.

Because of the hour, the innkeeper could offer us only the remains of yesterday's bread and mutton, and some wine and water. I saw to it that Jesus ate his share, then I saw him to sleep. I ate my share in my room next to his, then took my cup of wine and water out to a small paved circle round a well where there was an old but sturdy wooden bench.

This place of Jews, Samaritans, and gentiles was dead and unstirring in the darkness of the moonless night. I sipped from my cup of wine and water. Large clouds, outlined in part by slivery curved shavings of pale silver, passed by overhead, covering many stars. I became aware that I too was very tired.

I heard the slow approach of another, then tried to make him out as he stood near me in the dark. I saw that he was gray-haired, some years older than I, sleeveless in the warmth of the night. I saw that he had a withered arm.

"I seek Jesus," he said.

His voice was almost a whisper, as if the night to him was a sacred place where spoken supplication should not be made.

"Your Lord is resting," I said. "It would be wrong to wake him. He is very much in need of this rest."

"Perhaps tomorrow," the man whispered, and turned away with a sad bow of his head.

"The Lord cannot restore your arm," I heard myself tell the man.

He turned back round.

"It is not my arm with which I wish to impose on the Son of the Father."

"What is it then?"

"My daughter. A man does her harm in secret."

"That is a matter for the authorities."

"He is of the authorities."

"A Jew or a Roman?"

"He is a Jew."

"Then act according to your God's law. Kill him. But not openly. Not with your good arm and a good blade. His fellow vermin would be upon you. You must kill him in secret, just as he has violated your daughter in secret."

"But your master, whom I hold to be my master, has said to us only in the light of a few heartbeats ago that not only shall we not kill, but even anger is forbidden. This is why I seek his counsel. I cannot bear the suffering of my daughter, and yet I want not to sin."

I felt much compassion for this man, and hatred for myself and the consequences of my careless rhetoric.

"But I say unto you, That you resist not evil: but whosoever shall smite you on your right cheek, turn to him the other also."

How could I have conceived such wicked and harmful words? Why, of all lies, must the lies of religion be the most antithetical to the truth of the world? Why must religion instruct men to be false, to become *hypokritai*, actors and pretenders, to pursue *hypokrisis*, dishonest play-acting, while preaching against it? I felt shame and guilt for having been party to cultivating and furthering the ruinous lies of what fools and evil men held to be holy.

I felt that I must help this man. For what small amends it might make for the wrong I had done, I felt that I must help him.

"Our master," I said, "would tell you that he meant killing without true justification, anger without true justification.

"Come," I said, "follow me."

With the innkeeper's iron key, I drew back the night-latch of the manger door. I went to our good dun Faith and fetched a phial of liquid opium from one of the money-sacks of his packsaddle.

"Do you wish with all your heart to see mercy and justice brought to your daughter, and do you make oath unto God and his Son to remain forever silent of this?"

"I do."

"This is the blood of our Lord," I whispered then to the whispering man. "It is the blood of justice. It is the blood of love."

I held the phial to him, placed it in his good hand, wrapped his hand around it.

The whispering man looked into my eyes.

"When he is very drunk, pour all that is in this phial into a cup of wine and see that he drinks it fast and fully. Then to yourself say the Lord's prayer, as he has instructed it to you. Do you recall it?"

"'Our Father which art in heaven, hallowed be thy name. Thy kingdom come, thy will be done, on earth as it is in—'"

"Yes. Good. And feel no remorse. Never. As you would feel about ridding yourself of a despoiling rat, so much the less should you be concerned with this act of goodness you perform for God, our Lord, and your daughter."

"Are you a priest of the Messiah?"

"I am, under him, the one true priest of the Word and the Way."

Grasping the phial, he looked into my eyes, peering in darkness, through darkness, from glinting darkness to glinting darkness.

"Go now," I said. "Go now in the peace that rightfully will be yours. I will tell the Lord of you, and of your good work."

I felt better then, about myself and my fool, artful words, the whispering man with the withered arm and unfortunate daughter.

There were still wine and water in my cup. The sun was still far from rising above the black sphere of the earth. I had damned one to the hell he deserved, saved two from the hell they did not deserve. I felt good, and I slept well.

In the first full flush of the morning light, I saw that it had rained a great deal while I slept. But the sky now was good.

I led the three donkeys to a livery-stable, and rented a two-wheeled dray with sturdy shafts, traces, crossbar, and breast-strap. With the help of the stable-man, I harnessed it to good dun Faith, loaded the heavy packsaddles and sacks into the box of the cart, covered the load with an old blanket, and roped it well.

"Tell me, Gaius," said our Lord. "How would you feel if it were I who were going forth alone with our wealth, to return with a report of having been robbed? Or to not return."

"You can come with me—"

"You know that I cannot. You know that I am increasingly recognized wherever we go. There are shadows from my past in Caesarea who might tie this pious fraud to the Iesua they once knew."

"Caesarea is a great city. You know it well. You could await me at a distance. If we entered the capital individually, we would not be seen as associated with each other."

He smiled, turned, and strolled away.

The runt Andreas appeared and asked Jesus what we were doing. The Lord told him to remove himself to the rabbi, that he might learn.

"You are my only rabbi," said the runt.

"Then I have taught you wrong," said Jesus sternly. "I will not have your presence at this time. Go."

The runt retreated, sulking, glancing to me as he passed. I exhaled a low laugh, more a snort than anything else.

Narbata was little more than sixty stadia from Caesarea, and the road was level and wide, with long stretches of good paving. It was a journey of but three hours or so.

The road was well-peopled; the sun, pleasantly bright. Still, I kept my thumb hooked uneasily on the hilt of my dagger more often than not.

It was long before the sun reached its noon zenith that the

capital, and the Great Sea beyond, could be seen. Both shimmered where the plain ended: the domes of the city, with reflected colors whose rays were like gold; the sea, far bluer than the blue of the sky, with dancing light and argent spumes.

I made my way to the palace.

Producing the rolled document sealed with the mark of the princeps, I introduced myself in Latin to the two guards, saying:

"I am Gaius Fulvius Falconius, equestrian of Rome, son of Marcus, grandson of Lucius. I seek the proconsular auxiliary."

One of them left his post, returned, and bade me follow him. We came to an antechamber of the praetorium. The guard turned and left me there, looking on a solitary figure in white finery who sat at a wooden table whose highly polished surface showed not even a speck of dust, let alone any object that might allow it to be called a desk.

I bowed slightly, and just as slightly extended to him the rolled and sealed letter.

He did not reach out his hand to take it from me. He merely let his eyes linger long—and sadly, it seemed—at the seal. He invited me to sit opposite him. He gestured to the rolled document.

"And what is it?" he asked, in a voice that possessed tired-sounding humor and a note of the sadness that was in his eyes. "A recipe for a stew of a creature of myth that he wishes to share with us? A dictum of a new self-bestowed deific title by which he henceforth commands us to refer to him?"

As he raised his eyes to mine, I did my best to show the same wearied humor and measure of sadness that were his. I dared not place the sealed letter on the gleaming dark surface at which we sat. I lowered it to my lap.

He had spoken to me in Latin rather than Greek, and so I spoke to him in kind. It felt good to speak again in Latin, one displaced Roman to another.

"It is a letter of introduction and little more," I said, as if discounting it. "The princeps gave it to me in a moment of…"

I purposely did not finish my sentence, in a subtle show of wishing to avoid any disrespectful sentiment to him who still reigned, if in title alone.

"Madness?" said the adjutant, providing the word I had with purpose omitted.

"Yes. Strong lunar influence, you might say." At this he laughed aloud and smiled on me.

"And how is it that you know our…?" And it was he who now did not finish his sentence, but, as I remained silent, it was also he who did in the end finish it, with the word "princeps," uttered flatly and without spirit, except perhaps for the merest wisp of chagrin.

"I was, in better days, his advisor and speech-writer." I paused. "For some years, a member of his court."

"Before the increase of the…lunar influence, I assume. Before the reclusion to Capreae. Before the usurpation of the throne by Sejanus."

"Yes. As I say: in better days."

The adjutant audibly expelled a sigh from his long-haired nostrils.

"The last I saw of him, he gave me orders hence," I said. I raised from my lap for a moment the rolled letter of assignment bearing the seal of Tiberius.

"We have no use of a speech-writer here," he said. "The procurator gives but one speech a year, in Jerusalem, during Pesach, to express Rome's amity toward the Jews. And it is always the same speech, year after year, and there is no need for a new one."

"It has been my impression that he wished me to serve as a clerk, not as a flourisher of oratory."

"That is even more absurd," he said. "Financial matters are

our only concern here. We collect taxes. We allocate revenues for public works. We administer sums. We assess. We levy. We impose duties and excises. We calculate tariffs. We pay salaries. We add. We subtract. We multiply."

There was further audible breath from his nostrils. He gazed away, his fingers steepled.

"Our government of Judea is one of arithmetic. We count. We tally. We record. We report. We transfer income to Rome. There are more Roman clerks and tax-collectors here than there are Roman soldiers. That is a fact. This bureaucracy cannot bear the weight of another clerical reed-pen."

"I had taken as much for granted," I said. "This is why I have not until now intruded on you. It is not the matter of a position, or of any document given me by Tiberius, that is the cause of this imposition."

His eyes seemed occupied with searching the dark polished surface for a possible mote of dust, or worse, a thread or smudge brought to it by me.

"So what is it, then?" he asked, his eyes still fully absorbed in their inspection of the immaculate gloss.

I told him that I had come to Judea with considerable funds, and that while here I had engaged in enterprises and endeavors that had proven to be quite profitable.

"What sort of enterprises and endeavors?" he asked.

"The representation of litigants in the Senate was what brought me to the attention of the royal court in Rome. I have here acted as a consultant to the scribal representatives in cases brought before the Jewish courts."

At this, he raised his eyes and looked to me. "They allowed your involvement?"

"Not within the courts. I advised the legal representatives privately."

"But their laws are strange, and surely as ill-understood by you as by me."

"Yes, this is quite true. But oratory and logic and the power of persuasion are universal forces. Inventive premises and disjunctive or horned syllogisms produce dilemmas and verdicts alike. You might say that I was a shaper of soft, wet judicial clay on the spinning potter's-lathe of innocence and guilt.

"In words to that effect, anyway, was I described by one of the consuls who brought me long ago to the attention of the palace on the Palatine."

He stared at me for several moments, during which a smile slowly came over his face. Then he said:

"To hear you is to understand why." He paused. "But you encountered no problems with the Jews?"

"No. As I said, I never entered their places of judgment. And I never acted in consultancy to proceedings in Jerusalem. The high council there advised me against it, and I deferred to their wishes. I did not much venture at all into the southern region."

"This is good to hear. Beyond the endless arithmetic and registering and ledgering of our clerical duties, our making of buildings and roads and aqueducts, our primary duty is to keep Judea placated and well-disposed toward Rome. The fine line between ruling and riling is to be kept in mind at all times. Discontent and revolution are the bane of empire."

Then, with little pause—just enough to let a brief smile appear and disappear—and as if continuing in the same course, he said:

"And so, you are in need of an argentarius."

"Precisely. I need to deposit my money here for collection in Rome. I plan to soon return there, to my home and family."

"I wish I could say the same," he said, and there was yet another sighing through those nostrils of his. Then his voice was again one of business:

"Here," said the adjutant, "where such transactors are overseen by the provincial prefecture—that is, by us—rather than by the urban prefect of Rome, the proper term is *mensarius,* or often simply *negotiator.*"

The prefect of the city of Rome, the commander of the Praetorian Guard, was Sejanus.

"You cannot use our nummularius, who serves as assayer and officer of our mint here," said the adjutant. "He is ours alone. I can, however, recommend his brother, who is the associate here of one of the leading argentarii in Rome. And I can vouch for him."

"This is indeed very kind of you."

"Yes, it is," he reflected.

A tall gaunt man entered, as if, lost and wandering through the halls of the praetorium, he had found himself at this antechamber and decided to seek directions from those whose voices he heard. He had a certain benign but distinguished air about him. I soon realized that this dignified air was the result of his being bald and not trying to cover up his baldness with a wig, as was becoming the common practice among bald Roman men who felt their condition to be premature—that is to say, most of them. These wigs were as noticeable as they were ridiculous. I swore that I should never glue a wig to my pate should I go bald, and I never have done so. I write to you now completely bald but for three obstinate white hairs that seem intent on going with me to the grave. I am proud to have you know this of me.

The adjutant looked on the tall gaunt bald man with what seemed a familiar indulgence.

The tall gaunt man said to the adjutant: "Where are the most recent ledgers for Syria?"

The adjutant waved to a shelf among many shelves set into a wall across the room.

The tall gaunt bald man walked, apparently without purpose,

to the shelf. He then ordered the more aloof man to have the ledger brought somewhere to be examined by a certain calculator.

"Bring me a piece of papyrus, a pen, the ink, and my writing-board from the corbel beneath that shelf," instructed the adjutant, and the gaunt man did so.

"You have this beautiful desk here, and yet you use this schoolboy's writing-board," said the gaunt man, shaking his head. "Never will I understand you and your desk."

The adjutant glanced at him reprovingly. When he finished writing, he waved the papyrus in the air, allowing the ink to dry, and then he passed it to me. He told me the name of the financial agent, and where to find him.

"Just give him that note of introduction, and all will go well for you."

The tall gaunt man looked on me with curiosity.

With a turn of his hand toward me, the adjutant said to him:

"One Gaius of Rome, a fellow equestrian, formerly of the court of Tiberius."

"Very formerly, I hope," said the man.

"Yes, as I have told—"

"Now," interrupted the adjutant, to whom I was about to refer, "perhaps you two equestrians have matters to discuss. Horses, or horse-shit, or whatever indeed it is that distinguished equestrians such as yourselves do discuss when one of them comes upon another. It is time for my midday rest."

"You do nothing," said the other man, "and yet you require respite from it. Two hours of nothing, followed by an hour's sleep; and on and on."

The adjutant waved him away, stood, and, with the words "An honor and a pleasure," left the room.

The other man, the tall gaunt man, smiled to me, then spoke. On hearing his words, I experienced one of those sudden lurching stillnesses in the chest that cause sleeping men to jolt awake with a gasp, and strollers in public to be overcome with sudden faintness.

"I am Pontius Paulus Pilatus," he said, "equestrian of Rome, son of Septimus, grandson of Servius, of the Pontii of the Abruzzi. As you can see, I am the much feared and respected procurator of this province. I will call you Gaius, and you will address me as your god."

Then he smiled to me affably, to coax from me a smile. I told him that the mother of my father was a woman of the Abruzzi.

"Do you know the region?" he asked.

"Yes."

"Then you know how much I miss the grain, the olive oil, the forests, the mountains, the fields."

"The finest bread and olives in all the empire."

A wistful look passed over him, and when he broke his quiet, it was with a voice that was wistful.

"Yes," he said.

Then he spoke matter-of-factly. "So, the court of Tiberius, eh?"

I was thinking of the waiting donkey-cart of riches. I was thinking that the man with whom I spoke had been raised to his position by Sejanus, the killer of the son of Tiberius, the scheming usurper whose cunning machinations, and my knowledge of them, had caused a raving Tiberius to evict me in his refusal to heed my warning. I was thinking of the financial agent and the arrangements that needed to be made. I was thinking of the flight of the day. I was thinking of Jesus peering out from Narbata, anxious to glimpse my returning figure in the distance. I was thinking that this was no time for the tall, gaunt, bald Pilate and me to be discussing the swaying grain-fields of the Abruzzi, and most certainly no time for us to be teetering so precariously on the brink of talk of Tiberius and Sejanus.

"Some time ago, as I was telling your adjutor. In the years before..."

But, unlike his auxiliator, the procurator did not complete with his own words the sentence I had intentionally left unfinished. What was worse, he pressed me to finish it myself:

"As you were saying?" he said. "'Before'? Before what?" He did not appear so affable now. "Before madness befell?" There was a pause. "Before Sejanus?"

"Before many things," I said, with composure.

Once again he seemed affable, then once again wistful, then once again forthright.

"Tiberius was driven from the throne," he said. "Sejanus, our fellow equestrian, will die in it before his time. Madness and death were the fates allotted them by the divider of destinies and days. So be it. To hell with them, I say. To hell with both of them."

These words unburdened me of my worries. But I could not resist:

"I had been led to believe — mistakenly, it seems — that you were a favorite of Sejanus's."

"No, your belief is not mistaken. It is Sejanus who was from the outset mistaken. He mistook my manner for my substance. Men such as he favor only those whom they feel they can mold into disposable tools of their designs, which serve them and them alone. This is as evident to me as the vein that brings blood to my wrist."

"Your words are safe in me," I said sincerely.

"If I cared a whit for their safety, I would not have spoken them," he said. Then he spoke as if musing to himself:

"Yes. Rome grows impatient with Sejanus: with his persecutions, his plottings, his tyrannies. Diminished as he is, Tiberius is still princeps. Sejanus will never see the overripe fruit of age. It is not as in that strange tale of the Jews, that tale of the first murderer. Not all killers live for a thousand years. Sejanus will die soon. The world will be better for it.

"Sometimes I feel that the world is better for every death. Then I remember that for each who dies, two are born...."

Then he smiled again and spoke directly to me:

"But whither has my courtesy escaped? Will you let me call for some good Roman wine and good Roman food?"

I declined, and with circumspect ease, I bade him farewell.

"Will I see you again?" he asked.

"I will come again to the palace of your hospitality, and the pleasure of your company, and a cup of that good wine, before I depart for Rome."

He smiled with a subtle distant kindness, then walked with me until there was within hearing a guard whom he summoned to escort me.

Though his talk of Sejanus was assuring as to there being no enmity between Pilate and me, I believed there to be no truth in what he foresaw. Already the most influential and feared citizen of Rome, the usurper was to be raised to the consulship a few years thence.

But then, in October of the seventeenth year of the reign of Tiberius, Livilla would meet her end either by her own hand or the hand of another, and on that evening, the Senate would convene at the Temple of Concordia, at the western reach of the Forum. Amid accusations of conspiracy against the princeps, Sejanus was summarily condemned, apprehended, and executed by strangling at the Gemonian Stairs, where the body was left to be torn apart by crowds.

Mobs hunted down and killed anyone they could link to the regime of Sejanus. The Praetorians resorted to looting when they were accused of having conspired with the former prefect. His statues were torn down and his name obliterated from all public records. A few days later, Sejanus's eldest son, Strabo, was also arrested and executed. On hearing of his death, Strabo's mother, Apicata, the first wife of Sejanus, killed herself after addressing a letter to Tiberius saying that Drusus had been murdered by Sejanus with the complicity of Livilla: a charge corroborated by the testimony of Livilla's slaves, who admitted to having administered the poison to Drusus.

How had Pilate foreseen this? Perhaps he merely knew Sejanus better than most. Perhaps he knew and understood many things better than most men. Or maybe he was given to outlandish predictions, a few of which were bound to fall true.

On that day in Caesarea, I had a donkey-cart filled with wealth, a man to see, and arrangements to make. The future extended no further.

Having said this, I return immediately, like a fool, to what then was the future; but only to tell you a very small tale in which lies a very big lesson. When Tiberius at last did depart this life, he left his heir and successor, Caligula, with an almost inconceivable inheritance of more than two billion and seven hundred million sesterces. Caligula squandered this vast fortune in less than five years' time. This shows that there is no true value in inert wealth itself.

True wealth lies in the squandering of it. A good loaf of bread and a jug of good wine could be had for a single sestertius. Before deductions, a legionary's wage was barely three sesterces a day, about the same that a laborer was paid for a day of hard toil. The finest Greek slave could be purchased for a few thousand sesterces. A luxurious villa, for a few hundred thousand.

Now think of throwing such sums and more to the winds of every morning and every night. Think of idly hurling two billion and seven hundred million sesterces to the winds and raging seas of five years' living. That is wealth: the lavishing of it beyond reckoning; not the hoarding, the mere having, the prudent spending of it.

Our fortune was nothing by comparison, but we needed to insure that we could squander ours as well. I led Faith and the cart to the agent, whose place of business was close to the palace, and I presented him with the papyrus sheet given me by the adjutant. I loosed the ropes from the cart, threw back the blanket, and together we hauled the sacks and packsaddles into a curtained area of his stall. He betrayed no sign that he was impressed by either the bulk or the weight of what we moved from the cart to the curtained room.

Two assistants were called into the room, and the hoard was sorted into four piles: Greek coins, Hebrew coins, Roman coins, and coins of a more exotic nature.

The few jewels and pieces of gold virtu collected by us were kept apart from the coins and not included here.

The piles were subjected, under the charge of a third and especially expert assistant, to the simultaneous processes of permutation and computation, by which the current values of coins of different kinds, sources, and denominations were reckoned into Roman equivalents of commensurate value, with the ongoing calculations being stated aloud by the third assistant and entered on wax tablets by the other two.

The small pile of strange and exotic coins was treated last, and several of these coins required closer examination and deliberation. In the end, only one coin remained unaccounted: a very ancient electrum stater of Lydian origin, as the third assistant explained it, saying that he had encountered only one other example, and while he felt its value to be considerable, he could not responsibly appraise it. He excluded this small pale-yellow coin from the reckoning and handed it to me. Also excluded were several crude counterfeits bestowed on us with a show of piety in the course of our mission.

The two men with wax tablets then added the figures on their respective tablets, and, when they finished, gave the tablets to the agent, who compared them to establish that their individual arithmetical results were identical.

He wrote on a piece of papyrus, and presented it to me. I saw the symbol IIS with a line drawn through it, followed by the numeral DCCC with a line over it, followed by the numerals XMMM and DCCLIII.

"Eight hundred and thirteen thousand and seven hundred and fifty-three brass sesterces," announced the agent.

Though the sestertius was the standard unit of account, and thus always used formally, this sum was equivalent to eight thousand and one hundred and thirty-eight gold aurei, plus or minus a few handfuls of silver denarii.

Dividing this amount by two, it was plain that both the Lord and I were amply rich men. The requisite wealth of the two hundred or so Romans of senatorial rank was eight hundred thousand sesterces. It might be said that the Prince of Peace and I were now each worth half a senator. And more riches lay ahead. Jesus had been right. We should ride our mare farther and farther on, rather than quit, vanish, and make for Rome. These fleeting days were for the seizing. Rome awaited always.

The agent and I discussed the matter of how the deposit was to be held by him: as vacua pecunia, bearing neither interest nor risk, or as creditum, to be lent out by the argentarius at the conservative fixed legal rate of twelve per centum per annum.

Here he was quick to bring to my attention that while this fixed legal rate was enforced in Rome, with due penalties provided for violations, the rates commanded by usurers in the provinces were not so easily overseen or controlled. Lending through Jew intermediaries here in Caesarea could bring rates in excess of twenty per centum, and through certain usurers at the Holy Temple in Jerusalem, rates as high as forty per centum or more.

After much deliberation, I instructed him to invest half the fortune through usurious lending, and let the other half lie unturned. I did this because I could not speak for the Lord's share. If he felt comfortable with the increase afforded by usury, I would grant him half participation in the half of the deposit that I had designated as creditum.

The agent and I settled on his fees and his percentage of the creditum profits. There was paper-work: details of arrangements whereby the deposit could be claimed in full or in parts either here, in Caesarea, from him, or at his argentaria in Rome, in person or through prescriptive draught authorized by me.

"Where is your place of safe-keeping?" I asked him at last, not because I had doubts over his methods of security, but because I was quite curious.

"It is safe because I do not speak of it. It is unknown to my assistants and my associates, even to my brother, and to the provincial government for which he works." There came to his face a smile. "To have my fun, I make as to confide in the Jew usurers that it travels by my own manned war galley, moving from one feared and uncharted sea, one unknown port to another. They believe a large shark is painted on its hull, and that its mainsail is black, and some of them claim to have seen it, or to have heard reports of its sighting, on this distant horizon or that."

So my curiosity was not to be satisfied. But he did leave me with these words:

"You see, wealth is not a material thing. All these heaps of various coins you have brought me are but the tangible token-pieces, the roundel-chips of that which is impalpable. The values represented by them are affected by many things: changes in composition, changes in denominations and denominational tables, artificial manipulations of politics and marketplace, decreed or fortuitous debasements, decreed or fortuitous appreciations.

"Ships are loaded heavy with these tokens whose transient

values exist only in the minds of men. But wealth has no weight. It is so light as to be transported invisibly by the breath of Fortune. As it is good to increase the number of these tokens and chips, it is better to transmute them into nothing. Only when they become that which does not exist is their safe-guarding absolute and complete."

Hours had passed in that curtained room. I knew that I would not be returning to Narbata that night.

I found the inn of long ago, where Jesus and I had spent our first night together. The dark winding streets were still filled, even more so than I remembered them, with furtive shadows, lurking presences, the phantoms of old gods, the mad howlings of new messiahs. The increasing strangeness in the air was thick.

I saw to it that Faith had his feed and water. I ate pig jowls, rich with tender fatty meat beneath charred skin, and ocean fish, and good bread with vinegar, and good dry-salted cheese and summer figs, and I drank my share of good Roman wine.

I remembered his delight in the oysters. I remembered his telling me of the bread of affliction. I remembered our laughter. I saw my right hand slowly raise my knife and just as slowly lower it vertically to cleave in twain the air between us, to answer his question as to how any hypothetical gains were to be divided between us; and I heard my voice, as if from very far away: "Straight down the middle." So long ago, all of it. And, yes, considering the distances we had traveled, so very far away.

Faith and I entered Narbata well before the day's meridian. I found Jesus in the shade of a tree, telling a group of children about why it was important for them to honor their fathers and their mothers.

"For they gave you," said he, "the one gift without which there can be no other gift, and without which nothing can be possessed or enjoyed."

The children were young, and some of them turned their heads sideways as they looked to him and listened. Some of their mothers stood behind them, looking warmly to the Lord.

"They gave you the gift of this breath," he went on. "The gift of life itself, without which you would sing no song or hear the song of no bird in the sky. The gift without which there could be for you nothing."

"The old rabbi told us that it was God who gave us life," one of the taller children said.

"Then that rabbi respects not his father and mother. That rabbi disobeys the God of whom he speaks."

The mothers seemed to give this more thought than the children gave it.

"You are better than the old rabbi," said one of the little children.

"If that is true, it is because I am grateful for the gift of this breath, and for the happiness it allows to come."

"And how must we honor our parents?"

The mothers awaited his answer expectantly.

"By heeding them, for they know more than you and want only for you what is good. But more by caring for them as they become old. For as they gave you the gift of life, so you must return it to them. Life will become wearisome for them, and you must replenish it. If you grow to have good fortune, you must share it with them. If you grow to have children of your own, you must let them hold and cherish them. If you have nothing, you must give to them the love and care within you. As they gave you the gift without which there would be nothing, so you must honor them with all that befits this priceless gift."

I saw that, off a way, near the livery-stable, unburdened of his packsaddle, Hope had mounted and was fucking Charity.

We should have shoved a skipping-stone up that jenny's cunt.

The last thing we needed was a pregnant or foaling donkey. As the livery-hand and I unharnessed Faith, the old dun jack looked to Hope and Charity as if his turn were next. I gave a good push to Hope, but he went on with his humping, and Charity stood firm and impassive.

Jesus was alone now. I told him that all had gone well in Caesarea, and I told him of the sum of our wealth, at which he rejoiced.

I asked him if he wanted to share in the half that was to accrue interest through usury.

"No," he said, and he asked me the duration of the period to which I had committed my half of the deposit to be put into creditum in this way.

"Semi-annuum. Payment after six months. The Roman month of Januarius."

Jesus thought and muttered the name of the corresponding Jewish month, Shevat.

"That is good," he said. "Whatever you do, be sure that the term expires as arranged, and is not renewed."

"Why are you so concerned about this?"

"Because there may very likely be an upheaval among the usurers come next spring."

I looked at him and told him that I had heard nothing of the kind.

"You have heard it now. Just do as I say, and your money and your profits will be safe. But you must do as I say."

I told him that I would. His mood lightened considerably, and we celebrated our wealth.

"Good is the greed that is fulfilled," he said, as if from on high. At this he laughed as if reborn.

We walked in aimless good spirits.

"You missed a good funeral," he said. "One of the Temple publicans. The weepers could barely hide their gladness."

So, I thought, the whispering man with the withered arm had acted. It felt good to know that he and his daughter were no longer among the meek of the earth who would go to their deaths in the futile expectation of their inheritance. But again I regretted the fool and dodgy words I had written.

The priest and the rabbi, Aaron and Ephraim, welcomed me back. Jesus spoke to them, surprising me with his words almost as much as he surprised them.

"We have been together a long time. Throughout that time, I have looked upon your sectarian tenets with respect, understanding, and at last tolerance. But I tell you now that the time for every sect is done.

"The God who is my Father will have no more of Pharisee, or of Sadducee, or of Essene. All of these are as Philistines before him, and their division of the house of David will no longer be suffered. The Way is not to be argued. The Way is not to be contended. The Way is not to be cleft. Rock that is smitten and sundered has no strength, and only of solid rock will the new temple be built.

"To God the Father, the noise of your worship is more like the squabbling of hens than the voices of the righteous joined as one, and it is abhorrent to him.

"Renounce your sect, dear brothers, as God has renounced it. There is one Word, and there is one Way. Embrace them, or be gone."

They were stunned, speechless, as was I. I marveled at how his words, his own words, were becoming ever more powerful. I told myself that he had learned well from me.

"And you, Andreas, or Judas, or Judah, or whatever it is that you are called, what is it that you do? Fisherman who does not fish, boy who does not grow to manhood, disciple who does not follow my discipline—what is it that you do? The others pay their way, or they earn it. But you do not."

The young man's response came fast and in defiance of all deference.

"You tell us to consider and admire the lilies of the field, which toil not, and now you preach to me of toil."

And the response of Jesus met his just as quickly, and was without ruth:

"You are no lily of the field whose beauty is a blessing to behold. You are to be likened more to a carbuncle, a curse most dreadful to consider."

The young man's jaw was slightly lowered, and it slightly trembled.

Some of the newer disciples, whom we barely knew, backed away and withdrew, and were not to be seen again.

"And you, Peter, and you, Gaius." He paused long amid the bated breath all round. "You are good men," he said at last.

Things were not the same after this day.

The Sadducees did, with some reluctance, renounce their sect, and the priest did put away his priestly sash; but, at the same time, they seemed more remote. The young fisherman did indeed occupy himself with meeting the quota of donations imposed on him by Jesus after his drubbing, though the resentment in him was often apparent. Even Peter looked differently on his Lord at times.

It was like a new strangeness in the air within the greater and growing strangeness in the vaster air of the world through which we moved.

No, things were not the same after that day.

25

N EW MIRACLES WERE ATTRIBUTED TO THE LORD, AND THESE
fictions were spread far and wide, taking on revisions and
embellishments as they traveled by the telling. The disciples
themselves often believed in these tales, taking them as accounts
of wonders that Jesus had worked at times when he was not in
their presence.

Our Lord had come to disparage his miracle-workings, both
the feigned and the fabulated. He had quit perpetrating the former, and he had quit responding to rumors of the latter. He no
longer reacted to the tales of his miracles with a pose of humble
modesty. He reacted with a stern countenance and disapproving
silence.

He likened miracles to entertainments for those who sought
signs of his divinity through cheap tricks. The very idea of them,
he told me, was a vileness.

"Your Messiah has not come to you as a juggler, or as a con-
jurer, or as a presenter of prestiges. Your Messiah has come to you
to reveal the Word and the Way of your salvation. He who is my
Father has given you signs enough, and now would forgo them.
There is no meaning in them. The meaning is in the Word and
the Way."

These were his words to the many who gathered around him
as we made our way from Narbata, when one among them asked
him the meanings of his miraculous signs. His tone was adamant.

I had brought from Caesarea a whimsical gift for him: one of those amphorae encountered in Rome, by which clownish prestigiators bedazzle audiences of aristocratic children. You surely witnessed it when you were a little boy: the so-called magical amphora that, by means of a hidden belly within its belly, and an occult lip-hole, is seemingly filled with clear water from a fountain pool, then, when tipped—*praesto!*—flows with water that appears to have been turned to vibrant liquid gold, which is in fact the saffron-imbued water that was already concealed in the hidden outer belly of the amphora.

His words about jugglers' tricks were heartfelt. But he took delight and found laughter in the magical amphora I gave him.

"Ah!" he said. "A true miracle at last!"

We meandered south, and found ourselves on the eastern slope of Mount Olive, approaching Bethany, the house of misery, where long ago, at the beginning of all that came to pass, we had prepared the key-of-David narrative he delivered outside the gates of Bethlehem. It was like returning to a vision vaguely retained, vaguely remembered.

The people of Bethany preferred to interpret the name of their town as "the house of unripe figs" rather than "the house of misery." The accommodating flexibility of the recondite language of Judea never ceased to amaze me. That "misery" and "unripe figs" could be construed from the same allophones of the name by which the Judeans called this place, Anania, whose root, *anan,* was a verb meaning "cloud over" or "bring" or perhaps a thousand other things unknown even to those who lived here. But figs, unripe or otherwise? As I have said, I had learned enough of the rudiments of the language of the Book to know that I would never understand it, and to know that no one truly understood it.

It was not long after entering Bethany that we were approached by two familiar figures. They were lovely to behold. We soon recognized them as Maria and Martha, the sisters of our erstwhile disciple Eleazar, who was also known as Lazarus.

The sisters did not approach the Lord with the lust that had been so hard to resist when they followed him with their brother for a while in the days before the Magdalen Hag. They approached now not in lust, but in distress.

Martha, who seemed to believe that Jesus had arrived here on purpose, lamented that he had not come earlier. Her brother, his dear disciple, she said, had been so very terribly ill. She said this as if she felt that Jesus was aware of Eleazar's sickness, and that this was the assumed purpose on which he traveled here.

"You could have healed him," said Maria.

This was not a time to be speaking of healings, not after Jesus's recent denunciation and renunciation of all such miracle-doings.

But he forbore the sisters, and looked kindly on them. I did not know if this was out of fond remembrance or a lust of his own.

A mass of people grew around us. We saw that most of them were in mourning. One of them cried to us that Eleazar—Lazarus—had been claimed, and was now four days in his tomb.

"You must raise him and return him to us," this person pleaded.

Jesus did not look to her, but instead to Martha and Maria, who clung to him and wept. He seemed to enjoy the weeping movement of their breasts on him.

"After three days, the spirit flees the body," he said. "One cannot ask the Father to relinquish what he has taken up into his eternal embrace."

"Our brother is dead," sobbed Martha.

"You who are the Son of God must restore his spirit to him," said the woman in the crowd.

Jesus raised the heads of the sisters Martha and Maria. He wiped at their tears with his finger. He said to them:

"I am the resurrection, and the life. He that believes in me, though he be dead, yet will he live. And whosoever lives and believes in me will never die."

It was then that I witnessed what I had not witnessed before, and what I had not imagined I ever would witness.

Jesus wept.

As his weeping continued, there could be no doubt that his emotions had overtaken him. His weeping grew more uncontrollable, and more inordinate. His emotions had more than overtaken him. He was coming apart. He was not well.

He followed the mob to the tomb of Lazarus. He stood and commanded that the covering stone be rolled away from the tomb.

Martha covered her face and wailed anew, imploring the Lord to replace the stone and go no further. Jesus seemed to be praying, or incanting.

The terrible stench of decomposition caused all to cover their noses with the wadded cloth of their sleeves. Most backed away. A few swooned and fell. Some retched and vomited.

The sun entered the tomb of Lazarus. His putrid corpse lay in gray grave-clothes in a slime-pool of foul decay that drizzled from the shelf of rock. The face protruding from the grave-clothes was grossly bloated and black. Greasy slippages of the skin marked the holes in his cheeks and forehead where fat white maggot-worms fed, squirming in the holes they had eaten into him. These fat white worms also filled one of his eye sockets and churned a thick pus-like substance that foamed in the open sore that had been his mouth.

A few moths fluttered and a few flesh-flies buzzed near the corpse in the sun-bared thick dust of all that was horrid.

"Come forth!" commanded Jesus, from beneath the wadded cloth of his own raised sleeve.

Maria fainted to the earth. Martha screamed: "No!" The woman who had implored Jesus to raise Lazarus, now implored him to let him be. Others in the dispersing mob besought the same. There were cries even among the disciples.

I shouted to him amid the uproar: "This man is man no more!"

Jesus stood there, staring at what others could not bear to look upon. He spoke no more to the corpse. He spoke no more to anyone. He turned away finally, and went to place his hand on the shoulder of the fallen Maria, who now sat and sadly wept as Martha held her. When Jesus put his hand to her, she withdrew from his touch.

Many of those who were there looked on him with awe. Many looked on him with confusion. Many, with fear.

I later heard that some were said to have reported the incident to the religious authorities in Jerusalem. I also heard, among other things, that the remains of Lazarus now walked the hills dragging behind him the tatters of his winding-sheet, neither dead nor alive.

Leaving Bethany, we were very close to Jerusalem. But Jesus said that it was not yet our time to enter there.

We moved west, and then south, to Callirrhoe, on the eastern shore of the Dead Sea. I advised Jesus that he must rest. I told him that he would rest in Callirrhoe, a place of beautifully flowing hot springs, a place whose name in the Book meant "the splendor of the dawn."

As we made our way, we passed through a snowfall. Most Judeans had never seen one in all the winters of their lives. It was brief, but for an evening and a night, our path and the fronds of the tall palms glistened with a dusting of soft purest white.

The sense of distance and drifting apart that had settled on all of us in the recent months was lifted in the jubilation that overcame us for this rare wonder. But by morning, the pleasant warmth of the sun had returned, and the path and the broad fronds of the high palms were as they had been on any other day.

It was in the late afternoon of that buoyancy of falling snow, as the others frolicked about, that I asked him about what had happened in the house of misery.

"I do not know," he said.

"What did you mean to accomplish by calling forth that monstrous, rotted thing to rise?"

"To show the people the ugliness of their hungering for miracles, for what is against nature."

"The sisters had no such hungering."

"Was it not they who spoke of healing? Exorcism, healing, raising the dead. It is all the same."

I sighed. I did not know if what he said and what he truly believed were one and the same; I did not know if he himself knew.

"It was a perfect performance," he said.

I was sure this notion had come to him only just then, but that he wished to make it sound as if he were stating the obvious.

"How so?" I asked him.

"They wanted me to raise that stinking, swollen, leaking black sack of worms. I began to do so. Or so it seemed to them. Then they stopped me. This was proof of their belief that I could perform the miracle they sought of me. In beseeching me to desist, they affirmed their faith in me."

"But I thought that you rightly wanted nothing more to do with the trumpery of miracles."

"I accomplished that as well. As I said, I showed them the detestable atrocity, the utter ugliness, of their hungering for miracles, for what is against nature."

I countered him with calm silence. I made it seem calm, in any case. As far as I was concerned, this conversation was ended. I hoped that the biles of his spleen and gall-bladder had been vented through his mouth, and that my studied quiet might be conducive to a repose from, rather than an increase in, this bilious venting.

After some time had passed, I said:

"We departed that debacle without one shekel for the new temple."

I thought that this reference to "the new temple" of our own personal pursuits might bring a smile to him, or at least a lightening of his umbrous spirits.

"Is that what this is all about? Money?" he demanded.

"Yes," I said. If he would not smile, I should; and so, then and there, I did.

"We are already rich," he said flatly, yet with an ambiguity lurking somewhere beneath that flatness.

Men complain when they are destitute. Men complain when they are rich. That is the definition of a man. He is a creature of complaint. A finite being with an infinity of complaints.

"Then why not draw the curtain?" I said. "Why go on?"

He did not answer. I thought that he might be feeling anger toward me. I thought that there was something I was failing to understand. Then at last he answered, with no trace of anger.

"I do not know," he said. "I do not know."

The little miracle of the snow was ending. The others were returning from their private little worlds nearby.

"I do not know," he repeated.

With my eyes I sought the eyes of the Jesus I knew. The eyes of the loiterer. The eyes of the Lord. The eyes of my friend. I found something like them, and peered into them.

"You will rest," I said. "You will rest well, and you will know."

26

IT HAS BEEN SOME WEEKS SINCE I HAVE BEEN ABLE TO WORK ON this history that I write for you. I fell badly, and was bedridden and in pain. It was the sort of pain that, in my sleepless torments, took me beyond my acceptance of death, to a welcoming of it, and at times even beyond that, to a wishing for it. I could take only bread soaked in milk, and the concoction of opium and bitter herbal brew that was given me did more to make me vomit than to ease the pain. And thus I lost more blood and became all the weaker in my misery. When I could at last stand again, tremulously and with the aid of a staff, the first thing I did was dismiss my physicians. To me, such men are worthless. I now believe that they always were. A man's life is his life, with them or without them; and so is his death. They call themselves healers, but have more in common with the death-worms that feasted on Lazarus. They are a waste of time and money, and they are more adept at removing those two things from us than they are at ridding us of ailment and disease. Death cannot be stayed by learned-sounding double-talk, foul poultices, and fouler medicines. After a thousand years, these charlatans still cannot cure the common cold, yet they would have us believe that they can save us from the common end.

We dwell under the ruling shadow of Caesar and his whims and headsmen. Beyond that, we are the makers and breakers of our own lives. Neither implore nor cast blame on the fates, for the fates are you.

As much as I welcomed and sometimes wished for death, the prospect that I might not live to finish this account for you was what brought me through. But I am frail, even more frail than I thought. There is now beside me always a shade: the shade of myself.

I must not fall again. For no shade can tell you what I must. Good wine is the best medicine. Just a cup slowly drunk in the morning, a cup slowly drunk in the evening, set beside my bed. And whatever of raw fruit and cooked flesh my gums can mash and pulp. And the good air of the breezes in my garden. With my strong oak staff and the help of the two trusted old slaves, now faithful freedmen, who attend me, I have my wine and my food and my garden breezes. And, in these words to you, I have my reason not to recede from these things.

There are moments, when sleep eludes these exhausted bones, that I think I may be setting down this history, this story of my life, to remove it from my memory to a safer place, before the breezes in the garden bear it away from me. Thus, the thought unwinds, the story is as much for me as it is for you. But why, I ask myself, should this be? Of what use is the memory of a man's life as he fades from it?

Or could it be a confession? If so, what an odd confession that would be. The confession of a man who believes in no judge above him; who believes that, in this world predicated on wrongdoing and little else, culpability and forgiveness are mere fancies. The confession of a man who believes in no confessor but himself.

I do not understand.

Considering this simple declarative sentence that I have just set forth, I am prone to burst out in laughter, were I hale enough to do so without risking the splattering of fine vellum with a spray of blood. A life of long and deepening understanding, leading me to the realization that I do not understand. It is said that wisdom is measured by the degree of our awareness of how little we know. If this is correct, I truly have attained wisdom. Yes, just in time to leave my instructions that only rosemary be used to perfume the flames of my cremation, I have attained wisdom.

I lead you nowhere with such talk. But I do not lead you astray, or at least not for long; for my narrative now continues. If I stop its course again before its end, I promise you that it will be only because I myself have been stopped and ended, removed forever from the breezes, or become one with them, if only as a few unseeable ashen particles too light to settle, destined for all time to be borne in the sweet air. May other fading old men find solace in them. May young lovers find passion and peace. As all of life is endless substantiation, may the transformation of substance be endlessly wrought by the breezes of those things that are without end.

It is true. I do not understand. But nor are the natures of all things to be understood. By the everlasting breezes, perhaps. But not by us; not by we who are born and who die, and the sum of whose lusts and desires and inspirations and journeys and sighs and gold are reduced to the scent of rosemary burning.

27

THE PLACE OF IDYLLIC RETREAT KNOWN IN GREEK AS Callirrhoe, and in Hebrew as Zareth-shahar, had lovely meanings in both tongues: "beautiful flow" in Greek; "the splendor of the dawn" in Hebrew.

Beyond it, to the east, lay the lands of the Arabian nomads. To its west, the vast gloom of the Dead Sea. The hot springs of Callirrhoe, like the deep sea where the Jordan ends, were thick with bitumen. So very dense with bitumen was the Dead Sea, that the bodies of horses, camels, and even bulls would float upon it and never sink.

But the hot springs of Callirrhoe were rich too in living sulphur and rare minerals, and were as legendary for their restorative and curative powers as was the Dead Sea for its power to float the heaviest of carcasses. Herod himself had traveled from Herodium to frequent these hot springs in his late years. And many men of lesser wealth, Jews and Greeks and Romans alike, had also made the beautiful flowing and the splendid dawn of Callirrhoe their destination.

The richest of the Jewish aristocracy were given to making the greatest show of their austerity, such as by girding their fine tunics with unfolded sashes to ostentate that their waist-strips could not be used as keeping-places for something so unholy and defiling as money. Many such men, in making much fuss over their dutiful pilgrimages to the Holy Temple, stopped only briefly in Jerusalem to attend to financial affairs, then made straight for the hot springs near the farther shore of the Dead Sea.

There was thus no want of luxurious accommodations in Callirrhoe. I found for my Lord a comfortable and well-appointed upper room in a secluded inn. The food and drink at this inn were exceptional, no less Roman than Jewish, no less Arabian than Greek. Honeyed camel-milk and date-wine, not commonly encountered outside Arabia. It was a quiet room in a quiet inn, with little sound entering through its windows but for the soft calls and songs of the swallows and the sparrows, and the wintering woodcocks and the wintering turtledoves. Captured by net and roasted, the migrating woodcocks were one of the delicacies of the table here.

As pleasant and peaceful a room as I chose for Jesus, I chose for myself a neighboring upper room that was every bit as peaceful and every bit as pleasant. As for the rest of our retinue, I left them to their own devices. They knew that, though I was supposedly a follower of our Lord, I was still a Roman of equestrian rank, and they thus always had assumed that there were still personal funds in my purse, which at times I shared with the Lord.

Peter still fished the streams at times, for food and for sale. To the others, as well as to our elder fisherman, Jesus sometimes gave a few coins when they brought in especially good collections for the building of the new temple, though we suspected, and had indications, that most of them already modestly stole or skimmed from these collections, either occasionally or regularly. Simon Peter and the rabbi seemed of the most probity in this regard. Andreas and the priest who had put aside his Sadducee sash seemed the least trustworthy, though it worked in our favor that they strived to collect all the more so that they could pilfer all the more.

In Callirrhoe, some of them lodged at a humbler inn, some at a stable, and a few of them in the open. Having a suspicious mind, it occurred to me that those who slept outdoors were the biggest pilferers, and therefore the most intent on concealing this by exhibiting beggarly ways.

Jesus and I took the hot springs alone before daybreak after the night of our arrival. There were four large springs, and several smaller springs among and around them. Warm sulphurous vapors rose from all of them. We chose one of the smaller, outlying springs. At first light, an attendant appeared, bringing us wooden ladles and asking if we should like to have laundered the clothes we had placed aside before entering the spring. We told him yes, and he neatly carried our clothes away, leaving behind clean white robes for our temporary use.

Through some trees, in another spring, a fat man luxuriated alone as his slave ladled water from the spring over his master's big bald head.

"When we board the ship to leave Judea for Rome, you will have to play the part of my slave," I said.

"Fuck the ship," he said. "Fuck Judea. Fuck Rome. Fuck the world. For this one moment, let us both be slaves to this. Let there be only the beautiful flowing of this splendid dawn."

"You sound as if you slept well," I said.

"That I did," said he.

I said nothing else. I knew he needed many moments, many days, and many nights of sleep and rest and of these good recuperative hot springs and good food and good drink.

My eyelids began to lower in aimless, vacating reverie. It was then that I saw in the nearest spring, sitting upright in vaporous water to his neck, rotting Lazarus and his writhing plump maggots. With a start, my eyes opened wide. It was in that unsettling instant that I knew that I too needed rest.

"You look as if you've seen a ghost," he said.

He closed his eyes, leaned back his head, and ladled water on himself.

"You will rest," he said, sardonically. "You will rest well, and you will know."

The springs were most popular at the midday and sunset hours. It was in the warm winter sunsets that Jesus and I walked the many paths through the good-smelling pines. In these twilight hours, we could sometimes see the disciples taking the waters: alone, in pairs, in groups. Here, at Callirrhoe, they seemed quite apart from us.

At the inn where we stayed, there was a small library of papyrus book-rolls, most of them in Greek, but some in Hebrew, some in Arabic, and some in Latin. One night, after a stew of turkey-flesh, barley, dates, and root vegetables, with big-torn pieces of fresh hot bread to soak in the stew's broth and wipe clean our bowls—I will not forget this meal, or the Roman wine we drank with it—I settled into a reading-chair by the library lamp and drew open the first scroll of the epistles of Horace. This was an old book, published in the tenth year of the reign of Augustus; but I was unfamiliar with it. I was absorbed well into the night, and in the hot springs at daybreak, I told Jesus of the seven words of Horace that could be translated into Greek as: "Shame is not in having played, but in not knowing when to break off the play."

Jesus looked straight ahead, into the rising vapors and trees, quite intently. After a while, he said:

"I wonder where the fat man and his slave are. They are usually here by now."

He did not speak again until we heard the approach of the fat man and his slave.

"The slave looks to me like a Jew," he said. "Yes. He is a very dark-complexioned Jew. I am certain. But what of the fat man? Do you think the fat man is also a Jew?"

"His features are much distorted and deformed by the fat of his face," I said. "It is hard to tell what he is."

"Is he circumcised?"

"I cannot tell from here."

"Nor can I. And what of his nose? It is a prodigious snout, to be sure; but I cannot say if it is a Jewish or a Roman snout."

"It is, as you say, prodigious, but it is difficult to distinguish beyond that. Again, all his features are deformed by his fat."

"If only we could hear him speak. We should know then, by his language, or by the inflection of it. But he is a very silent man."

"Yes," I said. "That he is. A very fat and very silent man is he."

"And does this Horace still live?" he asked, in the same tone he had been using, and still looking straight ahead, into the vapors and the trees and late-most dark and early-most light.

"No," I said. "He was born under Pompey, in the time of the Republic, before the first triumvirate. He died in the twenty-third year of the reign of Augustus, leaving behind him the most beautiful lyric odes in all of Roman poetry."

I told him more about the poet, his life and his poetry, and how the two were often inextricable.

"So," he said, "we were both born by the time this Quintus Horatius Flaccus breathed his last."

"We were."

"And what sort of playing do you feel he was talking about? The sort of play we knew as little boys, or this grander play that we have undertaken as men?"

"I believe his words struck me last night because I took them to refer to grander play. He was talking of the ways of men, not of boys. He was, of course, not speaking of our game, but it was my own preoccupation with our game that brought his words to bear on it, and on us."

He slowly and thoughtfully repeated the words as I had given them to him.

"Are you once again," he asked, "thinking that we should end the game? I am not saying that there is not much sage truth in what your Horace said. I am saying only that his *when* is a very big word, vast as the horizon and unclear as the moment that day turns to night, or night to day."

We closed our eyes to the world, surrendering every atom of ourselves to the balmy, limb-loosening spring.

"You have rested well, these recent days?" I asked, my eyes still closed.

"I have," he said, sounding as if he, too, spoke with closed eyes.

"We have rested well. We have eaten well. We have slept well."

"Yes," he said, sounding as if not only were his eyes closed, but there was also a far-away smile on his lips.

"So tell me what happened at Bethany."

To my surprise, he answered as if his eyes were still closed, the smile still on his lips.

"One plays a role too intently, and for too long. He becomes subsumed by the role. Unseen by him, unknown to him, the role enters him, takes tendril-hold, and grows within him. It conflicts with the truth of his nature. It causes an imbalance, a turmoil, in him. This conflict, this imbalance, this turmoil, is a madness of sorts.

"In Bethany, I played no role. I told you that in threatening to give them what they wanted, I showed them the detestable wrong-ness of their craving for miracles, their desire for what is against nature. When I told you this, I half-believed it. And then I told you that I did not know why I did what I did. And when I told you this, I fully believed it. I did not know. Now I know."

I heard the sound of him ladling spring-water over his head, once, then again.

"In Bethany, I acted madly."

I let him hear the sound of me ladling spring-water over my head, once, then again.

His voice came again, in a different tone:

"The fat man's slave," he said, "is as thin as the fat man is fat."

I opened my eyes to find him peering once again, now in increased light, through the vapors and trees.

"When do you see the play ending?" I asked him.

"At the moment we spit in the eye of God, in the eyes of all who believe or pretend to believe in God. At the moment we break into the Holy of Holies in the Temple of Jerusalem, and spit on the Ark of the Covenant."

As he spoke, I thought: His madness has not passed, but has deepened. It took me a moment to realize that there was no substance in what he said. One could not spit in the eye of that which did not exist, nor could one spit in the eye of every Jew. And there was no way for any man but the high priest to enter the sanctum sanctorum of the Holy Temple, and even he, the *cohen gadol,* could enter it only once a year, on the Day of Atonement.

In the instant after he spoke his madness and these thoughts came upon me, I immediately saw that there was not only no substance in his words, but also no gravity; for he burst out in laughter, and his bright eyes danced.

I shook my head in relief from the momentary distress he had brought me, and my own laughter followed his.

"Just a gesture," he said. "That is all. Just a small, fanciful bead of spittle well-aimed."

"And what might the manifestation of this fanciful spitting be?" I asked him.

We were no longer laughing, but still we smiled. We took to ladling water on our heads again.

"You are the designer and the composer," he said. "You tell me."

I said nothing. After a while, he spoke again:

"Maybe that is what your Horace meant: that one must know to end the play before folly becomes a madness that does not pass."

We watched the dim figure of the fat man rise laboriously from his spring with the aid of his slave.

"I do not wish to pursue madness," said Jesus. "You might say that I wish merely to test the limits."

I made a show of weighing and pondering this comment with due consideration; but all the while was merely waiting to tell him what I said next:

"Soon after the epistle containing those words of Horace, he ends another epistle with a statement of even fewer words."

Jesus looked to me.

"And what is that?" he asked.

I gave him in Greek the meaning of the poet's terse, blunt words:

"Death is the limit that ends everything."

Now it was his turn to weigh and ponder words with due consideration. But his weighing and pondering were no show, but real.

"I thought we were in the business of eternity, which has no limits."

"No man, nor any of his gods, nor any living thing, is in that business. Not unless one thinks of wind and storm and sky, of cosmos and chaos, as living things."

"What business, then, are we in?"

"There is only one business. Call it what you would. Deceit. Greed. Filth. It is all the same. He who does business is he who lies. He who does business is he who steals. All business is shit, and he who does business is he who wallows in shit: eating it, regurgitating it, and, all the while, squealing deceit.

"We are men of business, like all the rest. Business. That is all. Simply business.

"To live, unless one is wealthy, one must be either a whore or a slave. Both whores and slaves can buy their freedom and be wealthy. Fortunate are we who have a choice between whoredom and slavery. But there are dangers."

"Dangers," he said, lackadaisically.

"Riches are beautiful things." I was certain that these too were the words of Horace. They were not from my reading in the epistles the night before. But I was sure that he had written them, though I could not remember where. I said them as if they were my own.

"Riches can buy us freedom. The danger is that greed and the love of money overtake all else. The danger is that we lose sight of the freedom we set out to buy, forfeit it, and instead become enslaved to an endless whoredom."

"There was a time," he said, "when you spoke of riches unimagined. A time when you spoke of shaping a new sect that would subsume all other sects, and would collect share and tribute from all the usurers of Jerusalem. That would displace even the gods of the gentiles. You spoke of a temple in Rome.

"These things made me then to think that you were mad. Now it is you who see me as mad."

"Maybe I was mad. Maybe we both have been mad. The control of usury. Priests and temples. All my wild talk back then. But we do have the riches of which we dreamt."

"And do you recall what we said of dreams? That there are no sweet dreams?"

"We spoke of sleeping-dreams, not of day-dreams, reveries, imaginings in the air."

"You were rich when we began," he said.

"And now I am richer more than twice over. And you. You who were sleeping with mice and rats in the dirty doorways of Caesarea. You now can sleep in a villa befitting an aristocrat in Rome. And you can have your asshole groomed every day."

His chest and lips moved with a slight wan laugh. "But Rome is your home," he said.

"And it will be yours."

He shook his head sadly. "I have no home. I was born here, but there is nowhere here that feels to me like home."

"Rome will be your home."

Again he shook his head sadly.

"And how," I asked, "should home feel?"

"Good," he said. "Home should feel good."

"That home is inside you. If you feel good, your home is good. If you feel bad, your home is bad. We have nostalgia most for what we have never known. We most miss what we have never had."

"But we have had our delicious times, haven't we?"

"That we have. And let me assure you, my friend: you make a damned good Messiah."

"Do you not want to go on for just a little more? A bit more money, a few more delicious moments, before sailing away?" he asked.

I confessed that I did. I recalled the feeling that had struck me when I took our money to Caesarea, the feeling that we should ride our mare farther and farther on; the feeling that these fleeting days were for the seizing, and that Rome awaited always.

"How much longer do you want to go on?" I asked him.

"Not much longer."

"Before, when I was talking in a lofty way, I spoke of dangers. There are more down-to-earth dangers, I think."

"Such as what?"

"Such as those rumors following your escapade at Bethany. The rumors that you had been reported to the religious authorities. What if such rumors are true?"

"Raising the dead is not forbidden in the Book. It is told that the prophet Elisha raised the dead. And if the modern priests of the law in Jerusalem now look down upon it, those who were to report it would also be implicating themselves and their fellow townsmen, as it was they who implored me."

"I mean to say only that such rumors can serve as thorns," I explained. "I feel that the noise of your renown has reached the ears of the religious authorities in Jerusalem. I feel that they frown on a Messiah who is embraced by the people of Judea. I feel that they find him something of a threat to their sovereignty over the people. Such thorns could prick them and stir them to strike out."

"Strike out in what way?" he asked.

I shrugged, and he seemed to dismiss any and all concern for the authorities.

"So, then," I said. "How much longer?"

I could not tell if he was thinking or hesitating. Then he gave me his answer.

"Pesach."

This seemed a poetically fitting end.

And, in truth, it was impractical to think of returning to Rome until the Pesach, after the calends of April, the feast-day of Venus the Changer of Hearts.

You will soon witness this, I hope. It really is something to see her cult image brought from her temple to the men's baths, disrobed, caressingly bathed in warm water by her alluring female attendants, and garlanded with sweet-scented myrtle. What a lovely way to welcome the warm, verdant days.

It was impractical for reasons of nature. The long northwest passage against the wind from Caesarea to Rome, which could take more than seven weeks — far longer than the leeward passage of ten or so days from Rome to Caesarea — under the best of conditions, in late spring and early summer, could take much longer before then. Furthermore, the late fall and the winter months were so fraught with violent, wrecking storms and rages of sea and wind, that the number of sailings was much reduced in number, occasioned only by essential communications. Crossings were simply too bitterly dangerous in winter. We had not endured and thrived this long only to perish at sea while watching the land we had looted turn into a speck and disappear on the horizon.

And, as I have said, Pesach seemed a very poetically fitting end.

"He who is the Anointed One wishes to extend his ministry until the Pesach," I said, and felt a smile spread slowly on my face. "And so Pesach it will be."

He appeared quite contented, and he laid back his head into the water, looking into the morning sky above.

Through the trees, others could now be seen making their ways along the quiet piny paths that led to the springs.

The caw of an unseen crow could be heard.

"And where should the Messiah like to spend the Pesach?" The smile still lingered on my face.

"Jerusalem."

I said not a word. I hoped that I had not put this into his head with all my talk of the authorities, which he had dismissed out of hand.

"And why Jerusalem?" I asked.

"Why not?"

28

AND, TO BE SURE, THERE WERE MORE GOOD TIMES. DELICIOUS times, as he called them. One dark starry night, in the cool, gently sloping hills east of Moab, I administered, under cover of wine and dainty-cake, a considerable dose of opium to the tick Andreas. I did this for my own amusement, and in the hope that he might unwittingly reveal something of his true nature, which he did his best to keep hidden.

I told Jesus what I was up to. We agreed that, if the tick's behavior became too strange, we should play it by ear as to how Jesus would explain it to the other disciples, by declaring that Andreas either was possessed by a demon or, depending on the direction of his strange behavior, was entranced by divine rapture.

Alas, our Andreas was so tightly closed in on himself that, after a brief phase of noticeable ataraxy, he merely entered into a state of panic. His eyes wide, his breath rapid but wordless, he was immobilized. "Something tries to claim him," Jesus said. The others gave their theories, some of which did indeed involve the demonic, but none of which ventured rapture.

The tick remained in his rigid panic for a good while. The peace of sweet dreams was not open to him. Then, in cold sweat, he fell fast asleep.

The entertainment I had anticipated turned out to be slight at best. And, no matter how much Jesus and I tried to lure him, he revealed nothing of what was within him. Nothing, that is, of

what lay beneath his fear, dread, and terror, which were manifest
in full. Otherwise, he was as a dull stone unmoved by a passing
earthquake. Looking down on him, the Lord said, seemingly for
lack of anything better to say:

"May the beloved disciple learn from this that, while evil and
dangers lurk all about us, those who would follow the Word and
the Way are not easily snatched up."

"Amen," said I.

The next morning, Andreas spoke much of his struggle with
the demon, and his conquest over it.

"It was the presence of our Lord that made the demon flee,"
the rabbi said to him.

"Yes, of course it was," said the tick. There was in his voice a
momentary hint of awkward reticence, which vanished as he said:
"And my faith in our Lord did not waver through the battle."

There was a wedding at a place near Salim that some called
Cana and others called by different names. Looking toward the
small feast, Jesus recognized the groom, a young man he remembered from our visit to Nazareth. Then his eyes fell on another he
knew from Nazareth.

It was his own mother on whom his eyes fell.

Before being seen by any at the feast, Jesus told us to go ahead
of him and join those who feasted. He would return after a solitary prayer that would be his spiritual gift to the handsome young
bride and groom. He veered off with Hope in tow, and soon was
among us again.

His mother looked to him with melancholy, and seemed ever
on the verge of saying something to him.

I could not keep from smiling with playful malice as he
brought forth from Hope's packsaddle the magical amphora that
I had purchased in Caesarea as a jest.

The feast had fallen quiet, as word had passed among them

that the Messiah was with them, and their blessed event was now doubly blest.

With two hands, he placed the brightly glazed amphora on the ground, and he removed the lid from it. He called to the servant of the feast to bring water to fill the vessel.

"I wish to share a cup of most precious wine with the bride and groom," he announced.

I watched him, then looked all round. I wondered if any of these rustics knew of the juggler's trick of the magical amphora. It was familiar to many in Rome, but I had been told by the merchant who had sold it to me that it was the only one in the province.

"Please," our Lord said to the steward, "fill well the jug." The servant returned with a waterskin and poured water from it into the false belly of the amphora. Jesus replaced the lid and bowed his head for a moment. Curiosity rippled through the hush.

"Please," our Lord said to the steward, "bring three cups. The bride's, the groom's, and one for myself."

The cups were brought. Slyly plugging the hidden water-hole with the thumb of his right hand, and bracing the amphora between his knees, he tilted it, and lovely red wine flowed from its open lip into the cup he held to it with his left hand.

The feast was suddenly quiet no longer. The rejoicing for the bride and groom became rejoicing for the Nazarene who was the Son of God.

Blessing all, Jesus raised his cup and drank. The bride and groom raised their cups and drank, and proclaimed that never before had there been a wine of such delight and grace. Jesus filled his cup again and gave it to an elder to be passed round and tasted. And all agreed that never before had there been a wine of such delight and grace. In truth, the wine was from a barrel of common Roman draught with which we had filled our wineskin at a shop in Aenon.

Yes, the Nazarene who was the Son of God. And of the aging woman who looked to him with melancholy, and who seemed ever to want to say something to him. Did others here know that he was her son? Did she claim to others that he was her son? Did those in Nazareth who remembered him as a boy, remember him as her son? Had she laid the past to silence, as he had done?

It was the sound of her voice that ended my thoughts. She was near him, the both of them somewhat apart from the rest. Her voice spoke only his Hebrew name. What lay in that voice was hard to discern. Love? A desire to forgive, or to be forgiven? Regret? Need? Perhaps even doubt as to his identity? It could have been a longing for something, or an expression of something. Whatever it was, that something that was to be heard in the utterance of her voice, it was unknowable. It may have been unknown, unknowable even by her son, even by her. All it evinced was a vulnerability, and nothing else.

What happened next was like a dazing blow. It must have stunned her to the quick.

From where I leaned, I could see him turn to face her; and those eyes of his were no longer like those eyes of his. They were the cold, untelling brown eyes of a hooded cobra roused and risen to strike. And strike he did.

His voice was one of low, chill, cadenced heartlessness, devoid of mercy, or pity, or any human quality other than inhumanity, that most defining trait of what we loftily call humanity:

"Woman, what have I to do with you?"

Her weeping was terrible to witness, but he beheld her as if her tears and sobs were sweet rain and song.

"I never knew you," he said. "Depart from me." Then he turned his back to her and drew close to me. "Judge not"—he spoke sternly, seeming to believe that I had pronounced silent sentence upon him, and that I had done this in ignorance and in prejudice — "lest you be judged."

His low voice now came through clenched teeth, like an aggressive hissing.

"Lovely words," he concluded in that same voice. "I seem to remember them from somewhere."

I should have slapped him. But I could not, because of the disciples, some of whom were walking toward us; because of the rest who were present.

His apologies came only after the day turned to night, and the wedding feast was well behind us. He neither explained nor offered excuses, but simply asked my forgiveness.

I thought of that nonsense of mine about turning the other cheek. I thought of the whispering man in Narbata: the whispering man with the withered arm and the unfortunate daughter.

My curiosity was such that I asked him to tell me more than he had about his mother and him. But all he would say was that there was nothing more to tell. He stared into the little dancing flames of our modest fire. Or, more accurately, he kept his eyes trained on them.

I studied him that night for a long time. He was conscious of my scrutiny. Finally, with a deep sigh, he walked off by himself. Later a few of the disciples asked me where he was.

"He went in solitude to pray for his mother," I told them.

"Is she ill?" one of them asked.

"I believe so."

"It is difficult to picture him as having a mother."

"Yes," I said. "It truly is."

"I shall pray for her as well," said the tick. "Oh, how our Lord must love all mothers, and most dearly his own."

"Yes," I said, "let us all pray for her before we sleep this night."

I spat casually into what was left of the fire. I longed for the springtime, and for that galley bound for Rome. I thought of what Jesus had said of his behavior in Bethany: "I acted madly." Did he feel that he had acted madly against his mother and me at the wedding feast? There was no telling, even, if he was or was not drifting into madness outright, full and fulsome. Why did I ally myself to men prone to madness? Was I one of them?

These were unpleasant musings. It was an unpleasant night, a humid and unpleasant and sleepless night.

No, not all of our times were delicious times, as he called them. Far from it. But they were times such as few men have ever tasted.

The month of Janus was on us: the month of the old two-faced god of the beginnings and ends of wars and peaceful respites from them. It was time to return to Caesarea. Payment was due on the earnings from my deposit of creditum. These earnings must be placed in a separate account, apart from the shared fortune belonging to Jesus and me in equal parts, his half on deposit, by his decision, as vacua pecunia, accruing no interest through usury, and my half, by my decision, as creditum, which benefitted, with small risk, from the ways and wiles of the money-lenders.

My interest amounted to more than sixty thousand sesterces, representing a return of fifteen per centum after the subtraction of the fees of the argentarius and the share of the profits claimed by the usurers. All of this was minutely detailed in the agent's ledgers. I did not care if these ledgers reflected the truth. Sixty thousand sesterces was sufficient truth to satisfy me. I arranged to have the principal of my creditum redeposited as vacua pecunia, and the interest from the principal to be deposited in a new account as creditum. I also deposited into the account of our mutual riches what new-temple money we had collected in recent months, an additional hundred and three thousand sesterces, which brought the total sum of our fortune to almost nine hundred and twenty thousand sesterces.

I left Caesarea this time carrying no jestful gifts from the jugglers'-goods shop.

As arranged, I met him at Hyrcania, east of the Dead Sea. He wanted to give a sermon to the Essenes. Hyrcania was very close to their main community, at Qumran.

I had questioned him about the prudence of this. These austere men had no money. But he was adamant.

"We both know that we have enough money. And in the towns after Qumran, there will be more money, a great deal more. We shall leave Jerusalem with Faith, Hope, and Charity burdened full."

"If money is not your motive in preaching to the Essenes, what is?"

"I am sick of the rabble who seek miracles. I am sick of those who want the dead to be raised, and demons to be exorcized. I am weary of those who believe in a God who shows himself through cheap jugglers' tricks."

"If you are sick and weary of the rabble, let us breathe free of everything and await spring in feasting and ease. We are as good as in Rome now, but for the storms at sea and your desire to visit Jerusalem.

"Besides," I said, "is not God himself but a cheap jugglers' trick? What do you expect from those who believe in him? All of the fine orations of the Word and the Way, they are taken to mean all manner of things by all manner of fools. The time for silence is at hand."

At Hyrcania, when he heard of the Lord's intention, even Aaron, our former Sadducee priest, modestly advised him that the tenets of the Essenes were held by them with such inviolable self-righteousness that the Word and the Way might be met with hostility at Qumran. The rigor of their beliefs could very well offer no tolerance.

"Nonsense," said Jesus. "Minds that pursue the mystical are always, by nature, open to that which is unknown to them." After a pause, he spoke again: "Furthermore, as you know, the Essenes forbid themselves the expression of anger."

Aaron held his tongue, sighing instead of saying whatever more was on his mind.

Simon Peter remarked that the idea of being surrounded by Essenes intimidated him, but added that when he was with Jesus, nothing frightened him.

I found it odd that, after our rest at Callirrhoe, on the other side of the Dead Sea, instead of winding down and looking toward Rome, Jesus seemed to be increasing his energies toward a climactic conclusion preceding our departure.

His self-aware confessions of acting madly, speaking madly, and being subsumed by the role he played were like vexing tidal currents, whose directions could not be predicted. Then a terrible notion struck me.

"Are you coming to believe in God?"

"Have you injured your head? Of course not." He laughed softly but deeply. "But I am beginning to believe in something," he said, looking off into the dusk. I followed his eyes and saw rosy wisps lighted with golden hues, and blue becoming violet-blue, and the colors of nacre imbuing the white of clouds.

"In what are you beginning to believe?"

"A truth," he said. "A certain and absolute truth."

"Do you wish to share with me this truth, so that I can make composition on it, or do you wish me to invent one on my own, or re-state one of the many fanciful absolute truths of our established repertoire?"

"The means to express it are almost risen to my lips. When I can express it, you will know it."

"Oh, come now. What is this?" In exasperation, I threw to his face with sarcasm the lofty lying words he had used so long ago, in Simonias, to tell the priest of how God spoke to him: "The voice speaks in elemental tones that are not words and yet are words."

He did not bristle at the exasperation or sarcasm in my tone. He merely continued to behold the changing colors and light of the dusk. To me, these were the changing colors and light of those unpredictable tidal currents that vexed me. In them, like a haunting, were the tints and shades and hints of madness and the insinuations of unfolding futures at play.

"This has nothing to do with any God," he said. His voice could not have been more calm or more gentle.

I looked into his eyes, which did not respond to my gaze. They were not the eyes of the man who once upon a time, at the inn at Caesarea, had run his dirty fingers over the handle of the dagger in his sash. I well remembered the lie of innocence in those soft, pale-brown eyes that had struck me the moment I chanced on them, those eyes that did not see the greater games, the greater gains that were their destiny.

The eyes I now beheld were even softer, more luminous, more mesmerizing, more deeply wed to destiny. We had won our great game, and the gains were ours. But I had an unsettling feeling that I had been drawn into another game, a game whose essence eluded me, a game whose movements were not mine to control.

"So," I said, "your pronouncement to these high holy cave-dwellers will be written. I shall begin composition tonight. Should the elemental tones of your certain and absolute truth come to your lips, do be so kind as to let me know."

"Please, my friend, take your rest tonight. My words are not so fine and well-wrought as yours. It is your words that have carried us to where we are. It is you who are the true and undenied master of the means by which we have prospered. But, please, tonight, take your rest.

"I will let issue from my mouth at Qumran that which will issue from my mouth."

I was displeased, and also felt a twinge of dejection. It was as if I were being dismissed. He had taken increasingly to extemporizing his own words, and to revising mine. But this was unprecedented in all of our journeying together. Was the puppet dispatching the puppeteer to the audience? Was I of diminished importance to him in this vague new game whose essence escaped me?

"It matters not to me," I said with a shrug. We had started out together as untrusting strangers, but we had become close and friends. I should have made known to him my true feelings, but I did not. Things are not always as they should be. It was not good, in the moments of that dusk, that I knew not what was in him, and he knew not what was in me.

I felt a sadness, and there seemed to be a sadness in him, too.

Hyrcania was unfortified, and after dark became a lawless sort of place. There were roving bands of drunkards, and of Zealots, and whores of both sexes called out from dim-lighted windows. From the inn where we stayed, with some of the disciples sleeping in the stable to look after Faith, Hope, and Charity, we could hear sporadic yells, whoops, and wicked laughter through much of the night. After one disturbance, I heard Faith bray. We had been so long with our three beasts that we had come to distinguish their noises, one from another, especially those of our old dun jack, Faith, who had been with us since we had set out on the road.

The growing strangeness that had long been felt in the air was back upon us: that eeriness of days whose every breeze seemed to whisper foreboding, whose every stillness seemed to bear presentiment, and whose every aspect seemed to possess a darkening shadow. There were nights when it seemed that the sun would never rise again, and black eternity, or death, could be heard like a distant groan deep down in the ground. Dogs barked at what men did not see.

29

AFTER YOU HAVE LEFT THE WAYS OF YOUTH BEHIND YOU, MY cherished boy, you will see that people are like sheep to the shepherd's crook. To possess and wield well the shepherd's crook is to hold sway over the herd of sheep that are those who believe. It matters not in what they believe.

How similar the crook to the *lituus,* the rod used by our Roman augurs in their divinations. And how similar, in turn, to augury and divination are the religions of men's folly. Sheep are sacrificed, and the quivering entrails of sheep are read to divine the future.

Wolves swim among the sheep, as Ovid says. Be always a wolf, never a sheep.

The Essenes we encountered at Qumran were like all other sheep to the slaughter. They differed only in the chosen mode, or fashion, of their bondage and their sheepishness. The thousand or so of them, from Qumran itself and from the En-Gadi caves to the south of Qumran, did in fact resemble a vast gathering of sheep. Their plain woolen garments were all of the same once-white weathered gray. They were all bearded; and no matter their ages, their beards and the hair on their heads seemed to be of the same drab gray, or streaked with it. Their countenances, of earnest and sullen castings, were all the same. Indeed, to look at the thousand or so of them was to see one, and to look at one of them was to see the thousand or so of them. This effect of their sameness was increased all the more by the fact that they were all men, as the Essenes allowed no women among them.

Jesus stood before them and raised his staff. Why had I not until now noticed that it was a shepherd's crook? Was it new? If it was, I was not with him when he had bought it, or been given it, or had stolen it from a shepherd asleep in a pasture.

Behind him rose the limestone cliffs of this place, and the plastered marl caves that were like silent open mouths in the pallid faces of these cliffs.

He spoke in a way that lent each of his words a monoepic gravity. This manner of speaking seemed reflective of the manner of their own solemn thought patterns, and lulled them into expecting the sum of his words to be other than it was:

"I have come here, among you, because I have heard that this is a good place to seek a wife."

There was silence, like that from the mouths of the cliff faces. Then one in the thousand or so of them laughed deep from his gut. Then others of them laughed. Then many of them laughed. Then the air shook with resounding laughter like a roar.

These earnest, sullen men appeared suddenly less earnest, less sullen. They seemed to seek more laughter in his words. But it was not to be.

Jesus did not smile to them, even as they smiled to him. The rhythm of his speech did change, however, forsaking all affectation as he resumed, after the last of their laughter fell to stillness:

"The God who is my Father will have no more of Pharisee, or of Sadducee, or of Essene, or of any sect. All of those who are of sects are as Philistines before him, and their division of the house of David will no longer be suffered. The Way is not to be argued. The Way is not to be contended. The Way is not to be cleft. Rock that is smitten and sundered has no strength, and only of solid rock will the new temple of my Father be built.

"But, I have said to the God who is my father, the men known as Essenes, the silent ones, the pious ones; they are of no sect, for they are seekers and keepers of truth, which is of no sect and can be not hewn and can be not sundered.

"To all, I have said: Renounce your sect, dear brothers, as the God who is my Father has renounced it. There is one Word. There is one Way. Embrace these, or be gone.

"To you, I say: I have within me messages that I have been entrusted to deliver. I would that all the world might understand the truth of their meaning. But I feel that only you, my brothers who are gathered here today, might understand this truth. If only some among you do, and reveal it to those whom it escapes, I will not have spoken in vain. This is why I have come here on this day.

"I say unto you these things as they have been given unto me to say them:

"The Pharisees and the scribes have taken from people the keys to knowledge, and have hidden them. They have not entered, and nor have they allowed those who want to enter to do so. Woe to the Pharisees. As for you, be you as clever as snakes, and as innocent as doves.

"May all who have ears to hear, may they hear.

"If it is said to you, 'Whence have you come?' say 'We have come from the light, from where the light came into being by itself, established itself, and appeared in an image of light.'

"May all who have ears to hear, may they hear.

"A disciple has asked me: Is circumcision meaningful? I have answered him: If it were, a father would produce children already circumcised from their mother. But rather, it is the circumcision of the spirit that is meaningful in every regard.

"May all who have ears to hear, may they hear.

"Blessed are the poor, for theirs is the kingdom of heaven. If you have money, do not lend it at interest. Give it, rather, to someone who will not return it to you.

"There was a rich farmer who had a great deal of money. He said: 'I shall invest my money so that I may sow, reap, plant, and fill my storehouses with harvest. Then I shall have everything.' These were his plans. But that very night, the farmer died.

"May all who have ears to hear, may they hear.

"Whoever does not hate father and mother cannot follow me; and whoever does not hate brother and sister, and does not bear the cross as I do, will not be worthy of me.

"Whoever recognizes father and mother will be called the child of a whore.

"May all who have ears to hear, may they hear.

"Whoever has come to know the world has discovered a carcass, and whoever has discovered a carcass is worth more than all the world.

"May all who have ears to hear, may they hear."

"A woman in a crowd did say to me: 'Blessed are the womb that bore you, and the breasts that fed you.' I said to her: 'Blessed are the womb that has not conceived and the breasts that have not produced milk.'

"May all who have ears to hear, may they hear.

"Give Caesar what is Caesar's. Give God what is God's. Give me what is mine.

"May all who have ears to hear, may they hear."

He stopped. There was no movement but for that of the soft white clouds in the deep-blue sky. Slowing slightly the pace of his words, so that it seemed to be one with that of the clouds, he said,

"If you bring forth what is within you, what you bring forth will save you. If you do not bring forth what is within you, what you do not bring forth will destroy you."

Like all who were there, I was swept away, mystified, by the sublime majesty and terror of these final words. If this were madness, I thought, what a beautiful madness it was.

The weathered gray men in their weathered gray garments converged gently toward him, and many bowed, and many embraced him, and some knelt and made strange signs unto him.

Most of what he had said, I understood, if only because I knew him so well. Some of it I had heard before. Some of it I recognized as nothing more than flourishes of the decorative abstract ambiguities he had found in my compositions for him, and had taken to imitating. Some of it I recognized as my own words.

But the final two sentences he had spoken were what had swept away and mystified us all with their sublime majesty and terror. So great was their effect that it took some time for those present to come to the realization that they had no idea as to the meaning of these words. It occurred to one of the gray men to humbly ask him for clarification, but he responded only by telling him that there was no mystery in the words of his closing sentences.

"Seek," he told the man, "and you will find. And you will be saved, or you will be destroyed."

Later, I asked him, less humbly, as much as the gray man had asked him. I was not pleased to hear him tell me as much as he had told the gray man.

"Did you speak of something or of nothing when you said those words?" I demanded of him.

"I spoke not only of something, but indeed of something in you that will either save you or destroy you. Something within me that will either save me or destroy me. Something in all that will either save them or destroy them."

"So you would play your game of riddles even with me," I said.

"It is no riddle," he said. "It is the way I found to express the truth I told you about. It is the sum of that truth. Please, Gaius, do not think about the words. Let them flow through your mind. You will feel their meaning, and you will tell it to me."

We came away from Qumran with a new disciple, one of the younger Essenes, not yet so gray. Jesus called him "the twin of none." This became simply the Twin, the Aramaic and Hebrew words for which were then rendered into Greek as Thomas, the name that I and the others often knew him by. He was a studious man, but the air about him was not heavy with the usual dust of scholars.

Fishermen, the former Sadducee priest and rabbi, a Roman gentile, who knew what else; and now a strayed Essene. Our motley band grew ever more motley.

We made good money at Selim, and at Sychar, and at Arus, and Mahnayim, and at Tirathana.

In the hills near Arus, we came upon a small group of naked foragers who spoke no known tongue. At a pond near Mahnayim, we saw a two-headed snake. In the woods south of Selim, we heard a baby crying, but we could find no baby.

Once again, my composings became his pronouncements; and it was in these towns that Jesus spoke of our sheep to the slaughter, saying at Arus:

"The thief cometh not, but for to steal, and to kill, and to destroy. I am not that thief. I am the thief that bears the key, the thief that giveth. I am come that you might have life, and that you might have it more abundantly. I am the good shepherd."

And saying at Tirathana:

"My sheep hear my voice, and I know my sheep, and they follow me. And I give unto them eternal life; and they will never perish. Neither shall any man pluck them out of my hand. My Father, who gave them me, is greater than all; and no man is able to pluck them out of my Father's hand. And I and my Father are one.

"I am the way. I am the truth. I am the life. No man cometh unto the Father, but by me."

The more we belittled them, the more we called them sheep, the more they liked it. For they were sheep.

People seemed to give not according to their means, but as if they were governed by the phase of the moon, or by some immanence in the air they breathed.

His bewildering words about that which was within us that would either save us or destroy us stayed with me, like a haunting.

One moonless night, in the Beth Shan Valley, when silver clouds obscured many stars, we sat together searching the sky to find the Ear of Wheat in the Virgin's left hand, which the Jews see as a Branch, also in the hand of a celestial Virgin.

We were as true brothers in blood beneath that sky. As our eyes journeyed through it, together seeking, we seemed to breathe beyond time and place. I recalled the melancholy dusk at Hyrcania, when I should have made known to him my true feelings, but I did not; when I knew not what was in him, and he knew not what was in me; and this was not good, and I had felt a sadness, and there had seemed to be in him a sadness as well.

"The truth," I said now, under the stars of the Virgin that could be seen. "It is the truth."

"What is?" He smiled to me.

"That which if you bring forth from within you will save you, and which if you do not bring forth from within you will destroy you."

"Yes," he said happily. "It is the truth of one's self. It is that which most men never find; that which most of the few who do find it, do fear to bring from secrecy to open light.

"Most men live their entire lives without once ever meeting

themselves; and when one does encounter one's self, he keeps him unseen and imprisoned in the dark within."

"Know thyself," I said. The words of Thales. Or of another. Or of many.

"And then expel thy self," he said. "Reveal thy self. Let loose the shame of thy self."

The words of Jesus. The words of no other.

"Free your self," he said, "that you might live in full and without knowing cowardice or fear; that your breath might be your own, liberated, unburdened by bondage, and strong. Set free the truth, and it will set you free."

Some nights later, the first slender light of the moon of Nissan appeared. In the mornings that followed, the pink and crimson flowers in the buds of the Judas trees, whose branches were still bare of leaves, began to be seen. Returning steppe eagles and ospreys became numerous in the skies. White storks became numerous in calm waters; small, flitting, bright warblers, numerous in the trees. The zephyrs of the spring caused every emerging blade and leaf to dance. The rains that fell were light and pleasant. Almond trees and apricot trees began to flower with white petals that drank the dew.

The unsettling sense of strangeness, the foreboding in the air of a world descending to dark, wild madness, that Jesus and I had felt increasingly for so very long, almost from the beginning, was a feeling we shared. We spoke of it often. Was it us, or was it something very real, this adumbrated world that we perceived around us, and through which we felt ourselves to be moving, toward what sometimes seemed in fact the end of days? We wondered if others, those who traveled with us and those we encountered in the cities, towns, and settlements of our journeys, felt this growing strangeness in the air. Was it possible to be amid the wild twilight howlings of the ominous Messiah-mad streets of Caesarea, and not sense it?

Surely it was felt by many. Surely this was why crowds stirred as if ghosts swept past, caressing them with cold, deathly fingers, when he pronounced:

"I am the Alpha and the Omega, the beginning and the end, the first and the last."

It was the triad of unknown finality—the Omega, the end, the last—that chilled them, that evoked the ghosts. Here, shepherds and sheep were alike in the approach of dark, untelling clouds.

For a while, in the bud-shaking zephyrs of that spring, the deep strangeness was gone. Then we realized that we were only becalmed in the heart of it. The zephyrs were gone, and there was a vague, terrible stillness, an enveloping presentiment that made even the birds look about them.

The moon was waxing full. The days of Pesach were nearing. Descending to Jerusalem, through the foothills of the Mount of Olives, we entered, beyond Bethpage, a place of many burial caves. An old narrow bridge traversed a ravine. About midway on this suspended bridge of old boards and rope, the afternoon sky became dark as night, and we were overtaken by a great wind out of blackness.

The bridge, and all the world, shook. All seemed claimed, and about to be consumed, by this tremendous wind of blackness.

What the Jews call *kalil,* the Greeks call *olocaustos:* a whole, pure, and perfect sacrificial burnt offering to God.

This was not holocaust. It could only be called what was known in olden-most Hebrew by an obscure word connoting complete devastation, catastrophe, a laying waste, a destruction and a desolation. This Hebrew word of rare might and occurrence was unknown to most Jews. There is no Greek equivalent or rendering of it, but, unlike most Hebrew and Aramaic, it can be easily pronounced in our tongue: *soua,* with a long *o,* consonantal *u,* and short *a.* It is a word used by our dire Isaiah: "and *soua* shall come."

When I had first heard and learned of this word, I was struck by how alike its two syllables were to the penultimate and final syllables of the true name of Jesus. It was as if doom were embedded in his name.

No, this was not the beauty of holocaust. It was the horror of *soua.*

The wind from blackness ended, and the blackness lifted, and we had not perished, as we were sure we would perish. None of us, not even Faith, Hope, or Charity, lay broken on the rocks below.

We knew then that it was not *soua,* but only its gentlest hasty kiss of recognition and of welcome.

Soon Jerusalem rose before us on the spur of a plateau.

Jesus rested under a laurel tree. He instructed the disciples to seek a good spring and fill our skins with good water, that we might enter Jerusalem refreshed. For them to hear, he directed me to remain with him, to receive other instructions.

"Let us take the packsaddle from Hope. I will enter the city astride him."

I looked to him with tired confusion.

"It was written in the Book long ago," he said. "Long ago it was written that the true Messiah would enter Jerusalem astride the colt of an ass. I will fulfill prophecy. We do not have an ass-foal, but Hope is at least younger than old Faith. He will have to do."

"Don't you think that this will be overstating things a bit? Don't you think that such a show of fulfilling prophecy will appear to be, as it indeed is, too obviously of calculated design? I mean, there is a lack of subtlety here, to say the least."

"These people are fools."

I looked to him, no longer confused, but still tired. My questioning of his judgment showed in my face.

"They expect it," he said. "They want it."

He attempted a smile, but he was as tired as I. The passing bitter kiss of wrathful desolation had taken much from us. There were yet tremors in our hands.

"Trust me," he said.

The soft sunlight and breeze through the laurel branches belied the vanished black tempest.

"How do you feel about the composition? It will be your valediction."

"It is too mild. It says nothing, really. You have given me words for a politician, not a prophet."

"Heed me," I said. "This is neither the time nor the place to spew damnation on the Pharisees. Or to denounce usury. Or to speak of a new temple.

"You will enter Jerusalem as the Messiah and you will leave as my dutiful slave, bound with me for Rome. From here, moving at ease, we shall be in Caesarea in three days. Thence to Rome. Think of this as a farewell feast, nothing more."

Exasperation and calm reason alternated in my voice as I spoke.

"It ends here," he said.

There were slight insinuations of reluctance, reflection, and resigned acceptance in this simple statement of fact.

"Yes," I declared, trampling these insinuations flatly. "The meticulous grooming of your asshole lies ahead."

He laughed his light silent laugh.

"We are visiting Jerusalem only because you wish to do so. If entering it on a donkey makes you happy, so be it. Were it up to me, we should bypass it and go directly to Caesarea and the sea. Spring is here. A galley for Rome is likely weighing anchor right now, as we sit preparing to mount you on poor Hope so that you can play-act at fulfilling some lie of a nonsensical prophecy. I really do not understand this." I slowly shook my head. "For a wise man, you at times are like a child."

"Verily, I say unto you," he intoned, in light mockery of his accustomed pronouncement voice, "unless you become like little children, you will not enter into the kingdom of heaven."

"I was more than a bit drunk when I wrote that line. I hated it then, in Capernaum, where I wrote it; and I have hated it since."

At this, his light laughter was no longer silent. He made as if to murmur something. I made as if to murmur something. Then we fell quiet awhile. As the others began to return, I rose slowly and went to our Hope. I stroked his head, ran my fingers through his shaggy coarse mane, and unbuckled his cinch-strap.

I bent and kissed the donkey's forehead, and I threw the heavy packsaddle toward Jesus.

"Perhaps," he mused aloud, "the beloved disciple shall offer to anoint the beast's hooves with oil so that they might shine, and tend to the proper grooming of the beast's fundament as well."

The disciples looked to their Lord, then to me, then to one another. None of the self-fancying beloved disciples stepped forth. I cast him an evil eye, which had no evil in it.

"The bread of affliction awaits us," I said to the donkey, giving him one last pat.

The disciples looked to their Lord, then to me, then to the donkey, then to one another.

Jesus asked the disciples for directions to the nearest pure water, then went off to bathe and to prepare himself. He took with him the wooden comb I had given him a long time ago.

"Do they have good Roman wine in Jerusalem?" I asked Aaron, the former priest, who was of this city.

But the priest said nothing, and it was the rabbi Ephraim who answered.

"Yes" was all he said.

A fair soft rain began to fall. I closed my eyes and raised my face to it. I knew that it would soon end, and I took it as the pink and red petals of the Judas trees and the white petals of the almond trees and the apricot trees took the dew.

We entered Jerusalem late in the day after the last Sabbath preceding the full moon, as the colors of sunset began to come forth, in the sky and through the city. I saw Jesus try to draw deep breath, but his lungs or his ribs denied him. Then the masses were upon him, enclosing him.

30

O N OUR WAY TO THE CITY, WE HAD PASSED A FIG TREE. IT was not the season of figs, which would not come until the westerly breezes wove through the late summer heat. Even the first small green fruit-buds and leaves of fig trees would not appear until spring neared its end. Jesus knew this. Yet, when we came to the bare fig tree along our way to Jerusalem, he cast a curse on it because it bore no fruit. His curse on the tree was vehement. I should have taken this as a warning.

This happened not far from the grotto and gardens of Gethsemane, at the foot of Mount Olive, close to the ridge road that led to nearby Bethany, the house of unripe figs, the house of misery, where Jesus had committed atrocity at the tomb of Lazarus. In these peaceful natural gardens were many fig trees that were, as always at this season, also bare. Jesus cursed them as well, and all else that was unbloomed in this place of beauty. I should have taken this as further warning.

From the garden we could see the Holy Temple high above us. We crossed the Kidron Valley, and ascended the path to Jerusalem.

Entering Jerusalem, I saw that Jesus had spoken rightly when he said that these people were fools. Word moved very fast among them that the man astride the donkey was Jesus, the Messiah, of whom they long had heard, and whose arrival they long had expected here, in the city of the Holy Temple.

They came on us in a frenzy, like hyenas converging on a gazelle. Some pulled their cloaks from their shoulders and threw them to the ground, that the donkey that Jesus rode might make his path on them. Others strewed the path of garments with branches of sweet-scented rose and myrtle. In making this path, they also blocked it, so that movement forward on it was torturously slow. From the oppressive swarm came a yell:

"Hosanna to the son of David! Hosanna in the highest!" These people were wild with this cry of salvation, and it came from all round, resoundingly, repeatedly: "Hosanna!"

Another yelled:

"He comes as Zechariah prophesied: astride an ass! It is as the prophet said it would be."

Those who had cast their garments to the ground struggled to retrieve them after the donkey had trodden them, but thieves made off with many of them. The owner of one of the robes, finding a big stinking lump of donkey shit sticking thick and fast to it, interpreted this as a sign that he was blest.

The mob forced our direction and path, allowing us no way other than that which their confining, narrow parting permitted. We found ourselves beneath the towering Holy Temple, on the broad stone steps of the Temple mount that led to the first of the northwestern gates, the gate of entry for the line of Davidic kings. The mob pushed us onward, until we ascended the uppermost step to the courtyard terrace of this, the fifth of the Temple's thirteen gates. The crowd then spread out from Jesus on the paved expanse of the terrace, giving him air and freedom at the gate's colonnade. The mob overflowed onto the steps of the mount and into the streets below.

The people fell quiet. From where I stood, in the front row of those who surrounded him, I looked at their faces and wondered what they expected from him.

Jesus dismounted the donkey. He raised his shepherd's crook.

"Oh, Jerusalem!" he proclaimed. "Oh, you who have been made holy by this city! Oh, you who have made this city holy!"

The people hosannaed and roared anew. They reminded me of the crude, plebeian crowds at gladiatorial games, drunk with wine and blood-lust. Veins and eyes bulged in ugly, pock-marked faces. The smell of sweating, unwashed flesh was acrid.

"Hear me!"

Again they became quiet, tense, expectant.

He spoke to them in strange, skewed parabolic allegories. A tale of two sons, one of whom tended his father's vineyard and one who did not. A tale of evil tenant farmers who attacked and killed the servants and son of their landlord. A tale of an uninvited guest at the wedding feast of a king's son. A tale of a bridegroom and ten virgins, five of them wise, five of them foolish.

He tied these tales to the kingdom of God, and to the fallen, faithless ways of Israel.

These odd-cobbled little tales were simple and unclear at the same time. The people showed great enthusiasm for them, especially after Jesus told them what they were supposed to illuminate. I thought again of the plebeians at the games, roused by any action whatsoever, be it fatal or fumbling.

Hope had wandered off after Jesus had dismounted him, and I searched for him. Peter was tending the other two donkeys near the wall where we had entered the city. I wanted to find and bring Hope to him as well.

Suddenly I heard a great commotion. I turned round. Jesus was making for the open gate of the Holy Temple.

I rushed to him through the noisy crowd that followed him. He disappeared through the gate. Except for a daring few, the crowd did not proceed after him, but halted all at once, slowing the progress of my hurried steps. Finally, I was past the gate, in the inner courtyard, where money-lenders and sellers of sacrificial doves were busy with customers. Jesus was wandering in the midst of this commerce. He looked like one who was lost and confused. I was very close to him, almost close enough to reach out and place my hand to his shoulder, when, oblivious to me, he bellowed with such force as to frighten all around him, and me along with them.

"Defilers! My house will be called a house of prayer, but you make it a den of robbers."

With a loud storm of outward breath, he overturned the table of the money-lender nearest him, sending it crashing down. Coins flew, scattered, rang, and spun in every direction.

The money-lender drew back, as did other money-lenders at other tables. Some of the bird-sellers raised their cages to them so quickly and nervously that doves escaped, fluttering wildly, low and high and all around.

But several of the money-lenders converged on Jesus, took him down, beat him with fists, and kicked him. I could not risk using my dagger in this place, but I struck out at the men, and did gouge the eye of one and deliver good blows to another before I too was overtaken. Jesus had the worse of it, but he bled only a little, from his nose, and none of his bones were broken, so that together we were able to wrest ourselves free and take flight.

No one ran after us, and when we were out of the courtyard, we were safe. But still we hurried, breathing hard; and it was in our rush down the steps that we both fell and suffered greater injury than had been inflicted on us by the fists and sandals of the money-lenders. It was dark by this time, and we made our way to Peter without much notice. I had hurt my hip either in the scuffle or on the steps, and I was limping as we approached Peter. I heard Jesus laugh out loud. Thinking that he found my limp to be an entertainment, I felt anger rise within me. It was anger that emanated not only from the pain in my hip, but more from the events of this day, from the cursing of the fig trees to the outburst in the Temple. Or did it emanate from the day before? Or a year ago? Or when I first laid eyes on him? Now, in the very moment that I was about to turn my anger on him, I heard him say:

"I always wanted to do that."

His tone was one of serene and tranquil satisfaction.

It was then that I laughed too. I believed it meant that all was now done and over with: that we could piss on the walls of this city, get rid of these tiresome disciples, go to Caesarea, drink and feast, and sail finally for Rome.

But this ending was not to be.

Under moonlight, with Peter, we returned slowly to the gardens of Gethsemane. We had expected the other disciples to be waiting with Peter. He had expected them to be with us. None of us really cared where they were. Peter asked us about our time in Jerusalem. We told him about the money-lenders in the temple. He enjoyed hearing of it, and said that he wished he had been with us.

A few moments later, rubbing his shoulder, Jesus spoke in a different tone:

"I think one of those money-lending sons of bitches used a cudgel on me."

Nearing Gethsemane, he spoke again, in a third, yet again different tone:

"Now we will see how the fig trees have died and withered, never to bear fruit again."

Both Peter and I looked to him, then to each other. We could not tell if he was serious or not.

It turned out that he was. In the dim light of the moon, he pointed to one perfectly healthy fig tree, then another.

"There," he said. "Do you see? They are gray-gnarled and wasted with death."

Slow-witted Peter was about to comment to him that all fig trees were gray-barked, and that the trees he indicated were vigorous and strong. But he thought better of it, and said nothing.

Sore and tired as I was, and as much as I drowsed, it was difficult for me to sleep that night. It was not the discomfort in my hip alone that kept me awake.

As I lay beneath the stars, I felt that it was time to depart from him, to abandon him to his own designs, whatever they might be.

For, unless they both be fools and mad, friends cease to be friends when one of them endangers the other through obstinate folly and madness.

But I did not leave him. I stayed. I was still young, and I still had in me a sense of adventure. Maybe that is why. Or maybe it was something else. I have asked myself about this many times, and I have received from myself many answers.

31

THE STREETS OF JERUSALEM GREW MORE DENSELY CROWDED every day, as the pilgrims arrived in increasing droves from all over Judea to visit the holy city at Pesach.

Overnight, the incidents of the previous day became much exaggerated and embroidered. Jesus no longer had overturned a money-lender's table. He had overturned all the tables of all the money-lenders in the Temple courtyard. He had physically assaulted the money-lenders. He had denounced not only them and the dove-peddlers, but the Holy Temple as well, cursing it and prophesying its destruction and downfall.

Some of the rabble sought to instigate Jesus to fiercer words and deeds. None of them was ignored. One called out loudly, asking him about his well-known teaching that we should do unto others as we would have them do unto us. Had he himself followed his own teaching when he attacked the money-lenders?

"I did unto others as I should have them do unto me," he answered. "If I lived in darkness and was filth in the eyes and temple of God, I should wish that I be brought to light and cleansed by my brother, and I should be most grateful to him who did so."

Another called to him, asking if he still believed that it was right and lawful under God that they should pay taxes imposed on them by Rome.

He disliked and thwarted this baited question by using the words I had given him long ago.

"Why put me to the test, you hypocrites?"

He demanded that someone in the crowd bring him a coin. Someone did. He held it high between his thumb and his forefinger.

"Whose likeness and inscription are on this coin?"

The man who had brought it to him, and many men all round, said: "Caesar's."

"Then render to Caesar the things that are Caesar's, and to God the things that are God's."

No more did he allow them to lead him to the Holy Temple. Instead he led them to it.

At the outer altar, lines of pilgrims stood with the caged doves they had purchased, waiting to make burnt offering. Others stood in line to give money offerings to the treasury agent of the Temple. To one side of him, on a plinth, was a wide crater wrought of gold; on a plinth to his other side was a crater of silver. As he took the money offerings, he separated the silver coins from the gold and put them in one bowl or the other. Coins of lesser metal were tossed by him into big woven baskets on the ground.

Jesus went to an elderly woman in rags who moved slowly toward the taker of the money offerings. She had but two small copper coins, which together were worth almost nothing.

"Truly, I say to you," he proclaimed, "this poor widow has put in more than all those who are contributing to the treasury. For they all contribute out of their abundance, but she out of her poverty puts in everything she has, her whole living."

Later I took him aside and told him that he was acting like a self-righteous old fuss-pot, a common *ardelio,* as we say in Rome: a pest of a meddler.

"No, you are acting even worse than that," I went on. "You are acting like the arch-hypocrite that you are."

He took offense.

"And how do you know that she is a 'poor widow'? For all you know, she could be a miserly rich aristocrat, a crazy old hag with ten thousand coins of gold buried in her floor."

But he was right to take offense. I thought of the fraudulent cripple I had seized upon in the settlement of the Jezreel Valley. I thought of the widow's poisoned son I had pronounced dead at Nain. I thought of all the self-afflicted and pretenders I had chosen to suit our purposes. Yes, he was right to take offense. Choosing to make his point through this old woman with her two copper coins was nothing compared to my own past machinations. And this was to say nothing of all the lyrical lies and plain pastoral deceptions I had contrived. Who was I to criticize him? Who was I to call him hypocrite?

I was, in my way, as out-of-hand, as out-of-control, as he in his way. I was tired. I had been through enough of this. I was sick of it all, impatient to be done with it; impatient for him to be done with it.

His ranting at the Temple colonnade grew wilder, much to the malicious pleasure of the rabble.

For every believer, every follower, every seeker of the Word and the Way, there must have been five who thirsted for perverse entertainment alone, delighting in every farther thrust of his incendiary words.

"These are sheep gone rabid," I warned him. "Your shepherd's staff will do you no good here. And you will do yourself no good."

But he would hear nothing.

I thought of all the mad messiahs howling in the shadows of dusk in the windy, winding streets of Caesarea.

Except for slow, stalwart Peter, the disciples were not much seen, and most of those who were seen did appear as fleeting apparitions, obscure and scurrying, glimpsed from the corner of an eye. Our despised young rodent, Andreas, who had been so ardent in his craving to gain his Lord's favor, was still about, but he now could be found at the far edge of the crowd. Our Essene seemed to have vanished.

When Jesus was confronted by a group of Sadducees, we were not so very surprised to see Aaron the priest and Ephraim the rabbi in the back of their group, with Aaron once again in his priestly garb. Jesus smiled and waved to them, greeting them by name. They reacted in a most ridiculous manner, turning their heads as if to see whom he might be hailing.

The Sadducees, who did not believe in resurrection, put a puzzling question to him, seeking to entangle and entrap him in confusion regarding his own beliefs, of which Aaron must have well informed them. It was the eldest of their priests who posed this question:

"Teacher," he began, "Moses said that if a man dies, having no children, his brother must marry the widow, and raise up children for the brother. Now, let us say that there were seven brothers among us.

"The first married, and died, and, having no children, left his wife to his brother. So too the second and third, down to the seventh. After them, the woman died. In the resurrection, to which of the seven brothers will she be wife? For they all had her."

"You know not the Book, and you know not of what you speak. For in resurrection none marry or are given in marriage, but are like angels in heaven."

He obfuscated further, until it was they who were entrapped in confusion.

"Thank you," said the eldest priest, and the rest of the robed Sadducees, including Aaron and Ephraim, followed him, the poser of the problem, in his retreat from Jesus. As they did so, Jesus waved good-bye to Aaron and Ephraim, once again calling them by name; and once again Aaron and Ephraim turned away their heads.

Only Peter returned with us and the donkeys every evening to Gethsemane. When we had first entered Jerusalem, innkeepers were eager to have Jesus as their guest, and we were offered good lodging and food without cost. Now these same innkeepers would not have us, saying that their inns were filled with Pesach pilgrims.

To both Peter and me, there seemed a new change in Jesus. By day, in the holy city, he was excited, impulsive, foolhardy, and very often mad-speaking. But by night, in the garden, he was subdued, peaceful, and often quietly pensive. There was no more cursing of fig trees; nothing like that.

One night, while Peter slept and the breezes brought us the luscious scent of daffodils, I turned to Jesus.

"When will this end?" I asked him, as one might ask for mercy.

He was sensitive to the cry for mercy in my hushed, weak, and imploring voice. He ceded a moment to the daffodilly breeze and the sound of crickets before answering.

"Soon," he said. "Very soon."

My eyes fell on Peter in his slumber, and I found myself in reminiscence.

"He was the first," I said. "Do you remember?"

"Sepphoris. The Feast of Trumpets."

"What a fine night that was," I said. "I can still hear the ram's horn blasting."

"He will betray me," said Jesus, indifferently. "He will betray me and renounce me."

I waited to hear the soft sound of his laughter, but there was none.

The next day, I found myself studying Peter repeatedly. His words. His movements. His eyes. I could not get the words of Jesus from my mind. I told myself that the breezes of the night before had stirred up a bit of his madness, and that was all. But this did not keep me from again and again looking to Peter with a searching eye. As attuned to, and wary of, his demeanor and behavior as I was, all I could see was good-hearted Peter. I decided to dismiss the matter. Jesus had spoken figuratively, and I had taken him literally.

It was Andreas whom I did not trust. It was the Sadducee priest of the reversible cloak whom I did not trust. It was Thaddeus, the nowhere-to-be-found drifter of Canaan, whom I did not trust. It was Levi, the errant tax-collector, whom I did not trust. It was the two who joined us in Jerusalem, a Greek gentile and a Jew from Damascus, whom I did not trust. It was he who had fallen from us before we entered the city, he whose name and face I could not recall, whom I did not trust.

Jesus damned the Pharisees, and he damned the Sanhedrin. If a fly or bee came near to him, he damned it. There was no danger in the damning of bugs. This was not so of Pharisees and the Sanhedrin.

"They sit where Moses sat," declaimed Jesus, the Temple colonnade behind him and the masses before him, "so observe and practice whatever they tell you. But do not as they do. For they preach, but they do not practice. They bind heavy burdens, hard to bear, and they lay them on the people's shoulders, but they themselves will not move them with their slightest finger.

"They do all their deeds to be seen in public. They make their phylacteries broad and their tassel-fringes long. They love the places of honor at feasts, and the best seats in the synagogue, and salutations in the marketplaces, and being addressed with reverence as priestly doctors of the law, grand rabbis, and masters.

"They devour the houses of widows, while for pretense they make long prayers. They say: If anyone swears by the Holy Temple, it is nothing; but if anyone swears by the gold of the Temple, he is bound by his oath.

"Woe to you, scribal judges of the law and Pharisees! Woe to you, hypocrites and fools! Woe to you! For you are like white-washed tombs, which outwardly appear clean, but within are full of dead men's bones and all uncleanness. Woe to you! For you outwardly appear to be righteous, but within are full of hypocrisy and iniquity. Woe to you! In your streets, there is not to be found the most wretched of whores who is undeserving of more glory than the high priests and judges of this place.

"Oh, Jerusalem, killing prophets and stoning those who are sent to you! Oh, Jerusalem, defiling all wisdom and all truth and all good. Behold, your house is forsaken and desolate."

Dark figures looked down on him, listening to him, from vaulted windows in the Temple tower-reaches high above us. There were those in the crowds who drew away, fearful even to be seen as members of his audience.

Again he cursed the Temple, and prophesied its destruction and its downfall. But now he foretold the end of the age as well. And then he simply said:

"You will not see me again."

His voice was now a ghastly dry rasp, almost painful to hear. He would take no food and no wine, but only small swallows from cups of water offered to him.

"What are you doing to yourself?" I asked him.

"I am purifying myself," he said. Not only was his voice rough and croaking. His lips were pale, parched, cracked, and swollen.

"Purifying yourself?" I stared at him and laughed. "You'll be shitting dust at this rate."

I reminded him of the good food and wine at the inn at Caesarea, and brought back to his mind the sea-fresh oysters served there.

He smiled. There was blood in the cracks of his lips.

I had ceased pretending in the presence of others that he was the Messiah. I had ceased pretending that I was his follower. I had ceased pretending that we were anything more than two men who were friends.

No one seemed to notice this. Not even Simon Peter, who was among those who were with us when the woman called us into her home.

She was a woman of hardened looks, which robbed beauty from her. She wore the clothes of a common wife, but there was no evidence of a husband in the furnishings or the few decorative elements of her home.

She welcomed us to sit, then brought out an alabaster jar and unsealed it. The aromatic scent of balsam-oil of precious nard was taken up from the opened jar by the spring breeze through the window. The jar of veined white alabaster appeared to be the most costly of her belongings.

Pouring the oil into a wooden basin, she used her hand to ladle some of it onto the forehead of Jesus, massaging it into his temples and across his brow. He slowly closed his eyes. She applied some of the oil to his lips.

After anointing him in this way, she knelt before him with the bowl, removed his sandals, and rubbed the rest of the oil into his dry and callused feet. Jesus appeared transported, and uttered several long and audible sighs of pleasure.

It was the Jew of Damascus who dared speak and interrupt this pleasure.

"This jar of ointment," he said, "could have been sold for three hundred denarii or more, a huge sum, which could have been given to feed a great many of the poor."

Jesus opened his eyes and glared at him. Then he rebuked him sternly.

"The poor," he told him, "will be there always."

On the eve of the Pesach, there was at the main gate of the city a commotion like that which had met the arrival of Jesus astride his donkey.

Preceded and followed by curtained and elaborately fitted carpenta drawn by pairs of yoked and fine-plumed stallions of exquisite chestnut color and black flaxen manes, there came a litter that shone with gold and gleamed with ivory, its carrying poles borne on the shoulders of six brilliant-muscled men. The red veils that enclosed the carriage of the litter blew and billowed in the breezes. Through a windblown parting of the veils, I saw and recognized the tall bald man who sat on the raised cushion seat within, distractedly playing upon his white-robed thigh with a golden scepter he held in his right hand.

"Who is this?" asked Jesus.

"It is Pontius Pilate, the praetor of the province, come to make his annual address."

There was no encroaching or directing this manned and stallion-strong retinue, as there had been with our scraggling bunch and sluggish, confused donkey.

The litter was brought to a platform near the base of the Temple steps. The awning-cloths above the platform were of black and purple, the colors of the Jews. The bunting round the platform was of Tyrian scarlet, the color of Rome everlasting.

The litter was lowered, the carriage curtains were drawn aside, and Pilate stepped forth. Awaiting him was Joseph Caiaphas, the ruling high priest of the Holy Temple and the Sanhedrin. The two men embraced.

Pilate was cheered loudly by many, and jeered loudly by some. Or it may have been Caiaphas who was cheered and jeered. Or it may have been the both of them. Or, more likely, it may have been their embrace. As I have said, these people were like the crude, plebeian noise-making crowds at gladiatorial games.

Pilate ascended the platform. Caiaphas followed him and sat

to the rear of where Pilate stood. The crowds became quiet. The prefect raised his scepter, and then bowed his head slightly, with formality, first to Caiaphas, then to the masses.

"Oh, Jerusalem! Holy flower of a holy nation, whose guest I am privileged and proud to be. When I first came to this land, I sought the guidance of the good and venerated man who sits with me before you on this day.

"It was he, through his sagacity, righteousness, and selfless love for the people of Israel and the welfare and prosperity of Judea, who brought me to share with him in this love. Together, with the rulers of the territories of this land, we forged a government, new and strong, soldered and welded of Judean vision and Roman goodwill; a government of and for the people. Your voice is the voice of your land, and we heed it as we cultivate and build.

"The peace of mutual benefit between Judea and Rome is manifest to all who travel our new highways, enjoy water from our new aqueducts, and are protected by the benevolent presence of legionaries who bring freedom from danger to where menace and lawlessness once threatened you. This peace of mutual benefit is so firm and flourishing that the Syrian legate has been dispatched.

"You who embody the glory of your past are the glory of the future. I salute you. May this Pesach deliver you from all that is evil to all that is good, and may all the days of your lives do the same."

At this, there was much cheering. Pilate stood properly, and, for a moment, he smiled properly. Then he resumed his properly dignified countenance. He turned his head toward Caiaphas.

"Will my good friend be so kind as to come forward." There was no questioning tone in these words. They were more of a stage-signal, or a command.

Joseph Caiaphas rose properly and stood properly beside the

much taller man. For a moment, he smiled properly. Then he resumed his properly dignified countenance. The two men looked to one another, then embraced. Again there was much cheering.

"I thank you," said Pilate, waving his scepter once through the air, then lowering his head in a cursory way.

Caiaphas said nothing, and nor did he bow his head to the rabble.

I remembered what Pilate's adjutant in Caesarea had told me: "We have no use of a speech-writer here. The procurator gives but one speech a year, in Jerusalem. It is always the same speech."

So this was Pilate's speech. It was not a bad speech. It was not without some effect. But it was indistinguishable from the usual stale political fare. It was perfectly fatuous, blandly fraudulent, and woven of drab rudimentary rhetoric.

The maker of this speech was not the same honest, sharp-minded, and outspoken man whom I had met in Caesarea. It was my hope that I would have a chance to meet that man again, here in Jerusalem.

During the first part of Pilate's speech, I saw in the eyes of Jesus, as they looked here and there and to the platform and then here and there again, that he entertained a notion to disrupt the speech by diverting the crowd from Pilate to himself, by breaking out with some sort of loud pronouncement of his own.

"Render unto Caesar," I said to him.

He seemed surprised that I had read him so well, and there was in him no further sign of mischievous intention. But after Pilate and Caiaphas were no longer to be seen, and the crowd dispersed and began to wander, Jesus drew them back with a cry:

"Out of Egypt did Moses lead you, and to Egypt you have returned!"

This was enough to bring them back, gathering as quickly as they could to him.

"Look well at your Holy Temple, and see the palace of not of God, but of Ramses."

I did not know what to think. I grew anxious. I wished he would shut up.

"You are of tepid blood, you who with timidity offer up your wrists for bondage."

Some were made uneasy, felt threatened and affronted, by what was said; and they hid behind a noise of protest and jeering. Some found truth in what was said; and they made a noise of enthusiasm and agreement.

"You are lukewarm. You are neither hot nor cold. I shall spew you out of my mouth. I shall vomit you forth from me, and God will not receive you."

He spat with violence upon the ground.

It was he who took leave of the crowd, not the crowd that took leave of him. He merely turned and walked away, and left them there behind him, alone and afraid, or stilled by the truth that hung in the air.

The sky became dark with coming storm. But no storm came, and the darkness passed.

A second darkness approached: the nightfall of the first day of Pesach. Watching the sun descend behind the tower of Psephina, I was slow in seeing that the emerging colors spreading through the twilight sky were the purple of the Jews and the red of Rome.

We were found by Peter and Thaddeus and the Greek who was new to us.

"Where will you have us prepare for you to eat the Pesach meal?" asked Thaddeus.

"I have no hunger for unleavened bread," said Jesus.

"But you must," said Peter.

"Is that so?" He looked at Peter very oddly, and there was also a cryptic oddness in his voice. "Must I, now?"

Only very slowly did he let go of Peter's eyes. "Anywhere," he said to Thaddeus. "Find a place. Anywhere. I do not care."

An hour or so later, we sat at a long table in the upper room of an old inn on the southeast hill of the Lower City, above the houses of the poor, whose part of Jerusalem this was.

We were alone in this room. There were nine or ten of us: Jesus and myself, Peter and Andreas, Thaddeus and Levi, the Greek and the Damascene, one or two others. Thomas the Essene had returned to us, of a mind that he could be both an Essene and a follower of the Word and the Way. He was there. We sat on long benches at a long table, which the innkeeper had set with a lamp, unleavened bread, some cured tilapia, some pickled olives, a jug of water, a jug of wine, and wooden cups. The poor, in their crumbling, dirty limestone dwellings in the streets below, likely had finer and more sumptuous feasts before them.

Jesus looked with little interest to what was on the table. I told one of the disciples to give me a piece of fish and some wine. Jesus did the same. I ate mine down, emptied my cup, called for more. But my friend ate but a morsel, and took only a sip from his cup.

"There is at this table someone whom I detest," he said. In his voice there was little emotion other than a hint of torpid disgust. "He is foul and rotting within. It would have been better if he had not been born. He has betrayed me."

Moments passed in excruciating silence.

"It is I," said Levi. "I have never prayed the prayer you taught us to pray, the prayer to our Father who art in heaven."

Jesus looked at him, waved him away with a dismissive, weary turn of the hand.

"I have no prayer to any Father who art in heaven," he said to Levi without bothering to look at him. "It was Gaius here, who sits by me, my fine pagan friend and Roman of rank, Gaius; it was he who wrote that prayer for me.

"He who believes in God, believes not in himself. He who prays to God, prays into the shit-hole of the bottomless latrine pit of his own meaningless being."

Andreas looked as if he was being taken by the paroxysms of apoplectic seizure. His left hand became claw-like and rigid, and struck at his neck repeatedly with tremor. His upper body convulsed, most of all his shoulders. He stood suddenly, raising a piece of unleavened bread in his right hand. There came from him choked attempts to speak, and when he succeeded in making coherent sounds, it was as if his tongue were a fat unruly snake in his mouth and throat.

"Our Lord would have us eat of this bread, for it is his body."

He grabbed and raised a cup of wine, spilling some of it on the table and himself. The spasms of his body were less pronounced, but his speech was still halting.

"Our Lord would have us drink this wine, for it is his blood."

He brought the cup to his lips with both hands. A small, fitful stream of wine ran down his chin as he drank.

I found these antics of the tick to be quite entertaining. It was as though he felt that he was losing his Lord, and his discipleship, and that his mind broke at this. Jesus was not entertained. On this night, there was nothing in the world that could entertain him.

"Shut up and sit down," he told the tick.

The others ate and drank, with little enthusiasm and less talk.

"Are there any words that you will gift us with?" asked one of them.

Jesus needed no time for thought, and he did not hesitate, but simply, straightforwardly, and straightaway said:

"If you bring forth what is within you, what you bring forth will save you. If you do not bring forth what is within you, what you do not bring forth will destroy you."

He then ceased to speak, and would say no more. Such was our Pesach feast in Jerusalem. I ate the last of the olives, drank the last of the wine, and stood. Jesus, too, rose and stood. We walked from the room, saying nothing to those we left behind. None of them followed, and there was no sound but the creaking of the floor beneath our footsteps.

We made our way to Gethsemane under the light of the full paschal moon. The host of stars were in array. My eyes became lost for a while in the Big Bear, trying to see the leopard that he saw in those stars.

A big gray long-eared owl with yellow eyes looked at us from his bough, and we looked at him.

Peter, who had returned with us to the gardens every night since we arrived here, was not with us tonight. We were alone.

"It is over now," he said. "Come morning, we can leave for Caesarea. Then to Rome. I am done here. It is a new life that I want."

I was soothed to hear this. I was very soothed to hear this. I breathed the good night air, freely and deeply. It was the first peaceful breath I had drawn in a while.

"You said some nights ago, as he lay sleeping nearby, that Peter would betray you. I thought you to be speaking fancifully. But when you spoke of betrayal again tonight, I saw that you were speaking plainly and without fancy. How could you foresee that Peter would betray you?"

"I saw him speak twice, covertly, to authorities at the Holy Temple. He did not suspect that, while I could not be seen, I was nearby, watching him, hearing him, trying to make out what was being said.

"From these authorities, he sought to discover if there was a price on my head. It was bounty, reward, that he sought."

"We should have dispatched him to his grave with a cup of dark wine. There is still opium in the packsaddle of Faith, enough of it to kill him twice over."

"In the morning we shall be gone. Enough of death.

"Enough of God. Enough of the Word and the Way. It is done, behind us, all of it."

"He showed nothing tonight. The tick, Andreas or Judas or Judah or whatever be his name, was like a mechanism whose gears, cogs, spindles, and pins were all awry. But Peter, or Cephas or Simon or Petros or Petrus or Simon Petros or whatever his name be, was as cool as a fish in the sea."

"Would that he were a fish in the sea, with a jagged iron hook deep in his gullet."

"I mistrusted them all, but him no more than the others. He seemed merely a simple fool of a fisherman, benign and gentle."

"Between what something seems to be and what it is, there often lies a chasm. How many harmless brown spiders is the deadly long-legged recluse fatally mistaken to be?

"But enough. May he be curst. May they all be curst. May they be taken as mares by the prefect's stallions. May they be trampled by them. I am done with them all. It is over, all of it."

"If you truly have been betrayed, and the authorities decide to make a scapegoat of you, or to punish you to set an example before the people, would it not be safer, just to be sure, to put distance between this place and us tonight, to leave for Caesarea now?"

"No one would be apprehended during the Pesach, unless it were for murder or robbery or some other violent crime. No. I have given thought to this. No man would be seized by the Sanhedrin during the holy Pesach unless he did great harm to another man."

My gaze returned to the stars, the bear and the leopard who were one. We entered the garden, and tethered Faith, Hope, and Charity to the same twin-trunked pomegranate tree to which we had tied them every night that we spent in this garden. As we did this, we looked to the tree, as we did every morning and every night, hoping to see a sign of flowering, the first early peek of red blossom, the first early peek of minuscule fruit. We saw nothing. Maybe in the morning, before we left.

"I am beginning to see the leopard," I told him.

There was more of exhaustion than of anything else in his soft and all but silent laugh.

"And I, the great bear," he said.

We felt no need for a fire that night. The moon was full. We were not hungry. We wanted only sleep.

I drowsed pleasantly, feeling sleep come over me. Sleep was always sweet, even if the dreams it brought were not.

My eyes shot open. There were unfamiliar sounds about. I heard movement on the path, then a brief thrashing through the rosemary bushes where the path narrowed. My heart beat fast at the prospect of a wild boar or lion. I saw that Jesus too was sitting upright, his eyes open and alert.

Then I knew, by the nature of the sounds, that it was no wild beast that approached. It was a more dangerous creature; and it was not one, but several. The sounds were those of men moving in stealth. They were the sounds of men trying to make no sound. We stood and looked toward where the pathway ended, at the garden's edge.

The sounds of men trying to make no sound grew closer and more pronounced, and then there were figures before us in the moonlight.

Three enforcers of the Sanhedrin. A Roman legionary. And close behind them, cowering as if they might not be seen, the older fisherman and the younger.

The temple enforcers wore robes and turbans of black. From their wide leather belts hung sheathed daggers, slings, pouches of shot, and coils of rope. The legionary wore a military tunic and belt, from which hung the scabbards of his dagger and sword. The fishermen, besides their usual ragged garments, wore only cowardice and shame.

The eyes of the three temple law-men passed over me, then were fixed on Jesus.

"Is this the one?" asked the foremost of the black-robed men.

There came a hesitant affirmation from behind him. It was difficult to tell whose voice it was.

"Step forward, both of you. Identify him properly."

The betrayers came reluctantly into the open. Their heads were slightly turned and downcast, and they averted their eyes from the eyes of Jesus.

"Look at him," ordered the black robe. "Is this the man who would be brought to trial in the Hall of Hewn Stones? Is this your Jesus of Nazareth?"

The fishermen stole glances at each other. "Speak! Identify him or forfeit your reward."

The tick rushed forward, no longer shunning the eyes of Jesus. He pointed a shaking finger at the man with whom he had so tried to ingratiate himself, the man whom he had so eagerly called his Lord.

"And you?" the black robe demanded of the other betrayer, who did not come forward.

"It is him."

"The night is dark. Put your eyes close to him."

And when the fisherman did this, Jesus whispered low to him: "My curse on you is strong. You will die most terribly, and soon."

"It is him," said the fisherman.

From the fold of a black robe, a hand brought forth two paltry cloth pouches of coins and tossed them toward the fishermen. They fell to the dirt with little sound.

I spoke to the legionary in Latin. One of the temple-men asked us to speak in Greek, that our words might better be understood by all present. The legionary looked at the black-robed man in a manner that showed displeasure at being interrupted. He glanced with mean ridicule upon the man's turban, then resumed speaking in Latin.

The legionary was of long-standing experience in these parts, and answered directly and only to Pilate, who, as the provincial governor of Judea, was also the legate and commander of the forces of the Roman military here. This military presence in Judea consisted only of one cavalry unit and five cohorts, or about three or four thousand troops at any given time. Most of the troops here were auxiliaries, and most of these auxiliaries were Jews, recruited from the native population. The Roman standing before me was proud to say that he was a legionary in full, and honorably decorated.

After introducing myself by name and rank, I told him that I was a former member of the court of Tiberius, and that I knew Pilate from our private meeting at the Palace of Herod, in Caesarea. I told him that, as Pilate knew, I traveled with a document of identification bearing the seal of the princeps.

I told him that this man, Jesus, was my slave, whom I had acquired to serve and guide me in my journeying through Judea. He was a good and faithful slave, and a good man, I told him. I explained to him that it was my plan to bring my good slave to Rome with me. I was, in fact, preparing to leave with him for Caesarea in the morning.

My good slave had done no harm or wrong. His accusers were jealous and driven by mendacity and petty greed. They were liars and not to be trusted or given the merest credence.

The fishermen now hurried away into the night.

"See how they flee with their little bags of dirty coins," I said to the legionary.

"Jews" was all he said.

This was a word of Latin that the temple-men knew, and the tone of voice in which it was said was one that all men knew.

The foremost of the black-robed men informed Jesus that he was hereby charged with blasphemy, sedition, and demonic acts.

"I am guilty of none of these things," said Jesus. "I have sought to bring men closer to the truth of their God. I have sought to have men render unto Caesar that which is Caesar's, and unto God that which is God's. I do not even understand what you mean by 'demonic acts'; but I can assure you that I do not believe in demons."

"You can save these claims for your trial. They will be heard."

"And what of God's law against bearing false witness? Is it now to be rewarded rather than punished by the protectors of God's law? And what of covetousness? You let the transgressors escape freely, and I am detained to defend myself from the crime of their lies, and not from a crime of my own, for I have committed none."

Nothing was said. There were only the crickets. Then one of them spoke:

"Shall you come with us peacefully, or shall you be bound and led?"

"I am a man of peace. Even when trespassed against, I am a man of peace. Please lead the way."

So, having come from Jerusalem for what we believed was the last time, we were brought back to it, with Faith, Hope, and Charity in sluggish tow, their tether-ends gathered in the fist of my right hand.

"This is absurd," I said to my fellow Roman. "This man is innocent. Furthermore, he is my property."

"You will have him back. The men in long beards and black rags tied round their heads will have their little pantomime with him, then impose on him a few lashes and a fine. Then you will have him back."

"I should much rather just pay the fine now, and get it over and done with. Here. Now. Without the pantomime. Without the lashes."

"That is not how they do things here. And we must allow them to do things here as they do them here."

The pebbles and pine needles of this familiar path appeared in the light of the full moon as they had not appeared before. In this light, they seemed to shine.

I thought it best to remind Jesus that he should now be playing the part of my slave; but this had already occurred to him, for he called to me over his shoulder:

"Please tell me, good master, what do you see in the stars tonight, the great bear or the leopard?"

"I see, my good servant, a beast of indeterminate nature," I called back to him.

The Roman was curious about this, and I explained that our Ursa Major was seen by the Jews as a great leopard in the night-time sky. He grimaced his acknowledgment of what he took to be an enlightenment of some interest.

He asked me if it was true that my slave had preached and made pronouncements through the land. I answered that in my free time I had taught him something of oratory and rhetoric; that he had a natural gift for it; and that he had made some little orations here and there, based on tales from these people's Book. I said that I soon would begin teaching him Latin as well, for I anticipated his being of increased value to me in Rome. I reiterated my indignation at this confiscation of my property, my time, and my dignity. It was unconscionable, this whole matter.

My outrage, though based not on what I pretended it to be, was real, and it was long-winded:

"How can the property of a Roman citizen of rank, in a province of Rome, be stolen from him and brought against his will to a court governed by the corrupt provincial priests of a barbaric provincial god?"

"Jews" was all he said.

I looked at the back of Jesus, flanked by the two black-robed men who followed the foremost of them. I looked for the yellow-eyed owl on his bough, but he was gone. It was the part of the night given to the hunting of prey. The temple-men had theirs. The owl, his field-mouse; the Jews, their Christ. I looked at the pebbles and pine needles that shone in the light of the moon.

32

WE WERE LED TO THE PALACE OF THE HIGH PRIEST, Caiaphas, on the Maccabean Path. Here the priest lived with his family, which included his father-in-law, Annas, who had been high priest before him, and who some said still controlled the Holy Temple through him.

Awaiting us at the palace of the high priests were some of the temple elders, Sadducees and Pharisees, who left soon after Jesus was delivered. They studied him with their eyes as one might view a strange and exotic animal, but they said nothing.

When they had left, Annas appeared, and did with his eyes as the others had done before him. He took the jaw of Jesus in his hand, turning it to the right and to the left, as if examining the features of a slave he was about to buy, or a whore he was about to procure. He removed his hand from the jaw of Jesus and walked away, passing two shadows at the far end of a hall. One of these was Caiaphas. The other, we soon found out, was the chief justice of the Sanhedrin, whom the black-robed officers addressed as *nagid,* which meant "ruler" or "prince." He was very old and very tall. He seemed to hate all the world except for himself, and there seemed to be little love lost there either.

"You are Jesus of Nazareth?" he said.

"I am," said Jesus.

"You are accused of blasphemy," said the prince.

Jesus opened his mouth and made a slight sound, as if about

to say something. But the prince of the Sanhedrin was already on his way to the door, which was opened for him by one of the palace attendants. It was then that Caiaphas appeared. He was even shorter than he had looked to be in public. He had seemed taller just a moment ago, as a shadow in the distance. He conferred in Aramaic with the officers of the Sanhedrin. Then he spoke in Greek to me.

"Your slave has caused much distress," he said.

"My good servant has done no wrong to any man," I said to him. "He is without blame, and no blame can be laid on him."

"You are a Roman, and you know little of this place and its ways."

"I know enough to know that, under their ostentations of piety and endless suffering, they are people like all others."

"Ah, but there you are wrong. They are not people like all others. They are Jews. And what seem to you to be ostentations are not. As empire is to you, so God and our history are to us. It is your arrogance, your Roman perspective, that causes you to misunderstand us, and that will prevent you always from understanding us."

There was not the least hint of harshness or hostility in what he said. He spoke with grace, in a manner that was genteel but not at all haughty. He seemed sincerely to want to correct me, to enlighten me, and nothing more.

"Do you truly believe this man, who is my devoted servant, to be guilty of anything?" I asked.

"I know nothing of him, but for what I have been told," he said.

"And, knowing nothing of a man, you would believe what you have been told."

"It is not a matter of what I believe."

"But you are the high priest of your people. Surely you would have them be led to the truth, is that not so?"

"It is so. But it is not always I who lead them. There are times when I must allow them to lead me. I must place their happiness before all. A priest is a servant of God, and therefore servant as well as shepherd of God's flock."

It now was clear to me that, for all his cultivated grace and genteel manner, he was a most devious and treacherous man. I decided it was best that I say no more to him. But he would not let our conversation end there. He would have it end in a way befitting the powers of darkness in the night that surrounded us.

"Surely, there is one thing about our ways that, as a Roman, you do understand."

"And what is that?"

"The principle of expiation."

I looked at him. He smiled and recast his words: "The need for sacrifice."

Only then did he look long and well at Jesus, and with sudden violence the high priest summoned phlegm from his lungs and spat into his face.

He laughed as he turned his back to us and walked away, down the hall, becoming a shadow once again. Jesus watched after him, wiping the priest's spit from his face with the sleeve of his tunic.

There was no sound for some time, except for a few words muttered between two of the black-robed officers. The legionary and I exchanged glances. Jesus and I exchanged glances. Night became day. There was the crowing of a cock.

Jesus was grasped by both arms and led from the palace. As we passed through the courtyard gardens in the faint early morning light, I saw him look down into the ravine of the Hinnom Valley, then to the sky, then straight ahead.

"I am behind you," I called to him, as I followed with the donkeys through the quiet streets.

There was no movement of his head as he was led forward, and he said nothing.

33

IN THIS LAND WHOSE PRIMARY RESOURCE AND SUSTENANCE were misery, I was by now accustomed to the dire, dour faces of long-bearded men in robes the color of death and mourning. But I had not before seen such dire dourness as I saw on the faces of the many Sanhedrin before whom Jesus stood in the Hall of Hewn Stones.

He was asked to state his name. He stated his name. He was asked to state his profession.

"Bond-servant to Gaius Fulvius Falconius, Roman citizen of the equestrian order and former member of the court of the princeps."

"A slave."

"Yes. As are all men who live."

"And is it true that on many occasions you have claimed to be the Messiah?"

"No, that is not true. I have encountered many who have made such claims, but I have never been one of them. A few fools moved by my little orations of stories from the Book may have thought me to be the Messiah, or any number of other things. That was their doing, not mine."

"There are those here who would contradict you."

"There are those who would contradict that the sun sets in the west. Contradictions of the truth do not turn black to white or white to black, truth to lies or lies to truth."

Ephraim the Sadducee rabbi was brought into the hall. Most of the Sanhedrin were Sadducees. The rabbi affirmed that, yes, Jesus had on many occasions claimed to be the Messiah.

"Who is this man, and how would he know?" asked Jesus.

"I observed him in his travels," Ephraim answered directly.

"My travels? My master is a good and kind man, but he allows me no travels without him."

"He was there too. I saw him."

I stood and declaimed:

"This is preposterous! It is a travesty. You summon one of your own to testify against my servant. Enough of this."

"Silence!" demanded one of the Sanhedrin. "Many of us did hear and observe you ourselves from the windows of this very temple."

"And what wrong did I utter?" asked Jesus.

"You blasphemed all that is holy."

"I said only that sects are a strife unto God. Do you, the Sanhedrin—Sadducees and Pharisees—constitute all that is holy? To me, other things are holy as well. God, for one. Purity of heart, for another. Do you not hold life itself to be holy?"

"And did you not teach strange ideas unto the peoples of the land?"

"I said only that they were fruit of the true vine, and that their Father who is in heaven is the vine-dresser. I told them to love one another."

"And did you not stir the people to rise against the Temple, and also against Rome itself?"

"I said that all men should render unto Caesar that which is Caesar's, and unto God that which is God's. Are these words that inspire or advocate revolution against God or government?"

"And what is it that you mean when you speak of the Word and the Way?"

"I mean the Word of God as revealed in the Book. I mean the Way that God instructs us to live as revealed in the Book."

"And nothing else? Nothing that is presented as emanating from you?"

"Yes, there is a belief that is mine and not to be found in the Book. I believe that if you bring forth what is within you, what you bring forth will save you. If you do not bring forth what is within you, what you do not bring forth will destroy you."

Murmurs flowed among the ranks of the Sanhedrin. Where there were no murmurs, there were silent stares directed at Jesus, if not as a defendant before them, then as the source of the elusive wisdom heard but not grasped by them.

Again silence was demanded, this time by and of the court itself.

"And did you not speak of the building of a new temple? What did you mean by this?"

"I spoke of a temple of the spirit, not a temple of rock and mortar. A temple that could be felt but not touched."

On saying this, he slowly raised and placed two fingers to his chest.

"And then why was it that you solicited funds for the building of such a temple?"

"I never solicited funds for anything. When people gave me alms, I gave them in turn to the poor. My master treats me well. I have no need for alms. I hope to earn my manumission by teaching in Rome, and there to continue in service to my master as a freedman."

"And did you not raise the dead?"

"I once resuscitated with my breath a man who was taken for dead but was not. I did no more than what midwives do with newborn infants who are blue and purpling for want of air in them."

"And did you not commune with demons that dwelt in men?"

"No. There are no demons. I helped a few drunkards to see the error of their ways, so that their shaking and howling might end. Is it a culpable act to feel compassion for one's fellow man? I should think not. I should think the lack of compassion to be culpable."

"And is it not true that you did travel to Egypt as a youth, and there apprentice yourself to a mage?"

"No, it is not true. I have never been to Egypt. I have never been beyond Judea and Syria."

"And did you not profess magic by advising others, most sinfully, morbidly, and horrifically, that they should eat of the bread of Pesach for, through magic, you had transformed it into your flesh, and that they should drink of the wine of Seder for, through magic, you had transformed it into your blood? Why should you wish others to eat your flesh and drink your blood, if not to effect godless magic most dark?"

"I never said any such thing. I never had any such wish. I should like to know why whoever concocted this incredible nonsense for you isn't standing here instead of me."

I stood again, declaimed again:

"This surpasses all decency. These insults to the nature of my good servant greaten to where they overflow onto me."

"Master," said Jesus. "Be not concerned. These men mean right, but they know not what they do."

Lassitude was starting to show in his performance. "Silence!"

I exhaled with audible disconcertion.

"And did you not...."

So it went. Whatever his refutation, and however reasonable and convincing it was, the assembly ignored it forthwith and moved on to the next accusation. This effectively rendered the refutations to be as mere interruptions of the accusations, and the accusations to seem as statements of fact rather than questions. This was not a trial. It was a ritual formality preceding a predetermined verdict. These high holy judges had from the start been sitting with their thumbs already turned.

This was jurisprudence and justice as practiced by the Sanhedrin in the Hall of Hewn Stones.

Jesus eventually became so worn down and discouraged by this hopeless pretense of a proceeding that he relinquished his attempts to assail their charges. One of the judges was in the middle of some vague accusatory question about desecration when Jesus, in a voice too tired to convey anger, resigned himself finally to whatever inevitability might be at the end of it all.

"Whatever you want me to be guilty of, I am guilty of. If you want me to be innocent of anything, I am innocent."

"Are those your final words in this matter?"

"Should you wish further words from me, I respectfully ask that you speak them for me."

In Rome he would have been acquitted on the grounds of eloquence alone. But this was not Rome.

"I have one question," I said. "If it is not in your jurisdiction to try a citizen of Rome, how comes it that you have the power to try the property of a citizen of Rome?"

"Because your property is a Jew."

No, this was not Rome.

The black-robed elders who sat to either side of the prince of the Sanhedrin rose. Together, in a monotone, they uttered some formulaic lines of Hebrew. After they sat, the chief justice of the Sanhedrin stood and for the first time spoke:

"You are guilty of blasphemy. You are guilty of sedition. You are guilty of embracing that which is forbidden. You are guilty of teachings that are contrary to the laws of God and men."

He sat; again the elders that sat to either side of him rose and, in their monotone, enounced further formulaic words in Hebrew. As soon as these elders sat, all of the many Sanhedrin, except for the chief justice and the elders to either side of him, said as if they were one:

"Amen."

The prince of the Sanhedrin slowly stood and began to make his way from the chamber. I called out to him:

"Wait! When shall you pronounce my man's punishment, that I might pay it?"

As they had spoken as if they were one, there now could be heard from them, as if they were one, a stunned low sound. I apparently had committed an unspeakable act in asking the chief justice to pause and hear my question. He himself turned, regarded me blankly, then moved on. All the Sanhedrin stood and bowed their heads as he passed them. He made no acknowledgment of them.

The officers brought Jesus to the entrance of the chamber that led to the street. There he was handed over, by the legionary, to a group of soldiers. The legionary explained to me that these soldiers were auxiliaries of the Roman force stationed at Antonia citadel, close by the Temple and looking onto the Temple mount. They were all Judeans, he said, save one, who was Syrian. The daylight was quite harsh after the dimness in the Hall of Hewn Stones.

The three-towered palace-fortress that Herod had built in Jerusalem was in the Upper City, at the northwest corner of the First Wall. Though the king was dead, it was still called Herod's Palace. The grand praetorium of the palace was now used as the prefect's residence when he came to Jerusalem during the Pesach.

It was to this palace praetorium, and to Pontius Pilate, that Jesus was taken. We were kept waiting for some time under guard before being summoned. During this time, my hope grew. Surely the prefect, my fellow equestrian, would resolve our difficulties. My heart fell to find Pilate in cordial company with the prince of the Sanhedrin and his "good friend" Caiaphas, the high priest who had spat on Jesus earlier in the dark of this day. But when we were brought into the praetorium, he stood and wished these men good-bye.

"I thank you for bringing this matter to my attention," he said to them.

He and Caiaphas did not embrace, as they had at the public platform.

Pilate did not at first remember me. I gave him my name again. I reminded him of our talk at his palace in Caesarea. The bread, the olive oil, the mountains, the fields of the Abruzzi, our shared heritage there, and our shared rank. Tiberius and Sejanus. My rolled document sealed with the mark of the princeps.

"Of course," he said at last, with recognition and pleasure in his voice. "Yes, of course. Now I recall our meeting very well. For a good time afterward, I reflected with laughter on the nature of our world, that a mad ruler should direct a sane man to compose his orations for him."

Then he smiled at Jesus, looking him over, and turned again to me.

"Your man here seems to have gotten himself into some trouble," he said.

"Yes, but he has done no wrong."

"That may be, but he stands convicted.

"You are from Nazareth, are you not?" he asked Jesus.

"I am," said Jesus.

"And Nazareth is in Galilee, is it not?"

"It is," said Jesus.

"I have an idea."

Residing in the palace at this time was Herod Antipater, who also had come to Jerusalem for the Pesach. This son of Herod the Great, the builder of this palace, was tetrarch of Galilee.

Pilate called for one of his attendants, and told him to ask the tetrarch to join them.

"Antipas," said Pilate to the tetrarch, greeting him by his nickname, "my countryman's servant here is from the region you govern. He is Jesus by name, Jesus of Nazareth."

"I have heard of him," said the tetrarch, "and have often wished to meet him."

Antipas extended to Jesus his right hand in fellowship, but Jesus did not extend his.

Pilate's face showed disapproval and discontent, and the tetrarch became a different man.

"Why do you behave as if I am not before you?" he said, loudly and indignantly.

Jesus said nothing.

Even in these straits, he was being the fool. Even in these straits, he had the capacity to anger me and fill me with an urge to leave him, abandon him, relinquish him.

"I was told that you were a wise and humble man. You are in fact an insolent and ill-mannered child." He turned then to Pilate and said, "When next you ask to introduce me to someone, please be so kind as to see to it that it is someone who will acknowledge my presence."

"Accept my apology," said Pilate, as Antipas strode away in anger.

Tired-looking, bald-headed Pilate put his hands on his knees and leaned forward toward Jesus.

"That was not good," he said. "I was going to ask that man to grant you refuge in Galilee." He looked then to me. "Is this the sort of comportment you countenance in a servant? In anyone?"

"He is not himself," I said. "They have made him to suffer

through an ordeal that has been most unjust, and he is the worse for it."

"Tell me," he said to me, "is there any truth at all to what they have told me about him? That he has blasphemed his God? That he has preached sedition? That he has dealt in demonry? That he has made corpses sing and dance?"

"He has never blasphemed his God. He has shown only honor toward Rome and toward his homeland. 'Give unto Caesar that which is Caesar's, and give unto God that which is God's.' Those are words that I first heard from him. As to the rest, surely you know that there is and can be no truth therein. There is no truth to any of this."

He leaned again toward Jesus.

"Tell me," he said, "why did you not speak to Antipas, the tetrarch of Galilee? Why did you not accept his hand in fellowship?"

He did not answer. I was on the verge of striking him, striking him very hard, as I would an obstinate, ill-tempered slave. But then he spoke.

"It is as my master says. I do not feel well from all this."

"For what reason, do you believe, have these authorities from the Holy Temple persecuted you?"

"For the reason that they will not tolerate the slightest comment on their wealth and power. They are corrupt. Their devotion is to themselves, not God. They care more for the money-lenders than for the poor of their flock. But they would pluck out the eyes of anyone who sees this. They would sever the tongue of anyone who remarks it."

The prefect turned to me.

"He is not only outspoken, but also well-spoken. I believe that what Antipas heard is true, that he is a wise and humble man. And a most perceptive one."

"I am proud of him," I said. "And I stand by him as he has stood by me."

"Tell me, Jesus," Pilate said. "What have you sought in life?"

"The truth."

"That is a noble-sounding thing. But, surely, if what you say of the men who have persecuted you is the truth, as I believe it is, it must be that they, too, know the truth of things, and of themselves. Do you not agree that truth is neither good nor bad, but simply the truth?"

"Yes," said Jesus, "I do."

"The truth may be that, given the opportunity, you might seek what those men seek: wealth and power."

"That is not true."

"Truth is nothing," said the prefect. "It is a word used by liars, fools, and wise men alike. And no man is only one of these. Every man is all of them. And if a man finds the truth, he is better not to look at it too long, for he might see the truth."

Jesus looked long into Pilate's eyes. When Pilate next spoke, it was to say: "I find no crime in this man."

My heart lightened. The world seemed to lighten.

"Please, then," I said, "let him free. Whatever fine must be imposed, I will pay it. Free him from this worst of dreams."

I told Pilate of my plans to set sail for Rome, bringing Jesus with me.

"Tell your prefect," I said to Jesus.

"I hope to earn my manumission by teaching in Rome, and to there continue in service to my master as a freedman."

Pilate revealed understanding, compassion, and pity in the troubled features of his face. Slowly, gravely, he shook his head; but, it seemed to me, as much in consideration of his own situation as ours.

"Caiaphas is a detestable and despicable man," he said. "But it is my duty to appease him, that concord between Rome and Judea be maintained. For that one small detestable and despicable man, the high priest of the status quo of the aristocracy that is called the Holy Temple, constitutes a greater threat to the stability of Rome's government of this province than all the Zealots and rebellion-minded paupers in these parts. Caiaphas has held the throne far longer than any other high priest. The people of Judea will not allow Rome to depose him. He could, from his throne of lies, bring about an insurrection with ease and alacrity. But, as Jesus has so much as said, the only insurrection he cares about is one that might be against him, his wealth, and his power.

"He has heard Jesus speak. He has heard reports from others who have heard Jesus speak. He sees Jesus as a threat. He sees him as a small spark with the potential to start a widespread conflagration. So that spark must be extinguished.

"That is why Caiaphas has had him convicted of crimes against God, Judea, and Rome. That is why he has turned the minds of Jews against him, recasting him as their enemy, and the enemy of their God and their nation as well. And that is why Caiaphas has had him brought here, to me."

"But in having him brought to you, has he not effectively surrendered to you the determination of the fine, or dismissal of it, and the mandate of prompt and rightful return to me of my property?"

"On the surface of it, yes, what you say is true. But only on the surface."

"I do not understand."

"He was brought here because the will of Caiaphas—and of his Sanhedrin and Pharisees—can wreak itself only through me. He—and his Sanhedrin and Pharisees—can have his appeasement only through me. And, as I have said, it is my duty to appease him.

"He—and his Sanhedrin and Pharisees—cannot by law do certain things. The benevolence of the Roman government is then called upon to accommodate him by acting on his behalf, often with the appearance of acting independently on its own behalf."

"You mean to say that Jesus was brought here so—"

"Yes, precisely. So that I might, in the name of Rome, order his execution."

Jesus became faint. Pilate reached out and braced his shoulder, saying:

"It is my sorrow to share the truth with you."

All the strangeness in the air of the past seasons, all the haunted howlings and descending ominous darkness. It had led here, to this tranquil palace, on this clear and sunny day.

I heard myself speak numbly:

"But you have said that you could find no crime in him."

"I was speaking for myself, not for Rome. And I spoke honestly. I believe this man to be guilty of nothing, except perhaps of innocence."

"You do not have to comply. You can disallow it."

Jesus had said nothing And he would say nothing now. For all I know, he said nothing ever after.

"I can delay it. Nothing more. Of all people, my Gaius, you should understand this. You, who once abided the mad dictates of a mad princeps; you, if anyone, should understand. But for a man to be caged to have but a spell of dank breath and anguish before dying—this is not an act of mercy; it is an act of torture. Where is the life, the dignity, the good in that? Do you not agree that to postpone death in such a situation is to postpone deliverance?"

"How long can you delay it?"

"The prolonging of his suffering?"

"Yes."

"A while. A few months perhaps."

"To whom in Rome do you answer?"

"Why do you ask me this? You know that it is Sejanus. But he would grant no reprieve. I can only defer the inevitable, I cannot avoid it. There will be no reprieve."

"Ah, there you are wrong," I said. "By the decree and seal of Tiberius, this man shall not die. The decree of the princeps of all Rome and its imperial provinces cannot be denied. He may be insane, but he is still the supreme commander and ruler of the Roman Empire."

Jesus turned to me. His eyes were red and watering. I had once reckoned that he was about ten years younger than I. Now he looked the same age, or older. Loiterer, savior, slave, captive, condemned. But soon to be freed. I swore that I would hear his laughter again.

"You will bring him with you to Caesarea when you leave?" I asked.

"That will be impossible. He must remain here, in Jerusalem. I can see to it that he is put in the Antonia. There are good Romans stationed there. The Jewish auxiliaries there might wish to see him suffer, but the Roman legionaries will see to it that they do not have their way, and that he is treated with kindness."

I asked Pilate to grant me two documents bearing his seal, and the use of a carpentum and steed-driver who could get me to Caesarea as fast as possible.

"What kind of documents?"

One was to be a letter instructing that I be given passage to Neapolis on the next trireme bound for Rome. The other, simply a note of good wishes to the princeps, was to be folded in such a way that it could not be opened without breaking the seal. Its brief message mattered very little.

I embraced Jesus and told him neither to worry nor to count the days. I would return to free him.

I had the palace livery-man remove the packsaddles from Faith, Hope, and Charity, telling him to put them in the carriage of the carpentum. I made a gift of the dear creatures to him, telling him to care well for them, or give or sell them to one who would. I should have told him to tend to them until my return. This would have insured their good care. But I was not thinking. My body stumbled and stammered. My mind raced.

Though the lashings of his whip were few and seldom, the carpentarius who drove the carriage gave the stallions no slack of rein and little rest. Making fierce speed, we were in Caesarea the next day. From lack of sleep, my vision was all flash and eclipse.

I delivered the packsaddles to our argentarius for deposit. I did not linger for the sorting, permutation, and computation of the wealth they held, but hastened to the harbor-master and presented him with my letter of instruction bearing the prefect's seal. I also showed him, without words, the folded sealed parchment that was addressed, in the hand of the governor, to Tiberius.

The navigator of the trireme had many years of experience on the Great Sea, in every weather of every season. The course he chose seemed unusual. Consulting no periplus-book, but looking only to shores and stars and the colors indicating sea-depths, he directed the ship straight toward Rhodes.

I had to close one eye and squint through the other to see, even as a blur, the moon in the afternoon sky, or any other thing. My legs trembled, and I fell. The dry burning in my throat made it impossible for me to speak.

When we were beyond sight of all land, I collapsed, and the frenzy of flash and eclipse that was my vision succumbed to blackness.

34

THE NAVIGATOR WAS A ROMAN. HIS CREW AND ITS ROWERS—
two hundred of them, all but twenty of whom manned the
oars at any given time, while twenty rested—were mostly
Egyptians.

When the island of Rhodes could be seen as a mote on the
horizon, the navigator turned the ship west, passing between the
northern shore of Crete and an island south of the Peloponnesus,
and evading the strongest of the winds that blew against us. We
made for the Sicilian Sea, to sail through the Strait of Sicilia,
between Agrigentum and Cossyra, and thence to the Tyrrhenian,
and directly northeast to Neapolis, where I was to board a light
craft for the brief crossing to Capri. Then, having gotten what I
wanted from Tiberius, I would come back to Caesarea as hastily
as possible.

The urgency of my mission was beneath my skin always. The
return voyage, I told myself, would be a matter of days, not weeks.
These same winds we now faced would then be leeward, filling
our sail.

Like the crew, I slept on the deck. As I had with me no food at
the time of our setting forth from Caesarea, the harbor-master
had seen to it that provisions for the sailing were brought to me
aboard ship before the gangway was raised.

On nights when sleep would not come, I watched the white
froth of the sea at the ship's prow and the breaking of distant

waves in the unimaginable cold black depths, which were so forbidding and so enticing at once.

My thoughts were on Jesus. I remembered all that we had done together, from our first encounter in Caesarea to the bad dream of our time in Jerusalem, where I never should have indulged his perverse desire to make known his presence. I dwelled on this perversity in him, and on the very nature of him. These things were as mysterious as the churning white sea-froth, the distant waves, the cold black depths. Who was this man? He was my friend. I knew him as a brother. But I really knew him not. Ultimately he was as unknowable as this sea and the winds that blew at times with us and, more often, against us. I had seen in his eyes a kind of magic that I associated with the powers of the elements. I recalled him describing, with artful cunning, the source of his words as the voice of another. A different voice, one that was not audible to others; a voice that spoke in elemental tones that were not words and yet were words. But, at sea, as much as I pondered the elements, and as much as I pondered him, there were no answers.

Or, usually, when sleep would not come, I just lay and looked to the stars, which at sea were myriad, a lushness and luxuriance as one never sees from the firm earth of civilization.

Have you ever seen a two-headed snake? I have not, though all my life I have heard that they are not uncommon. I saw the form of one now, in the stars of this voyage.

Your grandmother once told me a little tale that had scared her so in her youth. In this tale, a girl lying naked by a pond one summer afternoon has drifted off to sleep, and while she sleeps, a water-snake, one of the little live-born ones, wanders newborn from his brood and enters her.

I saw one night the image of this little tale in the stars as well.

Were there snakes in the skies? Yes, wisdom is a serpent. But I felt little wisdom.

As many souls as there are stars. So Plato said. Each soul to its star, destined and allotted from the soul-brew of the universe by the making-force of the gods and all things. And mounting each soul on its star, as on a chariot, the making-force revealed and instilled deep in all of them the nature of the universe and the laws of destiny. And anyone, on his incarnation, who lived virtuously for his appointed time, mastering his passions and his fears, would return home to his native star and dwell in bliss forever. And anyone who failed would be changed into a woman on his second birth. And if that soul still did not refrain from wrong, its mortal shell, on its third incarnation, would be reduced to that of some creature that was suitable to its particular kind of wrongdoing.

Maybe Plato was not such a fool. Maybe Plato was right. Maybe this is why there are more women than men, and more lower creatures than men and women together. All those cold and vacant stars, all those wandering homeless souls. Some stars did seem to glow more warmly than others, regardless of their distance, regardless of their size.

And what of the cascades of shooting stars that fell from the dark heavens? Whose souls were these?

Usually the movement of the sea, no matter how rough it might be, lulled me to sleep like a babe being cradled in his mother's arms.

The moon waned, then waxed, and then again was full, and still we sailed on.

I wondered if the moon could be seen from his cell. In my mind, I tried to enter that cell, that I might also enter his heart. But this was impossible. I could muse and brood on winds, the cold black deep and its waves, the myriad stars, and the souls that pulsed in them, and I could peer into the imaginings inspired by my musings and broodings. But into him, there was no peering.

No man can ever truly see into another. This was doubly true of him. Loiterer, pretender, wise man, fool. Which of these was he, this false savior who could now be saved only through the intercession of a madman, or should I say a fellow madman, or fellow madmen? Loiterer, pretender, wise man, fool. Was he all of these?

In a way, I had made him; had cultivated him, as the vinedresser his vine. From a petty thief, I had made a master thief; had taught him the honeysuckled oratory of deception; had from a dirty backstreet cutpurse groomed an immaculate illusion to whom men offered up their purses as eagerly as they offered up their souls.

Yes, in a way I had made him. But in no way did I fully understand him. I had once believed I did, but I was wrong. For there was in him something that had taken flight, or been borne away by breezes, one petal at a time, to a distant, unknown place.

35

H E WAS SPUTTERING CURSES ON ALL FIG TREES, AND ON THE
gods that had given them their season.

"I am Tiberius, supreme ruler of all the Roman Empire. I
could procure half the Negroes in Africa and have them brought
to me in silver chains; but I am not to have a single ripe fig. It is
absurd."

It was unpleasant to look upon him. He had been abhorrent
enough to behold when I had last seen him, on the day he had
dismissed me from his court at Rome. He then had been an old
man trembling with madness, bent and emaciated, destitute of
teeth, with sores and scabs on his withered bald head, and a face
of red blotches that could not be hidden by the cosmetic plasters
on them.

His condition had worsened since then. One of his eyes could
not open, but was like a sallow unhealing wound, a sunken slash-
mark sealed and caked with crystalline yellow, and oozing foul
matter. Under an ear, a white fungus grew profusely, with dark
blood trickling from it. Slender tatters of dead skin hung here and
there, revealing open pustules. I could not imagine the unseen
parts of him.

He moved stiffly, hunched over and contorted, with visible
difficulty. The cosmetic plasters were gone, but there was around
his neck a strip of muslin soaked with some kind of lotion and
spotted with blood. He wore a wig that seemed to be made of a

woman's auburn hair, and it made him appear all the more grotesque. This display of fair locks on a death's-head was the most incongruous and egregiously ridiculous indulgence of vanity I ever saw.

He looked at me with some bewilderment, squinting at me through the one eye that was not sealed.

"And what is it that you want?" he said.

"I come to save the life of a man," I said.

From somewhere in the palace, far-off and faint, there were the desperate piercing cries and wails of children.

Irritation came over him like a storm.

"That bawling maddens me," he said. Summoning one of his servants, he ordered him: "Silence those little squealers, and prepare them for the sty. Right now, this moment. Be done with it. Go."

He smiled easily.

"If there is anything better than acorns and chestnuts for the diet of wild boars, it is the soft flesh and vitals of the little ones. A diet of these three things will produce the most succulent meat imaginable."

I told him that there was unrest in Judea. There were those who would rise against Rome. The man whose life I sought to save was a defender of Rome. For this, the other Jews had condemned him to death.

"I care not about unrest in Judea. I care not about the affairs of Judea or any other province. I am now fully absorbed by my inquiries into the sciences. They alone command and occupy my time."

A man entered unannounced. He was dressed in finery more befitting an imperator than what the imperator himself wore.

Seeing that Tiberius was engaged in conversation, he excused himself and turned to leave.

I saw a ring of gold in the lobe of one of the man's ears, and rings of gold on his fingers as well. He looked oddly familiar. It was him, the soothsayer, the dark Egyptian of Greek blood named Thracyllus.

"Gaius," he said to me, turning round again for a moment, "it is good to see you."

I could hear the falseness in his voice.

"You know this man?" the imperator asked him.

"Why, of course," said the soothsayer, "I remember him well, from our court in Rome."

Tiberius looked at me.

"At least someone knows who you are," he said. He looked then to Thracyllus, and said to him:

"Your memory of things past is, as always, as acute as your foresight of things to be. Go now."

The folded, sealed parchment that Pilate had given me, and which I had shown to the imperial guard who had led me from the harbor to the palace, now lay on the desk where Tiberius sat. He raised it in his hand, brought it very close to his one good eye, and studied the seal.

Then he looked from Pilate's seal to me.

"And who is this man?" he asked.

"He is your governor in Judea."

"Ah, yes, of course."

I dared not mention Sejanus. I knew not how the princeps felt toward him these days.

"I believe he was an appointee of Sejanus," he said lucidly. He seemed abstracted for a moment, then again spoke lucidly: "I know that Sejanus plans to kill me. What I do not know is why he waits so long to do it."

He was very still then, as if deep in thought, or as if he had expired.

Perhaps Sejanus waited because he believed that death was already fast at work on this diseased and desiccated stick of birch loosed from the fasces. Perhaps it was simply because no princeps had ever been assassinated. That distinction would belong to the successor to Tiberius, his nephew and adopted son, Caligula.

His head rose with a jerk.

"Well, what is it that you want?" he said.

He had already forgotten what I had told him; and so I told him again.

"And it is ripe figs that I crave," he said sharply. "It seems that neither of us is to have our satisfaction."

I recalled to him his custom of visiting the Tullianum, where he strode before the row of prisoners who were to be executed that day, and sometimes ordered that one or two of them be set free, saying that their innocence had been revealed to him in dreams.

"I dream no more," he said.

"You can save this good man with a stroke of your hand," I said.

"I can do many things with a stroke of my hand."

"He increases your fortune, and the fortunes of Rome. He tells all Jews to render unto Caesar that which is Caesar's. He says that, were it not for you, the greatness of Rome would be much diminished."

"If this is so, he is a fool."

"If it is folly to worship you, and respect and admire you, and to love Rome, then, yes, he is a fool, as am I."

He cackled with sickly laughter.

"You are full of shit," he said. "You always were."

"I beg of you."

"I remember you now."

"Then you know that I always had your best interests in my heart, as I do at this moment."

"I remember many things. My memory of things past is as acute as my foresight of things to be."

"I beseech you. Do us both this favor. Spare the life of this rare good man."

He waved the back of his hand to me, then showed interest in my words.

"What are the preferred forms of public execution among the Jews of Judea?"

"Stoning. Burning. Hanging. Slaying by sword. Immersion in mud. Strangling. They have also taken delight in crucifixion, brought to them by Rome."

"Imagine being so benighted and unimaginative as not to conceive of a manner of execution on one's own. Imagine having to have it introduced."

"A most interesting reflection," I said.

"And what of the *poena cullei,* the punishment of the sack? Is it known to the Jews of that land?"

"I believe not."

"Ah, surely that is the sublimest of inflicted deaths. And surely it is ours alone, as truly as is Virgil. Such are the things that make us great." He looked away. "There is much poetry in pain."

He seemed startled to see me standing there. "Go now," he said.

"I shall not move until I have your written order for the life and liberty of this man under seal."

He was so incensed by this that spittle sprayed from his toothless mouth and he tried to stand upright.

"How dare you!"

Then complacency came over him, and he said in a tone of reason:

"What does it matter in this world, one Jew more or one Jew less?"

He regarded me with the one eye of his reason.

"Go, then," he said, "I have my inquiries, my experiments to pursue."

At this time, there entered a servant who excused himself and respectfully informed the autocrat that his afternoon meal was ready.

There would be boar and stewed apples, pie of garlic and herbs, dried figs in honey, and his favorite white wine of Liguria.

It was then, for a moment, that he seemed to be not a monster, but merely a pitiable old wretch with the remnant of a smile on what was left of his face.

"So who is this Jew that we must save from the Jews?" he asked. "A name, a name; he must have a name."

Parchment, ink, and reed were before him. I saw the seal of his ring press into soft bitumen.

36

THE AIR OF CAESAREA WAS HEAVY WITH HUMIDITY, RIDDEN with a foul humor that strong gusting winds could not drive away. The morning sky was a pall of gray. The sun, a hazy glare. This atmosphere disquieted the guts, and troubled the intake of breath through the nostrils.

I placed the sealed decree of Tiberius in Pilate's hand. The prefect did not examine it, but asked after the condition of the emperor.

I told him.

Neither his voice nor his countenance changed. He looked me in the eyes and said:

"It is too late."

I said nothing.

"Three days after you departed, Caiaphas and the Jews of Jerusalem gathered at the Antonia and demanded that your servant be executed as ordained. They were adamant, hostile, and caused a growing disturbance.

"I was forced to wash my hands of the matter; and their will was wreaked.

"He was taken with other criminals to Calvary, the Hill of the Skull, beyond the walls of Jerusalem; and there, with the others, he was crucified."

Still, I said nothing.

"We should have counterfeited a decree. Or simply made as if there were one," he reflected absently.

It was then that I spoke.

"If only you had suggested that before I left."

"I did not think of it," he said. "And as I think of it now, I dismiss it. For it would not have satisfied the eyes and suspicions of the high priest. No, yours was the only way. But time and events were against us."

I stared at him. From me came these words: "A man's life is a man's life."

"Yes." He sighed testily. "But you can always buy another man."

He seemed to regret the petulance of his manner.

"If it is of consolation," he said, "I was told by the Roman legionary who befriended you that, much to the displeasure of the Jews, he pierced the side of your man deeply with his spear, so that his suffering on the cross would end in a span of hours, not days.

"Aside from that, it was just another crucifixion. The Jews, as usual, spread their robes and enjoyed their family meals while witnessing the agonies of those crucified. Through the mercy of the legionary, your Jesus was the first to be delivered from pain to death, the first to be taken down."

I tried to picture it, but withdrew from what I pictured.

"He had no family present at Jerusalem?" asked Pilate.

"No," I said.

"Then the iron spikes of his crucifixion would have been sold by the auxiliaries to medical men. They are much in demand for their alleged healing properties, in the treatment of the falling disease and other illnesses. Some people carry them about with them, even on the Sabbath, or wear them as amulets to prevent sickness.

"He would have been put in an unmarked tomb, perhaps with others, in the rocks to the west."

There was in me a dire oppression like that which filled the sky and air of this day.

"It may also be of consolation," Pilate said, "to know that in the end he denounced and betrayed you. He claimed that he was not your slave; that you had enticed and directed him in his pronouncements, that your fortunes might profit by them."

I could hear the voice of Jesus, and his words about that which was within, which if you brought forth would save you, and if you did not bring forth would destroy you.

"A man who seeks to save his life will utter anything," I said.

"This is true," said Pilate, seeing that, at this moment, there was, for me, no consolation.

Nothing remained to be said. Nothing remained to be done. But still I stood there, saying nothing, doing nothing.

As he who passes from us is mourned, so passes mourning for him.

There was in me a feeling of guilt, and my first thought was that, somehow, I was responsible for his death. I shook loose this thought.

My second thought was that all his money was now mine. I did not shake loose this thought.

37

S UCH WAS THE END OF MY FRIEND. SUCH WAS THE END OF MY fortune-hunting days. Such was the end of the Word and the Way.

He is dust, as I soon will be ashes, unremembered. That the memory of me might dwell in you, as his has dwelled these fleeting years in me: this is all that I could ask. A young man wants the world. An old man wants only that the spent light of him glow for a moment after he is extinguished.

So it was that I returned to Rome, where sadness awaited me. My wife and my son, I discovered, were dead and gone, without a chance for me to have kissed them good-bye.

I became a sedate member of the Roman aristocracy. I did what rich equestrians do. That is to say, I did whatever those who are not rich equestrians are unable to do.

There was only you, my progeny and my heir-at-law, my heir of blood.

Sejanus was killed. A few years later, Caiaphas died. Then, at long last, Tiberius died. Some years later, Pontius Pilate died. Caligula came, and Caligula was killed. His uncle Claudius then was raised to the throne of Rome. I write this in the third year of his reign.

Is there a lesson to be learned from any of this? I do not know. Is there to be found in my life anything that might benefit you in yours? I do not know. If there is, I leave it to you to find it, or to believe you have found it. You are the sole heir of my estate. You are the sole heir as well of the truth of my life.

There is a cameo of some skill, carved by an artisan of Caesarea. It is, I think, a good likeness of me as I was before age made me hideous. That, too, is yours, if you want it.

I bade farewell long ago to those fools and betrayers of my story. Now I bid farewell to all fools everywhere. And I bid farewell to you, whom I love, and to the spirits of the others whom I did love; and to the breath of this life, and to the colors of this world.

We find the name of the Greek goddess Hera—our Juno—enclosed in the name of the Shemites' goddess Asherah. So we see that the gods are one. We see that all things are enclosed in other things; and that which encloses all, we shall never know. It is beyond us.

For we are, all of us, nothing more than finite beings who seek to understand infinity; and this understanding shall never be ours.

The Jew and the Roman are one: a Janus who gazes at chaos from two different directions and sees different gods where really there are none. None. The Great Mother and the Great Father are one. At the same time, they are none. All gods are but phantoms, figments of the minds of men.

Trust no man, and trust no god. For, as all men have their birth in mortal flesh, so all gods have their birth in the minds of mortal men, and that source is never else than a marsh of disease and ill. Know that every prophet is a false prophet.

Only the weak, the meek and wretched of the earth, need the palliative of hope. Shun it. It is a lie and a self-affliction. Where you find misery, there will be hope; and where hope is found, there will be misery. The strong have their heaven in this life. And, for all its greed, all its corruption, all its evil, injustice, and filth, this world is all of heaven we shall ever know.

ABOUT THE AUTHOR

Nick Tosches lives in what used to be New York.